"Such unnecessary exertion," he commented, looking on as her rapid breathing threatened to force her breasts past the confines of the lacey scooped neckline of the gown that had teased him all during breakfast. "A simple kiss won't take nearly as much out of you," he concluded.

Jacinta strained against his hold about her wrists. "Surely, you don't make a practice of resorting to such tactics to obtain kisses from helpless women." She shuddered.

"I don't," he conceded, tightening his hold on her wrists to draw her closer. "But, love, I don't usually encounter such beauties as yourself and you are certainly no helpless lady."

Jacinta's lashes fluttered in rapid succession as her chocolate stare searched his dark one for some clue about his true intentions. "How do I know I can trust you?" she asked in a tiny voice. The wolfish grin she received in response was answer enough.

"You don't know that."

Jacinta expelled a sigh of desperation and defeat. "Just get it over with," she commanded softly.

Of course she'd expected something brutal and nauseating. Her lashes fluttered closed over her eyes in a resigned fashion. Solomon's smile was sweetness and wonder personified as his stare trailed the curving loveliness of her doll face. He took both her wrists in one hand and removed what little distance remained between them.

PASSION'S FURIES

AlTonya Washington

Genesis Press, Inc.

INDIGO

An imprint of Genesis Press, Inc.
Publishing Company

Genesis Press, Inc.
P.O. Box 101
Columbus, MS 39703

ISBN: 13 DIGIT : 978-1-58571-324-0
ISBN: 10 DIGIT : 1-58571-324-4
Manufactured in the United States of America

First Edition

Visit us at www.genesis-press.com
or call at 1-888-Indigo-1-4-0

DEDICATION

For those who lived and struggled
through those days of long ago.

PROLOGUE

"Damn fine speaking."

"Powerful words, who is he?"

"They call him 'the old man'."

"Not very original," Solomon Dikembe argued, his black stare narrowing toward the front of the lean-to shanty. The 'old man' standing there appeared as though he should be reading stories to his grandchildren instead of speaking fiery words to an impassioned audience.

Moses Cuffe dipped his head in slight acknowledgement. "Perhaps not original, but no less respectful. Some say they fear this man more than God."

Solomon shot a sideways glance towards his ship's captain before looking back upon the old man with renewed interest. Solomon's interest, however, had been heightened since he stepped foot inside the shanty that was nestled deep within the woods along the Santee. Should the meeting be discovered by the owners of the powerful plantations along the banks of the mighty river, it would mean death to all in attendance. Solomon Dikembe, a man born free, found it admirable and impressive that the gathering had drawn such a following. The old man's words riveted far beyond the rickety boards of the dwelling. It was as though he hadn't a care for the consequences of voicing his opinions.

"Does this old man, who the people fear more than God, have a name?"

Cuffe shook his head at the sarcasm evident in his friend's voice. "Denmark Vesey," he answered.

Solomon nodded. "He sways a crowd like no one I've ever heard. I should hope his owners remain ignorant of his speaking engagements."

Cuffe cleared his throat, while tugging at the knotted scarf around his neck. "Prepare yourself, friend. Denmark Vesey is a free man."

Solomon's lips parted and his handsome vanilla-toned face clouded with surprise and curiosity. "Free man?" he inquired, his already raspy voice growing soft.

Cuffe heard him perfectly well above the melee of the crowd. "Free man," he confirmed.

"Why would he involve himself in something like this?"

"No one knows," Cuffe answered with a one shoulder shrug. "Some have said it's as simple as the man wanting to see what he can do for his people."

Solomon folded his arms across his massive chest and tuned in to the old man's insightful words. This time, he was interested not only in the man's opinions, but also his motivation and reasons.

In truth, Denmark Vesey was an enigma to most everyone who knew him or knew *of* him. The man, who was well into his late fifties or early sixties, had been a slave who obtained his freedom with winnings from a lottery ticket he'd purchased. In Charleston, he kept a modest house on Bull Street and worked as a respected carpenter. Still, leading such a comfortable lifestyle had only driven the man to want the same for his people, who lived their lives in chains so close to his own home.

Over the last two years, Vesey had gained something of a supernatural reputation among the people. His words, which encouraged those in bondage to shake off their shackles, rise up and smite their oppressors, had been embraced by all who heard him speak. It was believed that Vesey was in the process of organizing a great rebellion. If successful, freedom would be a reality and no longer an unrealistic dream.

"We should be on our way," Cuffe decided, a smirk coming to his rugged, dark face. He could tell that the owner of his ship had become mesmerized by the powerful stirrings of old man Vesey's words.

Solomon responded with a slow nod while rising from the creaking ladder-backed chair. The two tall, powerfully built men headed out into the dusty woods, which were further shadowed by the onset of the evening. Cuffe had ventured a slight distance ahead of Solomon, whose way was suddenly impeded by a body that raced across his path.

"Beg pardon," Solomon whispered when his larger form collided with the person, sending the smaller man to the ground. The man's hat fell from his head and Solomon bent to retrieve it.

"Dammit," the tiny man hissed.

It was then that Solomon noticed waves upon waves of black hair tumbling across the person's shoulders and back. Solomon's deep-set onyx gaze was awe-filled as he beheld the small woman in his midst. She never looked up at him, but when she raked her hair away from her face, his eyes narrowed and he took in every aspect of her beautiful, dark brown face.

"Dikembe!"

Solomon looked in the direction he'd heard Cuffe's voice. His attention diverted, the young woman snatched her hat from his hand. When Solomon's head whipped back around, he saw no trace of her.

"Solomon!" Cuffe called again.

"Coming!" he snapped, his temper heating over the realization that she was gone. "Coming," he whispered that time, his ebony gaze scanning the area once more before he walked away.

CHAPTER 1

Nambia Sula cleared her throat and glanced up with uncertainty. "I never done nothing like this, Jaci," she told the young woman seated across the rough wooden table.

Jacinta McIver reached over to pat the woman's hand in a reassuring fashion. "It's all right, Miss Nambia, just pretend you don't see the book. We're just having one of our talks. It's all right," she softly urged.

Nambia closed her eyes as though summoning the courage from some place deep within. "The day was so alive. There were people everywhere. I had never seen so much going on at one time. Being the age I was, I think it's something good and I was happy to be there." Her eyes misted with tears as her face reflected old pain. "Happy 'til I feel my mama's hand leave mine. I look up. I could hear her call me—I didn't know where she was. I try to go to her but . . . couldn't. I feel something 'round my ankle and I see the shackle."

Jacinta pressed her lips together as she recorded the woman's words. Silently, she demanded her own tears to remain at bay.

"I b'lieve I be a woman that day," Nambia was saying as she sat straighter in her chair. "As a child of five I think

I'm at a happy ball. As a woman I see it's no ball, but a sale and we was the goods. I 'member thinking my mama, my papa, my brother . . . one of 'em be gone with me. I was jus' a child of five. What a child of five gone do, Miss Jaci?" she asked, gazing across the table as though she expected an answer. Then she relaxed against the back of her chair and continued to speak. "I soon discover what I could do," she supplied, her black eyes snapping brilliantly from her face, which appeared far older than forty-one years.

Jacinta jotted a few more words on the crisp, beige pages of her leather-bound journal as she listened. At last, she raised her head and fixed the lady with a dazzling smile. "I think that's enough for today. We'll talk more later."

Nambia sighed as she smiled, slowly regaining her relaxed demeanor. "Was that good?" she inquired with a doubtful expression.

Jacinta recapped her ink bottle and pushed it into the pocket of her simple brown riding dress. "It was very good," she assured the grandmother of five.

"Why you put that in a book, Jaci? What you gone do with it?"

Jacinta eased the pen into her pocket and tapped her slender fingers against the brown cover. "I think I want others to read it. I keep thinking that somewhere, there is someone who doesn't know what's happening here. If they did, they'd come and stop it, wouldn't they?"

Nambia shook her head while reaching for bowls and pots to begin supper. "I think it take the good Lord above to decide when or if somethin' to be done 'bout it."

Jacinta rolled her eyes, her soft, full mouth curving into a pout. "You sound just like Poppa."

"And he gone whip your behind good for being over here like this," Nambia warned, flicking a tattered dishtowel in Jacinta's direction. "Ol' Wallens and his men can't be trusted round black womens, and you know what I mean," she said, referring to the owner of the plantation, Charles 'Chuck' Wallens.

Again, Jacinta rolled her eyes, her long lashes fluttering in dramatic sweeps against her high cheekbones. "I understand the danger, but the reward could be so great. If Poppa would only . . ."

Nambia continued with her pots. "Only?"

"Hear Mr. Vesey."

"Jacinta McIver!" Nambia cried, finally turning to face the petite young woman who watched her with defiance in her eyes. "You know not to speak that name on the grounds of this plantation. They git word of any of that and it mean death to a great many of us. 'Sides, t'aint nothing but a mess of talk."

"You don't believe that, Miss Nambia."

"Might as well. It's been talk for years now."

"It takes time to organize something this great," Jacinta argued.

Nambia Sula leaned against the wooden counter top and folded her arms across the white apron that covered her dusty, black work dress. She looked out past the windows at the children playing so innocently in the dirt yard and enjoying the work-free Sunday afternoon. "It take a lot of courage, too, and I don't know many who got courage enough to stand up to death."

Charleston was a beautiful city and well deserving of its title as the cultural Mecca of the United States. It was a recognizable force in trade of indigo and rice, while the city's architecture left many speechless.

The famed white palm-tree-lined streets of Charleston left those who viewed the spectacle breathless. The unmatched beauty—a collaboration of sand and crushed seashells—gave the city's main streets a gleaming, ethereal allure. Of course the white sand in all its beauty was further confirmation of the race that possessed complete authority.

The slave woman Nambia Sula and scores like her outnumbered the white population by staggering amounts. The pristine, untouched elegance of the city only masked the horrors that lay just beneath its surface. The black population of Charleston was a diverse group. Though the majority was enslaved, there were a number of freed men. Blacks with their own businesses and homes were in existence. They were well respected and several held their own share of white patrons. Of course, the majority resided in modest dwellings in town. Bull Street was a popular address for the free black class.

Away from the city, where the white sand faded to brown dust and the magnolia and hanging moss trees practically shielded the roads, the plantations reigned.

"My suggestion is that you make use of that land, and soon."

Jason McIver continued to scan the map lying on the pine desk in his study. He met the advisement with a smug look. "I plan to do just that."

Scurvy Logan appeared unconvinced. "You've earned no income from that island property since your father passed the land to you, may he rest in peace."

Jason retrieved a document from beneath the stock of log books sitting catty-cornered on the desk. "I believe that is about to change," he said, passing the page across the table.

Scurvy retrieved his horn-rimmed spectacles from the breast pocket of his three-quarter length linen suit coat. "Dikembe," he stated. "Michigan," he added as he read further.

"It appears he wants to add to his holdings and is interested in oceanfront property."

"That might bring a hefty profit," Scurvy predicted, pulling the spectacles from his wide nose.

Jason laid his hands against his protruding belly when he chuckled. "Indeed!"

Jason McIver's holdings in real estate were unmatched among both his own people and the white population. He was a beloved man who attracted his own share of envy. His white neighbors thought it an outrage that a black man should hold such power. Unfortunately, they had to accept the fact that there was little they could do to change it.

Jason was born a free man when his father's master repaid his most trusted slave by leaving him in charge of the property—estate and holdings—upon his death. Roland McIver had only one son, who died at sea. Roland's wife had died several years before and the man swore he would never remarry and never father another child. Jason's father, Mtumbo, was a young, strong and, more importantly, intelligent man. When Roland retreated from the world, it was Mtumbo who kept the plantation running.

Roland recognized this and grew to respect the young African more with each passing day. As a result, he rewarded Mtumbo with his freedom and, along with the last name McIver, gave the man the post of overseeing all his holdings. Of course, this infuriated Roland's associates. They were as shocked by the man's decision as they were to discover a black man possessed a business intellect which equaled or surpassed their own.

Mtumbo ran the estate with an iron fist. Still, that sternness did not extend to his people who still worked the land as slaves. Less than twenty worked the McIver Plantation as Roland preferred to pay to have his property maintained. His business was buying and selling property, and he frequently stated he had no need to keep a hoard of slaves. There were those, however, who said the man simply believed the entire institution was degrading, which accounted for his small number of human possessions. Mtumbo knew that the few slaves working the plantation would be free once Roland gave him complete control over the land.

Jason McIver saw much of his father in his own child. Jacinta's passion for the plight of her people and their freedom was admirable. But Jason knew that passion could get her killed or wishing she were dead. Her spirit and beauty attracted scores of interested suitors –black and white. Of course, Jason found none of them suitable candidates for marriage. The sons of the slaves freed after Roland McIver's death now lived and worked the estate. Those young men, fine as they were, were a far cry from Jason's perfect match for his only daughter.

Crawford County, Illinois

A round of applause carried on a, surprisingly crisp, late June wind as the newlywed couple jumped the long broom placed at their feet. The ten acre spread of land was home to Henry and Minnie Wise. The couple's lovely farmhouse had been packed with guests since early that week. Of course, none of the more than fifty guests were happier than the proud parents who had just seen their eldest daughter married.

"Mistuh Solomon, I got three more awaitin'. You keep actin' shy they be gone, too."

Solomon chuckled at Henry Wise's tease. The man had been determined in his intentions to see at least one of his daughters marry into money. Henry Wise, however, was not the only father who hoped to have Solomon Dikembe for a future son-in-law.

Of course, the fathers were interested in Solomon Dikembe's financial statement. The young man had obtained a startling inheritance from his father's family, but Solomon was determined to carve out his own legacy. He was almost obsessed with obtaining unprecedented amounts of land. He had accumulated amounts that far exceeded the holdings of the Hampton family in Michigan. Solomon's paternal grandparents had always lavished their only grandchild with the best of everything. The Hamptons, however, would have known nothing of Solomon had it not been for tragedy.

Solomon's mother, Sheba Dikembe, was sold to the Hampton family when she was a child. The Hamptons had no desire to keep the young girl as a slave, however. Instead, they adopted her as their own—teaching her to read, write, think, and know her history. Sheba was an apt pupil and brilliant teacher for her only son. Kenneth Hampton, Solomon's father, fell in love with Sheba as they were reared in the same household. He feared his family and their friends would never understand or accept his bi-racial child, or its black mother.

Young and desperate, Kenneth set out to make a life for him and his family. Both he and Sheba were almost fresh into their teens. They set out on a stormy night; the carriage lost a wheel and toppled into a ditch. Kenneth was thrown and his neck was broken.

The Hamptons were grief-stricken, yet simultaneously overjoyed to discover the new life about to greet them. They fell in love with the tiny new Hampton and swore he would never want for anything.

Solomon did want, however, and as years passed he became increasingly disillusioned with his family. It wasn't long before other children made him aware of his differences—the fair skin and silky wavy hair. Solomon heard the stories of how 'real' Negroes were treated and he hated the white man more with each passing day. More importantly, he began to hate himself.

Solomon's would-be sweethearts, though, found nothing to hate. The man left women breathless and captivated by doing little more than entering a room. He had grown into a handsome man with an intelligence and self assurance that practically radiated from his six and a half foot frame. Powerfully built, he possessed a quiet intensity that caused his gravely deep voice to harbor a softer, soothing quality. His eyes were the most mesmerizing black and set deep beneath long, sleek brows of the same color. His hair was soft to touch, a mass of close-cut waves. The wide mouth and strong set of his somewhat squared jaw was softened by silky whiskers that gave him a rugged look and kept him from appearing too "beautiful". His nose was long and wide, combining with his other features to give him a rather fierce impression depending on his mood. Solomon Dikembe possessed an astonishing amount of self awareness and self control without striking one as cocky or arrogant. He was well liked and had many friends and many more female acquaintances. Of course this lifestyle was more than suitable for the handsome bachelor, much to the sorrow of every woman who ever met him.

"Dammit, where is it?" Jacinta hissed. She perched on her hands and knees and peered beneath the crisp, silver colored skirt that surrounded her four-poster Chippendale bed. Only gleaming floorboards greeted her sharp gaze.

"Damn!" she thundered, unable to think of another place to look. Surely, she hadn't been so careless as to leave it lying around another room. Sighing with aggravation, Jacinta flopped onto the high mattress and began to fiddle with one of the silver, satin curtains that hung from the canopy.

If Poppa finds that missing notebook, I'm done for, Jacinta acknowledged. He would never allow her to leave the house if he knew she'd been visiting the Wallens plantation to record the stories of the slaves there. Thankfully, nothing about her other excursions were noted there. The mere mention of Denmark Vesey's name was forbidden, as was any discussion of his ideals. Jacinta knew her father would waste no time sentencing her to a lifetime inside the walls of the McIver estate, should he discover her jaunts. Jacinta understood her father's concern. After all, subscribing to such subversive thoughts would bring dire consequences. Those consequences certainly extended to women and Jacinta shivered as thoughts of the punishments came to mind. Of course, Jacinta was no fool; she knew the attention she roused. She knew her fearless, outspoken manner could be her downfall. Unfortunately, the passion she possessed for wanting to see her people out of bondage usually overruled all rational thought.

Jacinta McIver, however, would have roused just as much interest had she been the demure submissive her father felt more befitting a lady. Her beauty had the power to arouse the most basic of instincts in every man she met. A flowing mane of thick ebony locks rippled across her shoulders and back upon the few occasions she left them unbound. The waist-length tresses encircled a round lovely face many likened to a hand made doll. Rich, dark brown skin was as flawless and smooth as a sliver of chocolate. Her eyes were expressive, almond-shaped orbs of the same color and positioned above the smallest nose and full lips which were most often set in an unconsciously alluring pout. She was exceptionally small, hence her further comparison to a doll. Most everyone who met her was intrigued by the amount of compassion and bravery that existed in someone so petite and fine-boned. Jacinta believed the misconception to be her greatest ally. No one would ever believe someone so sweet and outwardly unsuspecting could play a major role in the greatest rebellion to ever take place.

An unladylike snort of laughter passed Jacinta's throat as she flopped back onto the bed. Her chances of her playing a major role in Mr. Vesey's rebellion were about as likely as her father attending one of the man's meetings. No, Jason McIver was far more interested in overseeing his land and being a businessman. His intentions for Jacinta were even less revolutionary. He was determined to see her married off and raising a house full of screaming tots, Jacinta thought with a grimace.

Never! That would never be her life, she vowed. Besides, she couldn't think of any man in all her dozens of suitors with whom she'd want to spend an eternity.

Jacinta gasped suddenly, bracing herself on her elbows as her eyes widened. There was another possibility of where the notebook may be located. She recalled a meeting in March along the Santee. She had begged her father to take her with him on the business trip. Jason, who much preferred his daughter be involved with his business than a dangerous uprising, happily allowed it. Jacinta was more interested in hearing Denmark Vesey speak.

In truth, she hadn't had time to write anything about the meeting in the notebook. The hour was growing late and she had to get back before Jason's keen suspicions prompted him to send searchers. In her haste to return to her father's side, she recalled colliding with a man on his way out. Jacinta felt a familiar shiver race up her spine. It was the same feeling she'd experienced when the man assisted her from the ground. She remembered her breath catching in her throat when she saw his massive hands— white hands, she vaguely recalled before shaking off the unsettling vision. The sound of his voice as he offered an apology was like a roll of faint thunder as it retreated after the storm. She never looked into his face, but she doubted she would ever forget the sound of his voice.

"Stop girl," Jacinta ordered herself and left the bed. She had no place in her life for another controlling male. Her father was quite enough.

CHAPTER 2

"Shh!"

"What?"

Zambia Sula tugged on her friend's hand. Soon both young women were standing, out of sight, just behind one of the splintered wooden porch beams.

"Zambia what—"

"Shh! They fightin—"

"Who?" Jacinta cried, desperate to know what had her friend in such a mood.

"Mama and Poppa," Zambia explained, laying one hand against the side of her dark cheek. Her light brown eyes were wider than usual as she watched her parents.

"What's happened?" Jacinta inquired in a whisper.

Zambia only shook her head.

"If they find out, you be killed, Mingo!"

Mingo Sula raised one hand to cup his wife's cheek. "At least I die fightin' to save my family."

Laile Sula watched her husband in disbelief. "Save your family? How, Mingo? With talk of this supposed rebellion?"

"Talk can be powerful, too, woman!"

"Indeed," Laile agreed, not a bit daunted by her large, fierce-looking husband. "Talk *can* be powerful, and if the wrong people hear this talk, we all be dead."

"Hush," Mingo ordered, already turning his back on his wife.

"Mingo, you a smart man. I always pride myself on havin' a smart man," Laile continued, following behind her husband. "But you lettin' yourself be taken in by fool talk. They been talkin' 'bout this thing for years."

Mingo's steps slowed as though Laile's words were beginning to seep through his determined veneer. Then, his back straightened and he continued on his intended path. Laile stared after him, then bowed her scarf-covered head and turned in the opposite direction.

"Another meeting," Jacinta breathed. She'd forgotten about the talk she'd arranged with Nambia Sula.

"I'll get Mama Nam," Zambia offered, trying to mask her feelings over the scene between her parents as she went to find her grandmother.

"Does it have to be South Carolina?"

"*Charleston*, South Carolina?"

Solomon chuckled at the disbelief on the faces of his associates. "Gentlemen, do I sense hesitation?"

"Damn right you do," McCall Riley expressed, backing up the sentiment by slamming one fist to his polished pine desk.

"Solomon, this is insane," Geoffrey Staley added, his brown eyes gleaming with concern for his business associate. "Charleston is the capitol of slavery," he added.

"You do realize that several free blacks live there? Many even own businesses," Solomon pointed out.

McCall shook his head. "These 'free blacks' you speak of earn only what their former masters allow them to earn."

"I believe you're just taken away by the beauty of it," Geoffrey drawled.

"Mmm, I hear the place is quite a sight to behold," McCall agreed.

"For all that beauty, I'm certain the horrors are just as captivating," Geoffrey decided with a flippant wave.

"Solomon, I must voice my firm disagreement to this idea of yours. Think about purchasing this seafront property elsewhere. Solomon?" McCall inquired, noticing the far away look in his friend's eyes.

Solomon was definitely miles away. The moment Geoffrey mentioned the beauty of Charleston, his thoughts carried him back to that dusky March evening when he collided with the beauty who possessed the sensual mane of ebony hair.

"Solomon?"

"My mind is set, gentlemen," Solomon responded, his mouth tilting upwards in a smug smile. "The number of blacks in that area is staggering. Think of the opportunity that would arise should I make a reality of this venture. People there could advance their earnings ten-fold instead of working for scraps as they do now."

McCall and Geoffrey exchanged bewildered glances before shrugging off their advisements. They knew Solomon well enough to know he never turned away from obtaining something he wanted, no matter how unrealistic it seemed.

Ⓢ

"Where is that girl?" Jason McIver's round, handsome face was a picture of aggravation. He peered out past the large paned windows, taking in the approaching evening. "Beta, what did she say before leaving?"

"Oh! Uh, Mister Jason, she only said she was stepping out for a walk."

"Mmm," Jason grunted, sending a sideways glance toward the young maid. The ready excuse more than confirmed his suspicions.

Just then, Jacinta hurried into the library. Breathless and disheveled, she checked that her hairpins were secure while brushing wrinkles from the folds of her rose blush riding frock.

"I'm so sorry, Poppa. I must've overslept."

Jason's thick brows rose just slightly. "Overslept? I suggest then, that you check with your accomplice, who claims you set out for a walk," he mused, pushing one hand into the pocket of his worsted brown lounging coat.

"I found a quiet place to nap during my walk," Jacinta explained, unflustered by the man's sharp mind.

Jason nodded, amused by his daughter's attempt at cunning yet angered by her disobedience. "Excuse us, Beta."

"Yes, sir," the young Creole woman whispered, sending Jacinta a quick look before she curtsied and left the room.

"This must stop, girl."

Jacinta lowered her eyes to trace the elaborate design of the rug covering the polished hardwoods beneath. "Stop what, Poppa?"

"Continue along this course, Jaci, and I'll see that you never leave this house."

Taking a deep breath, Jacinta dropped the façade. "Poppa, won't you even allow me to enjoy my writing?"

"Not when it puts you in harm's way."

"How can *talking* to *my* people about their experiences be harmful?"

"When it takes place on Chuck Wallen's land it can be very harmful!"

Jacinta gasped, realizing her father was more aware of her outings than she gave him credit for.

Jason tapped his fingers along the edge of one of the tall mahogany bookshelves. "You see, I am not the only one who can be cunning."

"What will you do?" Jacinta phrased the statement in a monotone as she settled onto a burgundy suede long chair.

"I'm hoping you will change your ways and I won't have to do anything."

"Oh, Poppa, can't you see how important this is!" Jacinta cried, her warm brown eyes pleading as she half turned to face her father from her sofa.

"Jaci, your life is the only thing of importance here!"

"But no one has threatened me!"

"And I'll not wait until they do before I take action!" Jason bellowed. "Jacinta, my plans for you reach far beyond anything in this godforsaken city. I'll see you wed and living the life your mother and I dreamed of for you."

"Wed?" Jacinta repeated the word as though it put a bad taste in her mouth. "Wed and swollen with babies for the rest of my life? No, thank you!"

"Jaci—"

"Poppa, how can you expect me to focus on such things, when not ten miles from here innocent women and children are being treated so horribly?"

Jason retrieved his pipe from the cherry wood tea table set between two armchairs. "I suggest you think about *your* freedom, sweet daughter. Continue to test me and you'll not care for the consequences," he coolly threatened, leaning down to press a kiss to her forehead before strolling from the room.

The meeting that Mingo Sula fought with his wife over attending took place at a quaint house on Bull Street. Marcus Wells had all interested attendees enter his home through the back and assemble in the basement.

That evening, the meeting was presided over by one of Denmark Vesey's chief lieutenants, Ned Bennett. Others included: Rolla Bennett, Peter Poyas, a strange little man named Gullah Jack and Monday Gell. Mr. Poyas was on schedule to speak first that evening. The subject of arms was most important. The rest of the lieutenants followed with their reports. Mr. Vesey himself offered no words that evening, and he didn't need to.

Those in attendance were completely riveted on the words of the lieutenants. Most were awed by the fact that these men were willing to throw away the trust and comfort of their lives to join such a dangerous undertaking.

Ned Bennett was the possession of Governor Thomas Bennett and Ned was both a trusted and beloved slave. Monday Gell, though a slave, was allowed by his master to keep a shocking amount of the earnings he'd acquired from his 'side job' as a harness maker, and Peter Poyas was a highly skilled ship's carpenter.

Still, these men had recognized the need for change. They appeared to have no qualms over spilling blood to bring about such change. That dedication afforded them scores of supporters, all ready to take up arms and fight.

"Gentlemen, brothers! Your attention at this time!" Marcus Wells called, his broad hands held high above his head as he bellowed. "We are honored this night to hear from Mr. Vesey's top men in this great event! First, let me address the concern voiced by some that this uprising is a hoard of talk and no action." Marcus nodded, allowing the volume of conversation to swell as attendees expressed their agreement.

"Let me simply say, gentlemen, this rebellion is to be the greatest uprising for the liberation of our freedom since the great revolt led by Mr. Toussaint L'Ouverture in 1804! But nothing, brothers, nothing can take place without planning. This must be done right and not pushed along by hasty measures. Only by practicing prudence and patience will we obtain victory!"

"There. What do you think, Asa?"

"Beautiful."

"Are we talking about the art or the lady?"

Sheba Dikembe and her houseman turned at the sound of the deep voice filling the music room. Sheba's dark eyes sparkled merrily when she saw the tall, handsome young man leaning against the gleaming pinewood piano in the corner.

"Solomon!" she cried, extending her arms toward her son.

Solomon relished the hug from his mother and kissed her cheek three times. "I'm sorry, Asa, I believe the lady is far lovelier."

"As do I," Asa replied with a gracious bow.

"You two!" Sheba scolded playfully.

"Good to have you home, young man."

Solomon shook hands with the proper fifty-year-old Haitian. "Good to be here, Asa."

"Have you eaten?" Sheba inquired, folding her arms across the front of her lavender and blue Asoke dress.

"I'm fine, Asa," Solomon addressed the man who was all set to head off to the kitchen.

Instead, Asa nodded and left mother and son alone to visit. Sheba reached for Solomon's hand and they sat together on a satin-cushioned settee near a window.

"I have bad news," Solomon began.

Sheba's flawless blackberry face softened with knowing. "I figured as much. Another trip?"

"I'll be leaving by the end of the week."

"And where are you off to this time?"

"South Carolina. Charleston."

"I hear it is lovely."

"Among other things."

"Are you certain you want to go?"

Solomon nodded, leaning forward to brace his elbows upon the knees of his trousers. "Tremendous opportunity in that town."

"There are many things in that town, as I'm sure you are aware," Sheba mentioned, sensing a slight melancholy in her child's mood.

"There's a man. A free black man who owns an estate. A black man," Solomon felt the need to reiterate. "He also possesses island property he is willing to let go. I am curious as to what good I can do in such a place and with such holdings."

Sheba leaned forward to pat his cheek. "I understand your motivation, but just be careful. You know what it is like in the North. The South is far worse."

"And Charleston is the capitol of evil," Solomon interjected in a teasing manner, while leaning forward to kiss his mother's cheek. "I've heard all the talk."

Sheba was serious and clutched her son's hand in a firm grip. "The racism within our own culture is far more pronounced there, love. Your intentions, no matter how admirable, will not be readily accepted or appreciated," she cautioned. "Being mulatto will not put you in a favorable light with your people."

Solomon kissed the back of her hand and held it close to his chest. "Has it ever, Mama?"

21

Jacinta frowned at Dot Simons, the woman who had raised her from infancy. "Dot, why is Poppa so rigid about this? I refuse to believe he is one of those free blacks who is so concerned with his own welfare that he casts a blind eye to the plight of his people."

Dot tightened the knot securing her white apron and shook her head towards Jacinta. "How long will you upset yourself over this, Jaci? Your father is just as settled on his opinions as you are in yours."

"Why is everyone so against something that has the potential to be so great?"

Dot left her bedchamber to begin the long trek from there to the third floor to the kitchen. "It is not so much that, Jaci. Personally, I believe what Mr. Vesey is doing is quite courageous. Your father believes that, too."

"Humph."

"He does," Dot confirmed, her round frame wobbling as she made her way down the carpeted staircase. "But he is a father with a daughter, a very beautiful *black* daughter, who is dabbling in things that could bring her great harm. I believe he has far more to contend with than allowing himself to become involved with another cause, no matter how great."

Jacinta responded with a tired sigh.

Suddenly, Dot stopped on the second floor landing. She bowed her head for just a moment, then pinned Jacinta with an angry glare. "You are such a foolish young lady. I can't believe I've been so wrong in thinking you had a bit of sense in that head."

"Dot?" Jacinta spoke in the tiniest voice.

Dot only waved her silent. "You have a life most negroes can't even envision. Your father has lavished you since you were a babe—too much for my liking, but thankfully it hasn't spoiled you. But this, Jaci," she raised her index finger, "this obsession with this rebellion is dangerous, and it is unfair for you to put your father in the position of having to worry so. Now," she huffed, gathering her heavy skirts in both hands, "I have work."

Jacinta smarted from the tongue lashing, her lower lip trembling as Dot's words hit home. The last thing she wanted was to cause her father a moment's unrest. She would just have to do a better job of hiding her outings, she thought with a decisive nod. If she could do no more than record the facts of the rebellion she would be content in doing so. Surely, her father could abide by that!

The *Sheba* was a stunning vessel that drew just as much attention by its appearance as it did by the fact that it was manned by an all-black crew. Solomon ensured that great time, effort and creativity went into producing the ship that would bear his mother's name.

"We'll dock the ship at Blake's Lands," Moses Cuffe explained, waving his hand above the map he studied. "We certainly can't sail right into Charleston Harbor and make port. Whites discover such a luxurious vessel belongs to a black man, it won't be yours for long," he teased Solomon.

"They wouldn't risk their lives by attempting something so foolish," he predicted calmly.

Moses chuckled amidst puffing on his pipe.

"So you're certain it will remain undiscovered?" Solomon inquired. His onyx stare was full of doubt as he scanned the nautical map.

Moses took another long drag from his pipe and blew more of the fragrant smoke into the air. "It's the best choice. The place is unkempt and unpopular. The land is marshy and, from what I understand, avoided by all who know its history."

In truth, Blake's Lands had a reputation as a killing field. The blood of white criminals permeated the soil, and the place had otherwise remained a desolate expanse of property. As usual, Moses Cuffe had conducted a thorough check of the land upon his last visit. He was content in thinking the *Sheba* would be unmolested there.

"You'll have to make the trek across the marshlands by horse," Moses informed Solomon while rolling the map. "A small thatch of woods lies at the edge of the area. A coach will be waiting to carry you the rest of the way."

Solomon nodded, following suit when Moses stood. "Good work," he commended, reaching out to shake hands with his captain.

"A few members of the crew will go the distance. Their horses are already packed with your belongings."

"I'll send word in a few days," Solomon told Moses as he left the deck.

Moses shoved one hand into the pocket of his navy coat. "God be with you, friend."

"Tonight, then?"

"Yes. Bulkley Farm."

"Use caution. If you think you're being followed, stay away."

"Bulkley Farm," Jacinta whispered, straining to hear more of the conversation taking place just past the barn doors. She recognized the voices of June Rawley and Rufus Sumter, two of her father's field men.

"Jaci? Jacinta?"

Jacinta muffled a groan of frustration when she heard her father's voice. She had gone to the barn to hide a fresh dress to change into following one of her escapades. The men's voices and hushed conversation beckoned her interest. Quickly, she completed her task of hiding the clothes and raced out to meet her father.

"I have a gentleman arriving this evening to take a look at some of the island property," Jason explained, once he and Jacinta were strolling away from the barn. "I'd like you to be part of the negotiations."

Jacinta stopped in her tracks. "Me, Poppa?"

"Don't sound so surprised," Jason urged, never breaking his stare. "You never hesitate to give me your opinions on business matters."

"Yes, yes I know, it's just—"

"Jacinta McIver, it's high time you begin to take an interest in what goes into keeping this estate profitable," Jason stated, holding his hands behind his back and turning to face her.

Jacinta's exquisite maple brown gaze narrowed in confusion, and then suspicion, as realization dawned. "This is just a ruse, isn't it? An attempt to give me some sort of diversion."

"You believe what I do is diversion?"

"Poppa!" Jacinta cried, taking a few small steps closer to the man. "You're doing this only to keep my mind focused on McIver Estate rather than more important—"

"*More* important?" Jason snapped, raking one hand through his thick, wooly gray hair as he fought to calm himself. "So Vesey and his supposed uprising are *more* important than your heritage, your livelihood?"

Jacinta felt her palms grow sweaty from agitation. "Poppa, don't you think others are entitled to this same heritage—a heritage that includes prosperity and happiness over hardship and death?"

"I'll not have this discussion with you again, Jacinta."

"Poppa please—"

"Now I want you in your room until dinner, and I will not have you behaving this way before our guest this evening. Is that understood?"

Jacinta dared not respond. She was so angry that she feared her words would land her in more trouble. Fist clenched and hidden in the folds of her gown, she stomped all the way to her room.

The carriage Solomon boarded at the edge of Blake's Lands would carry him directly to McIver Estate. Just before the vehicle reached its turn off point, Solomon heard the driver urge the horses to halt.

"You runnin'?"

"No, no sir, transportin'."

"Let's see your papers, then."

"Is there a problem?"

The carriage driver, and the two white men who stopped him, turned toward the one who had spoken from the interior of the finely crafted vessel.

"Beg pardon, sir," one of the men quickly apologized while tipping his hat.

Solomon's face was devoid of expression. "I'm on my way to a business meeting, and this is a waste of my time."

"Yes, sir," the other man agreed, already backing his horse from the path of the carriage and its 'white' passenger.

Jesse Morton, the driver, pulled off his cap and wiped beads of moisture from his brow. "That was somethin' else, Mister Solomon. Guess it pays to be on the lighter side," he said, watching the two horsemen ride off into the distance.

Solomon joined Jesse in laughing over the well meaning comment. Unfortunately, the laughter didn't reach his eyes.

"Have the bedrooms been aired, Dot?"

"Everything been done just as you instructed, Mister Jason!"

"Clara, I'll be stopping by for a sample of tonight's dinner shortly!"

"Yes, sir!" the head cook called back.

Jason McIver was more like the mistress of the manner than the king of the castle that afternoon. Since dawn, he had been checking in with everyone from the field men to the upstairs maids. He wanted to ensure the estate was in top shape when his houseguest arrived.

Of course, it was hard to find the home in anything other than pristine condition. McIver Estate was truly a beautiful vision. Its cozy elegance rivaled the lavish décor of homes owned by some of the wealthiest white Charlestonians. Though a great deal of the crafted wood furnishings were somewhat dated, they had been cared for to the point that each piece appeared as though it had been freshly carved.

Tapestries and Oriental rugs covered the polished hardwoods and walls. Each room was arranged with a loving touch and pulsed with a personality of its own. It was a house that boasted comfort and serenity.

Jason had been on the second floor, making his rounds, when he approached his daughter's bed chamber door. He knocked once upon the heavy maple door before entering.

"And how are we this afternoon?" he bellowed, intentionally overlooking his daughter's pouting expression.

Jacinta's gaze remained fixed on her writing. "I'm surprisingly well, Poppa, in spite of the fact that I was sent to my room like a child."

"Well, when you act like a child, I assumed it's the way you want to be treated," Jason countered, almost bursting into laughter when he saw her wounded expression.

"May I dine in my room tonight?" she asked, turning back to her work.

"No, you may choose your attire for dinner with our guest," he said and pressed a quick kiss to her forehead. "I meant what I said, Jaci. I want you to take more of an interest in the affairs of this estate. Now you have four hours to get ready."

Jacinta waited until the door closed behind her father. "Four hours . . . that gives me just enough time."

❦

With a knot securing the torn brown scarf covering her hair, Jacinta crept the short distance from the woods to the Sula family's quarters. Since her work recording the thoughts of Nambia Sula was complete, she hoped to speak with Mingo and Laile Sula next.

"Zambi!" Jacinta whispered, having spotted her friend across the clearing.

Zambia peered nervously across her shoulder before hurrying over. "This isn't the time, Jaci."

Jacinta frowned, looking past Zambia's shoulder. "Why not? What's happening?"

"Jaci, go!"

"No, what is it?"

"Mama and Poppa are fighting again," she whispered.

Jacinta's brown eyes sparkled with excitement. "Another meeting?" she guessed.

"Jacinta, please!"

Finally, Jacinta tuned in to her best friend's distress. She and Zambia had become friends the instant Jacinta discovered the pathway connecting the Wallens Plantation with McIver Estate. During the last twelve years, Jacinta had learned much about Zambia's life and, in turn, taught her much about her own. Unbeknownst to the Wallens group and even her own parents, Zambia had learned history, science, math, reading and writing all under Jacinta's tutelage.

"Zambi," Jacinta whispered, pulling her friend close when she saw the girl's eyes brim with tears. "I'm sorry, it's all right," she soothed.

"Poppa won't listen to Mama," Zambia explained, shaking her head against Jacinta's shoulder. "Mama's scared he'll be caught and beat if he go to that meeting. Jore!" she cried, having spotted her brother heading towards the woods.

Jore Sula began to wave his hand to urge her silence. He quickly closed the distance between them, constantly glancing across his slender shoulders.

"Where are you going?" Zambia asked, clutching the tail of his shirt.

"The old church, I—"

"What? Jore!"

Jore looked as though he wanted to confide more to his sister, but appeared suspicious when he realized it was Jacinta dressed in the ragged garb. Usually taken aback by her beauty, Jore's attitude that afternoon was distinctly hostile.

"What you done said to her, Zambi?"

"Nothing, I—"

"Keep your mouth shut, you hear?"

Jacinta stepped closer to Jore, unmindful of his attitude. "Keep my mouth shut about what?" she firmly inquired.

Jore's slanting brown gaze narrowed a bit more as though he were trying to read her thoughts. "You know dang well what, Jaci McIver. You just keep your mouth shut 'round them high yellow house folk of yours. Mr. Vesey don't need to be betrayed by them mulattoes."

"Jore!" both women called when the young man suddenly bolted past them.

Solomon's dark eyes were drawn close in concentration as he focused on the documents spread next to him on the cushioned black velvet seat. The carriage jerked to a sudden halt just then, sending the papers spilling to the floor.

"Dammit!" he muttered, "What now?" he grumbled, leaning forward to unlatch and open the side door. This time, his driver's way had been impeded by two men on foot. Two black men.

Solomon listened intently. The conversation was hushed and hurried, yet he heard mention of a meeting and a few names of those who would be in attendance. His dark, deep-set gaze sharpened when he heard the word "freedom." Soon, the men were rushing off and the driver was commanding the horses to 'giddy-up'.

"Sorry 'bout that, Mister Solomon!" he called, snapping the reigns feverishly as he spoke. "McIver Estate just 'round the bend!"

CHAPTER 3

"People are so strange, Jaci. People like you," Zambia clarified later that afternoon while she and Jacinta walked along their secret path munching on chinaberries until they found a spot to sit. "I'd think free people be wanting to stay away from slavery and death and beatin'. I know I would," she decided with an indignant huff.

Jacinta blew dirt from a berry before popping it into her mouth. "You say that now, but if you lived my life it would only make you angry to see those living such terrible ones. You'd want to do as much as possible to help them live your kind of life."

Zambia only shrugged.

"I have to know what's going on with the people," Jacinta suddenly blurted out of frustration. "I only happened upon that meeting in July and had to leave before it was over."

"Jaci, what could you do?"

Jacinta didn't misunderstand the question. "Maybe nothing. Maybe much. I told your grandma that I wanted to record the events in the hopes that someone would read them and offer help. *Real* help, Zambi," she stressed, pinning her friend with an unwavering stare. "Maybe then freedom would come for slaves."

Zambia studied her friend closely, and then looked away. Jacinta caught a glimpse of the same suspicion she'd seen in Jore's eyes earlier that day.

"I know that my upbringing would cause people to think I can't be trusted," Jacinta casually interjected, pretending to be entranced by the shape of the chinaberry she held.

"Then why keep trying to be involved?" Zambia challenged, drawing her knees up to her chin.

"Because I want to see us free," Jacinta simply replied. "This thing with Mr. Vesey . . . something is about to happen. Something that could very well bring us freedom."

"It's still dangerous, Jaci," Zambia softly warned, reaching out to grab her friend's hand. "What if the wrong eyes see what you write?"

"That wouldn't happen. I'd die before I'd let that happen," she vowed, recalling her lost notebook. She had decided to record all she heard mentally and then fill her journals upon returning home.

Zambia was not impressed. "You a fool, Jaci."

"Maybe, but I plan to be part of this, Zambi. I heard Jore say something about the old church. Was it the African Church? The one raided by the city guard six years ago?"

"No, Jaci," Zambia sighed, standing to brush dirt from the folds of her old cotton work dress.

"Then where?" Jacinta pleaded, gazing up at Zambia from her seat on the ground. "You know you're curious," she taunted.

Zambia chewed her bottom lip and appeared to be debating. Finally, she crossed her arms over her chest. "I have to go with you," she decided.

Jacinta clasped her hands and jumped to her feet. "Let's go."

ꝯ

"Mr. Dikembe! Welcome! Welcome to McIver Estate! My home is yours, please come in and make yourself comfortable!"

"Thank you," Solomon slowly responded, a genuine smile tugging at his mouth. The shorter, stout, dark-skinned gentleman shook his hand rigorously while pulling him towards the stately front porch. Meanwhile, some members of the house staff greeted Solomon while others retrieved his bags from the carriage.

Solomon had to admit that he'd never been treated so much like royalty and with such graciousness. He was certain to be shunned by Jason McIver or, at the very least, treated quite coolly once the man met him face to face. On the contrary, Jason took his topcoat once they entered the foyer and escorted him into the smoking lounge.

"What's your drink, Mr. Dikembe?" Jason asked, while heading to the impressive walled bar in the corner of the large room.

"Oh, uh, cognac if you keep it," Solomon hastily remarked, his attention more focused on the craftsmanship of his surroundings. Obviously the constructor of the estate had taken great time and care with its creation. "But please call me Solomon. Mr. Dikembe was my grandfather."

Jason chuckled heartily, almost letting Solomon's cognac spill from the confines of its beaded glass. "A hearty sense of humor, I like you even more! And you must call me Jason," he ordered.

"Agreed," Solomon replied with a nod and tilt of his glass. "You have a remarkable home, sir."

Jason took a sip of his brandy and relished the liquid warming his insides. "I thank you. I count my blessings each day for having such a roof above my head."

"And it is quite a roof," Solomon noted, taking in the artistry of the carvings among the claw foot sofas and armchairs which furnished the room. Not to mention the high ceilings and tall windows that offered breathtaking views of the tree-dotted landscape.

"You must be exhausted after such a long journey. Here," Jason called, reaching for Solomon's glass, "let me freshen your drink, then I'll show you to your room."

"My daughter Jacinta will be joining us for dinner. I believe that I've convinced her to participate in our business discussion as well."

"She has no interest in it, I gather?" Solomon queried while he and Jason strolled the mansion's long corridors.

Jason sipped a bit more of his brandy. "She has other things on her mind. More *important* things in her opinion."

Solomon chuckled, triggering the long dimple he possessed. "I see," he whispered.

"I won't be offended if you prefer she not join us."

"No, sir, I have no problem with it. She should take an interest in how she is cared for."

Jason laughed. "This way, my boy!" he instructed, leading the way to a curving staircase that would take them to the second floor.

The one-room shack nestled within the woods was barely noticeable from its cover of heavy brush and trees. The volume of raised voices was effectively muffled by sounds of crickets and other insects, not to mention the wind that rushed through the leaves and hanging moss that were barely clinging to the limbs above. The 'goings-on' inside the rickety dwelling seemed more along the lines of a religious revival than a political meeting. There were intervals of speaking followed by intense clapping and singing.

" 'Behold the day of the Lord cometh, and thy spoil shall be divided in the midst of thee!' This reading is taken from Zachariah fourteen, verses one through two, dear brothers. 'For I shall gather all nations against Jerusalem to battle . . .' "

Jacinta and Zambia arrived amidst the speech given by Denmark Vesey. Eager to hear the man's words as clearly as possible, Jacinta began to squeeze towards the front of the room. Though both women were garbed as men, Zambia was still concerned. Unfortunately, her attempts to catch Jacinta's sleeve were unsuccessful. The room was densely packed with bodies. Everyone was silent, save the short, rotund gentleman at the front of the room. Jacinta stood on her toes to catch just a glimpse of him.

"And so I say to you brothers, when? When, if not now? At this moment we must take full advantage of the opportunity. Our numbers are great, far surpassing those of our oppressors," the old man spoke, his eyes seeming to move over each face as though he were speaking to them one on one. "Some of you say 'no' to rebellion. I say, when? When, my brothers? When do we deserve freedom?"

"Freedom," Jacinta whispered, her voice mingling with the raised shouts and words of agreement. "I knew it!" She spoke a bit louder for Zambia's benefit. "It is really going to happen this time!"

"It is still talk, Jaci. It has always been talk, you know this!" Zambia reminded her friend, glancing nervously about as she was more than ready to leave the gathering.

Jacinta's rich coffee stare was still focused straight ahead. "There has always been talk, yes. But never before has there been one person to incite the crowd as this man does."

McIver Estate housed three dining rooms aside from the smallest one, which was located in the kitchen. Solomon Dikembe dined with his host in the one just off from the library. The rectangular, cherry-wood table was built to accommodate ten diners. That evening's menu consisted of smoked catfish with onion sauce, steamed rice with broccoli, cornmeal muffins and crisp cider.

"Why Charleston, Mr. Dikembe?" Jason inquired while expertly removing the long bone from his catfish.

Solomon shrugged, while debating his answer. "I'd traveled to the state several months ago after hearing many speak of its beauty—Charleston's beauty in particular," he recalled, spooning the fragrant, flavorful onion sauce over his rice. "Once I visited, I knew I wanted to own property here should the opportunity ever present itself."

"Well, my boy, you've been blessed, as the opportunity is very well presenting itself!" Jason bellowed, though his expression remained reserved.

Solomon noticed. "Why don't you ask your intended question, sir? I'm not easily offended," he said, tugging on the cuffs of his gray cloth coat.

Jason cleared his throat and set his fork aside. "Very well. I am aware of your other holdings. Quite impressive for a man your age. Farmlands and other property in Ohio and Illinois, not to mention your home in Michigan and a ship at your disposal. Obviously you are a man who can purchase property anywhere, and I'm sure you know that Charleston is a city whose beauty matches its horrors. Wouldn't owning land here be more trouble than it's worth?"

Solomon's black stare appeared more intense as he focused on the fire blazing from the hearth across the dining room. "My reasons are simple, sir. As you are undoubtedly aware, there is a high concentration of blacks in the area both free and enslaved. As you are also aware, many of the enslaved are permitted to hire out their services. Of course, they make next to nothing once their master obtains his share of their pay. Acquiring this land would allow me to hire my own people and pay them fairly. My hope is to see that they are able to purchase their freedom."

Jason's silver gray brows rose high on his cinnamon brown face. "Impressive words, admirable intentions. Quite admirable coming from someone so young and financially secure."

Solomon grinned while cutting a morsel of the succulent catfish. "Not to mention the fact that I am mulatto," he smoothly interjected.

Jason returned the grin and nodded once in acknowledgement. "Many of the mulattoes here care little, if anything, for their enslaved brethren."

Solomon didn't bother to mask his distaste over the fact. "I have dreamed of seeing my people free since I was a small boy," he said.

"Some work for a lifetime and never acquire enough money to purchase their freedom," Jason noted.

"Perhaps they won't have to *purchase* it. Maybe one day they will fight for it. Fight for it and win," Solomon challenged.

"Bah!" Jason cringed, leaning forward to wolf down a bit of rice and broccoli. "You talk as my daughter does."

Solomon chuckled. "Wasn't she to join us tonight?" he asked, noticing a fierce glare contort Jason's kind features.

"She wasn't in her room or anywhere else on the estate," Jason shared.

"Is there cause to be concerned?" Solomon inquired, propping his elbow against the arm of the spider-legged Hepplewhite chair.

Jason shook his head and continued to dine. "I doubt it. My daughter lives to defy me, but I'll not stand for it much longer."

Jacinta was returning home. A string of curses flew past her lips as she raced down the dusty back pathway. It was hopeless to believe her father hadn't noticed her absence, she decided while pulling off the tattered brown coat and beige shirt. Now she would have to create some grand excuse if she even hoped to escape his full wrath. Unfortunately, she believed her arsenal of excuses was empty.

She raced towards the barn and fell to her knees next to the weakened wooden slab she used to hide her change of clothes. Snatching the hat from her head, her black mane provided a partial cover for her back and breasts. Quickly, she stood to kick off the boots and trousers. She gave a fast shake to her fresh, informal evening dress and laid it across the wood fence that surrounded the barn. Completely nude, she tossed her hair across her shoulders and reached for the under things she'd packed along with the dress. She was about to slip into a white chemise, when she heard a throat clearing behind her. Forgetting her appearance, Jacinta whirled around and looked up. Way up. She found herself gazing into the face of a darkly handsome man who had the deepest pair of eyes she had ever seen.

She didn't know if it was fear, embarrassment or entrancement that kept her rooted to her spot. She didn't even think to cover herself with the chemise she clutched. At first, she thought he seemed vaguely familiar, but surely she would have recalled meeting him.

Solomon was thunderstruck. It was her! The woman who had captivated him months before. Now she was standing there before him in the moonlight and captivating him all over again. His smoldering onyx stare faltered to rake her tiny curvaceous body in a leisurely manner that was all too blatant in its approval.

When the beautiful stranger's dark gaze traveled progressively lower, Jacinta regained her senses. Her fearless demeanor quickly returned and her warm brown gaze turned stormy.

"How dare you sneak up on me that way?! Do you know that you are trespassing on private property, sir?"

"I could ask the same of you," Solomon challenged, his eyes leaving Jacinta's lovely face to scan her nude form once more.

Jacinta dismissed the shiver she felt attacking her spine. His voice was like—like a roll of thunder, she decided, her eyes widening as recognition dawned. Yes, his voice was like a roll of thunder grown faint after the storm. She steeled herself against collapsing at his feet.

"You could ask the same of me, sir. But then, unlike you, I could say that this is my home, and I don't think my father would appreciate knowing he has an intruder on his property."

So she was the daughter, Solomon realized. "Love, I think my being here is the least of your worries," he fore-warned softly.

Jacinta was outraged. "How dare you speak so familiar with me?" she blasted, praying that he not recall where they'd met.

"Seeing as we've met before, Jacinta, I think I should be allowed *some* familiarity."

He remembered, Jacinta acknowledged, her full lips thinning into a grim line. "How do you know my name? And what are you doing here?" she questioned, refusing to let him see her unease.

Solomon simply eased his massive hands into his trouser pockets while standing back on his long legs. "I'd like nothing more than to spend the rest of the night answering every question you can think of. Especially if you remain attired as such."

Jacinta gasped when Solomon's gaze lowered yet again. "Bastard," she hissed, while jerking into her che-mise and frilly drawers. "The very least you could do is look away," she chastised.

"Where is the sense in that?" he replied, his broad shoulders rising in a lazy shrug. "You forget that I've already viewed so very much." he teased, tilting his head to one side.

Jacinta felt her skin burn beneath the man's stare. Donning her clothing took far longer than usual, with her hands shaking beneath the unwavering intensity of his bottomless gaze.

"My father will see to you," she grumbled when she was done. Brushing past him, she stormed toward the main house.

"Poppa! Poppa!"

Jason was finishing off the last of his brandy and paperwork when Jacinta burst into his office. His expression was at once murderous.

Jacinta paid no heed to her father's expression. She was far more confident in approaching him now— believing to have found a perfect reason to divert his attention from her late arrival. She glanced across her shoulder and was a bit taken aback to find the soft-spoken stranger entering the front door of the house.

Jason noticed his houseguest heading toward the office door and stood behind the polished pinewood desk. "Forgive me for such an unusual introduction to my daughter and, unfortunately, the only successor to my business," he announced.

Solomon chuckled, taking in Jacinta's reaction to her father's words. Her extremely long lashes fluttered as she bristled beneath the insult.

"On the contrary, sir," he said, stepping further into the spacious room. "I was out for a walk and I, uh, met your daughter on her way in," he explained, once again raking her body with sweet familiarity. "She's the only person, save yourself and your staff, who hasn't mistaken me for a white man."

Jacinta's lips parted in surprise as her eyes narrowed. Her anger was now mingled with confusion and curiosity. She had, in fact, thought that very thing.

"Did you forget our dinner meeting this evening?" Jason asked his daughter while stepping from behind his desk.

Jacinta took a small step forward. "Poppa I—"

"This is Mr. Solomon Dikembe, our business associate and houseguest."

"Dikembe?" Jacinta whispered, scrutinizing the man who looked completely unsuited to the completely African surname.

"Answers, Jacinta!" Jason ordered, watching his daughter gasp and cast her eyes upon the rug. "But I already have the answers, don't I?" he continued.

"Poppa—"

"Don't I?"

Jacinta kept her head bowed. "Should we be discussing this before your guest?" she whispered, looking sideways at Solomon from beneath the heavy fringe of her lashes.

Jason's brows narrowed. "Oh? Embarrassed?" he guessed, propping both hands inside the small pockets on the front of his gold vest. "Perhaps you will think twice before disobeying me again."

"But Poppa—"

"Answers, Jacinta Paulette McIver! And don't use Zambia as an excuse. I'll deal with you about your trips to the Wallens plantation, but I know you weren't there this night."

Jacinta tilted her chin up in defiance, but she knew the time for truth had arrived. "There was a meeting."

"About?"

"The rebellion."

"Jacinta—"

"Poppa, I believe it this time," she cried, following her father across his office and splaying her hands across the top of his desk. "If you'd just let me tell you about it—"

"Foolishness."

"If only you would attend one of the meetings—"

"And that is where you were this evening?"

Jacinta winced and shot a quick glance toward her father's silent guest. She noticed the teasing light in Solomon's eyes had been replaced by an intensity she couldn't understand. Unfortunately, she had no time to dwell upon it.

"Do you think your name or your beauty would save you should you be discovered at one of those gatherings?" Jason pounded his fist to the desk with such force that it caused the pens and ink bottles to make a noisy clatter.

"The location and time of the meetings are kept in the strictest confidence," Jacinta explained, her molten brown gaze wide as she tried to convince her father. "You could attend a meeting and no one would be the wiser."

"Dammit girl, we are not speaking of my attendance, but yours!"

"Poppa, please calm down."

"How can I?" Jason silently commanded himself to lower his voice. "Not only would you be beaten but I have no doubt those devils would take the utmost pleasure in passing you around for a bit of dalliance before they hung you." He predicted coldly, hoping his words would put just an ounce of fear in her.

Jacinta, however, remained undaunted. "I am always cautious when I go out."

Solomon bowed his head in an attempt to hide his smile.

Jason gave up. "Go to your room, Jacinta."

"But Poppa—"

"*Now*. I don't want to see you again until we meet at the breakfast table in the morn," he clarified, strolling over to stoke the fire. "If I find you've disobeyed me again *I* will take the lash to you myself."

Jacinta inhaled deeply and let any further words of argument die on her tongue. She knew her usually indulgent, doting father was very serious about the threat. She bowed stiffly, cast one last loathing glare in Solomon's direction and left the room.

Jason's stoic resolve had vanished the instant Jacinta left the room. His shoulders lost a bit of their stiffness and he set the iron poker against the brick hearth. "That girl will be the death of me," he sighed, perching on the arm of one of the cushioned Thomas Hope chairs that flanked the fireplace.

Solomon chuckled, casting a glance toward the doorway Jacinta had stormed through. "She's quite headstrong."

Jason stopped massaging the bridge of his nose and sent his houseguest a knowing look. "You may be more deliberate in your opinions, young man. That is far more than headstrong."

Solomon shook his head while stroking the silken whiskers that roughened his jaw. "Definitely." He joined Jason in a round of hearty male laughter.

"Oh . . ." Jason sighed, as his laughter dwindled. "She inherited every bit of her compassion from her grandfather. She's been committed to the slave issue, or rather, to its abolishment, since she was a small child."

"Admirable."

Jason's smile held no trace of humor. "Admirable, yes. And I do admire her passion, but it could get her killed."

Solomon stepped over to refresh his drink and pour Jason another. "Does anyone suspect her involvement?"

"I don't believe there's a white person who even knows about what's being planned. These secret locations my daughter believes in would most certainly be rooted out if the City Guard had any idea talk of rebellion was in the air."

"I've heard some of this rebellion since I docked here and during my last trip." Solomon handed Jason the drink. "Mayhap nothing will come of it save the people having something to place hope in for a change."

Jason was uncertain. "Whatever the case, I know that I want her out of Charleston," he laughed shortly. "She'd never go, I'd wager. No matter how dazzling I made the trip sound."

Solomon shrugged. "She is a young woman, sir. She's seen nothing of this country, let alone the world, I assume?" He watched Jason shake his head. "Her attachments will change." He downed his cognac in one long swallow.

"I pray you're right, son. Otherwise, I may have to force the issue." Jason set his drink aside as though he'd lost his taste for the brandy. "Charleston is a city on the verge of great unrest." He crossed his arms over his chest as he looked out into the still pitch black of the night. "My daughter is right to believe something is going to happen." He turned to fix Solomon with a stony glare. "Still, I refuse to allow her to witness what is to come, or to be consumed by it."

CHAPTER 4

Jacinta was first to the breakfast table the following morning. She was already on her second plate of scrambled eggs, sausage and pan bread when her father arrived with Solomon.

"Ah, what a vision," Jason drawled, watching his daughter wolfing down the food. "I take this to mean your meeting did not offer rations last evening?"

Jacinta swallowed before placing her fork on the bread plate. Keeping her gaze downcast, she dabbed the corner of her mouth with a white linen napkin. "I respect you, Poppa, but I have to say that your teasing manner toward something so important is completely unfair."

"From what I understand there's been nothing more than talk about this for years now."

Silence followed Solomon's comment. Jacinta leaned back against her chair and regarded him with a stony gaze. She watched as he filled his plate at the buffet, her eyes scanning the breadth of his wide shoulders and back. The expensive cut of his deep beige suit coat and trousers flattered both his physique and complexion. "From what you . . . understand?" she inquired when he took a seat directly across from her. "And you've been in Charleston all of one day, is that correct, sir?"

"Jacinta!"

"She is correct, sir," Solomon confirmed slowly, raising his hand towards Jason. "However, Miss McIver, I do believe that proves my point. There has been an abundance of talk," he reiterated, his dark gaze never wavering from her brown one.

Jason burst into laughter upon seeing Jacinta open her mouth for a retort and then close it as though she could think of nothing to say. "'Tis a rare occasion to see my Jaci speechless!" he bellowed.

Jacinta was speechless more from outrage than embarrassment. Her hands clenched within the folds of her tanned dress with its ruffled white neckline. "May I be excused?" she whispered, already pushing his chair away from the table.

"You may," Jason granted amidst his chuckles. "But Jaci," he called, tapping his fingers against the lavender tablecloth, "you are to remain inside the house today. Is that clear?"

Jacinta's chest heaved and her maple gaze grew stormy at once.

"The lash is primed and ready," Jason warned when her lips parted to argue.

Refusing to allow her father's intriguing guest to see her riled yet again, Jacinta forced a sweet smile to her lips. "Actually, Poppa, I had already planned to spend the day inside. It looks very rainy and I would assume very chilly outdoors," she explained, before nodding once. "Good day, Poppa . . . Mr. Dikembe," she called as though it were an afterthought.

Jason slapped his hand to the table when Jacinta departed. The delicate dishes and silverware jumped at the gesture. "Headstrong, eh?" he asked Solomon, hearty laughter coloring the question. "And you are certain there's nothing more you'd care to add to my daughter's list of . . . attributes?" he teased.

Solomon's bottomless ebony stare remained focused on the maple wood door, still swinging in the wake of Jacinta's exit. "She is the most beautiful thing I have ever seen."

Expecting some witty reply or a round of boisterous laughter, Jason was stunned. His comical expression faded as he appeared intrigued, then thoughtful. The intensity of his light brown gaze didn't go unnoticed by Solomon, who smiled and set his napkin onto the dining table.

"I apologize if the comment seemed ill-mannered," Solomon spoke after a few silent moments.

Jason shook his head slowly, still taken aback by Solomon's candor. "Not at all, son. You have just paid a very high compliment to my daughter. I don't find such a thing ill-mannered in the least."

Solomon nodded once, then turned his attention towards the delectable breakfast before him.

Meanwhile, Jason was still in a state of concentration. For years, he had prayed for a time such as this. His daughter would be nineteen soon—far beyond the age when most young women were married with families of their own. Jason was determined to see his daughter living that life. Of course, it had been no great hardship attracting interested candidates. Jacinta was indeed a ravishing beauty, and he'd had offers from both black *and* white suitors.

While the later only lusted after her beauty and physical endowments, the former saw a smart, beautiful woman capable of producing and raising smart, strong handsome sons. Jason would never entertain the thought of linking his only daughter to a white man. Still, he could not see himself linking her to one of his own kind, either. At least, not one who resided in Charleston-or any place where slavery reigned supreme. Jason wanted his daughter far away in a world where she could live like the queen he'd always treated her. He wanted her to see more of the world than the tears, bloodshed and death that met her eyes the moment she left the protective walls of the estate. He looked back at Solomon. Yes, this was the young man, he thought. He would spend his life making her happy and he would give his life to protect her.

Solomon was in the process of slicing into another portion of the flavorful sausage when he took note of Jason's quiet. "Are you all right, sir?" he asked, his sleek black brows drawn close in concern.

Jason shook off his musings and favored Solomon with a cool grin. "Just recalling some unfinished business I should handle. We'll meet for lunch in the sitting room. Have one of the maids show you where it is."

"If it's all the same, Sir, I'd more enjoy finding it on my own. It'll give me the chance to study the artwork I noticed when I arrived."

"Perfectly all right, Son," Jason said as he stood from the table. "Enjoy the rest of your meal and we'll talk during lunch." He patted Solomon's shoulder on his way out of the room.

No one, save Jason McIver and the field men, ventured outside McIver Estate on that day. It rained incessantly and the temperature had dropped well past "chilly" to downright cold.

After breakfast, Solomon finished a few correspondences and then took a leisurely walk around the breathtaking mansion. He realized it would take some time to completely tour the home. Still, Solomon was impressed by all he had seen. He decided to make a point of learning how Jason McIver had acquired and maintained such a dwelling in the midst of such intolerance for black success.

He had never seen such exquisite artistry in one place. From the tapestries of the Charleston Harbor and sunsets off the coast of the sea islands, to the masks and statues with their obvious Gullah overtones, Jason McIver was a man proud of his homeland and his heritage.

Solomon's walk led him through several rooms, each one decorated by breathtaking artwork and impressive furniture. The paintings along the corridor leading to the library and music room held his attention for countless minutes. Clearly, the vibrant creations had been inspired by a person of African descent. The artist's love for the subjects within the bronzed frames was quite evident. It took Solomon close to two hours to travel that corridor. He became lost in the abundance of beauty as his soulful black eyes devoured every detail of the work. He was just entering the sitting room as the lunch hour approached.

The room's tall windows were left devoid of draperies to allow sunlight to filter the area. Due to the dreariness of the day, the room was lit by firelight from its multitude of oil lamps and the snapping flames from the stone hearth. Solomon took a moment to study the wet landscape, which appeared gray and lifeless beneath the dark storm clouds. Barely two minutes had passed before he realized he was not alone.

Jacinta had obviously ventured to the room to do some writing; her pads and other utensils were strewn on one of the round, three-legged cherry wood tables. She had fallen asleep in one of the large, hunter green armchairs. Solomon's handsome features were set in an intent manner as he watched her slumber. His deep, piercing stare memorized her sweet, chocolate face relaxed in sleep. The soft downward pout of her slightly parted lips seemed to beckon his kiss.

Solomon grunted and turned away to massage the bridge of his nose. He squeezed his eyes shut, tight, to ward off the ache of his loins tightening in response to the voluptuous vision in his presence. Choosing to direct his attention elsewhere, he focused on a small journal nestled between Jacinta's prone form and the arm of the chair. Gently, he extracted the book from its position.

He began to read. The smile tugging the curve of his mouth indicated his expectation to view some light-hearted piece of fluff. That easy smile, however, faded as his eyes traveled further down the page. The passages, written in Jacinta's elegant script, were, at times, humorous, comforting and unsettling. Solomon's fist clenched more than once as he read through the journal. Jacinta had managed to capture the spirit and the burden of the life of slavery and all its consequences.

"What the hell are you doing?"

Solomon continued to read, massaging his hair-roughened jaw as he paced the heavy black rug beneath his feet. Upon completing the passage, he turned towards her. Jacinta was awake and watching him with her property.

"I'm reading your work," he replied, slapping the book against the palm of his hand. "This is quite good."

Jacinta steeled herself against the feeling of pride washing over her. "I don't recall seeking your opinion, sir," she whispered.

Solomon shrugged. "Neither do I."

"Well?" She set her fists against her slender hips when he only watched her expectantly. "Will you please return that?" she hissed.

Instead, Solomon turned away once more with the book in his hand. "This is very good. You have a vivid imagination," he said, intentionally goading her.

Slowly, Jacinta stood from the deep armchair. "You horse's ass. Every word in that book is true. They are the thoughts of real people—slaves."

Solomon knew as much and was even more impressed by her interest in such a topic. "An interesting fascination for a young woman such as yourself."

"Fascination?" Jacinta repeated the word as though it were foul. "You think hearing stories of unimaginable cruelty fascinating? I can't count the nights I've cried while writing those very words you find so amusing."

"I never said I found them amusing," Solomon clarified, regretting that he had teased her so. "Still, I find it very odd that you would take such an interest in this."

Jacinta's luminous gaze narrowed sharply and Solomon held his breath. If possible, her reaction made her appear even more beautiful.

"Why would you find it odd?" she inquired, unaware of how she was affecting Solomon.

He simply thumbed through the book and strolled the spacious room. "Most young women raised as you've been, sheltered, pampered—"

"How dare—"

"Educated, but still spoiled, I'd think you'd be interested in something more tame, perhaps. The theatre, creating the nicest garden, how to be a gracious hostess . . ."

"Bastard!" Jacinta spat, closing the distance between them. "You know nothing about me, yet you've done nothing but try to belittle me since you've been here."

Solomon chuckled, sparking the lone dimple to splice his cheek. His gorgeous gaze narrowed almost to the point of closing and he appeared completely charming and roguish at once. "It has not been my intention to do so, Miss McIver."

"Yet you've done it quite well," she retorted, while extending her hand. "I'll take my property now."

"For a kiss," Solomon bartered without hesitation.

Jacinta closed her eyes for a second or two, then shook her head. "Beg pardon?"

Solomon behaved as though his request were nothing out of the ordinary. "Your property returned for a kiss."

"You can't be serious?"

Solomon perched on the corner of a windowsill. "I'm always serious when enjoyment is at stake."

Jacinta backed away, allowing more distance between them as the shivers along her spine grew more persistent. "My father is conducting business with you because he believes you are decent and forthright."

"But you know better?"

"I do."

"Well then?"

Jacinta lost her temper then. Forgetting the fact that this man unsettled her as no other, she charged for him. Prepared to do battle for her property and her pride, she was determined to slap the confident smirk from his handsome face.

Jacinta's fit of rage was met by Solomon's soft laughter. He held her at bay easily, his large hands encircling her wrists while he held her arms away from her body. His mesmerizing gaze caressed her face with a lover's gentleness before it lowered to appreciate the sight of her heaving bosom.

"Such unnecessary exertion," he commented, looking on as her rapid breathing threatened to force her breasts past the confines of the lacy, scooped neckline of the gown that had teased him all during breakfast. "A simple kiss won't take nearly as much out of you," he concluded.

Jacinta strained against his hold about her wrists. "Surely you don't make a practice of resorting to such tactics to obtain kisses from helpless women?" she shuddered.

"I don't," he conceded, tightening his hold on her wrists to draw her closer. "But, love, I don't usually encounter such beauties as yourself, and you are certainly no helpless lady."

Jacinta's lashes fluttered in rapid succession as her chocolate stare searched his dark one for some clue about his true intentions. "How do I know I can trust you?" she asked in a tiny voice. The wolfish grin she received in response was answer enough.

"You don't know that."

Jacinta expelled a sigh of desperation and defeat. "Just get it over with," she commanded, praying for some interruption.

Of course she'd expected something brutal and nauseating. Her lashes fluttered closed over her eyes in a resigned fashion. Solomon's smile was sweetness and wonder personified as his midnight stare trailed the curving loveliness of her doll face. He took both her wrists in one hand and removed what little distance remained between them.

Jacinta sensed his face close to hers and squeezed her eyes shut tight in expectation. The kiss, however, was not what she'd anticipated. It was unhurried and deliberate.

Solomon simply traced the supple curve of her mouth with the tip of his tongue. Then, his lips placed whisper soft kisses to each corner of her mouth before his tongue once again outlined its shape. Jacinta thought she felt a moan rising deep within her throat, but that was impossible. After all, this man she barely knew couldn't possibly wield such power over her, could he?

When Solomon applied a bit more pressure with his tongue, Jacinta's lips parted. He didn't invade her mouth greedily, as he wanted to. Moreover, he teased the dark, fragrant cavern with brief, darting strokes. Unconsciously, Jacinta responded, growing eager for the kiss and praying he would cease his teasing. Her prayers were answered when the final teasing stroke was followed by a leisurely thrust that forced the moan past her lips. Jacinta had no time to be preoccupied by the sound, though. She was far too enthralled by the possessiveness of his kiss. The slow thrusts of his tongue filled her mouth with a myriad of sensations. Solomon's kiss caressed and explored as it left her aroused and gasping her pleasure.

"Your property is on the sill," he spoke against her ear, pressing a kiss to the lobe before releasing her wrists and pulling back. He found that her eyes were still closed, her head still tilted back in anticipation of more.

Jacinta opened her eyes to find Solomon strolling towards the double doors of the sitting room. She pressed five shaking fingers against her mouth and could feel her lips throbbing from the kisses. Once again, her lengthy lashes fluttered in response to the sensations he had stirred someplace deep and unthinkable.

CHAPTER 5

"And you're this certain after knowing the man one day?"

Jason chuckled over his friend's concern. Scurvy Logan had been both friend and advisor to him since the days when they'd been young men hoping to change the world. Then, the heaviest topic on Jason's mind was how to court Pauletta Lichens, his future wife. Scurvy, of course, had been there offering his advice even then.

"I'm pleased by the way he handles her. She's so quick, but when he speaks he catches her off guard, and I know it has her intrigued."

"But intrigued enough to marry?" Scurvy inquired, leaning forward to pin Jason with a doubtful stare.

Jason acknowledged that improbability with a shrug. "Perhaps. I like him, and I think they'll make a fine match," he decided.

"Mmm . . . but will she?"

"Bah!" Jason scoffed with a quick wave. "She doesn't have to love him right away, but I wager that she will in time. Besides, the girl needs someone to take charge of her—to keep her from bringing harm to herself."

Scurvy was still unconvinced. "He must be quite a young man."

"You'll meet him at dinner this evening."

"And what of Jacinta?" Scurvy inquired, standing to fill a large white China cup with coffee. "Has she said or done anything to give you cause to believe she has any feelings for this boy?"

"Nothing's happened yet, but I know this is the man who will take my daughter out of Charleston. He is the one she should begin her adult life with."

Now Scurvy was more than doubtful, he was suspicious. "I sense an urgency in you, friend," he whispered, his long, dark face appearing more stern as he regarded Jason. "Are you sure there is nothing more going on here?"

Jason passed his cup to Scurvy and watched him refill it with the fragrant coffee. "Nothing more?"

"You're not being threatened, are you?" Scurvy knew the jealousy and hatred that was directed toward Jason and his success.

"No, no nothing like that," Jason was quick to correct.

Scurvy's round, brown stare still harbored concern. "You know if things are . . . unsettled we can always contact Mr. McIver."

"I'm well aware of that, but I'll not seek that sort of help until it is absolutely necessary. I assure you, my friend, that I'm not being threatened just now," Jason said to Scurvy, a smug smile warming his kind face.

Scurvy seemed convinced. "If you say so, my friend."

Jason set his mug on the tea table and reached for his pipe. "Believe me, there's no need to bother New York," he said, referring to Roland McIver's brother who lived there and constantly urged Jason to contact him if *any-thing* threatened his brother's chosen heir.

"In truth, Scurvy, it's Jacinta who worries me." Standing from the claw-foot Chippendale, he strolled toward the brick fireplace to light his pipe. "Talk of rebellion is growing stronger."

Scurvy's shoulder rose beneath his black linen suit coat. "That's nothing new."

"My daughter believes there is more to the talk this time. She believes it quite strongly."

Scurvy began to nod. "And you're afraid she may become caught up in something?" he guessed, knowing what an outspoken opponent Jacinta was regarding the issue of slavery.

Jason stood lighting his pipe and speaking as he took short drags from the stem. "I'll see her married and far away from Charleston before I die. This young Dikembe is the one. He is the only one who I believe can tame that girl and, by God, I do believe she'll let him."

⟨ornament⟩

Solomon had retreated to the solitude of the library, located a ways from the sitting room on the other end of the long corridor. The cool, confident demeanor he displayed for Jacinta vanished the moment he was out of her sight. Now his fists were clenched tightly and his broad chest was taut with emotion.

He leaned against a towering shelf filled to the top with books. A picture of consternation, he massaged the strong curve of his jaw. What had come over him? What was Jacinta doing to him? He smiled, amusing himself with recollections of stories he'd heard about the voodoo and witchery that were common among certain tribes. Perhaps Jacinta McIver was some sort of sorceress, for she was surely casting a spell over his body and mind.

Following a short grin, Solomon cast the notion off as utter foolishness. Still, he had to question his actions. He had never been so forward with any woman—especially no woman he had only recently met and, not to mention, the daughter of a business associate!

In truth, he had never been placed in the position of needing to be the aggressor. Women had always flocked to him, and he was aware of that fact without becoming arrogant or overly confident as a result. He had known the pleasures of women from many cultures, many shapes and colors. Jacinta McIver, however, had more to concern herself with than bedding a man of good breeding and great wealth.

Solomon was intrigued by her, and all he knew about her were the ideals she defended so strongly. She believed that slavery was a horror and deserved to be abolished. Moreover, she was prepared to play an active role in bringing about that change. Suddenly, Solomon found himself hoping that the business venture with Jason McIver would take more time to complete. He wanted nothing more than to remain in Charleston, uncovering the numerous facets to the cool, lovely young rebel in his midst.

Jacinta remained in the sitting room. She'd taken a seat on the burgundy cushioned windowsill overlooking the east side of the grounds. The day was still wet and rainy, the light outside fading fast due to the onset of the evening. The remaining leaves barely held on to their places on the tree limbs that offered massive amounts of shade in summer. Now they fought against the cold, invisible wind intent on snatching them from safety.

This all went unnoticed by Jacinta. She stared blankly past the window, her syrupy gaze pensive and unblinking. Again, she shuddered—for the fifth time since Solomon's departure. She knew her reaction had nothing to do with the chill in the air. *What's happening here?* She had certainly been kissed before, and had convinced herself that it was an act she considered quite disgusting. The way Solomon kissed, though . . . there was no disgust, only wanting—*her* wanting.

She shook away the thought, brushing back a lock of hair that slipped past the coil at the nape of her neck. She knew nothing about Solomon Dikembe. Nothing, aside from the fact that he was tall, incomparably gorgeous, self aware, self possessed, self made and free ... and kissed like the sweetest dream.

"Dammit Jacinta! Stop this!" she ordered, pounding one fist on the window pane. "I have far more serious matters to worry about than dreaming some silly fantasy." Yes, Solomon Dikembe was all those things. He was also a lot like her father. That was a fact she could neither deny nor accept. She had known him less than two full days and already she had arrived at that conclusion. He possessed the same reserved, yet powerfully alert and commanding, demeanor as her father. Jacinta would wager he possessed more of those qualities than Jason McIver had ever had.

She believed Solomon Dikembe was a man who would not stand for her allegiance to her principles. Like her father, he would stifle her attempts to be her own woman. Unlike her father, however, Jacinta suspected Solomon would use *any* means to have her succumb to his will—means she would be unable, or unwilling, to resist.

Suddenly, Jacinta's sharp gaze caught movement among the trees littering the yard below. She sat a bit straighter along the sill, her fingertips pressed flat against the panes as she peered intently from her heightened view. At last, a figure stumbled forward and collapsed into the clearing.

Solomon, who was being introduced to Scurvy Logan, bolted from the smoking room with Jason at his heels. Jacinta's screams for her father brought the entire house out into the corridors.

"Where is she?" Solomon demanded as he stormed into each room along the hall. He caught sight of Jacinta's skirts swinging as she ran toward the end of the wing.

Jacinta raced to the kitchen that encompassed much of the rear of the mansion. Double mahogany doors, usually left open during the day, had been bolted shut against the wind and rain that had churned since morning. Jacinta quickly unhinged the bolts, flung open the door, and rushed off the wide screened porch. The man she'd seen collapse from her view out of the sitting room window was still there. Venturing closer, she could tell that he was shivering, from cold or pain, she couldn't be sure. Without a care for the mud that was blackening her lovely tanned dress, she knelt beside the man to find that his shirt was bloodied and lay in tatters around his waist. Jacinta's eyes were riveted on his back, a mass of blood and sliced skin. He had been beaten.

Jacinta jumped in surprise when she felt hands fold over her upper arms. Blinking against the rain pelting her eyes, she looked up to see Solomon's face close to hers. Easily, he pulled her away from the injured man before taking her place at his side.

"Let's get him in the house!" Jason called.

Solomon wasted no more time. Carefully, he eased his arms beneath the man's body and lifted him. Scurvy was already holding open the screen door as Jason and Jacinta preceded Solomon and the stranger under the watchful eyes and whispers of the house staff.

"The sitting room is closest!" Jason instructed, already leading the way.

Inside the room, Solomon set the man face down on one of the indigo long chairs. His moans were soft, yet persistent. Again, Jacinta knelt beside him, wiping rain and dirt away from his face with a piece torn from her underskirt. Slowly, her head tilted and her eyes narrowed in recognition.

"Jore?" she gasped in disbelief, as she stared into the face of her best friend's brother. "Please Lord, don't let him die," she whispered, pressing soft kisses to Jore Sula's forehead.

"Jacinta dear, perhaps you shouldn't—"

"Poppa, please," she begged, her mesmerizing stare filled with tears, "I know this man."

The three men standing in the room grew silent and more observant. Solomon was especially curious, and his dark gaze narrowed as he looked from Jacinta to the injured young man. The intensity in his eyes was laced with just a hint of jealousy.

"Masta . . . Masta Chuck went fool when he saw me comin' thru da gate," Jore tried to explain, though his voice sounded weak and barely audible. The rest of the explanation was hampered by a coughing spell that succeeded in forcing more blood past his wounds.

"Jore, don't try to say anymore," Jacinta urged, pressing her fingertips to his mouth. "You need to rest," she said, and then looked up at her father. "Oh, Poppa, do something, please!" she cried, her fingers nervously clenching and unclenching the folds of her dress.

"Jaci, calm yourself or I'll have to ask you to leave," Jason urged, though he understood and sympathized with his daughter. "Scurvy, go fetch Doc Samuels," he instructed, referring to the man who attended the medical needs of the city's free blacks. Franklin Samuels was a former slave of one of the town's top doctors. Samuels had been an apt pupil whom his master showed kindness and allowed him to apprentice in New Orleans under the renowned Doctor Robert Dove.

"Solomon, if you would please carry Mr. Sula to the third floor," Jason asked once Scurvy had gone.

With Jacinta at his heels, Solomon handled the three flights of stairs, and his wounded burden, with ease. Jore's groans gained volume with every step. The mutilated skin of his back stretched and oozed blood as Solomon carried him across his shoulder. Several times, he appeared on the verge of losing consciousness.

"It's all right, just a little further and we'll be in your room," Jacinta assured him, patting his cheek with one hand while slapping Solomon's shoulder with her other. "You could try being more gentle with him, you know?" she raged.

Solomon grimaced and kept walking. "My love, nothing short of this man lying flat and motionless will ease his pain. His back has been ripped apart."

"I know this, do you?"

Solomon halted his steps, just before reaching the third floor landing. "I really think it's better that your friend not hear your annoying voice just now. Especially when he has far more pressing matters on his mind."

Jacinta cringed, blinking as though he had slapped her. Still, she stifled what remained of her argument and the journey continued in peace.

Members of the house staff began to prepare Jore Sula's room the minute Jason McIver ordered him taken into the house. They were tucking fresh linens into the corners of the massive, maple four-poster bed when Solomon arrived.

Jacinta wrung her hands and watched while Solomon placed Jore stomach down in the center of the bed. The housemaids took over from there and saw to removing

Jore's ripped and bloodied clothing. Jacinta took her place at the top corner of the bed and squeezed Jore's hand while whispering words of assurance.

Meanwhile, Solomon stood away from the scene. His deep stare was hooded, and probing, as he watched Jacinta. He observed her tender manner toward the man, the softness of her melodic voice, the way her soothing chocolate-toned eyes stroked his face as her fingertips grazed his temple. Solomon felt his slow temper beginning to simmer. His lips tightened into a thin line and he chastised himself for harboring such murderous jealousy towards a man in such a condition.

The house staff had almost completely surrounded the bed. They worked diligently to comfort Jore, and it was no easy task.

"Why don't you leave and let these ladies tend to your friend?"

Jacinta ceased her gentle words towards Jore when she heard Solomon's gravely brogue. Her stare narrowed sharply as she slowly turned towards him. "Why don't *you* leave?" she suggested.

Solomon slid one hand into a side trouser pocket. "They could do a far more efficient job if you weren't in the way."

Jacinta set Jore's hand on the pillow, lest she crush it within hers. Once again, Solomon Dikembe was succeeding in rattling her most sensitive nerve.

"Mr. Dikembe, I appreciate your concern for my friend, but you're sadly mistaken if you believe I'd leave him in such a state."

"He's right, Jaci."

Jacinta rolled her eyes, the full curve of her mouth thinning at the sound of her father's voice.

"It's best if you leave. The doctor will be here shortly, and Jore needs to be prepared for the examination."

"And I won't interfere with whatever needs to be done, but I can't leave him, Poppa," Jacinta argued, already standing with her hands upon her hips.

Jason barely acknowledged her mood. "You can and you will, Jaci. This is no time for stubbornness."

"Listen to your father, Jacinta," Scurvy Logan urged.

"For once," Solomon goaded.

"Oh, shut up," Jacinta spat, regarding him with scathing eyes.

"Jacinta, that's enough!" Jason snapped, pointing towards the wide door. "I want you in your room, now! Dinner will be pushed back a few hours due to the incident."

"But I—"

"I think that's a fine idea," Solomon muttered, closing the distance between himself and Jacinta. Surprising everyone and pleasing Jason, he flung Jacinta across his shoulder in one effortless motion.

"Dammit!" she hissed, pounding his back with her fists. "Poppa! Do something!"

"In your room until suppertime," Jason requested, laughter following his words.

Jacinta kicked and screamed the entire way, unmindful of the interested stares she received from the passing house staff. Solomon Dikembe had gone too far that time. It was bad enough to be humiliated by him before her father, now he had done so before guests and members of her household.

"You jackass! Let go! Let me down, dammit!"

Solomon grunted when Jacinta's elbow connected with the back of his head. In response, he brought his palm down hard upon her rump. The blow stung Jacinta's pride more than her bottom. Her lower lip trembled and her nails curved so tightly into the soft flesh of her palms that she winced from the pain.

The wing that housed Jacinta's bedchamber was deserted, as everyone was on the third floor with Jore Sula. The door was already ajar, so Solomon simply pushed it open using Jacinta's derriere to give it a nudge. His dimpled smile appeared when he heard her gasp. Once inside, he kicked the door closed with the heel of his boot. Then, slowly, he allowed her to slide down the length of his body. Jacinta grimaced at her reaction to the man. How could she be even the slightest bit attracted to him she thought, as the simple combination of soap and talc fused with his natural scent to produce a clean, spicy aroma that was very intoxicating.

Upon releasing her, Solomon stood there as though he were waiting for some argument or a sharp blow in response to his actions. Jacinta remained quiet, her head bowed.

"Humph," Solomon gestured, then turned and strolled towards the fireplace on the other side of the room. Covertly, he studied his surroundings while pretending to be more interested in stoking the low flames.

Clearly, Jacinta McIver was not the pampered princess he would have expected. After all, what princess would prefer dirtying her hands and placing herself in mortal danger over enjoying the lavish beauty of such quarters? Great time had gone into decorating the room that appeared to be part sitting room, part bedroom. Heavy oversized armchairs faced the fireplace and flanked a dainty tea table; a spacious writing desk was set before tall windows that were draped with gauzy white curtains. A stunning Chippendale bed occupied the farthest side of the room. The cherry wood four-poster had a majestic embroidered cream canopy and rose-colored curtains that swept the imported Turkish rug covering a wide area of the floor.

"Bastard."

Solomon smiled, his attention reverting to the young woman in the room.

Jacinta felt her heart lurch to her chest when he turned and she glimpsed the firelight outlining his devastating features. Courageously, she tamped down her unease. "You have no right to treat me this way. Who the hell do you think you are?"

Solomon, pleased with the look of the fire, set aside the poker.

"You can also forget about this supposed business deal with my father," she went on, her anger gaining more steam as she spoke. "He wanted me to take an interest in the business? Very well. My first job will be to convince him of how foolish it would be to . . . what are you doing?" she interjected, watching as Solomon walked right up to her and placed his hands beneath her under-arms. As though she were a child, he carried her to the inviting bed and dumped her to the center.

"Son of a bitch!" she hissed, her skirts flying over her head as she went down.

Solomon stood back to regard her with his cool, dark eyes. "You express yourself so eloquently, Miss McIver. I can tell you're an educated woman."

"Horse's ass!" Jacinta spat, tugging loose tendrils behind her ear as they unraveled from her chignon.

This time, Solomon leaned close pressing his fists against the bed's cobalt blue quilt. He took in her exquisite dark face, her features sharpened by anger.

"Such language," he whispered, his onyx stare straying toward her breasts, which were threatening to heave from their confines. "I can think of at least a dozen far more pleasurable things you could be doing with that mouth."

"Get out!" she ordered, exasperated by the fact that he had succeeded in overpowering her physically as well as verbally. "Get out!" she cried with a bit more urgency when his entrancing gaze focused on her mouth. Bracing on her elbows, she began to back away from him, moving toward the head of the bed. She continued to voice her request that he leave, but her voice was fast losing its strength. Finally, she had run out of room to retreat.

Solomon hadn't realized how thinly his temper was stretched until he had Jacinta alone in the room. Now he was left with two choices, either throttle her or kiss her. After a second's debate he concluded that he'd find far more delight in the latter.

Jacinta's gasp caught on a moan when his mouth crashed upon her own. This kiss was far less tender than the first, but no less exciting. Jacinta heard herself gasp each time his tongue thrust deep into her mouth. Someplace deep in her subconscious she berated herself for allowing this man such liberties without attempting to resist him. His hands never moved from their fisted position on the quilt, but his lips were very persuasive— very irresistible. He pressed soft tiny kisses around her mouth, before his tongue delved back inside. The quick forceful thrusts were now leisurely and seeking as he deftly traced the ridge of her teeth and the hidden area beneath her tongue.

"Stop . . ." she whispered, as her lips puckered to meet his during the kiss. She knew she should be fighting but could not summon the will. All she wanted was to give in to the desire stirring throughout her body. She wanted to let Solomon have his way.

He took full advantage, all the while hoping that she would protest just a little. She did not, clearly leaving it up to him to have the rational head. He decided to allow himself a little more enjoyment, knowing she would stop him if he shocked her a bit too much. His mouth left hers to tease the soft curve of her jaw and the sensitive area below her earlobe.

"Mmmm . . ." Jacinta moaned, tilting her head to allow him more room.

Solomon squeezed his eyes shut tight. He pounded his fists against the quilt in a desperate attempt to keep them away from her body. His mouth trailed her collarbone, the tiny flicks from his tongue forcing deeper moans past her lips. Those moans, combined with her tortured cries of arousal, brought an arrogant smirk to his gorgeous face. His mouth continued its downward trail.

The dark clouds encircling her nipples were just visible above the ruffle of her gown's bodice. Solomon voiced his own helpless cry when he noticed this. Surely, she would stop him if he . . . his head dipped.

Jacinta's eyes opened for a split second then drifted close again. Solomon was outlining the curve of one breast with the tip of his tongue, before it dipped into the cleft between, then out to caress the curve of the other. With a will of their own, her hands rose to cup his head, slowly her nails eased down to graze his hair roughened cheeks.

Solomon's fingertips ached with the need to caress the firming nipples so close to his mouth. Instead, his lips rooted against the bud that lay half in half out the dress.

"Solomon . . ." she sighed, knowing she would never again be able to look at him without recalling the splendid mastery of his mouth at that very moment. Of course, she would curse and criticize herself later for never even attempting to fight him. But there was no way she could when she completely wanted every bit of what was happening.

God, how he wanted her! Solomon suckled madly upon the satiny peak of the nipple. He moaned his satisfaction when it grew more rigid beneath his manipulations. His massive fists had unclenched and he was but a hair's breath from taking her in his arms. *And what then, man?* He silently questioned. Would he deflower her right there while her father and a house full of people stood worrying over the young battered man in their midst?

The thought gave him enough strength to pull away, surprising both himself as well as Jacinta. He didn't dare look her way as he left the bed, knowing his best intentions would be utterly forgotten if he did.

CHAPTER 6

Dinner was a conversation-filled affair that evening. The McIver mansion was alive with talk of Jore Sula. Doctor Samuels, who had tended many "back injuries" during his tenure, said the extent of the wounds warranted at least three weeks strict bed rest.

"I still think it would be better to keep him someplace aside from a bedroom." Scurvy Logan voiced his opinion while slicing a plump chicken breast. "Ol' Chuck's minions will surely come lookin' for that boy tonight, and I don't know what would stop 'em from comin' here."

"Mr. Scurvy's right," Jacinta said upon finishing the last of her turnips. "I'm going to see Zambia and let her know what's happened to her brother."

"You will not!"

Surprise registered on everyone's face at the sound of Solomon's outburst. Even members of the kitchen staff jumped in response to the heavy rasp of his voice.

Jacinta was first to look away, as surprised as she was curious about the man's concern.

"I agree as well."

"Poppa!" Jacinta snapped, her gaze fiery once again.

"And if I hear of you going off on any more escapades, you'll suffer a fate similar to your friend up there," Jason continued.

"Poppa, don't you think they should be told?" Jacinta questioned slowly, lacing her fingers as she leaned closer to the table.

Jason forked up a helping of the fresh turnips. "I think it's something you needn't concern yourself."

"If not me, who? It's important they know what's happened."

"And *you* are my top priority!" Jason snapped, finally looking up to glare at his daughter. "No more escapades!" he commanded.

Jacinta wouldn't be silenced. "They're not escapades! Poppa, you act as though I'm off to some celebration— that I go to hear these people tell me about how incredibly exciting their lives are!"

"Jaci—"

"These people—our people—are dying, Poppa, and it is time for some of you high and mighty free blacks and half whites," she paused, fixing Solomon with a pointed glare, "to get off your arses and do something about it!" She stood then, tugging on the sleeves of her emerald green gown. "Don't bother sending me to my room," she said, already stepping away from the table. "I am more than happy to leave!"

Despite his mood, Solomon felt the smile of admiration tugging at his mouth. True, Jacinta McIver held a far too careless attitude toward her own safety. Still, her courage and determination to uphold what was right could not be argued. Sadly, he didn't have long to appreciate the personality traits of the woman who was infatuating him more than he cared to admit. Jason McIver sat stone-faced and staring toward the corridor leading from the dining room.

"As much as that girl angers me with her stubbornness, I can't deny the point she's made," he admitted, looking as though he could still see his daughter's rigid figure as she bolted out the dining room. "Someone ought to get word to that family. They must be sick with worry."

"Well, just you don't forget, Jason, Chuck Wallens is worryin', too," Scurvy warned, his long face appearing more gaunt. "You best believe he's worryin' about where that boy is."

"I know that, but they need to be told," Jason argued.

"And alert every slave on that plantation that McIver Estate is offering a hide-out for runaways? You'd have all of Charleston on your back!" Scurvy cried.

Jason set his tankard of ale back to the table with more force than needed. "Dammit, Scurvy, didn't Jaci's words unsettle you in the least?" he asked, his warm brown gaze hard and fixed on his old friend. "Despite my wanting to keep her away from this mess, she is right. It is *high* time for us free blacks to do something to help our brothers and sisters in bondage," he whispered, watching Scurvy wave off his preachings.

"You're sounding just like Vesey with that talk," he chided. "Are you certain you haven't attended a few meetings, my friend?"

Jason would not be swayed. "We have an obligation to keep that boy safe. We cannot allow him to return to that life," he decided, his soft tone brooking no further argument.

"Sir, if I might make a suggestion?"

Jason and Scurvy looked toward the younger man who, aside from his earlier outburst, had remained silent.

"Please, son," Scurvy urged, raising his hand to beckon Solomon's response.

"As soon as he can moved, I say he be taken to my ship. I'm docked at Blake's Lands and, as you well know, the place is scarcely visited," he said, watching the two older men exchange hopeful glances. "The next time Jore Sula's feet touch dry land he will be a free man."

Now Scurvy and Jason's expressions reflected astonishment.

"I really can't see a better way," Solomon added, taking note of their strange looks.

Jason clenched his throat. "Neither do we, son. It's just that . . ."

Solomon tilted his head. "Sir?" he prompted, waiting for Jason to continue.

Scurvy patted the area on the table before Jason's place setting. "I think what my friend is struggling to say, is that you've, uh . . . you've somewhat surprised us."

Solomon leaned back in his chair, his dark gaze studying both men intently. He was obviously confused.

Scurvy chuckled. "You certainly have no obligation to lend your assistance in this situation," he noted.

"I disagree. This man needs help," Solomon replied.

"Indeed," Scurvy confirmed with a slow nod. "Still, this is an extraordinary circumstance."

"And I pray that neither of you think I am treating it lightly?"

"No, no, Solomon," Jason confirmed suddenly. "But you are a stranger to us, to this part of the country and the reality of its politics."

Solomon smirked a little. "Unfortunately, the issue of slavery is not foreign in the north."

"Yes, but for you to go to such lengths for a man you don't know . . . lengths with dangerous, perhaps deadly, consequences."

Solomon's handsome face was softened with appreciation for the point Jason was trying to relay so diplomatically. "Well, as your daughter said, Mr. McIver, we 'half-whites' should get off our arses and help do something," he reiterated in a humorous tone that caused his dark riveting gaze to crinkle at the corners when he smiled.

Jason cleared his throat, allowing his uneasiness to show. "I should apologize for her disrespect."

Solomon barely raised his hand from the table. "There's no need. I took no offense to it."

"Still, she shouldn't have said it," Jason argued, his lips curling with distaste. "I am afraid such views are not uncommon here. Racism exists between black and white at almost the same level that it exists between black and mulatto."

"I'm aware of that," Solomon shared, his dark features sharpening in a sinister fashion. "But since I've been a small boy, I've dreamed of the day when I might be a factor in the freedom of my people. I have a ship and the means to get Jore Sula to freedom. You're right Mr. McIver, the boy cannot go back to that life."

Jacinta headed to her room most willingly earlier that evening. Of course, she had no intentions of remaining there. More than anything, she wanted to be downstairs out of eyesight, but within earshot, to hear the remainder of the dinner conversation. Men, she thought with a tired smirk, they didn't believe a woman had a brain in her head, much less a cohesive thought about the politics of the day. Jacinta was determined to prove that theory wrong. Through writing or speaking her mind, she would be heard, and one day her opinions would most certainly be valued.

But that was someday, Jacinta acknowledged with a grimace while cinching the rope belt around faded brown linen breeches. Now she had a far more important task ahead of her. She had to get to the Wallens plantation and inform the Sulas about the welfare of their kin.

Her fingers slowed as she buttoned the first of three cotton shirts she would don as part of her disguise. She had seen disappointment and worry in her father's eyes far too much for her liking in these past months. Should she become the ladylike, demure, obedient daughter that her father longed for, she would surely see the light of pride in his eyes that was absent now. To do that, however, would require that she suppress her need to be involved, to stop caring so deeply for those less fortunate. To get what she craved from her father, she would have to relinquish a part of herself. With a quick shake of her head, Jacinta forced the heavy thought out of her mind.

She had to be focused and settled. Once her thick hair was braided and forced beneath two caps, she checked her reflection in the oval looking glass fashioned next to the chiffarobe. Satisfied, she doused the candle lights and ventured outside her bedchamber.

Thankfully, the house was dark at that hour. She could faintly hear members of the house staff stirring on the third floor. She knew it was their nightly ritual of relaxation: reading, conversing and knitting, not to mention looking in on their injured visitor.

Holding her breath, Jacinta crept down the darkened hallway. Her fingers brushed the gleaming maplewood walls as she approached the stairway banister. By the light of the single oil lamp that burned throughout the night, she moved quickly down the carpeted steps. Her heart raced as a triumphant smile curved her full mouth and her lovely eyes were wide with anticipation. Jacinta almost expressed a yelp of glee when she opened and exited the front door without being discovered. She was off the front porch and down the wide front steps when she heard him.

"Trouble sleeping?"

Solomon's deep rumble of a voice roused a shriek from Jacinta. She whirled to find him leaning against one of the white columns supporting the stately porch.

"Dammit!" she gasped, pressing one hand to her throat. "Must you constantly sneak up on me this way?" she raged.

Solomon was a picture of cool sophistication as his hands remained settled inside his trouser pockets. His head rested back against the column and his onyx stare was hooded. "It appears that you're the one who is . . . constantly sneaking," he noted.

The simple observation removed what remained of Jacinta's resolve. "This is too much, it's too much now!" she cried in a fierce whisper, bounding up the steps to poke an index finger against his chest. She gave a start upon feeling the steely muscular expanse beneath the expensive fabric of his cotton shirt. She forced her attentions back to the matter at hand. "Now you listen to me, Mr. Dikembe, you have no right whatsoever to judge, order or to even *advise* me of what I should and should not be doing. You don't even have the right to question my actions. Don't allow yourself a false sense of confidence in that area simply because my father appears to agree with every word you speak," she informed him, her voice firm and unwavering. "Your constant interfering and bullying is as unwanted as it is inconsequential," she called over her shoulder once she was headed back down the steps.

Solomon caught her before she made it halfway down. In one deft movement, he took her upper arm and made her face him. "You are the most naïve, childish and disrespectful woman I've ever had the misfortune to meet."

"How dare—"

"Shut your mouth," he softly ordered, taking her other arm and forcing her to remain standing before him. "Naïve," he continued, fixing her with a scathing glare, "in that you have no idea of the danger you place yourself in despite the fact that your very dear friend had his back ripped apart and collapsed in your backyard less than ten hours ago. Childish, in that you obviously can not comprehend the context of the very stories you write. You believe none of what you hear could possibly befall you."

"Don't—"

"I'm not finished," he spoke through clenched teeth, his massive hands tightening around the bulky sleeves of her shirts. "Disrespectful. I think that's what sickens me most. Your father is a good man, a loving father and kind—*too* kind to a daughter who has no regard for his wishes or the anguish she puts him through for refusing to keep herself out of harm's way."

"You shut *your* mouth, Dikembe!" Jacinta blurted, her emotions overwhelming her. "You know nothing about my father or me and I'll thank you to—oh! Oh, no!"

Solomon noticed Jacinta's eyes riveted above his head and looked back and up. Candlelight danced against the drapes before a window on the second floor. Jason McIver's bedchamber.

"Damn you!" Jacinta gasped.

Solomon's chuckle began deep in his chest. "Damn *me*? I'm not the one who was ordered to remain inside the house," he reminded her humorously.

"Shh!" she ordered, her hands rising to clasp his forearms. For a time, she waited, her eyes focused on the window.

Solomon, in the meantime, enjoyed the picture she made. Her eyes wide and expectant, her chest heaving beneath the heavy shirts she wore, the huge hat covering her head. She was innocent and plain yet beautiful and provocative at once. The emotions she roused inside him were a mixture of desire and anger. Never had he felt more alive.

The light against Jason's window was doused and Jacinta heaved a relieved sigh. Her eyes closed and she bowed her head momentarily as though she were voicing a short prayer. Then, she jerked herself free of Solomon's loosened embrace, intending to continue her trip to the Wallens plantation.

Solomon took no chances on her escaping that time. He scooped her into his arms the instant her feet touched the ground. Immediately, Jacinta began to pound against the unyielding wall of his back. The way he held her, they were face to face. Her breasts crushed against his massive chest, her thighs nudged the unthinkable power below his waist. Jacinta gasped at the unexpected rush of sensation and prepared to blast him.

Solomon gave her a warning squeeze. "I don't think you want to get too loud."

"Let me go," Jacinta ordered through clenched teeth.

"I will."

"Now."

"In time."

Jacinta renewed her struggle, but Solomon's embrace was like iron. She fought fiercely, but scarcely felt as though she were moving. Shortly, she noticed they were heading away from the house. It appeared as though the barn was his destination and Jacinta quieted. Her mind was alive with thoughts on what his intentions were. She dared not question him, though. Solomon's very handsome face was contorted by some murderous glean. He looked like a man on the verge of completely losing his temper.

Inside the barn, Solomon kept walking. He seemed unmindful of the dark, using the faint streams of moonlight that shone through a few separate beams to mark his way. Jacinta's heart thudded in time to the fall of his boots upon the hay-covered floor and steps as he carried them to the loft. He set Jacinta to her feet and held her pressed against the wall instead of releasing her.

"Solomon—"

"If you can't see, or at least vaguely acknowledge, the danger you place yourself in each time you take these foolish chances, then you are as good as raped, beaten and killed—perhaps not in that order," he gravely informed her, wincing when he saw real fear sparkle in her chocolate gaze for the first time. He shook his head, bending a little to look directly into her face.

"When my mother was a young girl, she befriended a young woman who was a wash girl for a family who lived not far from my grandparents," he began, releasing Jacinta to lean against the wall next to her. "She was curious and fearless, like you," he said, glancing at Jacinta when she looked up at him. "Like you, she thought nothing could touch her. She was mulatto and thought that, in some way, would protect her. She was wrong, and one evening, after visiting a friend who was a farm slave on the other side of town, she was taken. Some of the farmers' sons had been watching her for a while and, now, they had a perfect opportunity. They kept her in a shed a ways off from the farm. For days, they kept her there. She was raped, made to do things . . . they beat her several times, before they let her go. The people she worked for were frantic with worry and had paid searchers to find her. She almost died." Solomon cleared his throat and pushed himself away from the wall. "I enjoyed long walks when I was younger. Once my mother told me that story, those long walks lost their appeal. I always wondered if she was simply trying to discourage me from going off too far from home or if such a horrible story could really be true."

Jacinta was quiet. More than likely the story was very true. After all, hadn't she heard similar accounts from the slaves whose experiences she had recorded?

Solomon saw the emotions crossing her face and cleared his throat. "I apologize if I frightened you," he said, his rough voice sounding much softer.

"It's all right. I'm fine," she assured him, even offering a small smile. "I understand why you felt the need to tell me that story. It might surprise you to know that I've heard similar."

Solomon chuckled as he nodded. "Your writing." He eased his tall frame down the length of the wall to take a seat on the hay-covered floor.

"Yes, my writing," Jacinta confirmed, following suit. "When I first began to record, I'd run home every night and either cry myself to sleep or vomit. Sometimes, I did both," she reminisced with a rueful smile.

Solomon sat with his arms draped across his knees. "Why'd you begin to do this?"

Jacinta inhaled deeply, removing her hat to lean her head back against the wall. "I had always been curious about the people in chains—what I called the slaves when I was younger. When I learned to read and write and . . . understand, I realized what their lives were and I wanted to know all that I could about them."

"Why not just go and ask them? Why write about it?"

Jacinta's smile, brought a deeper sparkle to her warm brown eyes. "Well, once I learned to read, I read *every-thing*. My favorites were the pieces by Briton Hammon, Phyllis Wheatley, Gustavus Vassa and Benjamin Banneker. Vassa, whose real name was Olaudan Equilano, wrote on his kidnapping and subsequent enslavement. He was sold countless times, endured and witnessed unspeakable horrors. I think the most horrible thing is being stripped of your very identity—your family."

Solomon listened, his onyx stare focused on her hands as they gestured in accordance to her words. The wisdom and emotion clutched her voice like a silken tether.

"I thought surely if this man had such a tale to tell, the same had to be true for the people in chains who lived so close to my own home."

"And you felt they should have the sort of life you were blessed with on McIver Estate?"

Jacinta nodded. "I did. I understand that people had to work, but why force them? My father had scores of people working his land and they weren't forced . . . obviously I was ignorant to the ways of the *real* world."

"No, your thinking was quite logical. Sadly, the world has and will continue to become an *illogical* place."

Jacinta sighed and toyed with a loose tendril from her braid. "Whatever the case, it sickened me to know people were being treated so brutally while I was at home safe in my bed."

"Now that I can certainly identify with."

Jacinta turned to face him. "You?" she breathed.

Solomon grinned. "I was in a constant state of guilt over my upbringing—especially as I grew older."

Debating, Jacinta chewed her bottom lip as she listened to his words. Finally, she decided to speak her question. "What is it like?" she asked, her gaze faltering when he stared at her. "Being . . . half white? Are you? Were you ever confused?"

"I was confused a lot. Sometimes I still am," Solomon admitted, massaging his neck as he spoke.

For a time the only sounds between them were the songs of the crickets in the distance and the soft banter of the horses in the stable below.

"I suppose that would be the greatest disadvantage, then? Being confused?"

Solomon almost laughed out loud. *If only that were true!* "You could say that," he told her, having no desire to speak of the circumstances he'd endured because of his heritage.

"And the advantages?" Jacinta's face wrought with curiosity.

"As a child, I was never separated from my mother," he shared, his voice carrying a refreshing air. "I can't think how many grown men I know who can't recall the woman who gave them life. What it must do to a man."

Jacinta nodded, thinking she knew just as many who suffered from a similar circumstance. "It must have been very hard for her to raise you on her own."

"It was no easy task, but she did have my grandparents."

"Yes, but I'm sure they kept busy working. Trying to make a life. It's wonderful that your mother wasn't torn from her family."

Solomon grimaced. "If only that were true."

"But you just said she had your grandparents to help with you."

"My grandparents. Not her parents. My mother was taken from them when she was a small child. The Hamptons, my grandparents, raised her."

Jacinta's eyes were wide. "I don't understand, how—"

"The Hamptons had a son. He and my mother fell in love and had me. They were running off to marry when they lost a wheel from their carriage. My father was thrown. The fall killed him instantly."

Now Jacinta was awestruck. "And his parents just accepted you? Raised you as their own?" she questioned, watching Solomon nod.

"They're not all bad, Jacinta," he spoke as though he were reading her thoughts.

"You think that because you came from a different place," she decided, leaning back against the wall as a cold expression masked her lovely face. "Your grandparents were maybe a better breed. The whites here are animals. It seems some sort of cruel joke that we are the ones in chains."

"And I suppose you feel this way about the McIvers, whose name you bear?" Solomon said, hiding his smile when Jacinta pinned him with a murderous look.

"I wouldn't expect you to understand." Jacinta sneered, her chocolate gaze studying his face with disapproval. "After all, you *are* mulatto. The mulattoes of Charleston think they are above everyone, even the free blacks, those who have never been enslaved. They are an untrustworthy lot, quick to jump to the white side of the fence to save their hides."

Solomon slapped his palm with a tuft of hay. "I won't believe they all think in such a manner."

"Ahh . . . the *charitable* mulattoes," Jacinta drawled with phony graciousness, "they're even worse. They would just as soon keep a slave themselves. After all, slaves receive a roof over their heads and a meal—three a day!"

"Jacinta—"

"Who could ask for more?" she continued, without regard for the warning chord in Solomon's voice.

"Jacinta," he called again, losing the battle at keeping a cool temper. He could feel his anger returning with every word she uttered. "You cannot lump everyone together in the same foul pot based simply on the behaviors of a few."

"It's far more than a few, Mr. Dikembe. Far more!"

Suddenly Solomon turned, bringing his index finger within inches of her small nose. "You're very intelligent, Jacinta, but very naïve. You speak when you should be listening and you are so determined to thrive off anger and distrust you won't let yourself see anything that might exist beyond."

Jacinta slapped his finger away. "I won't stand for you speaking to me like a child, dammit! I have seen things as a child that would have sent you scurrying back to the safety of your momma's embrace!" she seethed, her eyes narrowing as she glared directly into his. "Why don't you go back to the frills and luxury of your white life, Dikembe?"

Solomon let go of his temper then. Jacinta shrieked when he caught the collar of her shirt in his fist and dragged her beneath him.

"When I leave," his raspy voice grated close to her face, "Ms. McIver, you can damn sure rest comfortable that I will not be going alone."

Jacinta gasped, reading the intention clear within his intense, obsidian stare. She retaliated with a fierce slap to his face. She immediately regretted the action when his magnificent features contorted with murderous intent. His dimpled smile held no trace of humor, only wickedness.

"Stop," she whispered, her breath coming in panicked bursts when he ripped through the buttons of her top shirt. "Don't," she ordered, grimacing at her inability to force more strength into her voice.

Solomon barely heard her. He was intent on having what lay beneath the worn tattered clothing covering her nudity.

"I said stop!" Jacinta bellowed, finally regaining her voice. Regardless of the consequences she slapped him again, only to have Solomon take both her wrists in one hand and imprison them above her head. He leaned in to kiss her and she turned her face away. He took her chin with his free hand and held her still.

Jacinta moaned in protest, even as her lips parted to receive his kiss. His tongue probed long and deep, thrusting slowly until he felt her respond. Jacinta continued to moan against the kiss, though the protests had lost their power. Solomon resumed his task of unbuttoning the remaining shirts she wore. When, at last, she was bared to his gaze, he broke the kiss and caressed her with his eyes.

A voice screamed to Jacinta that she use all her power to resist him. When his thumb brushed the rigid peak of one nipple, the voice lost much of its volume. She whimpered from the sensation as Solomon added more pressure to the stroke. His head leaned close, his lips traveling the dark, flawless plane of her neck and collarbone. His massive hands rose to cup her full bosom, his thumbs caressing both nipples in unison.

"Please . . ." Jacinta urged, but didn't know if she pleaded for him to stop or continue. Solomon had released her wrists, but she had no strength to pull her hands from above her head. Unconsciously, she arched into his touch.

Solomon dipped his head closer, his nose tracing the cleft between her breasts before it encircled one full mound. He smiled at the sight of her straining nearer to his touch. The tip of his nose outlined the nipple before his lips closed upon the stiff bud.

Jacinta cried out into the lofty barn, the breathless sound echoing all around. Shamelessly, she pushed the extra sensitive part of her body deeper into his mouth. Solomon voiced a satisfied grunt when the peak nudged his tongue. Slowly, he began to bathe the firm bud, alternating between suckling and grazing it with his perfect teeth.

Jacinta was lost on a bed of sensation. Tentatively, her hands moved from their place above her head. Her fingers ached to test the close-cut waves of his hair. She had to know if it was as luxurious as it appeared. She hadn't long to wonder. She reached into a smattering of crisp silkiness and massaged her slender fingers all over his head.

Her soft gasps and strokes upon the nape of his neck forced tortured groans from Solomon's chest. Jacinta's lashes fluttered open when she felt him leave her. His lips burned a trail around the curve of her breasts to pleasure the satiny undersides with silken kisses. Then, he moved on-traveling lower. Jacinta chewed the nail of her index finger as the friction from his whiskers ignited a path of fire beneath her skin. Her body shook violently when he probed her naval with his tongue.

"Wait," she insisted unconvincingly as he ventured lower. "Solomon wait-"

"Shh . . ." he urged, his hands insinuating themselves beneath her bottom, which was outlined within the snug fitting fabric of the trousers. "Shh . . ." he soothed again, this time as his nose was tracing the triangular impression of her womanhood.

"Don't," she insisted even as her eyes widened in wonder and curiosity.

Solomon was lost in his desire for this woman. Faintly, he heard her protests and told himself that he should take heed. His reaction to her was too dangerous. He was sure it wouldn't take much more for him to cast all rational thought aside, remove his clothes and what remained of hers and take what he'd wanted from the first night he met her along that river. Just a bit more time with her, only a bit more, he reassured himself.

What in heaven's name is he doing? Jacinta asked herself, feeling the already overwhelming sensations steadily mount. Solomon's hands massaged her full buttocks in a scandalous fashion, his handsome face buried between her thighs. Of course, she was still secured beneath the material of her brown trousers. But that in no way lessened the stimulating caresses he applied at the junction of her thighs. She could feel his nose nudging her there and her legs began to tremble uncontrollably.

Then, Solomon pulled away suddenly as though he were snapping out of a daze. In one smooth motion, he rose to his feet and stepped away from her.

"Get dressed," he ordered, keeping his back toward her.

Jacinta lay motionless for several seconds. Her heart still raced frantically as her thighs continued their trembling. At last, she closed her eyes and ordered herself to save at least a shred of her dignity. Moving to her knees, she fixed her shirts and smoothed back lengthy tendrils into her unraveling braid. When she was presentable, Solomon led the way out of the barn. He spoke not a word as he escorted her back to the house.

"Jacinta McIver!"

"Oh, no," she muttered, hearing her father storming down the front stairway as he bellowed her name. She couldn't deal with this after . . .

"I've reached my limit with you, miss!"

"Poppa, I can—"

"Quiet. I'll entertain no more explanations," Jason decided, his round face appearing hard as granite as he approached his daughter. "You have finally backed yourself into a corner, and I'm done issuing threats."

"Jason, wait," Solomon called, as the man prepared to drag Jacinta down the hall. "She doesn't deserve your anger tonight. I was out for a walk and found her in the barn feeding the horses. I offered to escort her back here once she was done."

Jacinta's coffee stare widened in surprise, and her arms grew limp beneath her father's hold. Solomon's unexpected assistance was much needed and greatly appreciated.

Jason was obviously taken aback as well. But before he could speak a word, there was knocking at the front door.

"McIver, open up! It's Chuck Wallens!"

Jacinta's gasp echoed down the hall. She followed her father back to the front door.

"They didn't waste much time," Jason muttered, tightening the belt on his black, ankle-length house robe.

"Jore's owner, I take it?" Solomon guessed, grimacing at the nod Jason sent his way. "What do you need me to do?"

Jason clapped Solomon's shoulder. "Just stand there, son. This won't take long," he promised, then turned to Jacinta and jerked his head toward the hallway. "Out of sight, Jaci," he said, patting her hand when she pressed a quick kiss to his cheek and raced down the corridor.

Charles Wallens was a tall, lanky man in his early forties. He appeared far older. His face was usually beet red and slick with sweat. His brown hair was coily and thinning on the top and sides of his head. He wore a permanent scowl whether he was in the company of friends, family or enemies.

"Evenin', Jason," Wallens greeted as though he were doing the man some honor by appearing on his doorstep at such a late hour.

"Wallens," Jason returned, maintaining his stance before the doorway.

Of course, neither Wallens nor the three men who accompanied him expected a welcome greeting. They treated Jason McIver and the McIver Estate with reluctant respect. They acknowledged the fact that Jason McIver could not be touched. He was legally Roland McIver's sole heir, but also he had the protection of Roland's eldest brother, who resided in New York.

"The hour is rather late. What can we do for you?" Jason stonily inquired, regarding his neighbor with a look that practically oozed dislike.

Wallen's own gaze reflected his dislike as well. "Got a runaway on our hands," he announced as though Jason already knew. "Jore Sula," he added when Jason remained mute.

"And is there some reason you're here on my doorstep instead of out looking for him?"

Chuck Wallens and his men bristled. Meanwhile, Solomon bowed his head to hide the smile threatening to break through on his face. Clearly, Jason McIver had not an ounce of fear toward the men with their rifles clutched in their hands as though they were ready to open fire.

"We're here because we're puttin' out warnins."

"Warnings?"

Wallens, looped his thumbs beneath the waistband of the dingy gray trousers he wore. "Anybody knowin' where that boy is had better step for'd or suffer the consequences. And I mean anybody, Jason—powerful name and money won't mean spit if'n it's discovered they be hidin' my property."

"You threatening me, Wallens?" Jason's question sounded closer to a statement.

Chuck Wallens glanced toward the tall, fierce-looking man at Jason's side. "Just informin'," he quickly explained, his blue-gray stare filled with curiosity as he watched the stranger. "Just informin'," he repeated, as though he were trying to assure Solomon. "Evenin' to ya," he said, nodding towards the imposing man before looking back at Jason. "McIver," he grunted, then stomped off the porch with his men close behind.

"I'm going to check on Jore!" Jacinta called, emerging from her place behind the shelter of a tall, potted tree in the far corner of the foyer. Her steps slowed when Solomon turned his penetrating gaze on her. Immediately, her skin burned as it did when they were in the barn loft. Quickly, she dismissed the erotic images from her mind and glanced at her father. "Goodnight, Poppa," she whispered, nodding once before racing up the stairs.

Jason turned and leaned back against the cherry wood door. His arms were folded across his chest. "The sooner that boy is on free soil, the better," he said, appearing as solemn as the sound of his voice.

Solomon's long brows rose as he looked past Jason's shoulder. "The sooner we are *all* on free soil, the better."

CHAPTER 7

Jason sent word to Jore Sula's family the evening following Chuck Wallens's unexpected visit. Almost three weeks had passed since that night. Solomon undertook the task of preparing for Jore's departure with rigorous intensity.

"Are you touched, son? That's an even more dangerous idea than agreeing to give the boy passage on your boat."

Solomon nodded, appreciating Jason's words of concern. After all, his plan was extremely perilous with equally perilous ramifications should it fail. "I can't be party to a man gaining his freedom yet losing touch with his family," Solomon declared, shrugging as though his feelings were not surprising. "What sort of life could he have knowing they still suffer?"

"I don't argue with your reasoning, son," Jason clarified, leaning forward to help himself to more coffee. "But this thing you want to do . . . it could mean death if discovered."

Solomon grinned. "Then I suppose we should plan carefully so as not to be discovered," he teased, tapping his fingers along the edge of the table where he and Jason ate breakfast.

"I should like to share your easy manner, son," Jason confided in a light tone. He was constantly amazed by the young man. Solomon Dikembe saw nothing of consequeces, only an important matter needing to be addressed.

"I plan to visit the *Sheba* today," Solomon shared, stirring a pat of churned butter into a bowl of creamy hominy. "I'll make sure everything is prepared for the Sula family's voyage north," he said, shaking his head when silence greeted him. "I promise you, Jason, I'm of a mind to do this. The Sulas will be safe *and* free. Chuck Wallens will be none the wiser."

"'Tis quite a feat," Jason sighed, "and a dangerous one."

"I've been in worse situations and this is something that must be done."

Jason crossed his arms over his chest and rested back against the polished pine ladder back chair. "I pray for its success, then," he sighed, smiling when the double doors swung open in the dining room and Jacinta stepped inside.

His daughter had been noticeably quiet for the last few weeks. Jason figured she was brooding over being restricted to the house. He soon discovered there was more to her mood, and that whatever it was involved his houseguest. If only he could pinpoint the nature of the matter.

Jacinta greeted the two men with a slow nod and smile. "Good morning, Poppa. Dikembe."

Jason watched Solomon reply with a hushed 'good morning' and hid his grin over Jacinta's use of the man's surname. Of course, he knew she would be livid if he told her it sounded more endearing than formal.

Jacinta strolled to the long buffet across the small dining room. As usual, the breakfast spread was superb. Still, she only filled her plate with a light serving of scrambled egg and one small salmon croquette. Though her back was turned, she could almost feel Solomon's pitch black stare riveted on her. She set the fork to the silver tray carrying the croquettes, with more force than needed. Bracing herself, she turned to meet his gaze. Doing so, resulted in the same effect each morning. While his smoldering, dark stare raked her face and form, Jacinta felt every part of her tingle. His stare was all too knowing as it seared past the lavender button-down bodice of her dress. She glanced at her father then, taking note of the inquisitive gleam in his hazel eyes.

"Are you well this morning, Poppa?" she innocently inquired before he could ask the same of her.

"Quite," Jason replied with an easy shrug. "And you?"

Jacinta nodded while taking her place at the table. "I was up late with Jore," she mentioned, hoping that would keep him from reading more into her unease.

Jason nodded, seeming to accept the excuse. "Doc Samuels has approved your friend to travel."

"Travel?" Jacinta parroted, her fork poised over the golden croquette.

Jason looked toward Solomon. "Our guest has been kind enough to offer Jore refuge and transport to the north."

"Transport?" she repeated, unable to mask the dumbfounded expression plastered to her face.

"That's right," Jason confirmed. "We've been planning it for weeks now, but I felt it best to wait before sharing the news. And there is more," he added.

Jacinta could scarcely find her voice. "More?"

"Not only has our Mr. Dikembe agreed to relocate Jore on free soil, but he plans to take the entire Sula family once the ship sets sail."

Jacinta's brilliant cocoa stare was riveted on Solomon's handsome face. Her stunned expression clouded with a hint of suspicion and intrigue as her father relayed the magnanimous offer.

"What are you thinking, love?" Jason asked, seeing the look she wore.

"'Tis pleasing," she admitted, her eyes never leaving Solomon's face. "Thank you," she told him.

Solomon's rough voice barely rose above a whisper. "No need."

"May I be permitted to tell Jore?" she asked, looking toward her father after a moment.

Jason waved one hand above his head. "Please," he urged.

Jacinta gave a quick smile and excused herself from the table. Jason's keen eye was focused on Solomon, whose attention was focused solely on Jacinta. Solomon's black gaze, usually intense and observant, was now helpless and wanting. Jason could tell, in that moment, that the young man was hopelessly infatuated with his daughter. Of course, Jason was more than pleased.

"The girl's appetite wanes yet again," Jason noted, when Solomon looked his way. "She has little regard for all else, especially eating, when she's involved in a crusade," he said, shaking his head at Jacinta's barely touched breakfast.

"She's very dedicated," Solomon noted, clearing his throat at the emotion he heard in his voice.

"Yes, well, that dedication will ruin her health." Jason stood and reached for the black linen suit coat that hung from the back of his chair. "I'd be grateful, Solomon, if you would see to it that she eats something at lunch today."

"Lunch?" Solomon repeated, watching the man pull on the coat.

"Mmm," Jason grunted, already perching his top hat on his head, "I'll probably not return from business before this evening."

"Is there anything I might assist with?" Solomon offered, his deep voice carrying a vaguely hopeful tone.

Jason waved one hand, then continued buttoning his coat. "Nothing to trouble yourself with, son. Simply last minute preparations for our trip. There are a few arrangements I want to confirm," he explained, a smug grin coming to his face as he observed the younger man's disappointment. "Fret not, son. I can guarantee you'll have your fill of business once we set foot on that drab island property you're so eager to purchase. Now, don't you forget about Jacinta at lunch."

Solomon nodded, managing to appear calm and good spirited as Jason strolled from the dining room. Once alone, he allowed the façade to drop and clutched the edge of the table in an iron grasp. Solomon groaned. The very last thing he wanted was to spend any more time alone with Jacinta McIver. Clearly, she was a constant distraction. His every thought involved bedding her in some lengthy, ravishing manner. Those thoughts were so explicit, at times, his loins tightened as he grew aroused to an almost painful state. He certainly couldn't keep his hands away from her, not that he wanted to or had even tried for that matter.

No matter his desires, however, he had to remember that the woman was no fluffy tart eager for a quick romp. She was grace and toughness combined. She was the kind of woman a man wanted in the most basic way—yes. But she was also the kind of woman a man took for a wife. Wife? he questioned, the admittance astonishing him. Solomon shook his head as if to clear it, massaging one hand across his silky, close-cut hair. *Get a handle on yourself, man. Your thoughts are running away uncontrolled.* With those words in mind, Solomon pulled the white napkin from his lap and slapped it to the dining table. He decided to escape the huge house and check on his ship.

"I know you're still in pain, but I would have expected applause, laughter or, at the very least, a bright smile over the news."

Jacinta's words did manage to bring an easy smile to Jore Sula's dark, attractive face. "I'm happy Jaci, it just . . ."

"Just what?" she softly prompted, smoothing her palm across his shoulder while he lay on his side.

Jore closed his eyes and turned his face into the pillow as if that would remove the uneasy expression he wore. "It about to happen. It for certain this time."

Of course, Jacinta knew the "it" he was referring to. "So far there's only been talk. For years, Jore," she said, intentionally playing the doubtful role.

"It gon' happen, Jaci," Jore insisted, his expression now as adamant as the sound of his voice.

"How can you be so sure?" Jacinta whispered, her expressive gaze growing wider and more inquisitive. "Tell me what you know."

"You know as much as me, Jaci."

Jacinta straightened. "Me?" she asked, sounding confused.

Again, Jore smiled. "Jaci, I ain't no fool. E'rybody know you be at the meetins. Them ol' clothes you wear can't hide that beauty."

"Thank you," she whispered, patting his cheek. "But Jore, you know there are things you know that I don't."

"It's a good a reason for that, Jaci," Jore challenged. "Them men trust me, and I plan to be a 'portant part a this."

Jacinta sighed, entwining her fingers and placing them demurely in her lap. "Well unless the rebellion takes place within the next few weeks, I don't see your plans coming to light. Solomon Dikembe will have you and your family tucked away on his ship and off to freedom very soon."

"Solomon Dikembe," Jore said, trying to picture the man's face.

"Do you remember the man who carried you up the stairs the night you came here?"

Jore's heavy brows drew close as he concentrated. "I 'member a lil' bit. You was—you was fussin' at him."

Jacinta cleared her throat and patted the balled knot of hair at her nape. "He can be an aggravating man."

"He mulatto, ain't he?"

Jacinta gave a quick nod. "He is."

"Can we trust him, Jaci?"

"I think we can," Jacinta responded without hesitation, surprising both Jore and herself.

"These people should have stood up to fight long ago!"

"And risk their lives?"

"For freedom!"

"But how? These people have no financial backing, no weapons—"

"They have numbers! Numbers can outweigh lack of money and weapons!"

"You talkin' fool!"

Solomon had taken a stroll of the *Sheba*, speaking with members of the crew. He had been told that Moses Cuffe and his officers were eating in the captain's mess. Solomon walked in on the late breakfast to find the air alive with fiery conversation. Talk of the impending revolt was the topic of discussion. Solomon remained in the shadows, perching on the edge of Moses's massive desk, which sat catty-cornered in the spacious dark room. Solomon enjoyed the passion and anticipation in the eyes of the men as they debated. Obviously, more than a few of Cuffe's top men had inside knowledge of the coming uprising, which was still mostly talk.

"If these people are so intent on having their freedom, why have they not done more about it? Surely they've been in bondage far too long."

The verbal battle silenced when Solomon's calm, rough voice filtered through the meshing of voices. One by one, the men turned, their expressions softening when they realized who had offered an unsolicited opinion.

"Well?" Solomon challenged, playing the role of devil's advocate to discern the extent and seriousness of the revolt.

"That is precisely why it is taking so long, Solomon." Reese Caro was first to offer an explanation. "The people have lived this way for so long it will take much talk, powerful talk, to make them see that they are deserving of freedom."

"And this man they speak of, you believe he alone can persuade them?" Solomon asked.

Reese responded with an immediate nod. His head bobbed so quickly the cap he wore slid away to reveal his shiny bald dome. "This man incites the crowds—all crowds—with powerful words and truth. They say he speaks as powerfully whether at his home on Bull Street or down along the banks of the Santee where the majority of the French Negroes dwell. He says it is time for a great and bloody revolt."

Solomon pretended to be incensed. "And the people take him at his word on this? How gullible."

"He fortifies his talk with successes of past events," Reese challenged, leaning back in the chair he occupied at the food laden maple wood round table. "I cannot forget the very successful uprising in my native Haiti under the direction of Monsieur L'Ouverture."

"And a great revolt it was," Solomon acknowledged, silence filling the cabin as each man thought of the significant revolt led by Toussaint L'Ouverture in the early 1800s. The ex-slave gathered firm support from his black brethren, and in 1804 the island of Saint Dominique was formally declared the Republic of Haiti.

"So, Reese, are you saying Vesey and his top men are that well prepared?" Captain Moses Cuffe now questioned.

"'Tis only an assumption, but I would stand behind saying it is a fact," Reese sighed, his expression smug.

"The man has hoards of supporters and gathers more each day," first mate Humphrey Wiggins shared. "Vesey and his men realize this strike must be exceptionally planned and precisely executed."

"But Charleston is not Haiti," Moses pointed out.

"Aye, but its political climate is far more deadly. In Haiti, the blacks worked and fought together for one common goal," Humphrey went on. "Here there is a surprising and disturbing presence of racial dissention dwelling within the black race. One group thinking they are . . . better and . . ." Humphrey let his words trail away into silence as he realized the direction the conversation was headed.

"Please go on, Hump," Solomon urged, waving his hand above his head. "Please speak freely. I'm well aware how the mulattoes are regarded here."

Humphrey's small piercing eyes seemed to harden in their intensity. "Beg pardon, Solomon, but in light of some of the things we've heard about the mulatto population here, we'd not put you in the same class with those traitors."

Solomon nodded, thanking Humphrey for his candor and urging the conversation to continue. Inwardly, he didn't feel quite so at ease. He couldn't help but think of Jacinta and the disapproval when she'd spoken of the 'half-whites'. Her views—many of which he felt had been left unspoken—disturbed him more than he was willing to admit.

"Where's my father?" Jacinta questioned later that afternoon. The cooks had told her Jason decided they would have lunch on the ballroom terrace. When she arrived there only to find Solomon waiting alone, she grew cautious and uneasy.

Solomon helped himself to another swig of the flavorful ale filling his tankard. "Still away on business," he informed her, casting a quick glance in her direction. "He asked that I make sure you eat since you left the table so quickly this morning."

Jacinta blinked and cast her gaze toward the hanging moss trees in the distance. She'd never tell Solomon that it was his effect on her that hastened her departure from the breakfast table. "I couldn't wait to tell Jore about the good news of your offer," she said instead.

"He was pleased, I hope?"

"Oh, yes!" Her lovely, dark face illuminated with joy as she recalled how wonderful it felt to share such news with her friend. "I doubt they have ever dreamed such a thing was possible."

"No one should live in constant fear," Solomon said, his striking features growing sharper as his expression hardened.

"You're right," Jacinta whispered, folding her arms across the square bodice of her gown. The folds of lavender swept the stone floor of the terrace as she moved to lean against one of the white columns that outlined it. "One day it will be different. I know it. But," she sighed, turning to favor him with a soft look, "for the moment, I thank you for extending such a grand gesture."

Solomon, who leaned against one of the white stone columns at the opposite end of the terrace, continued to regard her closely. "You thank me, yet you are still surprised?" He smiled when he glimpsed guilt sparkle in her chocolate stare.

"It surprised me. It still does," she admitted.

Solomon finished what remained of his ale. "Why? Because I am mulatto and can't be trusted?"

"Because this is not your fight," Jacinta countered. "You are only here to acquire land and increase your wealth," she added, watching him with a look that radiated disapproval.

Solomon's easy expression began to reflect disbelief. "Good Lord, woman, you act as if we in the north have no inkling about slavery and its horrors."

"Still, to put yourself in such a position—"

"The position of aiding a man in his freedom?"

"Why?"

"Why not?"

"Do you have something to prove?"

"To whom?"

Jacinta rolled her eyes and looked away from Solomon's probing gaze. "Oh, what could be keeping Poppa?" she groaned, eager to bring an end to the conversation that was becoming a bit too personal for her liking.

As if on cue, two housemaids arrived and began to set out lunch. Jacinta kept her eyes trained on the glass doors leading through to the ballroom. There was no sign of her father appearing. It was then that she noticed the small round table on the terrace had been set for two. Clearly, her father never had intentions to join them.

"I should go eat with Jore," Jacinta decided in a small voice, once the maids had finished and gone.

Solomon was already strolling toward the table. "What is it between you two?" he asked, removing his tailored linen suit coat and hanging it across the back of a chair.

Jacinta was speechless. Her eyes lingered on the breadth of Solomon's chest and back. She had never seen a man so huge possess such cool grace. His movements were not awkward or overbearing. Moreover, they were unhurried and deliberate. He commanded full attention without having to utter a word.

"Jacinta?"

"What?" she whispered as though dazed. Shortly, she blinked and realized he was waiting on an answer to his question. "Jore and I have been friends since we were children."

"Friends . . ." Solomon drawled, while taking a seat. "Simply friends?"

Jacinta propped her hands on her hips. "I don't like your implication, Dikembe."

"Did I make one?"

"Jore is a man of principle," Jacinta declared, pointing her index finger in Solomon's direction. "He has high hopes for his people and he isn't afraid to take a stand against those who may be older, more established *or* white!"

Solomon remained unaffected, choosing a few medallion biscuits for his plate. "Does that in some way pertain to me?" he asked.

"I don't know. Does it?"

"I should pray not!" Solomon bellowed with a laugh.

Jacinta's lashes fluttered when she rolled her eyes. Ordering herself to dismiss his presence, she took her place at the intimate table and concentrated on the delightful late lunch. Aside from the medallion biscuits with fresh churned butter, there was saffron rice with herb potatoes, and green peas, and oven-fried chicken. The meal was expertly seasoned with fresh spices from the garden. It was the perfect accompaniment to such a lovely setting.

"Is Jore Sula the only man in your life?" Solomon asked, once they'd dined in silence for several minutes.

"There is no man in my life," Jacinta sang.

Solomon was quite pleased by her words, but that didn't cease his taunting. "I find that hard to believe."

Jacinta let her fork hit her plate with a clatter. "What? That there is no man?"

"No, that there is only one."

"But there isn't even one."

"Jacinta, you can tell me," he tempted, leaning back to persuade her with the hypnotic power of his gaze. "A woman like you—voluptuous, beautiful, full of . . . vigor. I'm sure you have appetites," he went on, sensing her temper heating across the table. "Heaven knows the life you lead—always out and about—leaves plenty of time for—"

"You bastard," Jacinta hissed, her fists clenched and firm atop the table. "I don't know where you came from, Dikembe, but I'd wager it was a place of ill repute and filth. For you to insinuate that I am a woman like that leaves no doubt in my mind that you are a man of the lowest nature. All your fine clothes, charm and money can't disguise the filth that follows you around like a shroud."

Solomon forked a morsel of tender oven fried chicken into his mouth. "You think I'm charming?" he asked between chews.

Jacinta pounded her fists to the table. "Damn you! I have my suitors, yes, but that is all they are or ever will be!"

"Strong words," he noted with a shrug. "You expect me to believe not one of those men has appealed to you in a more sensual way?"

Jacinta's eyes narrowed as she shook her head. "Oooo . . . how can you speak so . . . loosely with me?"

"Miss McIver, I do believe I'm offended. Already you've forgotten what we've shared? The places my hands have been, my mouth? The way you moan when I—"

"Devil!" Jacinta spat, seething with more anger than she thought herself capable of possessing. "You are no gentleman to remark upon such things!" she scolded in a fierce whisper. Her cheeks stung with embarrassment while visions of those past interludes filled her mind.

Solomon's sleek brows rose in mild surprise as he wiped his hands on a napkin. "Perhaps that explains why you have no man in your life—dealing with *gentlemen*."

"Disgusting jackass," Jacinta breathed, fixing him with a scathing glare as she stood from the table. The heavy, padded Chippendale chair she'd occupied skidded a bit across the stone flooring when she bolted away. Intent on getting as far away from Solomon Dikembe as possible, she stomped off the terrace. The crisp lavender material of her skirts swished loudly as she made her exit. Just inside the ballroom, Solomon caught her arm.

Jacinta balled her fists and fought with all the strength she could muster. Solomon showed no sign that he even felt the blows as he pulled her high against his chest. His head tilted at that familiar angle and soon he was kissing her deeply.

Jacinta continued to fight, moaning her anger as her soft lips weakened beneath the devastating kiss. Her struggles renewed with increased rigor, when his tongue delved past her nipping teeth to taste the sweet haven of her mouth.

"Stop . . ." she urged, still pounding his shoulder while intermittently shoving against his neck. Of course the whispered word only afforded him more opportunity to thrust his tongue deeper into her mouth.

Solomon squeezed his eyes shut tight, relishing the feel of holding her captive between his chest and the wall. He kissed her with unmasked desire and desperation. Small sounds of tortured arousal slipped past his lips before he began to kiss her all over again.

Jacinta's fists lost their power, and soon the deft blows resembled awkward massages to his broad shoulders. Once she yielded to his touch, Solomon allowed her to slide down the length of his towering frame. Little else mattered to Jacinta at that point. Her fingers curled into the collar of his shirt as she stood on her toes to enjoy the kiss more comfortably. Her tongue battled with his unashamedly, and her entire body tingled from the feel of his silken whiskers against her face.

Solomon's breathing came in rapid deep bursts that were mingled with soft moans. One massive hand cupped Jacinta's neck to hold her in place as his lips and tongue tested the supple tissue of one earlobe. Jacinta tried to speak his name, but could form no words as the pleasure of his touch left he utterly breathless.

"Marry me."

Jacinta's body went rigid and, already breathless, she felt faint. There was no reason to ask Solomon to repeat himself, she heard each word.

"Let me go."

"Answer me."

"You're mad."

"That's no answer."

"All right," she whispered, searching the deep, dark depths of his eyes with frantic intensity. "No, never."

Solomon smirked, triggering the striking dimple in his cheek. "Never is such a long time."

"Understand me, Dikembe. I have no intention of marrying. Anyone. Ever," she swore, her voice dropping an octave as she voiced the declaration.

Solomon gave a short laugh, his expression brightening with understanding. "You actually believe that?"

"Why any woman in her right mind would want to be legally bound to a man in this time is beyond me. Marriage is just another form of slavery."

"Ha!"

The natural arch of Jacinta's brows rose in response to his reaction. "It's true."

Solomon's sinfully handsome face expressed pure disbelief. "How do you figure?" he breathed.

Jacinta shrugged, her body growing pliant in his embrace as she considered her answer. "Well, of course, there are no lines between black and white, only man and woman," she began, her warm brown gaze focused on the distance as though she could actually envision the topic of discussion. "Women are expected to cook, clean, mate and breed while men boast of conquest and find other ways to satisfy their lust when they no longer fancy their wives."

"Humph, I see," Solomon replied, finding her viewpoint amusing yet disturbing. "And what would an innocent like you know of such things?"

Jacinta fixed him with a stony look. "I know plenty, Dikembe. You would be most surprised."

Solomon graced her with the gorgeous one dimpled grin and a shrug. "I think not—judging from your responses to me, I believe I'd be more pleased than surprised."

Jacinta slapped him. Pleasure and triumph flowed through her when she heard the blow echo in the room. The satisfaction was short lived when she saw that Solomon barely acknowledged any discomfort. She decided to repeat the gesture and raised her hand. Solomon caught her wrist and jerked her close.

"This exaggerated innocence of yours is becoming tiresome, and you will never strike me again. Is that understood?" he whispered, the intensity of his midnight stare leaving no doubt that there would be serious repercussions should she not take him at his word.

Jacinta wrenched her arm out of his loosened grasp and decided to strike with her words. "You truly believe your looks and stature give you the freedom to behave this way, speak to me the way you do? I am not the least bit impressed or excited by you."

"In truth?" he challenged, the harsh look in his eyes fading to desire. He stepped closer until she was completely immobile between him and the wall. "Then resist me."

"Wh-what?" she whispered, feeling his closeness hamper her breathing.

"Push me away when I kiss you."

"Push you away." Jacinta stated, her tone clearly sarcastic.

Solomon nodded. "I'll not prevent you."

Jacinta turned her face away when she felt the familiar tingle settle someplace deep. His softly seductive manner and deep whispered words were already arousing her. "Why are you doing this?" she groaned, frustrated by her inability to resist him. "I'm sure you could find any number of women in this town who would be eager to please you. Why waste time with me?"

Solomon's hand rose to her face, his thumb brushed her cheek, and then curved down to her chin. "If you saw yourself from my point of view, you wouldn't dare ask such a question. Now do as I ask and push me away."

"No."

"Just as well."

"Solomon, please."

"I intend to do so."

"Solomon—"

"Shh . . ." he urged, kissing along her neck. The sensuous curve of his mouth trailed across from her collarbone to tease and nip the base of her throat with his tongue.

Jacinta arched her neck to allow him more room to explore. Solomon continued to cup her chin, his lips gliding up to nudge his nose against the velvety soft skin behind her ear. When his mouth was inches from hers, he released her chin and placed his hands lightly at her waist. His tongue outlined the curve of her full lips, briefly darting past to test the sweetness inside. Jacinta gasped, but spoke no words as her hands clenched into fists. Solomon held her in the lightest embrace and simply pleasured her with his mouth. Jacinta never realized there were so many nuances to something as simple as a kiss. His tongue traced the even ridge of her teeth, the soft flesh inside her mouth then taunted her tongue into a sensuous duel. Jacinta was almost paralyzed by desire. She ached to join Solomon in the lusty kiss, and each time she moved to participate she summoned the will to resist.

Solomon didn't know whether he had ever been so aroused, or if he ever would be again. He actually felt the urge to beg her to return his kiss. The slow uncertain thrusts of her tongue, before she changed her mind, only brought him closer to the brink of madness.

One hand cupped her breast, which heaved provocatively against her gown's square bodice. His thumb brushed the nipple once and she whimpered. Twice, and she moaned. When he took the rigid bud between his fingers and manipulated it in a devilish fashion, she broke the kiss and gasped wantonly.

Solomon stilled his movements after a while. "You're not . . . excited by me, hmm?" he challenged, lifting his smoldering charcoal stare from the rigid outline of the nipple against her dress.

Jacinta turned her face away, commanding her tears to remain hidden. Solomon's expression turned sympathetic. He knew he had teased her shamefully, but knew she was indeed attracted to him. The rest would come in time. Without another word, he left her alone in the ballroom.

Jacinta blinked the moisture from her lashes and stared up at the glass chandelier in the ceiling. "Damn," she whispered.

CHAPTER 8

"Ol' Chuck Wallens and his crew more n'likely think that boy was the only recruit!" Reynolds Carter joked, taking a few long drags from his pipe.

"They are a dense lot," Jason agreed, enjoying the warmth from the fire and the comfort of the worn leather chair set before the hearth.

Reynolds continued to chuckle. The free man and local blacksmith enjoyed a quiet home life, though he was often visited by scores of friends.

"I'm surprised you heard about Wallens all the way in town," Jason noted, while lighting his own pipe.

Reynolds stroked the heavy salt and pepper beard that shadowed his face. "It's on everyone's lips. Talk is, the boy got a ticket to the Work House for another beating after the one Big Bill gave him," he shared, citing one of the overseers at the Wallens Plantation.

Jason shuddered in spite of the blazing fire warming him through to his bones. His kind, round face hardened as visions of Jore Sula's lacerated back came to mind. Yes, he believed that very thing had probably happened. The Work House had been the final destination for many men. For the black population, the Work House was the most feared place in all of Charleston. The imposing building located on Magazine Street was like a dash of foul reality in the otherwise pristine beauty that was Charleston. For a fee, owners could send their slaves to the former sugar warehouse to be beaten. It was common to hear that some unfortunate soul had been sent to the Work House "for a little sugar".

"He was Mingo's only son," Reynolds was saying, resting his head against the high back of his chair. "The man was sick with worry and grief."

Jason's mood lightened a bit at Reynolds's use of the word "was". He knew Mingo Sula's despair had been lifted with news of his son's pending freedom and their own. "It's an outrage," he expressed while shaking his head, "whipping that boy on suspicion that he's involved in something that is no more than talk."

Reynolds waved his hand. "They don't even have a suspicion. They know nothing of this uprising."

Jason grunted. "They will soon enough with all the talk that's been hurled about these long years."

"Talk is necessary," Reynolds argued.

"Talk is pointless without action."

"The old man is far more than talk."

"Well, let's *talk* about this supposed 'old man'. I've heard some identify him as Vesey."

Reynolds' bushy gray brows rose as to confirm the gossip. Jason set his pipe aside while he laughed. He chuckled until tears streamed his face.

"Vesey? That's preposterous!"

Reynolds shrugged. "It's very true."

"But he's a free man, and far too old to play at such a thing."

"Nevertheless, he is doing it, and he's gaining support wherever he speaks."

Jason scratched his gray bush of hair. "I can't believe it," he admitted. "Why would such a man risk his freedom, his life and the life of his family? He lives a good life, Rey."

"And perhaps he wishes for that goodness to be experienced by more of his people."

Jason seemed to consider Reynolds's argument. Unfortunately, the entire idea struck him as nonsense and he dismissed it with a shake of his head.

"Why don't you attend one of the meetings, Jason?" Reynolds urged, leaning forward to fix his friend with an expectant gaze. "Attend one of the meetings and judge for yourself, see that Vesey is deadly serious and a firm believer in what he speaks."

Jason stood from the chair and strolled closer to the fire.

"We need for more free black men to stand and be counted, Jason. A man of your stature and respect could wield unimaginable power and success for this crusade." Reynolds predicted, frowning when Jason chuckled.

"I'm an old man, Rey. So are you, so is Vesey. This is a fight best suited for young men."

Reynolds left his seat to prepare two drinks at the bar cart in the corner of the dim office. "Believe me, friend, Vesey most certainly has his eyes on the younger men. With the exception of those damnable mulattoes, the man wants and needs everyone's help."

"Cutting off possible support doesn't seem to be smart move, Rey."

"Mulattoes, Jason? We don't need their kind of help."

"And you can say that without hesitation. Without knowing what they'd have to offer?" Jason challenged.

Reynolds' small dark eyes reflected disbelief. "Jason, you know as well as I do how untrustworthy the half-whites are."

Of course Jason knew. Hadn't those views been shared and voiced by everyone, including himself? He had always considered the mulattoes to be a self-serving group. That is, until he met Solomon Dikembe. "I should think Vesey would be eager to accept any support if it is offered with a genuine heart," Jason expressed.

Reynolds reclaimed his seat before the fire. "Need I remind you, friend, that the half-whites would not hesitate to use their own kind to infiltrate and report back on any suspicious behavior."

"And must I remind you, Rey, that there are almost as many mulattoes enslaved as there are pure blacks?"

Reynolds would not reconsider his stance. "I've not forgotten the Charleston mulattoes who've found favor at the white man's table and prefer that side of their heritage. You yourself are aware of the mulattoes who not only keep slaves but treat them as cruelly as any white man ever could."

Jason sat back in his chair and offered no response. The displeasure on his face, however, spoke volumes.

A knowing smile crossed Reynolds's brown oval face. "I'm curious about your change of heart, Jason. Could it have anything to do with the fact that you're in business with one of them?"

"Solomon Dikembe is not one of them, and he's not from the South," Jason defended quickly.

Concern was mirrored in Reynolds's eyes as clearly as it was in his voice. "You're a fine judge of character, Jason, so I'll not argue your opinion that this boy is as upstanding as you think he is. Vesey's just being safe."

"Safety like that could be the downfall of this so-called uprising," Jason forewarned. "Vesey should embrace *all* his supporters, be they four-quarters black or otherwise."

※

"Cuffe," Solomon greeted with a smile as he shook hands with his friend.

"Settle in," Cuffe instructed, sliding over to make room inside the carriage that would carry them to the ship.

Solomon took his place, and then knocked on the roof of the cab to signal the driver to move on. He glanced at Cuffe, feeling the man's stare upon him. Sure enough, Cuffe's brown eyes reflected a curious, teasing light. "Speak," he urged.

"This . . . business trip appears to be dragging on a bit, is it not?"

"There is much to attend to."

"And you haven't even seen the land yet, correct?"

"I've visited the property on the mainland. We'll be on the islands for several days, and that excursion has taken a bit of planning."

Cuffe's dark brows rose. "Mmm . . . convenient."

"Convenient," Solomon parroted, fixing Cuffe with his most penetrating look. "What's really on your mind, old friend?"

"McIver's daughter is quite a beauty."

Solomon shrugged. "She is."

"And not yet a conquest, I gather?"

"A gentleman never tells."

"And I know you're no gentleman."

Solomon couldn't help but chuckle. "And you have no idea how difficult it is to pretend that I am."

"You desire her."

"In every way."

Cuffe let his confusion show. "Well, hell, man, bed her and be done with it."

"I want more than that."

Now Cuffe's handsome, dark chocolate face reflected stunned amazement. "What are you trying to say, Sol?" he softly inquired, having never heard the man speak in such a manner.

Solomon cleared his throat and focused his eyes on his leather boots. "I proposed marriage," he confided.

"What?"

"She turned me down instantly," Solomon shared, smiling as he remembered the scene.

"You're serious?" Cuffe breathed, his eyes widening. "Have you spoken with her father?"

"Not yet."

Still stunned, Cuffe sat back against the cushioned black velvet seat. "I know she's an incredible beauty. Still, there must be far more to her than meets the eye if you were moved to propose marriage."

Solomon shook his head. "There is more to her than I could begin to tell you."

"If she ever accepts your proposal, you'd be leaving a trail of broken hearts."

Solomon chuckled at the notion. "But she hasn't accepted. The woman's much more in love with the idea of chasing behind one dangerous escapade after another."

"Speaking of dangerous escapades," Cuffe switched conversations as his voice dipped to a lower octave, "when will we be ready to travel with our guests?"

"Part of the reason I wanted to meet with you this afternoon." He glanced out at the muddied landscape as they trotted down the back road. "His wounds have closed. The doctor says he can be moved in another week or so."

"Will you be joining us?"

"Obviously I have reason to stay, but it may be best to go along. Just in case," Solomon decided, with a grim smirk.

Cuffe nodded. "You said the boy was part of the reason you wanted to meet."

Solomon cleared his throat. "What talk is there of the rebellion?"

"As I told you before, it's far more than talk. Weapons are being gathered, finances accumulated."

"So it is to happen?"

"It is," Cuffe boasted, spying the unease tighten Solomon's profile. "You are concerned about your lady?" he guessed.

"She is so fearless," Solomon muttered, pounding his fist to his palm. "She has no idea how much more serious this situation could become."

"So will you travel with us or not? Perhaps you can have her come along."

Solomon burst into laughter. "There is no way I could get her to do that unless—"

"What? Sol?"

Solomon would offer no answers. He simply rested back against the seat and pondered the plan forming in his mind.

Ol' Mista Blake and his men come for Pa in the middle the night. Come right in the slave quarters and take my pa out. Say he was just thinkin' 'bout runnin'. Mista Blake say slave ain't 'pose to think. And if'n he thinkin' 'bout runnin' that all the worser. They take my pa and hang him in the night. Let him stay right in the middle of da clearin' where'n ev'rybody see him fo' days. Say it be a lesson to the rest of us who might be thinkin'. Later we find out it was Munro Caffrey who spoke ta Mista Blake 'bout a talk he had wit Pa. Pa talk to ev'rybody. Even when the rest tell him mulattoes not to be trust, he neva listen. He say they part black, part white—he talk to the black part. After Pa hanged, we all wonder what part of Munro betray him to the white man.

Jacinta brushed her fingers across the passage from her journal. She read that entry, and several more like it,

since retreating to her father's study earlier that afternoon. The recording from Lawrence Payne, now a free
man living in Charleston, never failed to cause her eyes
to pressure with tears.

"They're all the same," she chanted, closing the book.
"Solomon is just waiting to find some weakness he can
exploit."

Someplace deep in her heart, Jacinta knew she was
being unfair. True, Solomon had said and done things she
found shocking and unseemly, but she knew he was not
a cruel man. Should the time come to choose, she could
not be sure where his loyalties would lie.

"Good afternoon, love!" Jason called out as he
strolled into his upstairs study. "This is a pleasure to find
you here," he said, while searching his desk for a missing
document.

Jacinta chewed her bottom lip and regarded her
father with thoughtful eyes. Then, nodding once as she
made a silent decision, she set aside her journal and stood
from the settee as Jason retrieved the paper he searched
for. When he took a seat on the long chair across from his
desk, Jacinta smoothed her hands across the vibrant coral
skirts of her gown and took her place next to him.

"Poppa . . . has—has Solomon . . . spoken to you?"

"Mmm? Spoken to me, love?" Jason absently queried,
as he frowned over the papers he held.

Jacinta pressed her lips together and glanced toward
her lap. "Um, has he mentioned anything?"

"Such as?"

"Well . . . anything?"

"Business?"

"No," Jacinta sighed, feeling her frustration mount. "Never mind, Poppa."

Jason set his work aside then and turned to regard her closely. "Was he supposed to speak to me about something?" he asked, patting her hands to urge her to cease the nervous wringing.

Jacinta felt she had already said far too much. She also felt more than a little embarrassed by the fact that she had taken Solomon Dikembe's proposal even the slightest bit seriously.

"Jaci?"

"Poppa, I'm sorry I disturbed your work."

"But you haven't—"

"I'll let you finish," Jacinta interjected. She pressed a light kiss to his cheek before rushing from the study.

Jason's curious gaze followed her until she was gone.

Solomon had worn a fierce scowl since Cuffe ordered the carriage driver to stop. They were miles away from where the ship was docked. Still, Cuffe seemed certain about wanting to stop here. He and Solomon had walked quite a ways before Solomon noticed any hint of civilization.

Of course, it was quite a stretch to compare the shack in their midst to civilization. The place appeared deserted among the towering pine trees, brush and thicket deep in the woods they traveled.

"Man, where are we?" Solomon hissed, his dark features sharp with agitation.

"You're still curious about the revolt, so you may as well obtain your information from the source," Cuffe whispered, tugging his brown-brimmed hat further down over his head.

Solomon tugged upon the high collar of his black cloak and focused on the building ahead. As they neared, the sounds of voices grew audible. The gathering was well attended. So well, in fact, that Cuffe was barely able to shoulder a bit of space just inside the heavily weathered shack. Solomon had no complaints about listening in from the outside, as he was sure to garner more than a few curious, distrustful glares. Thankfully, he was able to hear the main speaker without having to strain his ears. Denmark Vesey, the 'old man' with powerful thoughts and words, captivated Solomon as he did all those long months before. The intensity of his opinions had not dwindled. Moreover, he seemed rededicated, as though he knew the time was fast approaching.

"July fourteenth, eighteen hundred and twenty-two! Gentlemen, that is the month, day and year of this great event. An event we will see through to the end! It is the day that we give our wives, our babies, ourselves hope! Peace! And dignity!"

The crowd cheered the old man's words and firm predictions for success.

" 'They devoted the city to the Lord and destroyed with the sword every living thing in it—men and women, young and old, cattle, donkeys and sheep.' "

Solomon stroked his whiskered jaw and listened reverently as the man recited the biblical passage from Joshua, sixth chapter, twenty-first verse. The shouting men were silent, their eyes riveted on the non-threatening, stately man at the front of the room.

In the midst of the speech, Cuffe turned to regard his friend with smug assurance in his cool, brown gaze. "Still doubtful?" he asked.

"They are still words, man," Solomon remarked, though the "words" had stirred the crowd like nothing he had ever seen.

Cuffe shrugged, looking back into the crowded, dank room. "That is true," he admitted, "but they are words unlike anything these people have ever heard."

Solomon offered no response for he agreed with his captain. The "talk" had the makings of emerging into some great event. As much as he applauded the fight for freedom, Solomon couldn't help but think of Jacinta, who would surely want to take part in that fight.

"Delicious!"

"Mistah Jason, I ain't even got the crawdads in yet!"

"Anell, this jambalaya is your best yet! Add anything more and I don't think I'll be able to stand swallowin' somethin' so good!"

Anell Handy covered her mouth as she laughed. "Mistah Jason, you too much!"

Solomon found Jason in the kitchen surrounded by at least three of his cooks. Leaning against the tall doorway, Solomon smiled as Jason talked and joked with members of the staff who appeared happy and at ease in the midst of their employer.

Jason spotted Solomon at the doorway and waved him forward. "Come have a sample of tonight's feast, young man!"

Solomon grinned, watching Jason hold up a saucer that teemed with shrimp, fish, tomatoes, onions, okra and other ingredients.

"I'll wait until Miss Anell adds her crawdads," Solomon decided.

Anell bowed her head at the gracious refusal. "A man who know good food take time," she teased sarcastically, her light brown eyes focused on her employer.

"Bah!" Jason growled, finishing his oversized sample amidst the laughing women.

"If I could have a moment, sir?" Solomon requested when he caught Jason's eye again.

Intrigued, Jason finished with the plate, urging his cooks to hurry with the scrumptious feast. "Come, boy," he whispered, clapping Solomon's shoulder as he rushed past.

Inside the sitting room, Jason watched Solomon take a seat on the long chair near the windows. He sensed the same uneasiness surrounding the young man that he had sensed around Jacinta earlier that day. Sitting next to Solomon on the long chair, he waited.

Solomon trailed his index finger along the inside of his collar in an uncharacteristic show of uncertainty.

"This is concerning your daughter," he eventually confided.

"I gathered as much."

Solomon's brows drew close. "How, sir?"

"What would you like to discuss, son?"

The young man's sinfully handsome features softened as he experienced a twinge of unaccustomed discomfort. "I am . . . I'm asking for your daughter's hand in marriage, sir."

Jason's expression illuminated with happiness. "So that's what it was," he breathed.

"Sir?"

"So do you love my Jacinta?" Jason questioned, feigning a firm tone of voice.

Again, Solomon appeared uncertain. "I have never known a feeling like this for another. I can not say it is love, though I do believe it could be so."

Jason focused on the embroidery along the edge of the cushioned seat. "And my Jaci? She feels the same?"

Solomon's expression reclaimed its fierceness. "The woman likens marriage to slavery. I do believe she'd rather drop dead than marry. Anyone," he shared, grimacing as Jason laughed.

"I know that she has certain . . . feelings toward me," he continued, folding his arms across the tweed suit coat he wore. "Still, sir, these *feelings* are hardly the ones required to sustain a long marriage."

"Yet you want her anyway?"

"I do."

"Her beauty has captivated you?"

"Yes, but only in part."

Jason nodded. "Her spirit?" he guessed.

"And determination," Solomon added, standing from the chair as thoughts of Jacinta evoked stirring sensations in the pit of his stomach. "Everything about her fascinates me. I would not see her with another," he vowed, his coal black stare smoldering with determination as he focused on the view from the windows. Then, realizing how the words may have sounded to Jason, he turned to explain. "Of course, sir, I mean no disrespect should you feel that I am unsuited to your daughter—"

"Nonsense!" Jason bellowed, moving from the long chair as well. "Boy, in all the suitors that girl has captivated, you are by far the *most* suited. Like you, I would not see her with another, either."

Solomon nodded, his long lashes closing briefly over his eyes as he experienced a jolt of relief. "She will fight this, sir," he warned.

Jason shrugged. "Then you should court her until she has no fight left." He clapped his hands and turned suddenly. "I have the perfect scenario."

"Scenario?"

"Our trip to the sea islands. It's the perfect place, and we sail at the end of the week."

"But we're going there to conduct business, sir," Solomon reminded Jason, though a tiny smile played at the curve of his mouth.

"True. But I guarantee you'll have no desire for business once you view the landscape," Jason declared. "It's lovely. The property owned by the family is very secluded, and a ways off from any civilization."

"Who maintains it in your absence?" Solomon perched his tall frame against the window sill.

Jason massaged his jaw and smiled. "A staff assumes care of the property. It is their home. I tell you, boy, it is such an enchanting place, one would almost believe the horrors of our world never existed."

"Mistah Jason, beg pardon."

"Come in, Marva," Jason called, waving towards the upstairs maid who had also been acting as night nurse for Jore Sula.

Marva curtsied to Jason and offered a bashful smile to Solomon. "Mistah Jason, I come to tell you Jacinta ask to dine in her room this evenin'."

"Is she ill?" Jason asked, his brown stare sharpening just a tad.

"Not ill in the way you mean, Mista Jason." Marva squeezed her hands tightly. "Her spirits seem low."

Jason and Solomon exchanged glances. Obviously such news had surprised them both. Jacinta's spirits being low didn't seem conceivable.

"What I tell her, Mista Jason?" Marva inquired softly, appearing far younger than her sixteen years as her dark eyes widened in expectation.

"Tell her it's fine, Marva. I'll look in on her later," Jason said. "What of Jore?"

Marva's uneasy expression brightened at once. "Oh, he doin' fine, Mistah Jason. He sittin' up in bed, makin' ev'rybody laugh and laugh. He eatin' good, too."

"That's good news, Marva," Solomon commented. "You're doing a fine job."

"Thank you, Mistah Solomon," Marva replied softly, offering a demure smile.

"Good work, Marva," Jason complimented as well.

Marva curtsied and backed towards the sitting room doorway. "Thank you, Mistah Jason. I best be gettin' back upstairs," she whispered, then hurried off.

"Good news about Jore," Jason remarked, reclaiming his seat on the long chair. "Are the arrangements set for that trip?"

"Confirmed earlier this week," Solomon said. "My crew's been informed. We're simply waiting on word from the doctor."

Jason nodded. "The sooner that boy's on his way, the better."

"Do you expect another visit from Wallens?"

Jason scratched his gray bush of hair and smirked. "I'm almost hoping for one. It would give me great pleasure to stifle his inquiries most firmly."

Solomon's expression grew curious as he tilted his head. "You sound as though you have a plan in the works?"

Jason folded his arms across the silver gray vest he wore. "Son, there'd be no need for revolt if this plan could be expedited by every free man in the South. I suspect you'll be wanting to take my Jaci along when you set out with the Sula family?" he asked, taking note of Solomon's confusion when he spoke of his "plan" involving the Wallens.

Solomon's thoughts fell immediately to Jacinta. "I've thought of that, but I know I'd be in for one messy fight."

Jason uttered a short laugh. "She'll calm, and it comforts me to know you want her away from this place."

Solomon focused on his hands. "I meant no disrespect toward your home, sir."

"I've wanted my child away from Charleston for many years."

"Still, it *is* her home, sir."

"And the older she becomes, the more rushed I feel to see her gone," Jason admitted, his expression hardening. "She grows more beautiful each day, and that fact invites a great deal of unwanted attention."

"I understand," Solomon's rough voice grated as his lips tightened.

"My daughter does not understand. She has no idea of the danger surrounding her each time she leaves my land unchaperoned."

Solomon's massive hands clenched into fists. "I'd die before I let anything happen to her."

"This I know."

"Sir, you have no reason to take my word."

"Yet I think I'm right in doing so."

"I appreciate your saying that."

Jason slapped his hands to his thighs and stood. "I best go on up and check on her," he decided, leaving Solomon alone with his thoughts.

Marriage! The word echoed in Solomon's mind. He had never entertained such a thought through all the lovely ladies who had frequented his life and bed. Jacinta, however, mesmerized him, and she didn't really have to try. He would certainly be in for a fight. After all, aside from knowing she was physically attracted to him, he knew little of any other feelings she might have. He grimaced then, triggering the lone dimple. He realized he knew little of his own feelings.

ᕫᑐ

Jason waited until after dinner to look in on his daughter. He knocked once on Jacinta's door before stepping inside. He found her seated along the powder blue cushioned window sill. Her vibrant coffee stare was devoid of emotion as she stared out into the night.

"Jaci? Love? What is this? What's wrong with you?" Jason questioned.

Jacinta offered a weak shrug. "I didn't feel up to eating downstairs."

Jason glanced toward her untouched dinner on the small round dining table in the corner. "Obviously you didn't feel up to eating here, either."

"Simply waiting for the meal to cool."

Jason closed the bedroom door. "Anell says jambalaya loses something once it's cooled."

Jacinta only shook her head and offered no response.

"You were right about Solomon," Jason called, as he leaned against the carved, white oak dressing table. He smirked when he noticed Jacinta's head turn slightly in his direction. "He did want to speak with me about something."

"Oh?" she questioned, remaining intentionally indifferent. She shielded her curious expression behind the heavy curtain of her black tresses.

"Mmm," Jason gestured, pretending to be interested with something on the heel of his dress boot. "He wanted to discuss the particulars of the island visit. I warned him of not being able to keep his mind on business once he sees the beauty of the place."

"Yes, it is beautiful," Jacinta responded absently, once again looking out into the black night. "The two of you should have a wonderful time," she added.

"And so will you."

Jacinta allowed the gauzy light curtains to fall into place across the window. A frown marred her soft, lovely features as she watched her father. "No, Poppa."

"Yes, Jaci."

"Poppa—"

"Now you know I can not leave you here."

"Why not?" Jacinta challenged, turning on the window sill to fix her father with a steady glare. "I won't be alone."

"Precisely. You have too many outside interests for my liking."

"But Poppa—"

"Jaci, my mind is made. Besides, it's time I put my foot down about you taking more of an interest in our business."

Jacinta realized it was useless trying to persuade her father to leave her behind. She let the subject drop and turned back to the window. When Jason left, she whipped the curtain back into place and bolted from the padded sill. Pacing the lovely woven rug in the center of the room, she cursed Solomon Dikembe. Then she reprimanded herself for allowing him to get the better of her. Clearly, his proposal was just a vicious tease and she should never have allowed herself to be carried away by it. Now she was moping around because he wasn't serious. Why?

"You know why," she answered aloud, tapping her fingers to her chin. The man fascinated her, she admitted that. He was physically devastating, yes. But there was so much more, and he plagued her thoughts at every turn.

"Dammit!" she raged, kicking out at the air. She had no place in her life for such distractions when there were far more important matters demanding her attention. Unfortunately, her attention, at present, was focused on one very intense, very appealing man.

CHAPTER 9

"And just where you hear 'bout this?"

"Slaves talk."

"What slaves?"

"Why, of your very plantation, sir. I'm certain any of them would know more on the matter."

"And you certain they was referring to *this* matter?"

"I am."

Chuck Wallens reclined in the worn black leather chair behind his cluttered pine desk. His blue gray stare regarded the short, rotund, light-skinned man closely. "Your assistance will be rewarded, Paul," he finally decided, nodding toward one of the four men in the study. The man stepped forward, waved in Paul Vinson's direction and escorted him out of the smoky office.

Alone with his remaining cohorts, Wallens grimaced and fixed them with a stony glare. "I do b'lieve it's time for another trip to that uppity darkie's *estate*."

While Chuck Wallens and his crew were plotting their next move, Solomon was seeing Jore Sula into a wagon that would transport him to the *Sheba* amidst the cover of trees, brush and the coming night. Also in attendance for the trip were Jore's parents, his sister, grand-mother, uncles, aunts and cousins. It was an emotional and joyous event.

"This is a great day, Mingo."

Mingo Sula's blackberry-toned face was a picture of pride. His dark eyes roamed the expanse of the covered wagon as though he beheld his salvation. "I never hope to dream a day like this find me, Jason."

Jason clapped the man's back and grinned. "Yet here it is, and your family is together here to take part in it."

"Yes," Mingo sighed, gazing out over the small crowd in the back yard, "my boy coulda been dead, Jason."

"Hush now," Jason urged with a quick wave, "don't think such things. Not this day."

"I don't think sad on it, Jason. My boy woulda died for a great cause."

Jason frowned. "Mingo, I know you don't believe in this talk."

Mingo smiled while shaking his head of short graying hair. "It easy for you to put it off as talk, but we slaves got to hold on to the dream——no matter what it be."

Jason nodded, his expression softening. "God be with you, Mingo," he whispered.

Jacinta pulled her best friend into a tight hug for the fifth time that evening. "I'll miss you so," she breathed.

Zambia laughed amidst her crying. "So will I. Oh, how I wish you could come with us!" she fiercely whispered.

Jacinta smoothed her hands across the sides of the burgundy scarf covering her friend's coarse, shoulder-length hair. "Now don't you think about that," she ordered, cupping Zambia's dark, oval face. "Concentrate on your new home and all the good things waiting for you there. My place is here and I wouldn't have it any other way."

Zambia rolled her eyes. "You sound just like my father," she muttered.

"Mister Mingo knows what's important," Jacinta said, folding her arms across the button-down bodice of her charcoal gray riding dress.

"Humph, important?" Zambia snorted. "I believe he'd rather stay in Charleston a slave just to fight in this revolt."

Zambia's fear and concern were obvious, and Jacinta regretted not being more sympathetic. "I'm sorry," she whispered, stepping forward to smooth her hands across Zambia's arms, which were covered by the long sleeves of her dress. "Your father's place is with you and the family—I agree with that. But try to understand, Zambi, he just wants a better life for everyone."

Zambia nodded once, her eyes drifting across the lovely scene in the yard. Suddenly her eyes sparkled and she smiled demurely before looking away. "He is so very handsome, Jaci," she commented, nodding toward Solomon Dikembe, who stood talking with Jore.

Jacinta glanced around in confusion, her lips thinning when she saw to whom Zambia was referring.

"He seems so different from the mulattoes here in Charleston," Zambia continued.

"Mmm . . . I pray you're right. Only time will tell."

Zambia watched her friend curiously. "He's been here for quite some time and you're *still* suspect of him?"

Jacinta rolled her eyes. "His kind . . . they're a self-serving lot. I still don't know what he's after."

"He can't stop looking this way for more than a few moments, Jaci," Zambia noted, her expression mischievous. "I'd say he's after you," she decided, then kissed her friend's cheek and strolled over to her mother and grandmother.

Jacinta stood there, her skin riddled with gooseflesh.

"Jore, please, for the twentieth time, your thanks are not necessary," Solomon was saying through his chuckles as the young man shook his hand yet again.

"I can't think a one person who would do what you doin', Mistah Solomon. You give me and my family somethin' most people got to die tryin' to git."

Solomon only nodded. He realized that while he looked upon the act as a gesture of decency, the Sulas saw him as the man who saved their lives.

"Take care of Jaci, Mistah Solomon."

Jore's words prompted Solomon to glance over at Jacinta as he'd done for the better part of the afternoon. She caught him staring and fixed him with a stern look before stomping off.

"I want to take care of her, Jore, but she seems more interested in fighting me," he admitted.

"I think it a act," Jore decided, smiling at the look of surprise he earned from Solomon. "I can tell by the way her face change when your name mention. You a good man, Mistah Solomon. Make me feel good to know that lady got men like you and Mistah Jason lookin' after her."

Solomon nodded. "Thank you. I appreciate you saying that," he shared, initiating a handshake.

Jore held onto Solomon's hand. "You just make sure you git her out this place fore all hell break loose. 'Taint no place for a lady, suh."

Solomon looked over at Jacinta, now huddled in conversation with a few of the field hands. A grim smile darkened his face. "I fully agree, Jore."

Jacinta, Jason, Solomon and the rest of the household collected in the clearing at the mouth of the back trail. The carriage was departing, and they all watched until it had disappeared down the tree and shrub lined lane leading past the rear of the estate. Some of the house staff whispered prayers of thanks and well wishes. Jacinta, meanwhile, stood with her hands clasped and her eyes brimming with tears.

Jason noticed and pulled her into a reassuring embrace. When he let her go, Jacinta stepped back and noticed Solomon watching her. She nodded once and smiled.

"Thank you," she spoke in a hushed, sincere tone.

Solomon only nodded. His ebony gaze was lingering and intense as he watched her head back toward the house. He followed in her footsteps while Jason stayed behind. He thought of his matchmaking scheme for the coming days.

"This will be quite an adventure," he mused.

Jacinta retreated to one of her favorite areas within the house following the Sula's departure. The main dining room had been constructed to accommodate diners when the estate held one of the great galas it was famous for so many years ago.

Though the area was hardly used now, Jacinta often dreamed of seeing the place filled with people. Her people—happy and free.

Because no one ventured there, especially at such an hour, Jacinta felt free enough to let her guard down. She strolled out to the enclosed balcony, kicked off her slippers and unbound her hair. She sat on one of the cushioned stools with her head bowed and her elbows resting on her knees. The evening breeze ruffled her dark locks. Jacinta bowed her head lower, allowing the tresses to tumble across her head so that the night air cooled the nape of her neck. She moaned a little at the exquisite relaxation the simple treat provided and envisioned staying there for hours. She was there with her head between her knees when Solomon found her.

For a while, he only watched her, feeling his body respond to the image she portrayed.

Jacinta whirled around as the sound of a clearing throat touched her ears. "Dammit, Dikembe!" she seethed. "Can't you find anything better to do than follow my every move?"

Solomon couldn't respond, not when Jacinta McIver was such an incredible sight. She had turned quickly on the round, cushioned seat and, in doing so, her hair whipped back across her shoulders. With the mass tumbling in midnight waves across her back, she appeared the most lusciously tempting vision he had ever seen.

"Solomon?" Jacinta called, trying to gain his attention.

He took a deep breath, determined to stamp down his basest urges. "I only came here to look in on you. You seemed very emotional when the carriage left."

Jacinta shrugged, causing a heavy lock to curtain one side of her face. "I was no more emotional than anyone else."

Her soft argument brought a smile to Solomon's face. "Perhaps, but the Sulas were your friends. Especially Zambia."

"She was my best friend," Jacinta corrected, thinking back on all the times they'd shared—good and bad. Zambia had shared her hopes and fears with Jacinta. Jacinta had done the same. "Where will the ship take them?" she questioned, clearing her throat as emotion had brought a touch of hoarseness to her voice.

"The ship will dock in New York and they'll travel the rest of the way by carriage," Solomon said, stepping further onto the balcony.

A shiver kissed Jacinta's skin and she knew it had nothing to do with the chilly onset of the night. "So far away . . ." she mused, her chocolate stare gazing out into the night. "Tell me about your home. Tell me about Michigan," she urged, watching him with expectant eyes.

Solomon chose his spot on one of the iron lounge chairs bordering the edge of the balcony. "It's my home. The home of my father and mother when she came to this country. When I was a child, I thought no place else existed but my home," he confided, the striking dimple appearing in his cheek when he chuckled at the childish assumption.

Jacinta leaned forward on her stool, bracing her elbows on her knees, as she propped her cheeks against her palms. Her expression was soft as she studied Solomon, listening to him speak with such compassion filling his gravely voice. His devastating features were relaxed as he spoke of the snow in winter, apple blossoms in spring, and the way in which the white pines dotted the landscape with their shade while filling the air with their smell.

"Tell me about your business," Jacinta requested, unconscious of how eager she was to learn more about the man.

"I have several interests, but I suppose my greatest would involve acquiring land," he shared, crossing his long, tan, trouser-clad legs at the ankles. "Aside from my family's home, I've managed to obtain a vast amount. A great portion of it I've sold to my people, who've either purchased their freedom or escaped to it. Now they want homeland of their own. I help to make that possible."

"And this is where the Sulas will be?"

"That's right," Solomon confirmed Jacinta's question, watching her reaction as her gaze drifted out into the night. "I have a good home, Jacinta," he assured her, hoping to take her mind away from worrying over her friends. "The land is suitable for everything from cattle and corn to oil and soybeans. It's said that the upper region is vast in iron ore, which is a good source of fuel. One of these days, there may even be canals to link the upper and lower regions of the state. This would only increase the success of trading these resources," he boasted.

Jacinta was in awe. "And you have interest in all of this?" she whispered.

Solomon's broad shoulders rose beneath the tanned fabric of his three-quarter suit coat. "Most, not all," he told her. "I'm working to change that."

"It shouldn't be too difficult for you."

A tiny furrow formed between Solomon's brows. "What makes you say that?" he asked.

Jacinta allowed her gaze to falter.

The response was telling enough and Solomon felt his hands clenched into fists. "Do you think my white blood makes my life any easier, Jacinta?" he snapped.

"Far easier than the lives of those of us who are one hundred percent Negro," she threw back.

Her blunt point roused Solomon's temper tenfold, yet he did an admirable job of appearing calm. "At least you are trusted. Your motives are not looked upon as self-serving or traitorous. As a child, no matter how much I ached to belong, I couldn't. White children didn't think I was good enough. Black children believed I thought I was *too* good," he shared, biting back more of his story, refusing to give Jacinta anything more she could use to stomp his feelings.

"So you held it against these children for teasing you as you went back to a cozy home and they returned to their shacks?"

Solomon decided it was useless to explain anything more. He threw his hands up in defeat and leaned back in the chair.

Jacinta stood, her hair snapping against the wind as fiercely as her eyes snapped with anger. "What a hard life you must've endured," she muttered sarcastically, as she sauntered off the balcony.

Losing the will, or desire, to restrain his temper, Solomon bolted from the chair. He caught Jacinta before she could step foot inside the ballroom, his massive hands folding over her upper arms to lock her in a steely embrace.

"For me it was hard. It was hell," his deep voice grated, matching the almost tangible anger that spewed from his black eyes. "You have no idea what it does to a child—wanting so very much to belong, knowing he has every right to belong but having to hear that the color of his skin makes him unworthy."

"How can you say I don't know what that's like?" Jacinta argued in a tiny voice, having no desire to anger him further.

Solomon's smirk was grim. "Imagine having to hear it from the race of people you identified with," he countered, his anger reheating when her gaze faltered. "Imagine having to hear that those of your skin color enslaved and dehumanized them. Imagine growing up hating half of yourself in spite of the fact that it's the half that has loved you, raised you, educated and provided for you."

"Solomon—"

"And what do you know of hardship, Miss McIver?" he spat, bringing his face closer to hers. "Living in your ivory tower," he sneered, "venturing out to hear slave stories for entertainment and fodder for your journal."

Jacinta couldn't stop the tears from pooling in her eyes. She wanted to argue his points, but she had never seen him so angered. She gasped when his grip grew unbearable as he drew her closer.

"Solomon, please—this hurts," she whispered, barely able to form the words.

Just then, the dinner bell rang and he released her. Jacinta closed her eyes in relief. She stood there massaging the soreness from her arms and watching as Solomon stormed from the balcony.

"The happiest moments of my life took place on that island. It was there I proposed to Jacinta's mother—there where Jacinta was born," Jason reminisced later that evening. He grimaced, seeing that his memories hadn't instilled the same warm-hearted feelings in his two young dinner companions.

Jason had expected dinner would be a quiet affair. He barely tasted the delicious roasted chicken with rice, fresh greens and cornbread.

"I think I'll go see what's keeping dessert," Jason finally decided, realizing his stabs at lightening the mood were in vain.

Jacinta and Solomon tried to appear interested and amused by Jason's stories, but they were clearly preoccupied by the earlier scene on the balcony. Jacinta kept her eyes on her plate and tried to focus on what remained of the delicious meal. It was useless, of course. Now Solomon Dikembe had come full circle in the ways he infatuated her. His looks, his intelligence, his accomplishments, his sensual appeal and now his anger and vulnerability. Her words had wounded him deeply and she knew there was far more hurt in his past than he had admitted. As he sat across the table, she could almost feel the tension and frustration radiating from his solid, powerful frame. Giving up on her attempts to finish her dinner, Jacinta stood to leave. Too late, she realized she would have to pass his chair to exit the small dining room. Tamping down her unease, she kept her eyes focused ahead and went to step past.

Solomon's deep-set gaze followed her every move. When she raised her hand in order to drop the linen napkin to her plate, he noticed her wince in pain. When she passed his place at the table, he caught her hand in a firm, yet gentle grasp.

"Forgive me," he whispered.

"You did nothing," she whispered back.

"I should never have touched you in anger. I am sorry."

"What I said—"

"I've heard worse."

"There was far worse I might have said—could *still* say," she forewarned.

Solomon felt his mouth tug against laughter. "Then I may very well be apologizing again."

Jacinta couldn't hide her amusement, either. She was about to smile when she caught sight of the intensity in his dark eyes and her breath stopped in her throat. She moved to pull away, but Solomon's grasp flexed around her hand and he urged her to bend towards him.

Jacinta could feel her knees weakening when she heard him utter a tortured cry when their mouths met.

For a time, their lips melded in the sweetest fashion. Then Solomon's tongue demanded entrance and Jacinta willingly complied. Her hair fell forward to shield their faces as the kiss intensified. Solomon thrust his tongue harder, deeper, as Jacinta met the lusty act with a fire of her own. Solomon's free hand curved around her neck and drew her in deeper. Jacinta was inches away from making herself comfortable in his lap, when the sound of Jason's voice in the distance pulled them apart.

"Gingerbread cake with hot cider! A dessert fit for kings!" Jason bellowed, rubbing his protruding belly beneath the tightly fastened vest he sported. "Have a seat, dear girl. The best is yet to come!" he promised.

Jacinta raked one hand through her hair and fixed her father with apologetic eyes. "I couldn't eat another thing, Poppa," she told him.

"*Another* thing? Love you've hardly touched your dinner," Jason noted, glancing at the food left behind on her plate.

"Poppa—"

"Alright, alright, I won't argue," he muttered, pressing a kiss to her cheek before he headed back to his seat. "I've never known the girl to lose her appetite regardless of what was going on," he muttered to Solomon.

Jacinta heard him clearly and fixed him with a soft look. "Poppa don't worry. You know I'll eat my fill once we get to Seabrook Island. Esa always keeps me eating," she said, referring to her friend there. "Now I'll be saying goodnight to you both," she spoke to her father, and then set Solomon a lingering look.

"Mistah Jason! Mistah Jason!"

Jacinta had scarcely taken two steps when the dining room door flew open. Rufas Wells, one of the yardmen, had rushed in from the kitchen's entrance to the dining room. His youthful features appeared fierce and matured by anger.

"Mistah Jason, Wallens and his crew ridin' up the front lane!"

Jason stood from the table and Solomon followed suit. Jacinta's sweet persona vanished instantly and she was at once on guard and ready for battle.

"Should I get the rifles, Poppa?" she asked, her brown gaze hard and steady.

Jason smiled at his daughter's fearlessness. "Love, I don't believe it'll be necessary. But keep the key handy just in case," he suggested, sending her a quick wink. "I've been waiting weeks for this chance," he added.

Jacinta and Solomon exchanged brief glances of confusion. Then they followed a very confident Jason McIver outside the dining room.

Mary Chapins, one of the downstairs housemaids, ushered Chuck Wallens and his three followers into the house. The men wore hard-as-granite expressions beneath the dust and sweat sticking to their faces. Needless to say, they appeared completely out of place within the cozy, elegant home.

"Evenin' folks," Chuck Wallens greeted in his casual manner, though his gaze was inquisitive as he studied the tall, powerful-looking, light-complexioned gentleman who leaned against the desk in the corner of the room.

"Miss Jacinta," he greeted, his eyes slinking across her body in open appreciation of her beauty and other physical endowments. His men repeated the greeting; the lust in their gazes was also unmistakable.

"Evening," Jacinta replied in her most regal tone. She met each of their gazes with a knowing glare that told them she could read behind their polite salutations.

Wallens cleared his throat, the harshness in his expression returning. "Lot a men posted outside, Jason," he mentioned.

Jason smiled. "You're right," he agreed.

"Make the place look like a armed camp. 'Spectin' trouble, McIver? Or tryin' to protect somebody?"

Jason threw back his head and laughed. "Is this what you came to see me about?"

"I came to discuss my property," Wallens sneered.

Jason folded his arms over his chest. "Land?"

"Slave. Jore? I b'lieve you know of him?"

"And why would you think that?"

"Got it on good authority."

"Whose?"

"That ain't 'portant—what is, is that my authority say you got that boy stashed 'way in this house."

Jason perched on the edge of his desk, opposite from the end Solomon occupied. "Your authority is mistaken," he said.

Wallens rocked back and forth on his dusty work boots, a clear gesture of confrontation. "We can search," he threatened.

"But you won't."

Wallens' smug expression seemed to freeze on his face. Of course, he wasn't bested yet. "Jason you may be a 'free' man livin' high, but don't you forgit who you talkin' to!"

"And don't *you* forget where you are, Chuck," Jason politely retorted, his voice low and steady. "Don't forget whose house this is," he added.

Wallens took a few steps closer to Jason. "This house b'long to Mister Roland McIver, and he be havin' a downright fit if'n he knew how uppity you done got! But he's dead now, ain't he, Jason?" Wallens sneered, his face gleaming with devilment. "Maybe you be needin' a lil' stay at the Work House?"

Jason grinned in spite of Wallens's taunt. "You're right, Chuck," he drawled, swinging one leg back and forth from his position on the desk. "Mister Roland is dead, but his possessions live on. Mister Roland had some power over almost every business or plantation in this town. One plantation in particular, ain't that right, Chuck?"

Cooter Wallens stepped forward. "Now-now Mister Jason, you can't be talkin' to my-my pa like that," the young man stuttered.

Jason's gaze remained fixed on the elder Wallens. "But your pa knows what I'm talkin' about."

Chuck Wallens's bottom lip trembled and his eyes were wide with unease. "You ain't got no power over me."

"But Roland McIver did, and he still does. His brother may live in New York, but he still holds the deed on several key properties in this town—including yours.

Now . . ." Jason sighed, finally standing from the desk, "this being his beloved brother's estate, I don't think he'd look too kindly upon it bein' barged in upon and searched. He might even be obliged to pay a visit to the offending parties and . . . take action."

Chuck Wallens's round, stubbly face was beet red with vicious anger and hate. Still, he knew better than to let his emotions place him at a disadvantage. Jason McIver was not issuing an idle threat. Chuck's hands shook as he turned steely gazes toward his men. "Let's get the hell out of here," he ordered.

The men left, casting last looks toward the dark beauty still present in the room. This time Jacinta let them all see the disgust in her eyes, and they shuddered beneath its power.

Once the front door slammed behind the Wallens gang, Solomon grinned and looked over at Jason. "So that was the plan you were referring to," he said.

Jason's hearty laughter could be heard all through the lower level of the house. "And a most effective and satisfying plan, I'd say! It's pretty hard for *any* man to reach out and bite the hand that's feedin' him."

Jacinta raced towards her father, flinging herself into his arms. "Oh, Poppa, you were wonderful!" she cried, pressing countless kisses to his cheeks.

Of course, the entire house had gotten wind of what was taking place in the downstairs office. As Wallens and his men rode away on horseback, McIver Estate was alive with laughter.

CHAPTER 10

Jacinta woke the following morning with a satisfied smile on her lips. She stretched languidly in her huge bed, thankful that her father decided to leave for the islands at midnight instead of that very morning. True, the change in plans had much to do with Wallens. Jason had no desire to alert the man to their departure. Whatever the reason, however, Jacinta was still grateful. After all the excitement with Wallens's surprise visit the night before, a peaceful night of sleep was a welcome treat.

Unfortunately, no amount of sleep could ease her mind in regards to Solomon Dikembe. Her thoughts of him ran rampant as she tossed herself to sleep the night before and awoke that morning. Her thoughts revolved unendingly around the man and his kisses. When he touched her, she never wanted him to stop; although she had no idea what else he could do to make her feel more wonderful than she did when he held her in his arms and his mouth—

"Stop! Stop this, Jaci!" she hissed, dragging her fingers through her hair as she lay sprawled in the center of the tangled sheets on the four poster bed. "Have you no shame, girl?" she chastised softly, flipping onto her stomach as she spoke the question.

No, a silent voice replied. No, she had no shame when she lost herself in Solomon's embrace. In his arms, she wanted to cast aside doubt, caution, suspicion and all her many causes. The man was so appealing and in so many ways.

She twirled a lock of hair around her index finger and recalled his heated proposal and her reaction to it. Marriage had never been the least bit appealing to her. When Solomon spoke of it, however, it was the thing she wanted most of all. Of course, she would never speak the admission aloud, much less to Solomon. He had already toyed with her once, and she hated the way it made her feel—weak and needy. The trip to Seabrook Island came to mind then, and she groaned into one of the pillows at the head of her bed. She prayed for just a fraction of will to resist his charms. With any hope, her father would keep him far too preoccupied with business to pay her any mind.

Around mid-morning, Solomon and Jason enjoyed hot ale on the back porch. October was approaching and, with it, came brisk mornings.

"You'll have plenty of time to take a closer look around the grounds while spending time with my Jaci," Jason decided, sipping the ale as satisfaction brightened his warm gaze.

Solomon shook his head. "Don't you think she may become suspicious?"

Jason shrugged. "If you court her as you should, she won't have time to grow suspicious."

Solomon couldn't resist chuckling over the man's candor. "Sir, I can't help but question your giving me such free reign over your daughter," he said, pretending to be more interested in fixing the cuff of his cobalt blue shirt sleeve.

Again, Jason shrugged. "I know that she is in good hands. I know you are a good man. I see that in you. I saw it long before your gracious gestures toward Jore Sula and his family. You are the man I would see her with," he declared, his brown gaze uncommonly firm. "I also know that I want her away from this place—away from the South and all its pain and cruelty."

Solomon's jaw clenched, triggering a wicked dance of the muscle there. "I share that sentiment," he breathed.

Jason looked out over the expanse of his property. "I also know that my girl is very strong willed and stubborn." He warned the young man of the work he had cut out for him. "She will have to be quite taken by you to let go of the so-called 'responsibility' she feels she has for this place and our people." Just then, the sound of a horse neighing caught his ears and silenced the rest of the conversation.

The horse drew a small black carriage behind with a lone rider seated atop. Jason grinned, buttoning his brown, cotton suit coat when he stood.

"Come Solomon, there's someone I want you to meet."

Paul Vinson waved when he spotted Jason heading in his direction. He left the carriage and hurried forward to meet his friend halfway across the clearing of the back pathway.

"Jason!" he bellowed, catching the man's hand in a hearty shake.

"Paul, good to see you! This is my houseguest, Solomon Dikembe, here to look over some property he may be interested in purchasing," Jason explained.

Paul's light hazel eyes shone with interest as he studied the powerful, intense looking stranger standing next to Jason. "Mister Dikembe," he greeted, extending his hand to shake.

Solomon nodded, catching Paul's hand in a firm grasp. "Mister Vinson," he replied politely.

"So, Jason, finally getting rid of some of your many holdings?" Paul teased.

Jason perched one hand inside the front pocket of his suit coat. "Solomon has great plans for the property. I'm content it'll be well managed."

"Content . . ." Paul sighed, almost reverently. "Many of us are not so content this morning, my friend."

"What's happened?" Jason questioned, immediately on guard.

Paul folded his hands across the beige suit coat which fit just a bit smug at the waistline. "Ol' Wallens paid several visits to our friends and associates."

"What for?" Jason probed.

Paul shook his balding head. "The man won't stop until his property is recovered. He's hell-bent on finding Jore Sula and his family."

"Humph," Jason gestured with a grimace. "The damn fool," he muttered.

"Fool or not, he's got a hell of an arsenal to back it up," Paul warned.

"Bah!" Jason drawled with a flippant wave. "I'm having far too good a day to waste a minute of it talking about that man. Now you, Mister Vinson, will join us for breakfast," he decided, already turning back toward the house. "I'll have them set another place," he called over his shoulder.

Paul shook his head, his expression a mixture of admiration and something else. "That Jason . . . he's a good man."

Solomon smiled. "I agree."

"So tell me about your business," Paul was asking as they strolled closer to the carriage.

"Real estate is my main interest. I don't believe you can ever have too much land," Solomon teased.

"A smart man!" Paul complimented, his laughter gaining volume. "Land is the most important thing any black man can own," he declared, a furrow forming across his high forehead.

Solomon bowed his head. "Again, Mister Vinson, I agree."

Jacinta had ventured out to the backyard after one of the housemaids informed her that several of her unmentionables were still drying on the short line outdoors. Jacinta decided to collect them herself and complete her packing for the trip. When she arrived out back, she noticed Solomon in conversation with Paul Vinson.

"Humph, they should find much in common," she mused, referring to the fact that both men were mulatto.

Across the yard, Paul Vinson noticed Jacinta near the clothesline. He threw his hand up to wave, grinning when she returned the gesture. "That is one beautiful lady," he remarked.

Solomon's sleek brows rose and he turned to see who had captured the man's interest. Finding that Paul's remarks were directed toward Jacinta roused his temper somewhat.

"Yes, she is," he managed to agree.

"Every man I know has sought the girl's hand in marriage," Paul shared.

Solomon's mouth curved into a deeper smile. "Every man? Including yourself?" he inquired.

Paul closed his eyes. "No stomach for having my heart broken," he teased. "It's a well-known fact the girl's unwilling to marry. Of course she's far too lovely and too desirable to remain unwed."

"Her feelings will change," Solomon promised.

Paul appeared skeptical. "Not with Jason allowing it. He's unwilling to give her to any man whose intention is to remain in the South. What any man wouldn't give to possess such a woman."

Solomon consoled Paul with a hearty clap to the shoulder. "You can rest assured Mister Vinson, and tell Miss McIver's other suitors to cease their worry. Her hand in marriage has already been promised to another, and she is in his complete possession." With those words, Solomon strolled in the direction Jacinta had taken.

Paul Vinson's mouth fell open from shock.

Jacinta hummed a light tune while ensconced in retrieving her things from the line. She handled the delicates in a leisurely fashion, shaking any clinging articles from the pieces before inspecting them and tossing them into the straw basket at her feet. She was in the process of inspecting a pair of frilly drawers when Solomon silently approached.

"During our trip, will you allow me the opportunity to see you dressed in such a delightful garment?"

Jacinta gasped the instant she heard his rough voice. By the time he was done issuing his lurid request her eyes were narrow with distaste. "I'm sure the person who raised you did a far better job than your manners give them credit for."

Solomon pushed one hand into his cream trouser pocket and stood back on his long legs. "Quite sharp in the morning," he noted, his seductive dark eyes tracing her face with blatant appreciation. "I wonder if that quality only applies in conversation."

Jacinta closed her eyes. "Would you please go?" she urged, desperate to stifle her temper.

Solomon shrugged. "What for?" he asked, feigning confusion. "Surely you can't be uneasy about my seeing your . . . undergarments in light of all that I have already seen."

"That's it!" she hissed, her palm connecting with the light beard covering his cheek when she slapped him hard.

Solomon chuckled upon feeling the tiny sting. Jacinta was already storming off, but he caught up to her within a few short strides.

"Surely you knew there would be consequences for hitting me again?" he breathed, once his arm snaked around her waist and he held her against his chest.

"Let go," she ordered through clenched teeth. Her luminous brown gaze scanned the yard for anyone that she might call out to. Incredibly, the yard was deserted.

"Damn you, I'm going right to my father with this!" she seethed, struggling against his iron grasp.

Solomon was silent until they were locked inside the barn. "Then I suppose I should give you something to tell him," he taunted, his deeply set onyx stare lowering to her chest. Intent on exposing the full, heaving mounds to his view, strong fingers began to unfasten the buttons along the front of the crimson riding dress.

Jacinta slapped his hands away, feeling a surge of power when she glimpsed the surprise in his gaze. When he approached her, she stood her ground, her chin rising in defiance.

Solomon's smile deepened as he quietly acknowledged the strength of her will. When he would have conceded her the victory, he noticed the slight unease in her expression and saw her retreat an inch. Unable to resist the delicious temptation she unknowingly exuded, Solomon continued to advance toward her.

A lock of hair had slipped from the high coiffure she wore, and Jacinta quickly tucked it behind her ear. The courage she felt drained away as she studied the smile Solomon offered. There was no trace of humor, only desire and a determination that would not be swayed. She believed the need in his eyes mirrored her own and feared what would take place if she allowed her needs to rule her mind. Soon, though, Solomon had her trapped in the corner of the stables. His knee was insinuated between the folds of her dress and she gasped at the feel of his hard thigh between her legs. "Solomon—"

"Shh . . ." he soothed, as his mouth slanted across hers. He smiled when his tongue thrust past her lips and he heard her moan.

"Don't," she cooed upon feeling his fingers resume the task of unbuttoning her dress.

The kiss deepened. Solomon stroked her mouth deeply, with slow thrusts that soon caused her to arch her soft form into his hard body. Satisfied by the amount of buttons unfastened, Solomon eased one hand inside to cover her breast.

Jacinta moaned shamelessly as the offending hand fondled and squeezed in the most erotic fashion. His thumbs grazed the nipple until it grew rigid against the crisp material of her chemise. The strokes of his tongue inside her mouth matched those of his thumb as it raked the firming peak into an extra-sensitive bud.

Jacinta responded, her tongue thrusting against his as she abandoned the inhibitions and embraced her needs. Solomon moaned in surprise, almost losing the strength to stand. The kiss intensified, growing hotter and wetter until their tongues fought a reckless duel. Jacinta's small hands splayed across his gorgeous cobalt blue shirt and she moved against him in an unknowingly sensuous manner that stiffened his manhood instantly. Jacinta felt his arousal against her belly and realized that her desire had most definitely taken possession of her better judgment. Surprising herself, she broke the kiss and stepped out of Solomon's weakened embrace. He didn't pressure her to return. Instead, he kissed her cheek, set her dress in place and left her.

On one of the hundreds of islands dotting the South Carolina and Georgia coasts, Denmark Vesey delivered another masterful speech. He had been questioned repeatedly about the significance of the date chosen for the rebellion: July 14, 1822. The question, however, was not addressed with a firm reply. Of course, Vesey electrified his supporters just the same while his top men informed the audience of the progress made in acquiring weaponry, finances and asylum. Many wanted to abandon Charleston for the North, while others wanted to return to their African homeland and others to Haiti.

"Jason McIver got a visitor these days—he come in on a big boat," Harth Simms, a runaway slave hiding along the island banks, shared with the group of men he stood closest to.

"Who is he?" one of the men asked.

Harth shrugged. "All's I know is he doin' business with Mistuh Jason. They say the ship b'long to him."

"I heard 'bout him," Coker Webb, a Charleston blacksmith, concurred, stubby fingers massaging his square jaw as he spoke. "They say he got that runaway family out of Charleston on that very boat."

"He mulatta," Harth shared.

"A half-white!" someone blasted.

"A half-black, too, and got a ship 'sides," Harth said.

"And you think that make the ol' man ask for his help?" Coker probed.

"Ain't you listenin'?" Harth retorted, waving his hand towards the pile of rocks where Vesey and his men conducted the rally. "Right now they talkin' 'bout transportin' and how we gone git out this hell after standin' up to them devils."

Coker stepped forward, slicing the air with an index finger. "Well, don't you go thinkin' they gone take that half-white in they confidence," he argued.

"That's the truth," Sammy Quarles, a local coachman agreed. "Mister Vesey know them mulattoes can't be trusted. Some say they just as bad as tha white man hisself."

"Humph," Coker grunted. "Worse. Some say it was a mulatta who told ol Wallens 'bout Jore bein' at the McIver place."

The small group of talkers silenced, each acknowledged the truth of the rumor. Silently, they reconfirmed their opinions that anyone whose blood ran 'half-white' could not be trusted.

"Poppa! Poppa? I need to talk to you!" Jacinta called, having spotted her father making his way down the long, red velvet-carpeted hallway on the second floor. When he spotted and turned to wait for her, Jacinta slowed her sprint to a quick walk. "It's about the trip," she said, when they were face to face.

Jason grinned, cupping his daughter's dark pretty face in his palms. "Are you as excited as I am?"

Jacinta's smile was weak as she patted her father's hands and pulled them away from her face. "I was hoping to convince you to let me stay behind."

"Jaci, you love the trips to the islands," Jason noted, his round, cinnamon brown face clouding with concern.

Jacinta couldn't meet his gaze. "It's just that . . . well, with Chuck Wallens and his group upsetting everyone, I thought it might be good for someone to remain behind."

"Mmm, hmm," Jason considered, watching his daughter suspiciously. "And you believe I would allow that *someone* to be you?"

"Poppa—"

"The estate is being watched, Jaci. My men are more than capable. You know that."

"Poppa, it's just—"

"I believe they can manage a few weeks without your keen ability."

Jacinta couldn't mask her frustration. She leaned back her head and closed her eyes. "Then can't you . . . just send Solomon Dikembe off with a guide who can show him the property?"

"Jacinta Paulette McIver!" Jason shuddered, intentionally overplaying his surprise. "I'm shocked at you. That would be a most inhospitable way to treat a guest. Especially a guest that has been so gracious."

"Gracious perhaps, but also ungentlemanly," Jacinta replied in a small voice, as she studied the tips of her black riding boots peeking out beneath the long hemline of her dress.

Jason hid the amused smile which threatened to curve his lips. "You really believe this?"

"He's kissed me several times," she blurted.

Jason willed himself not to chuckle, he was so satisfied. "And this was utterly displeasing to you?"

Again, Jacinta's maple brown gaze focused on her shoes.

"Jaci?"

"Well . . . no . . ."

"No?"

"Poppa, I didn't give him permission!" she snapped, desperate to protect her honor. "I didn't ask him," she saw fit to add.

Jason nodded. "Of course you didn't, love."

"Oooh! Solomon Dikembe just takes whatever he wants," Jacinta ranted, pacing a short distance down the mirror-lined corridor. "He thinks his skin color and money give him leave to behave any way he chooses. I don't trust him, and I don't like him in the least!" she swore, accenting the remark with an index finger pointing towards the floor.

"Trust does take time to build," Jason agreed, reaching out to enfold Jacinta's fist in his hand, "but love, I believe you may be fooling yourself when you say you do not like him."

"Poppa!" Jacinta cried, mortified by her father's keen insights.

Jason closed his eyes. "Shh . . . I won't ask you to admit that to me. I only ask that you be honest in here," he whispered, tapping his finger against her heart. "Hurry now," he ordered, kissing her forehead before patting her bottom to urge her on her way.

CHAPTER 11

The McIvers and their guest set out at midnight sharp. Barely a sound was made that would have alerted anyone to their departure. Jason and Jacinta remained inside the cab of the horse-drawn carriage. Solomon chose his place seated outside next to Geof, the driver. The cloud of shadows during the day delivered on their promise for rain that night. Just as well, since the imperfect weather added to the cover of the evening and kept most everyone off the back dirt roads.

Within three hours, the carriage was arriving at the dock where Jason's ship, the *Lariat*, was stored. Solomon admired the man even more in that moment. Though the *Lariat* was not quite as elaborate in its design as the *Sheba*, it was obviously in pristine condition. Jason had done an excellent job of protecting it from the evil hands of those who believed no black man should have ownership of such a vessel.

Jacinta noticed Solomon admiring the ship when she stepped down from the cab. "I've often wondered why Poppa never tried to help free some of our people with the use of his boat," she said, as she walked up beside him and stood watching the ship.

Solomon smiled, but didn't turn to look at her. "The time would have to be right for such a mission," he warned.

Jacinta pursed her lips while folding her arms across the black, ankle-length tweed coat. "Humph, Poppa doesn't think the time will *ever* be right."

"He is a cautious and wise man."

"He is," Jacinta conceded, taking a few steps past Solomon. "But there is a time and place for caution."

"And wisdom?" Solomon challenged, his sleek midnight brows rising when she sent him a sharp look.

"Come, come now you two!" Jason was calling then as he hurried toward them. "No time to dawdle or we'll have all of Charleston's City Guard upon us."

"By morning we'll be on Regal," Jason informed Solomon and Jacinta as they walked along the splintered dock.

"Quite a name," Solomon noted.

"Roland McIver claimed the island on a trip he took to Edisto," Jacinta explained, as her father hurried on ahead, "Regal sits on the southernmost tip of Seabrook Island. It's a most exquisite place," she sighed, her eyes sparkling as though she could actually envision it.

Solomon bowed his head, clasping his hands behind his back. The softness of her voice brought a smile to his face.

"It's a wonder the property's remained so long in our possession," Jacinta continued, tugging the high collar of her coat tighter about her neck.

"I can't wait to see it," Solomon said.

"I don't believe you'll ever find a more enchanting place," she boasted, making way for two crewmen who were loaded down with baggage. "It's fenced by the

Atlantic to the east and North Edisto River to the south. And all the great courtships of the family—black and white—took place there," she added, thinking of her own parents' incredible romance.

Solomon knew as much, but there wasn't much time to dwell on the pleasure the coming weeks promised. Jason was back, telling them that he'd planed for a spectacular before-bed snack, elaborate late breakfast and slumber in the most comforting quarters.

The *Lariat* was a beautifully crafted machine. The fact that it was mostly a coastal vessel and not really suited to high sea travel made it no less impressive. Though propelled by steam, the boat maintained its sails, which were most often used when the crew traded cargos of rice, wheat, fabric and other goods along the island markets.

Members of the fifteen-man crew went about placing baggage in three of the ship's five passenger cabins. Each cabin was furnished with a luxurious bed, armchair, desk and washstand. A beautiful claw-foot tub had been situated before the stone fireplace in Jacinta's cabin, and every cabin connected with its own balcony.

Jason instructed Solomon and Jacinta to follow him to the starboard deck, which offered a perfect view of the night sky. The galley crew had set out a delectable snack for its passengers. While his guests took their places at the small round table on the deck, Jason went to speak with the crew.

Jacinta was silent, hoping her father would keep his conversation brief. Solomon had settled his tall, muscular frame into one of the heavy ladder-back armchairs and rested the side of his handsome, vanilla-toned face against his palm. He watched her closely for the longest time, smiling when she finally met his gaze.

"Is there something on your mind, Mister Dikembe?" Jacinta asked, not bothering to mask the edge in her voice.

"There is."

"Dare I ask?"

"Are you certain you want to know?"

"I'm sure I already do, Mister Dikembe."

"Enlighten me."

Jacinta sighed, trailing her fingers against her collarbone as she contemplated. "I'm sure you're anticipating your plans for tormenting me during the trip."

"Torment," Solomon repeated, his dark eyes following the trail of her fingers across her satiny, dark chocolate flesh. "How could I possibly torment you during this trip, Jacinta?" he asked, his own fingers coming to test the supple area of her breasts, which were set high against the scooping bodice of her indigo blue gown.

Jacinta rolled her eyes toward him. "The same way you've been tormenting me since you've been a guest in my father's home. Only now, tonight, we are in closer proximity on this ship. And, as you will no doubt discover, Regal is quite . . . intoxicating."

"Is that right?" Solomon remarked, appearing pleased just to aggravate her. "I had no idea. Perhaps I *will* have time for more than business after all."

His leering gaze made him appear even more gorgeous, if that was possible. Jacinta felt her cheeks burn and looked away.

"Now you two are in for a treat!" Jason announced, rubbing his palms together when he returned to the table.

Two young men followed, each carrying a tray of food.

"Miss Jacinta," the short, muscular men simultaneously said, in an obvious show of adoration.

Jacinta beamed at each man. "Lucas, Hans. It's so good to see you both again."

Lucas and Hans grinned in appreciation and set their burdens to the table. Their expressions sobered a bit when they nodded towards Solomon. "Evenin', suh," they said in greeting.

"Lucas, Hans, it's good to meet you both," he replied, smothering his chuckle when the two men appeared stunned that he had thought enough to call them by name. He felt Jacinta glaring and sent her a quick wink.

"Who keeps watch over Regal during your absence?" Solomon inquired, as they dined off a tray loaded with shrimp puffs, finger sandwiches stuffed with thinly sliced roasted chicken and beef, baked apples and hot tea.

"Ibn and Esa Obu are in charge of the land there," Jason explained, adding more of the hot rum-laced tea to his cup. "Their families inhabited that part of the island long before Roland McIver ever knew it existed. Mister Roland paid the families there to help cultivate the land. They were employees, not slaves, and you can imagine

the talk he endured over that!" Jason laughed. "But that
was Mister Roland. Some say he had a soft spot for Esa's
great aunt Sonje who, at the time, was quite young and
very regal—hence the name. It was rumored that an
affair began and that Regal was Roland and Sonje's special place."

"In actuality, Regal and everything on it belongs to its
original inhabitants," Jacinta interjected. "Roland only
kept it in his legal possession to ensure its protection
from those who might seek to 'obtain' it after his death."

Solomon grunted. "Smart man."

"A good man," Jason added.

"Tell me how the families came to be there—undiscovered. Surely the island isn't their native home."

"The Saids and Obus," Jason sighed in reference to
Solomon's query. "Those families were only two out of
tens of thousands of families who were forced into the
horrific passage from their native lands. Such tragedies,
the unspeakable events that occurred on those devil
ships," he spoke with passionate distaste, his kind face
hardening as he continued. "The Saids and Obus traveled with crews of men who thought nothing and cared
nothing about them. Men who likened them to cattle—
less than cattle. They hoarded as many bodies as possible
on those ships, and then packed in even more. Once they
realized their error, the boat was in the middle of the sea.
That mattered little and to 'make room' they simply cast
bodies overboard—tens, hundreds tossed without a care
into the raging seas."

"Jesus," Solomon whispered, leaning back in his chair to stroke the silky whiskers shadowing his jaw. His taste for the delicious snack had vanished.

"This is what happened to the Obus and Saids, but they were cast overboard by an even greater force—a far greater man—and they were thankful for it."

Solomon's long brows drew close as he sat entranced by the story. Jacinta listened as well. Even though she'd heard the story more than a few times, the tale never lost its luster.

"A fierce storm threatened to rip their ship to shreds. The lower quarters of the slave ship were ravaged, many died. But many survived. On planks of wood that were ripped from the ship, many held onto their lives until the Maker brought them to land." Jason stood from the table and strolled across the deck. "There's over four hundred thousand acres of land here, Mister Dikembe," he boasted, waving one hand toward the dark water. "Hundreds, thousands of islands that have never been charted, let alone claimed by any white man." Jason smiled and shrugged in spite of himself. "I know it's an incredible story, son. I can only relay it as it was told to me. Sadly, there are no records to keep account of such great events, and there are times when you simply know something happened just as it is being told."

Jacinta smiled. "That's another reason I write," she spoke to Solomon, but her eyes were riveted on her father. "So that we might keep a clear account of our history—our horrors *and* our triumphs." With that said, she stood and nodded toward Jason. "I'll be saying goodnight to you both," she spoke softly, gathering her skirts as she moved away from the table.

"I think I'll be turning in now myself," Solomon decided, standing as well.

Jason slapped his hands to his sides. "Why, this is perfect timing. Jaci, if you would be so kind as to show our Mister Dikembe to his quarters, they are right next to your own."

Jacinta's easy expression froze into a hard mask and she watched as Solomon smiled his devious smile and offered his arm. A taunting gleam lurked in the mysterious dark depths of his eyes as he silently dared her to refuse her father's request.

"I know what you're up to," Jacinta mumbled once they'd entered the corridor leading to the passenger cabins.

"Up to?"

Jacinta extracted her hands from the crook of his arm. "Don't pretend to be confused."

Solomon grinned, his deep-set gaze narrowing playfully. "You know, you're far too lovely to be so suspicious."

"Humph. I have good reason to be in light of your disrespectful manner these past few weeks."

"Disrespectful?" Solomon repeated, concern flashing on his handsome face. "There's that word again. Why do you think so negatively of me?"

Jacinta's jaw dropped and she stopped walking to turn and glare up at him. "I can't believe you could question that."

"You *actually* believe I've been disrespectful?"

"What would you label it as?" Jacinta challenged, her hands propped against her slender hips. "Obviously every woman who interests you falls quickly and willingly into your bed. I haven't and you refuse to accept that I won't, so you use these tactics of yours to . . . persuade me." When her words were met with roaring laughter, Jacinta rolled her eyes and turned away.

"I seem to lose control of my actions when in your presence," he softly called out to her.

Jacinta stopped, knowing she suffered the same affliction. She managed to just barely turn her head and face him. "May I suggest you get a handle on these emotions, Dikembe?" she whispered, before continuing on to her quarters.

That evening, sleep was slow in coming. Jacinta tossed and turned, her thoughts riveted on Solomon Dikembe and his earlier admission in the corridor. Slamming her fists against the tangle of crisp linens on the bed, she silently cursed the fact that she had been ordered to take the trip to Regal, especially when she so feared her inability to resist her father's dashing guest. Whenever Solomon pressed the advantage, she found herself wanting to forget the fact that she'd been raised to be a lady. The thought forced a gasp to her lips, and Jacinta whipped back the covers and left her bed for the refreshment of the balcony adjacent to the cabin.

Outside, the sea air kissed her face the instant she walked out onto the polished pine flooring. She relished the feel of the breeze against her bare skin and through her loose hair.

Solomon had long since abandoned his cabin for the balcony. He'd been seated in shadow when Jacinta ventured out into the night. His dark eyes narrowed and shock registered on his face as he raked her petite, curvaceous frame. Her shift was transparent in the moonlight, the hem whipped around her thighs so that teasing glimpses of her bottom were revealed to his charcoal stare. He couldn't look away and prayed she wouldn't notice him watching her. He could feel his loins tightening beneath the fabric of his black sleep pants. One hand clenched into a massive fist when she stretched and trailed all ten fingers through her flowing, midnight locks. The flawless brown of her skin held him as mesmerized as the way her full breasts strained against the material of her white shift.

Then, just as suddenly as she'd appeared, she was gone. Solomon realized he'd been holding his breath.

Jacinta had heard knocking at her door and approached on tentative foot steps. "Who is it?" she called, feeling relief and mild disappointment when she heard her father's voice instead of Solomon's.

"Poppa," she said quietly, "is something wrong?"

"Nothing at all, love," Jason assured her, remaining outside in the corridor. "I only wanted you to know that I've decided to let you stay behind while I show Solomon the property on Kiawah Island. You can stay and visit with Esa. I'm sure the two of you have much to discuss."

"Oh, Poppa, yes. Yes, I'd like that," Jacinta breathed, her satisfaction genuine. Still, a peculiar look tinged her face. "Uh, Poppa if you don't mind my saying . . ."

Jason shook his head. "By all means, child."

Jacinta focused on her bare toes, hidden within the thick hand woven rug. "Well, it's—it's just that this trip seems less like business and more like recreation," she admitted, wincing when Jason's hearty chuckles filled the air.

"Are you complaining?" Jason taunted.

"Just observing."

Jason was still chuckling. "Jaci, someone so lovely should not be so suspicious."

"So I've been told."

Jason leaned forward, taking her upper arms in a light hold before pressing a quick kiss to the tip of her nose. "Get some sleep," he ordered.

Still, moments after Jason's departure, Jacinta stood in deep thought. Another knock sounded and she whipped open the door, thinking her father had returned. Solomon waited in the corridor.

Jacinta slowly retreated into the cabin as he approached. "What do you want?" she whispered, her gaze widening as she watched him close and bolt the cabin door.

"Out," she ordered, as he moved toward her.

"Soon."

"Now . . . Solomon . . . Don't."

"Why?" he challenged, one hand already closing around her upper arm. "Why? Because you find me so disrespectful—so unappealing?"

"Why are you doing this to me?" Jacinta whispered, trying to tug her arm free of his hold. She despised the helpless tone to the question. "Damn you, surely there must be scores of women who would gladly give you—"

"They don't interest me. I only want you."

"You know nothing about me."

"But what I *do* know has me in a constant state of need."

"Need," she sneered, her gaze knowing. "*Physical* need," she guessed.

Solomon conceded with a nod. "There's more. But yes, physical need, and I can barely think straight because of it."

"I can't—we can't."

"We could. We will," he promised, drawing her even closer to allow his lips to trail her temple and cheekbone.

"Solomon, please . . ." Jacinta's protests trailed away to be followed by as gasp when his mouth teased the curve of her jaw. In one lithe motion he settled her high against his body, allowing him a more comfortable position to tease her neck.

Jacinta smothered a moan, her hands sliding across the crisp fabric of his partially unbuttoned sleep shirt. She could feel the solid wall of his chest crushing her breasts and wanted nothing more than to see if it was as powerful looking as it felt. Her eyes widened when she realized Solomon had carried her across the cabin and was placing her in the center of the bed. She could feel her heart thud frantically beneath her breast when the bottom of her shift lay bunched around her waist, leaving the rest of her bared to his eyes. Solomon seemed even more powerful, more massive, sprawled above her on the tangled mass of linens and quilts. She idly fingered the collar of his shirt and held her breath in anticipation of his next move.

Gently, he cupped her chin. His thumb caressed the fullness of her bottom lip before his mouth mimicked the action. Brief flicks of his tongue, brought Jacinta's head from the pillow as she silently beckoned his kiss, a kiss he provided without restraint; the act was deep and full of emotion. Jacinta unconsciously arched herself into his iron frame, gasping each time his tongue stroked her mouth. She could feel something lengthy, firm and powerful nudging her belly. Instinctively, she moved against it, surprised by the helpless sound he uttered in response. Solomon broke the kiss to rain countless kisses across her face, his fingers disappeared in her breathtaking, luxurious locks before lowering to massage her back, shoulder, waist, then lower . . .

"Solomon . . ." she murmured, lost in a whirlwind of sensation. Her lashes fluttered each time his teeth tugged at her earlobe before his tongue suckled it in a sensuously slow manner. "Solomon, wait . . ." she begged, her legs quivering with a desire that was foreign, yet utterly pleasurable. She was but moments away from giving him verbal permission to do as he pleased, when his mouth ceased its magic and he rose above her. His incredible, bottomless black gaze was knowing in its intensity as he traced every inch of her face.

"This ache you feel," he said, a lone finger trailing the satiny dark length of her thigh to curve just slightly into her femininity.

Jacinta's luminous eyes grew impossibly wide and her breath caught in her throat.

"This ache will only grow," he promised, smiling when a soft cry slipped past her lips and her lashes fluttered in response to the sensation. "Only when you are legally mine will I properly tend it," he added, momentarily savoring the feel of her love before gently extracting his finger.

Jacinta didn't trust herself to move. She managed to keep her eyes focused on his devastating face as he coolly backed off the bed and left the cabin.

Breakfast was just as delectable as the late night snack seven hours earlier. Jacinta arrived on the deck, noticing that her father and Solomon had yet to arrive. She prayed they were involved in business and that she could complete her breakfast and avoid Solomon that morning altogether. Such was not to be. When she turned her back on the view of the Atlantic, Solomon was arriving on deck.

"Good morning," he greeted with a slow nod.

She returned the nod. "Morning," she muttered, barely able to focus on anything except the softness of his baritone voice. It took her thoughts right back to the encounter in her cabin.

"Good mornin' Miss Jaci, Mistuh Solomon!" Hans greeted him, setting out fresh juice to the sideboard.

"Hans, have you seen my father?" Jacinta asked the crewman.

"Oh, Miss Jaci, he ask to have his meal in the cabin—said he might sleep more 'fore we get to Regal," Hans explained.

Obviously distressed, Jacinta turned her back on the two men lest they see her expression.

"Thank you, Hans," Solomon told the young man. His stare raked Jacinta's alluring frame, which was encased in the beautiful pearl blue gown with its silver piping, fitted lace sleeves and embroidered bodice which gave her slender neck an even more elegant line.

Jacinta shook her head and decided to concentrate on having her fill of the grits with hearty onion gravy, glazed and perfectly seasoned catfish, cornmeal muffins and fresh fruit. "You're not eating?" she asked Solomon after glancing across her shoulder to find him seated at the table.

"Soon," he responded. "I'm more in the mood for watching just now."

Jacinta laughed, surprising both herself and the gentleman who teased her so sweetly.

"Mister Dikembe, don't you ever run out of such completely inappropriate things to say to me?"

Solomon shrugged, folding his arms across the front of the finely crafted hunter green shirt he wore with black trousers and leather boots. "You may not believe this, but I never say such things," he shrugged, stroking his shadowed jaw as though he were deep in concentration. "Perhaps I've been saving all this for you."

"I feel so fortunate," Jacinta drawled, setting her plate aside to reach for a cup and saucer. "At least have some tea," she urged.

Solomon's black eyes narrowed. "Is it my imagination, or are you being nice to me?"

Jacinta shook her head, her high ponytail bouncing between her shoulder blades in an adorable manner. "It's your imagination. I'm simply giving you something else to focus on."

"A cup of tea could never take my thoughts away from you."

"Ahh, but that would depend on what is in the tea."

"Surely you don't subscribe to such foolishness," Solomon questioned amidst soft laughter.

Jacinta gave a one shoulder shrug. "Well . . . I *do* know people," she shared, placing a cup of tea before Solomon before turning to retrieve her plate and glass of juice from the sideboard. "My friend Esa, you'll meet her on Regal, she's a wizard with potions and herbs."

Solomon was intrigued. "In truth?" he probed.

"Mmm . . ." Jacinta confirmed, drizzling a generous amount of the onion gravy atop the hominy grits. "She's cured many aching heads in her day."

"The place seems unreal the way your father talks about it," Solomon mentioned, propping the side of his face against his palm as he enjoyed the sun and breeze against his face. "It's amazing that Negro people could survive there for so long without having their way of life threatened."

"It's incredibly amazing," Jacinta agreed, forking a morsel of the succulent catfish into her mouth. "I was especially amazed by it when I was younger and Poppa would tell me those stories." Her smoky gaze misted with tears and blurred her view of the fluffy clouds overhead. "As I grew older and understood the horrors my people endure, I hoped Poppa's stories were true. I'd imagined an entire kingdom living happy and free."

"Even as a small girl you believed your father was spinning tall tales?" Solomon asked, leaning back to watch her. "So you've always had this suspicious nature?" he guessed when she only shrugged.

"Suspicion is usually justified," Jacinta snapped, mildly offended by his observation. "People rarely surprise me, Dikembe. Especially you—"

"Mulattoes?" he finished, smirking when she looked away without answering. He left the table then to prepare his plate.

The remainder of breakfast passed silently.

CHAPTER 12

Jason stood at the wheel of the *Lariat* when the ship docked on Regal the next morning. The sun had just peeked above the thick white clouds that maintained their place against the backdrop of a vibrant sky that rivaled the blue of the water below. Acres of lush green from the waist-high grass that fenced the outskirts of the property, to the masses of pine trees that sprinkled the landscape and smattered the area with cool shade, added yet another splash of striking color to the stunning portrait.

Solomon stood mesmerized, looking on from his place on the deck. He had never seen a more beautiful place. It even rivaled the beauty of his own home, to which he thought there was no comparison. Never had he seen such a vibrant meshing of color. In truth, the only objects that gleamed white were the huge clouds above and the grand, white mansion perched atop a hill in the distance.

While the crew unloaded the bags, the passengers left the ship. Jason talked nonstop, pointing out different aspects of the property and relaying different stories to their newest visitor.

"That was the place where I first kissed Paulie," Jason shared, his eyes gleaming as he reminisced about the moment shared with his late wife. "We spent several different occasions there after that," he confided, fixing Solomon with a quick devilish look.

"Poppa . . ." Jacinta scolded quietly. She usually enjoyed hearing her father speak so of her mother. Unfortunately, she felt such conversation might be a bit too suggestive to Solomon Dikembe's fertile imagination. "I hope Ibn and Esa are at the house," she said, already looking toward the stunning white house in the distance. Eager to see her friend after so many months, Jacinta sprinted on ahead of her two male companions.

"I've arranged for us to take a look at the property on Kiawah at the week's end," Jason announced, easing both hands into the pockets of his blue cotton trousers. "That should give the two of you more than enough time on your own."

Solomon's laughter rose quickly and his gorgeous eyes narrowed to the point of closing. "A person would be quite mistaken to accuse you of being subtle."

"Ah . . ." Jason drawled, with a wave of his hand. "My Jaci is desperate to hold on to that guarded demeanor of hers. It has never been so difficult for her to hold onto it before. Her feelings for you are deeper than you know, my boy."

Solomon only shook his head. "She is so tough. I've never met a woman more complex, and the more I'm around her, the more difficult it is for me to imagine being without her."

The skirts of the magenta gown swished and ruffled as Jacinta raced up the steps toward the beautiful, coolly elegant house that overlooked its fence of calm blue water. Regal Place had always possessed an open, airy feel. Every long corridor carried the scent of jasmine, pine and fresh sea air. Lush fern plants occupied most every corner of the house in addition to vivid portraits of land and family. In spite of its grand, spacious allure, a sense of warmth and security flowed throughout.

"Still toiling away, I see!" Jacinta remarked to the two young housemaids who worked diligently in the foyer.

"Jaci!" Bela cried, setting her water bottle aside as she left her task of tending the hanging plants.

Jacinta spread her arms wide to embrace both Bela and Sallie, who had been polishing the entryway mirror. The three young women greeted each other with hugs, kisses and more hugs.

"Where's Esa?" Jacinta asked after she and the girls had spoken for a few minutes.

"Where else but the kitchen?" Bela informed, her high voice kissed by the melodic accent of her native Barbados.

Jacinta was off like a shot. Sure enough, she found Esa tending at least five huge iron pots on a massive black wood stove in the corner of the bright kitchen. For a moment, Jacinta stood smiling, her arms folded across the front of her gown. Esa Said Obu was five years older than Jacinta. She had always been like an older sister to the young woman, who had no other siblings and had lost her mother at such an early age.

"Your cooks finally tired of your tyrannical attitude, I see!"

Esa slammed a lid down to one pot and whirled around. Her slanting black stare widened as far as possible when she spied her friend in the doorway. Without a word, she quickly closed the distance between them and pulled Jacinta into a hug. They embraced for the longest time. Tears welled in each woman's eyes, as they realized how much they had missed one another.

"I see I'm no closer to being an aunt?" Jacinta steadily teased, patting her hand against Esa's minute waistline.

Esa's eyes sparkled past her lovely blackberry face. "I assure you it's not for my husband's lack of trying."

Jacinta laughed. "Where *is* Ibn?"

"Oh, out in the fields somewhere," Esa replied, waving her hand toward one of the four large windows in the kitchen. "He'll be back in time for dinner."

"The house—the land looks wonderful as always . . ." Jacinta sighed, strolling over to stand next to Esa and peer out at the glorious view.

"I believe the land to be possessed," Esa said, her fingers trailing the smattering of baby fine hair that was visible at the edge of the red and gold silk scarf covering her head. "Regal seems to almost take care of itself. It's almost as if we have to find things to occupy our time," she mused.

"Mmm . . . how awful for you," Jacinta teased. She joined Esa in soft laughter while nudging her shoulder.

"Mister Jason's letter said he'd be bringing a guest. Are they outside?" Esa queried, as she left the window to resume her place at the stove.

Jacinta rolled her eyes, feeling her easy mood drifting away with the breeze. "He's here," she confirmed.

"Well, who is he?"

"Solomon Dikembe. He's interested in some property Poppa has on one of the islands," Jacinta went on, hoping the brief explanation would soothe her friend's interest. Esa was far too sharp and would soon ask questions Jacinta knew she was not prepared to answer. "The revolt is gaining fire," she said, hoping to change the subject. She watched Esa continue to stir the pot of vegetable broth and waited for her reply.

"We've heard a little from the ship's crew and some of the other workers," Esa replied.

Jacinta nodded. "Well, in Charleston it's on everyone's lips. Meetings are abundant and so much progress has been made, Esa. Of course there are those who think it's still a load of talk, but this time—this time something is to happen. Something great."

By now, Esa was turned from the stove and watching Jacinta with concern and suspicion in the dark depths of her stare. "How involved have you become with this, Jaci?"

"*How involved?*" Jacinta parroted, her coffee stare flashing with disbelief. "I'd like to be *very* involved. This is an important matter deserving of everyone's attention."

"I take it Mister Jason doesn't approve?"

Jacinta leaned back in the white oak chair next to the matching round table. "You know my father," she muttered.

"He wants you safe."

"None of us will be safe until we're free."

"You *are* free."

"You know what I mean," Jacinta snapped, pounding her fist to the table.

Esa stepped closer. "Jacinta—"

"My dear, I pray I'll be able to leave this place when the time comes! It grows more lovely every time I visit."

"Mister Jason!" Esa cried, forgetting Jacinta as she ran towards the handsome older man with her arms outstretched. "Oh, I've missed you!"

"Still a beauty," Jason sighed, hugging the laughing young woman and pressing a kiss to her cheek.

"Mister Jason, we have so much to talk about!" Esa went on, pulling the man into another hug. "Ibn's had a new attachment built onto the barn and—oh," she started, her expressive dark gaze moving past Jason's shoulder. A small gasp passed her lips as she gazed upon the tall, powerful looking, handsome man who stood just inside the kitchen.

Jason smiled and patted the small of her back. "Esa Obu, this is Solomon Dikembe, the business associate I spoke of in my letter."

Esa was already stepping forward to accept Solomon's outstretched hand. "So nice to meet you," she whispered, her expression full of awe.

"Good to meet you too, Esa. You have the most beautiful home," he commended softly. "I look forward to the coming weeks."

"Well, I can promise you this will be a wonderful trip, and you're sure to like my husband Ibn."

"Where is that young man?" Jason questioned, stepping further into the kitchen.

"Oh, out in the fields trying to find something else to . . . get into . . ." Esa said, her voice trailing away as she took note of her friend. Jacinta was still seated at the table, her expression tight. Realization registered in Esa's eyes and she tugged her bottom lip between her teeth to stifle a knowing smile.

"I can't wait for this supper, love," Jason remarked, settling a lid back on the pot of seasoned greens. "But right now, we need to have a little talk in private," he said to Esa, taking her by the arm and leading her out of the kitchen.

Solomon strolled across the polished oak flooring and enjoyed the gorgeous view from one of the windows. "This is an incredible place. I can't wait to see the rest of the property."

"I'm sure someone will be more than happy to give you a tour."

Solomon grinned at the dry tone of her words. "I'm sure of it. However, I've already requested that you be my guide."

"You what?" Jacinta hissed, sitting up straighter at the table. "Never mind. *That's* not going to happen, I'm sorry to say."

Solomon shrugged, smoothing one hand across the olive green of his suit coat. "Well, I'm sorry to say that you'll have to take this up with your father. He's already assured me there's no problem with you showing me around."

"Dammit!" she thundered, rising from the chair. "What the hell are you trying to do to me? Drive me insane? You stand there perfectly at ease about using my father and his kindness to lure me into some sort of-of—"

"Seduction?" Solomon supplied, his gaze lowered.

Jacinta's chin rose and her angry expression was replaced by a cool smile. "Know this, Dikembe," she breathed, stepping right up to him. "In spite of my . . . reaction toward certain things you've done, I have no intention to allow things to continue this way. You will never have me. Possession over me is out of the question, so feel free to continue to waste your time with these schemes. I'll enjoy continuing to foil them." She nodded once before brushing past him and strolling out of the kitchen.

"I knew it! Oh, Mister Jason, this will be so wonderful for her!" Esa cried. She was delighted to discover that the trip was to be so pleasurable for Jacinta.

Jason nodded, but raised his hands to quell Esa's excitement. "Now you know how she is. She won't be quick to find the *enjoyment* in this, I assure you. She is still completely against marriage, as you well know."

Esa shook her head. "I'm concerned for her, Mister Jason. This talk of rebellion—"

"And my daughter is intent on being a part of it," Jason brooded, his warm features hardening abruptly. "The air in Charleston becomes thicker with tension each day. I'll do what I must to keep her away from it."

Esa glanced across her shoulder. "And will this man take her away from it?"

Jason smiled. "He thinks as I do on the matter. He can give my girl a life a black woman could only dream of. More importantly, he loves her."

Esa tilted her head. "Has he said this?"

"I really don't believe he has any idea how deep his feelings are. I can see it, though," Jason declared, pouring himself a drink from the brass bar table at the rear of the sitting room. "The poor boy appears completely helpless whenever he looks at her."

"So in these next weeks—"

"We simply bring them closer."

Esa hid her hands in the oversized pockets of her white apron. "Mister Jason, do you really believe Jaci will agree to marriage in such a short time?"

Jason watched the sunlight shine through his glass of sherry. "Perhaps not, but with any hope she may stop denying how deeply she feels for this man."

The new guests slumbered through the lunch hour. Regal Place provided such a relaxing and refreshing atmosphere with the sound of the ocean rolling in the distance, which combined with bird cries and whispering grass to create an irresistible lullaby.

Jacinta awoke, happy to discover things so peaceful. Quickly, she left her white oak canopied bed, chose a fresh shift, put up her hair and set out for her favorite place on Regal. She tiptoed down the hall and winding staircase, praying all the while that the area was still as untouched as she remembered. Casting several glances over her shoulder, she hurried out the back entrance and across the fields of waist-high grass towards the cluster of trees and brush far off in the distance.

Her squeal of delight filled the air when she found the small pond. The area appeared even more secluded, shrouded by more trees and brush. After a quick look around the quaint spot to ensure her privacy, she discarded her dress, hose and slippers and tip-toed across the clearing until her feet touched the cool water. The moment was bittersweet; Jacinta acknowledged it would probably be her only opportunity to enjoy the indulgence. With the onset of winter, dips in an outdoor pool would be most uncomfortable.

The water seeped right through to her skin, causing the material of the white shift to adhere to her body. She closed her eyes, splashing water across her face. Her eyes opened and she met the unexpected sight of Solomon Dikembe leaning against a tree.

"Damn," she muttered, glaring at the man through her water-spiked lashes. "Do you receive some delight in scaring me out of my wits?"

Solomon bowed his head and smiled. "No, Jacinta. At this moment, my delight doesn't come from scaring you."

"Oooh! Go away!" she demanded, splashing water everywhere as her hands slammed against the crystalline surface.

Instead, Solomon inspected his surroundings. "Quite a place," he remarked, folding his arms across the mocha linen shirt that flattered his vanilla complexion. "Thank you for showing it to me," he added, just to further annoy her.

"I had no idea you were here," Jacinta replied through clenched teeth.

Solomon pushed himself from the trunk of the pine tree. "Then I'm happy I decided to follow," he rephrased, walking toward the pond.

"Leave!"

"And deprive myself of such a treat?"

"What are you doing?!" she shrieked, her smoky brown stare wide with unease as she watched him undo the small buttons along the front of his shirt. "Solomon?" she called, when the shirt parted to reveal the chiseled expanse of a broad chest. "Don't!"

The command came too late. The shirt fell to the short grass and was soon accompanied by the remaining articles of his clothing. When he stood nude before her, Jacinta was speechless. She had never viewed a man unclothed in her life. Shirtless, yes. But completely— *gloriously*—nude? No. Her long lashes fluttered with an uncontrolled urgency as her eyes raked his magnificent form. His torso looked as though it were carved from a stone slab. Every breathtaking inch was toned and riddled with an impressive array of muscles. Her heart thudded into her throat when she viewed the extent of his maleness. The lengthy rod of flesh appeared intimidating and unyielding even at a distance. Jacinta felt her palms ache with the desire to test its feel.

Solomon had walked forward until he was waist deep in the very cool water. When Jacinta finally thought to move away, he caught her wrist and kept her close. He wasted no time with words, only kisses. His lips showered her cheeks and the corner of her mouth with soft pecks that traveled the curve of her jaw, earlobe and neck. His hands molded to her scantily clad, molasses-toned body—squeezing her bottom while settling her against his arousal.

Jacinta cried out her surprise, realizing that part of his anatomy felt as rigid as it appeared. "Wait," she whispered, her hands curving into weak fists. "Solomon wait . . . I can't," she moaned, even as her fingertips explored his chiseled form. Her eyes were riveted on his body as she studied him intently. His body felt hard and impenetrable. It was like touching a smooth wall of rock.

Solomon's hands roamed freely as well. A small grunt lodged in his throat when he filled his hands with her round derriere. For a while, he settled his handsome face into the crook of her neck and massaged the firm expanse of flesh. When that wasn't enough, his fingers curved around her thighs, pulling her legs apart in an easy, undetected motion. Strong fingers curved into the moist, hot sheath of her femininity and thrust so lightly it may have been imagined.

Nothing was imagined for Jacinta, however. She could feel every movement of each finger and her lips parted as she moaned in pleasure. The sound spurred Solomon onward, and he allowed his fingers a bit more room to play. A surge of male satisfaction swelled within him when her cries filled the quiet air. Soon, he had her gasping uncontrollably while clinging to his shoulders in a helpless manner. Solomon felt his own arousal building to an even more fevered pitch and squeezed his eyes shut tight.

Steady man, he silently ordered. He willed his hormones to cease their raging. Though the gentle, repeated strokes into her sex were beyond stimulating, he knew those greedy thrusts could have easily deflowered her. Making love to this woman would be done slowly, he decided. Not because she was a virgin, but because he wanted to savor every moment she was in his arms.

"Solomon—"

"Marry me."

"No. Never," she promptly refused, her breath catching on a gasp when his thumb stoked the sensitive flesh guarding the entrance to her womanhood. "You don't love me," she moaned, lost in swirls of pleasure.

Solomon suckled her earlobe. "Would it change things if I told you I do?" he asked, raising his head to stare into her eyes.

Jacinta shook her head, tears beginning to pressure her eyes. "You wouldn't mean it."

"And if I did?"

"Stop!" she whispered in a fierce tone. She couldn't listen to any more, afraid that he would speak the words she found herself longing to hear. "Let me go," she requested quietly, blinking in surprise when he obeyed. Quickly, she left the pond, donned her clothing beneath his smoldering gaze and raced back toward the main house.

Dinner that evening was an exceptional treat. Esa and her staff of outstanding cooks prepared a perfect seafood feast. Shrimp and chunks of crab meat that had been broiled in a broth of fresh seasoned vegetables provided a perfect topping for fluffy white rice. Catfish marinated in herbs from the garden closest to the house, had been broiled over flaming coals and gleamed golden from a platter teaming with moist, hot corn muffins.

Jason had opted to enjoy his meal from the privacy of his bedchamber. Meanwhile, the two young couples dined on the enclosed terrace just off from the kitchen. Ibn Obu returned from the fields to greet his guests. He and Solomon became instant friends and chatted away as though they had known one another for a lifetime. When talk turned to the subject of Denmark Vesey, Jacinta involved herself in the conversation. As always, her opinions were witty and brash, but not overly emotional as men tended to expect from women. Moreover, her opinions were well thought and coolly expressed.

Unfortunately, Solomon had never been so angered. He sat quietly, directly across from Jacinta in his seat at the intimate square table they shared with the Obus. He realized how deeply involved Jacinta had become in the plot. She had used her writings to not only gain audience with those she wanted to interview, but also to spread word of the rebellion.

"So everyone has been receptive?" Ibn was asking Jacinta, his fork poised at his mouth as his handsome features softened in anticipation of her answer.

Jacinta was already nodding. "The people are ready. They've just not been properly swayed. Mister Vesey has an incredible gift for moving the crowds. People are riveted by his words and pushed to take action."

"Mmm . . ." Ibn agreed, "I know what you mean. You begin to believe freedom is a reality when he speaks."

Esa's dark eyes narrowed when she turned to glare at her husband. "You've been to hear him speak?"

"Several times," Ibn coolly replied, savoring seasoned morsels of shrimp and tomato.

Esa was unnerved by fear for her husband's safety and could say nothing more. Solomon's silence grew from anger, his features appearing more fierce as Jacinta voiced her remarks.

". . . he's made many appearances along the islands," Ibn was saying as he and Jacinta remained oblivious to the moods of their dinner companions. "Many of my men have attended most, if not all, of the gatherings. I've attended a few, but I know Mister Vesey plans to hold several more meetings before returning to the mainland."

"Good," Jacinta was saying, while nodding her satisfaction. "I plan to be there."

"Like hell!" Solomon bellowed, his usually soft voice now harsh.

Jacinta's gasp echoed in the confines of the small terrace. Her small hands clenched into fists beneath the long lace cuffs of her silver gray evening gown. "How dare you," she seethed, leaning forward to fix him with a hate-filled glare. "How dare you even fix yourself to speak a word in regard to *my* plans? You have *no right* to dictate *anything* to me."

Solomon clutched one hand around his tankard of ale and imagined the vessel were Jacinta's neck. "The day you even attempt to attend one of those meetings is the day *I* take the lash to you."

"You son of a bitch!" Jacinta raged, pounding her fists to the table.

Esa leaned towards her friend. "Jaci—"

"Careful with your threats, half-white," Jacinta sneered.

"They are threats sure to be followed by action," he whispered.

Jacinta rose from the table so quickly her heavy chair crashed to the floor. Her skirts swung just a wildly as the black braids which covered her head like snakes. She was enraged, fearless and moments from physically attacking Solomon, when Esa's hands closed over her upper arms and held her back.

"I need some help in the kitchen," Esa whispered against Jacinta's ear and practically dragged the woman from the terrace.

Members of the house staff ceased their eavesdropping and quickly dispersed when Esa and Jacinta stormed into the kitchen. Desperate to throw something, Jacinta reached for the freshly polished silverware on the buffet hutch and slammed it to the floor. She paced like a wild tigress, halting when she heard Solomon's and Ibn's hearty laughter in the distance.

"Oh, Esa, why has the Lord seen fit to allow that man to plague me so?" Jacinta moaned, dragging her fingers through her braids as she flopped into a chair at the table.

"Shh . . ." Esa urged, stepping around to massage Jacinta's shoulders. "It can't be that awful."

"Humph."

"Ohhh . . ." Esa drawled, leaning down to press a quick kiss to her friend's cheek. "Solomon Dikembe is beautiful, strong, charming . . . how much of a *plague* could he be?"

Jacinta let her forehead rest on the table. "Esa . . ." she groaned, thoroughly dismayed by the fact that her best friend had also been captivated by the man's appeal. "Those very assets you speak so highly of, and a few more, are the root of my troubles with the man."

"Troubles?" Esa inquired, her dark eyes twinkling as brilliantly as the curly blue black locks atop her head.

"Esa . . ." Jacinta breathed, turning to face her friend. "Esa . . . things-things have . . . happened between us."

"Things?" Esa parroted, her hands slowing in their massage.

Jacinta pulled Esa around and pushed her into a chair. "He's kissed me. I—I've kissed him."

"Oh Jaci, that's not—"

"I've seen him without his clothing. His hands have been places on my body . . . his mouth . . ." Jacinta buried her face in her palms. "Esa, I never stopped him. I didn't want him to stop. If he hadn't stopped himself, I . . ." she admitted, her voice trailing away.

Esa bit her lip to keep from smiling. "Honey, please don't. It's not the end of the world."

"How can you say that?" Jacinta cried, watching Esa with disbelieving eyes. "A lady doesn't allow a man to do such things, Esa. I wanted every bit of it every single time it happened."

"Sweetheart, listen," Esa ordered, cupping Jacinta's face in her hands and making her pay attention. "From what you've said, it's obvious you feel more towards this man than any of the dozens of suitors who've come your way. I believe this goes much farther than physical desire."

"But I don't want it to!" Jacinta left the table, smoothing damp palms across the folds of her dress. "Esa, Solomon is so much like Poppa that I can't stand it. He'll do anything to stifle me. To keep me from doing what I have to do."

"He's saving your life," Esa countered, standing as well. "Thank God, since you seem to be blinded to how dangerous your involvement is."

Jacinta rolled her eyes. "I wouldn't expect you to understand. Living in paradise far away from the horrors I witness every day."

"Oh, love, I understand. I understand all too well," Esa corrected, smoothing her hands across her arms left bare by the capped sleeves of her champagne evening gown. "Jacinta, freedom is a right, and for far too long it has been a dream for our people. This I both know and understand. Unfortunately, I am not willing to sacrifice *you* to the masses in order for it to become a reality. However Mister Dikembe intends to keep you safe, he has my complete support."

Jacinta successfully avoided Solomon during the following days. Still, she wondered how much avoiding Solomon had to do with her efforts or his. Perhaps *he* was the one keeping the distance between them, and she was glad. The situation was so frustrating in so many ways.

Finally, the day arrived for Solomon and Jason to leave on their two-day trip to the coast of Kiawah Island. The *Lariat* was prepared to set sail at noon.

"Impatient man," Jacinta grumbled when she heard the knock sound on her bedroom door. The noon day hour was approaching and she assumed her father had grown tired of waiting for her to appear down at the dock to say her goodbyes. Her vibrant smile faded when she whipped open the door to find Solomon on the other side.

"I thought it was Poppa," was all she could think to say.

Solomon fingered the brow of the black top hat he held. "Jason sent me to tell you we're about to board the ship."

"I'll be right down," she called over her shoulder, when she turned back to retrieve her shawl from the chair.

"November is definitely setting in," Solomon noted, when she wrapped the cream knit covering around her olive green riding dress.

Jacinta smoothed her hands across the shawl. "Mmm . . . I love this time of year," she shared, preparing to walk out into the hallway. When she approached the door, Solomon would not let her pass.

Slowly, she looked up at him through her heavy lashes. Her breathing grew labored and she prepared herself for one of his fantastic kisses.

Solomon leaned close and propped his index fingers beneath her chin. "Remember, Miss McIver, you even *attempt* to traipse off to one of those meetings and there will be hell to pay."

Jacinta felt her cheeks burn as her luminous gaze spewed fiery daggers at Solomon. Her lips parted to blast him fiercely, but she never got the chance.

"Jaci, come on or you'll miss your father!" Esa called, rushing by the door on her way to the dock.

Jacinta left Solomon with a hateful scowl, then stormed down the hall.

"Isn't it a bit early in the day to wear such a murderous expression?" Jason teased his daughter when she arrived to see him off.

"Poppa, that man," Jacinta breathed, her hands tightly clasped at her chest as she struggled to quell her temper.

"Oh . . . give the boy a chance," Jason urged, gathering her into a tight hug. "I like him."

Jacinta pulled away. "Of course you do. He's exactly like you."

"And I can't think of another man I would prefer seeing as the father of my grandchildren."

"Poppa!"

"I love you. Be good," Jason ordered, kissing her forehead before turning to hurry along the dock.

Jacinta stood with her hands still folded over her chest. She saw Solomon boarding and turned back to the house when he waved.

CHAPTER 13

Denmark Vesey's presence was as potent as his speaking abilities. He remained seated while his top men conducted their meeting, expressing their opinions on the need for rebellion—opinions which gained them even more exposure.

Solomon paid more attention to Vesey. He studied the older man closely, taking note of the similarities between he and Jason McIver. They were both freedmen, respected and financially secure. Yet for Vesey, there was still a void aching to be filled, an ache driven by the need to see his people free and to take part in the struggle.

The *Lariat* had docked on Kiawah Island some hours earlier. Through members of the crew, Solomon learned of a meeting which was to take place along a secluded area in the thick wood along the river bank.

The fact that he'd arrived with members of the crew and that they were of a darker complexion played a huge role in gaining Solomon access to the secret meeting. As he listened, Solomon could easily understand why Jacinta was so eager to be part of the rebellion. Vesey had indeed attracted quite a following. The speeches given were laced with anger towards their oppressors and their intolerance for the brutality against their women and children.

The location of the meeting was yet another dark, chilly lean-to, far too small to comfortably accommodate such a crowd. Of course, that mattered little to the masses desperate for any corner of space.

". . . streets is fill with them ev'ry night. There ain't no time to—"

"Our plan is to ignite fires in different places all over town. This should keep them busy!" Will Garner called in response to the question voiced from the crowd.

"And keep them scattered!" Jake Stagg, another of Vesey's men, added.

"That's right!" Jake McNeil agreed with his associates. "And this is why we need much assistance. We need every slave armed and ready to strike down any who think to keep us in shackles!"

Applause and cheer erupted amidst the audience. The words were riveting and did more than prompt a sense of urgency and readiness in Solomon. Moreover, it drove home his intentions to shield Jacinta from danger. The proposed rebellion was sure to be a bloody battle, and the aftermath would be just as gruesome whether or not the group achieved success.

Solomon went still then. For the first time, he realized how deeply his feelings ran for Jacinta McIver. Even though she had shown him little more than contempt over the last two months, he was in love with her. As deeply as freedom rang in his heart, as much as he wanted to be a force in what was taking place, he was glad to turn away from it to keep her safe.

The meeting dispersed a short while later. As Solomon left with members of the crew, he noticed the interested looks cast his way. He was less than surprised when they were stopped on their way out of the shack.

"Who this, Murph?" a dark, lanky man asked Murphy Hinnant, a member of the *Lariat's* galley crew.

"Mistuh Solomon, a passenger just come with Mistuh Jason, Sirus," Murphy told the man.

Sirus Keely's wide brows furrowed with a frown as he regarded Solomon with pure distaste. "Damn mulatta," he sneered.

"Y'all fools bringin' him here!"

"Damn half-whites can't be trusted."

Solomon kept his hands hidden in the deep pockets of his black, ankle-length overcoat. His temper was not roused by the harsh name calling and insults. He'd heard far worse before.

"Yo kind ain't welcome here," one man breathed, stepping right up to Solomon.

"There are slaves of every shade working plantations all across the South," Solomon said, once the steel in his onyx stare persuaded the man to back down, "for many the only *advantage* those of a lighter complexion have is that it makes the welts from their beatings easier to see," he continued, stepping towards the man who had confronted him until he'd forced him outside the shack. "The Charleston mulattoes may be a ruthless bunch, but they do not represent the masses. You would do well to consider that before turning away from valuable and much needed assistance. Good evening, gentlemen," he bade the men, dipping his head once before walking away.

"Jason, I know that you're in control of the land, but has Roland McIver's family in the North expressed any aversion to a black man assuming ownership?" Solomon was asking later that afternoon while touring the property on Kiawah. "Or have you told them about me?" he added when Jason's steps slowed.

"The rest of the family is aware that you and I are doing business," Jason said, regarding Solomon with his thoughtful brown gaze. "But you should know that all of Mister Roland's property in the South was left to my family. I have the authority to do with it as I please."

Solomon nodded, though his expression was still clouded.

Jason clapped the younger man's shoulder. "What is it, son?"

"I just don't know how I'd feel knowing the McIvers are granting me this property simply because half my blood is white."

Jason stroked his jaw and continued his stroll along the wooden fence skirting the eastern portion of the land. "Is that a concern to you?" he questioned.

Solomon shrugged. "It shouldn't be, but it is," he admitted.

"Why is that?"

"Because it is of such concern to others, I suppose."

Suddenly, a grin spread across Jason's cinnamon brown face. "You should not have gone to that meeting, son."

Solomon tugged upon a stalk of the waist-high grass as he passed. "Nothing was said that I've not heard before."

"Still, it vexes you?"

Solomon only clenched his fist and walked on ahead.

"You know that my Jaci shares many of those views."

Solomon's steps slowed. "I know."

"And you believe they would affect her ability to open her heart to you?" Jason guessed.

"I'm certain of it."

"And?"

"And I don't care. I intend to have her, sir," Solomon confessed, turning to fix Jason with a weary grin. "Abuse and all," he added.

Jason's laughter rumbled forth, filling the air as he slapped Solomon's arm. "All my prayers are with you, son!"

"Jacinta McIver!" Esa cried, spotting her friend amidst the hoard of men returning to the house with her husband Ibn. Her hand closed around Jacinta's arm and she pulled her aside. "You are such a fool! Involving yourself in such nonsense after your father—"

"Esa, please, I know how to handle my father," Jacinta whispered, patting Esa's hand while extracting her arm. "This was an important night. We've gathered so many signatures, Esa. The rebellion is gaining a staggering amount of support."

"Jaci—"

"There will be a huge meeting here on Seabrook in another day or two," Jacinta went on, tugging away the torn hat that hid her black locks.

"Jaci, Mister Jason told you—"

"Poppa will never know since he's on Kiawah."

"And what of Solomon?"

Jacinta's cocoa gaze narrowed, her features sharpening with anger. "As I said, my father is on Kiawah. Solomon Dikembe has no right to dictate where I may or may not go." She paused and took a step closer. "They won't hear of this from you, will they Esa? Esa?"

Esa folded her arms across the square bodice of her tanned housedress. "I can't promise you that," she retorted and brushed past Jacinta.

"Exquisite choice, sir. She must be quite a lady."

Solomon's devastating features softened when he smiled. "She is," he agreed while studying the perfect round diamond set high on a silver band. The ring was cool and elegant, and he could not wait to place it upon Jacinta's finger as she became his wife. He thought about how she would respond—not lovingly, he predicted. He also thought of how her reaction would affect his temper. Already he'd questioned his attraction to her. Perhaps it was only physical—she'd certainly sparked his basest desires like no woman ever had.

Jason noticed Solomon with the jeweler who traded his wares at one of the many seaside markets on the island. Jason smiled, knowing the young man was truly in love with his daughter. Why else would a man push aside business to spend time shopping for a ring—something he could have put off for later or leave to someone else?

"You are round the bend for that difficult young lady, my boy."

Solomon shook his head at the sound of Jason's voice. "I agree, and I can only pray her feelings run just slightly in the direction of my own."

"A Christmas wedding would be lovely," Jason casually suggested, pushing both hands into the pockets of his gray shirtwaist coat.

Solomon's brows rose and he turned. "Surely you mean next Christmas?"

"No, son, I don't."

"Sir, Christmas is little over a month away."

"Yes it is, isn't it?" Jason agreed, curving his hand into the crook of Solomon's arm to urge him along.

Esa found Jacinta seated on one of the long benches that skirted the portion of Regal that faced the Edisto. Esa smiled, spotting the journal, pen and ink next to Jacinta on the bench. Happy to find her friend writing and out of trouble, she waited a few moments before intruding on her solitude.

"Can I bring you a little something, Jaci? It's quite peaceful to eat before the sunset."

Jacinta stretched in her seat, before turning to glance at Esa. "No, thank you. I'll just wait for dinner. I'll probably eat in my room and retire early."

Esa nodded in understanding, though she was rather disappointed. Jacinta dining alone in her room meant that she would have to eat with the staff or eat alone as well since Ibn would be out for much of the night.

Jacinta continued to scribble away on her pad, her head bowed in concentration. Esa watched her only for a while longer, then bit her lip and took a few small steps closer to the bench.

"Jaci?"

"Hmm?"

"Are you . . . are you still upset with me?"

Jacinta ceased her writing and slowly turned a confused stare toward her friend. "Upset with you?"

"Jacinta . . . you must recall our conversation a few days ago? About your involvement with the rebellion?" she clarified when Jacinta still appeared confused.

Finally, Jacinta's eyes closed and she shook her head. "Oh, Esa, please don't tell me you've been upset about that this whole time?"

Esa's dark eyes sparkled with unshed tears. "The conversation wasn't very jovial," she pointed out.

"Still . . ." Jacinta sighed, rising from the bench. "Sweet, I feel terrible about this and that I made you feel so uncomfortable. You had every right to say what you did. You were just concerned," she soothed, pulling Esa into a tight embrace. "Everything's fine. I promise not to give you any more cause for concern," she whispered against Esa's cheek before kissing her there. The two shared a long hug before the setting sun.

"We must be prepared to take every ship in the harbor! We will need a hefty number of vessels at our disposal."

"Is it true Mister Vesey will obtain aid from the Republic in our fight?"

"Mister Vesey is determined to secure aid from Haiti. In order to get there, we need ships. Many ships!"

"How many?"

"And where will they take us? Haiti, Africa, to the North?"

"There are no definites, but we are confident that there will be transport available to any desired port!"

"These ships are manned by white crews. How do we—"

"No life, save the captain's is to be spared. The rest die!"

"As they deserve to!"

"The decks will be painted red with their blood!"

Thunderous applause and cheering followed the declaration. The meeting on Seabrook that evening was more than a lecture. Members of the crowd gathered in the cover of heavy trees and marsh, were given the chance to voice questions to the men closest to the rebellion leader.

Jacinta, disguised as a young boy, had arrived with Ibn and his crew. When she heard the speaker reply that no life be spared, her heart lurched. She wondered then if she had the stomach to take the life of another, regardless of the fact that the very life she spared would show no hesitation towards ending her own. She heard Solomon Dikembe's rough, authoritative voice in her head then. He was telling her she had no place amidst such conversation and actions. She shook off the words and the unyielding male certainty they were laced with. The freedom of a race depended on the fortitude of all those sworn to fight for it!

That very evening, Esa was racing out to the dock to meet the *Lariat.*

"I expected you all to be out yet another night!" she cried, flinging herself into Jason McIver's waiting embrace.

"Solomon was pleased straight away," Jason told her as he kissed both Esa's smooth cheeks. "We were able to strike a deal very quickly. Besides, the young man is in a terrible hurry to see that feisty daughter of mine."

"Mmm . . . Jaci decided to dine in her room this evening," Esa said, hugging herself as she cast a quick glance across her shoulder. "She's been writing most of the day so there's a chance she's still awake."

"Well go collect her, then. We'll meet in the first floor sitting room!" Jason urged, turning Esa in the direction of the main house. "Come along for a drink, son!" he called towards Solomon, who was leaving the ship.

"So have you settled on a time to present my Jaci with her ring?" Jason asked, while Solomon prepared drinks in the sitting room.

Solomon's gorgeous singular dimple appeared as he poured a second brandy. "Perhaps when she's in a more docile mood," he decided.

"Docile, eh?" Jason grinned. "Are you sure you can wait that long?" he teased.

Esa smiled when she walked in on the two men chuckling away.

"Is Jaci on her way, dear?" Jason called when he saw her in the doorway.

"Uh, no." Esa cleared her throat. "No, sir."

"What's that?"

"Um . . . Mister Jason, I—I think she may have left for a walk."

"At this hour?"

Esa wrung her hands. "I can't seem to find her, sir."

Solomon looked up then and exchanged a glance with Jason.

Jason stood from his chair, his hazel gaze riveted on Esa. "Where else could she be?" he asked, his tone vaguely knowing.

Esa was shaking her head. "I have no idea. I left her this evening, she said she was going to turn in early. Oh

. . . oh, no . . ." she breathed, pressing a hand to her heart as she sat in the nearest chair.

Solomon bounded across the room to kneel before the chair Esa occupied. "What is it, love?" he whispered, patting Esa's trembling hands. His tone was as soft and coaxing as the look in his dark eyes.

"Ibn," she whispered, then cleared her throat in hopes of forcing more strength into her voice. "Ibn left earlier with his men. They—they were going to a meeting," she explained, fixing Solomon with a look that made things perfectly clear.

"Dear God," Jason shuddered, his expression growing weary as he appeared faint.

The pained sound of the older man's voice alerted Esa and Solomon at once. Quickly, they rushed over to where Jason had taken to a chair.

"Solomon!" Esa gasped, not liking the drawn look on Jason's face.

"Is his room in order?" Solomon questioned at once.

Esa nodded and stood. "I'll see that the bed's turned down," she said, grasping her skirts and rushing from the room.

"Sir? Can you stand?" Solomon asked, smoothing his hand across the sleeve of Jason's deep blue suit coat.

Jason covered Solomon's hand with his own and squeezed. "My daughter cannot remain in Charleston. She will not listen to reason and continues to put her life in jeopardy," he moaned, closing his eyes, as though he hadn't the strength to keep them open. "I admire her courage," he continued, "but should her actions be discovered, it would mean her death." He looked upon Solomon with a foreboding glare. "I'm sure my lecherous neighbors would find a few other tortures to subject her to before putting an end to her existence."

Solomon refrained from clenching his hands, knowing it could mean crushing the bone in Jason's forearm, which he still stroked in a reassuring manner. "Sir, if I may express an idea?" he inquired instead.

"What are you thinking?" Jason asked, leaning back in his chair.

"I'll help you to your room and explain along the way."

"You—you don't want her aware that we know?"

Solomon shook his head toward Esa. He had just explained his idea to her and Jason. He stressed the importance of keeping Jacinta calm until the very moment the situation was revealed.

Esa clasped her hands before her waist. "She's going to feel most angry."

"What else is new, Esa?" Jason rebutted.

"They should be returning at any time," she sighed, preparing to leave the room.

"Esa? Remember, do not let her suspect that we know what she's been up to," Jason cautioned.

Esa managed a nod. "Yes, sir," she whispered.

Solomon waited until the heavy mahogany door closed behind Esa, before smoothing his hands across the worsted fabric of his tweed trousers and taking a seat in the armchair next to Jason's bed. "Sir, are you certain that this arrangement is acceptable to you?"

Jason's smile was easy to appear. "Son, I've wanted this for Jacinta longer than I can remember. I wish it could be more to her liking, but I understand that it is for her own good."

Solomon's silky black brows rose. "She will surely despise us," he predicted.

"Humph, *us*? 'Tis *you* she hates!" Jason bellowed, and then followed the teasing observation with hearty laughter.

The next morning, Jacinta was turning over to stretch lazily in the luxurious four-poster canopy. A satisfied smile graced her full lips and she felt content enough to purr. She had gotten away with last night's excursion and no one was the wiser.

"Mmm," she grunted, feeling her eyelids still weighed by sleep. Unfortunately, keeping such late hours had cut sharply into her time for slumber. She could only pray for an opportunity to rest through the day without having Esa grow suspicious.

As if on cue, a knock rapped upon the bedroom door. A few moments later Esa walked in followed by members of the house staff.

"Good morning, Jaci!" Esa called, rushing around the room placing toiletries and fresh bath linens on the washstand. "It's a beautiful day out, and quite warm, too. One would never know it's already November."

Jacinta fought to keep her eyes open as Esa rambled on and on. Several times, her head almost fell back to the pillows.

". . . yes, it promises to be a splendid day. Had Mister Jason returned this morn instead of last night, he would've had a marvelous day of traveling."

Sleep left Jacinta's eyes to be replaced by shock. "Poppa's returned?"

"Mmm, last night," Esa replied matter-of-factly. "Oh, but there's no need for you to jump up just yet. Your father is still sleeping."

"You say he returned last night?" Jacinta probed, already pushing herself up amidst the tangle of covers.

Esa pretended to be concerned with folding the bath sheets as she spoke. "Mmm, hmm, but I told him you wanted to be left alone last night and he understood. However, he does request your presense for a late lunch this afternoon, and he'd like you to be up and ready."

Jacinta yawned. "This afternoon? I think I can manage that," she sighed, preparing to lie back down. It was then that she noticed the tub being brought into the room.

"I think it's best that you go on and bathe before lunch," Esa suggested, noticing Jacinta's inquisitive expression. "That way you can get more rest," she added.

Of course, Jacinta would have preferred to remain in bed. Unfortunately, the tub was quickly filling with water, and the thought of an early morning soak did sound quite relaxing.

"Come on Jaci, up!" Esa ordered, clapping her hands as she whipped back the covers.

The bath was luxurious. Esa washed Jacinta's hair and toweled the mass until its riot of natural waves was a high gloss. From the tub, Jacinta saw a spectacular dress being brought into the room.

"Esa . . ." she breathed, her brown eyes riveted on the gown. "Isn't that a bit elaborate for lunch?" she asked.

Esa laughed. "Oh, Jaci, only you would complain about dressing so fine."

"Well, are we having guests?"

Esa wrapped a bath linen around Jacinta's hair to prevent it from getting wet again. "Are you forgetting Solomon Dikembe already, Jaci?"

"Mmm . . ." she groaned. "I was hoping he'd fallen overboard or something."

"Jacinta!"

"Dammit, Esa, can I help it if that man completely infuriates me?"

Esa braced her hands on the edge of the tub and stood. "I think you're feeling a sensation far removed from infuriation and closer to stimulation."

"Esa!"

"Hush," Esa ordered, flicking water at her friend. "Finish your bath and get some rest. Your father wants you downstairs by the three o'clock hour."

Whatever her father's reason for such a formal lunch, Jacinta wouldn't complain. It had been far too long since she'd had the chance to dress in such exquisite attire. The gown was a pearl white creation of silk and satin. The bodice was uneven, the lace neckline cut in a scooping pattern that emphasized the prominence of her full breasts. Beaded piping trailed from the seam beneath her arm to waistline. Lace sleeves contrasted in breathtaking fashion against her dark skin. A full hoop skirt with its silk lining fell past her ankles and only offered infrequent glimpses of the white slippers that adorned her small feet. Jacinta felt like a fairy princess, and prayed lunch would last for hours. She arrived downstairs to hear soft music filling the air as it mingled with the unmistakable sound of conversation.

"Jaci! You're ready!" Esa gasped, spotting her friend at the foot of the stairway. Esa's dark eyes sparkled with satisfaction as she studied the mesmerizing gown and Jacinta's long, thick hair upswept in an array of glossy curls.

"This sounds like quite a gathering," Jacinta breathed, already heading in the direction of the music and voices.

Esa caught her arm. "Your father's in the mood for celebration," she merrily explained, leading Jacinta in the opposite direction.

"Esa, what—"

"This way, Jaci."

"But aren't the guests *this* way?"

Esa pretended to be more interested with fluffing out the curls that cascaded along Jacinta's neck and ignored the question.

A frown married Jacinta's soft brow, but before she could comment on Esa's behavior, she saw her father in the front room.

"Poppa!"

Jason spread his arms and enveloped his daughter in the warmest embrace. "You look like a vision," he breathed.

"Poppa, what's going on?" Jacinta questioned as she pulled away to regard her father with inquiring eyes. "Why such a formal lunch? Are we celebrating something?"

"You could say that," Jason replied, pulling his daughter's hand into the crook of his arm as they strolled out of the room.

"Did you plan this before you left for Kiawah? And why did Esa lead me away from the guests?"

"Jaci, shh . . . all your questions are about to be answered," Jason promised, his smile as serene as the look in his hazel stare. He escorted his daughter down the short corridor which led from the front room to the sunroom. At the double glass doors, he nodded toward Jacinta urging her to look.

The grand expanse of the back lawn was filled with people. From the eldest person to the tiniest child—everyone seemed dressed in their finest white attire. Jacinta also noticed something else—they were all standing half-and-half, leaving an aisle between them. An aisle for a father to escort his daughter—the bride.

Jacinta's hand tensed within her father's and she strained against his hold.

"Jaci . . ." Jason warned, his grip tightening.

"Poppa, how could you?" Jacinta hissed, barely able to hear her own voice for her heart pounding in her ears.

Jason spoke through his smile. "First, this is for your own good and safety. Second, this is a fine young man and he loves you."

Jacinta stilled her movements and focused on Solomon, who stood next to Ibn Obu at the end of the long aisle. She studied the man who was about to become her husband. He was tall, sinfully handsome, and she could not deny his appeal. Yet, she had denied it. She had resisted him or, rather, he had allowed her to resist. Now she was to be his forever. He would bend her to the desires of his will and he would have every right to do so. She would be his wife and it would be pointless to resist.

Taking no heed of the fact, Jacinta began to struggle again. Desperate to pull away from her father, she gave one last tug before taking note of all the eyes riveted her way. The encouraging stares of all the well-wishers forced her to cease her struggling.

Jason felt her hand grow limp in submission and he gave it a reassuring squeeze. She was upset and felt betrayed, but he knew there were so many reasons why this union was necessary . . . and right.

The walk down the aisle came to an end and Jacinta felt her father relinquish his hold upon her hand and place it in Solomon's. Jacinta's lashes fluttered, her lips tightening. She wanted to use the very hand that rested so trustingly against Solomon's palm to slap the smug look from his face. Of course, she knew that he'd be expecting some form of retaliation from her and she commanded herself not to give him the satisfaction. The minister stepped before them and she felt her legs start to give beneath her. Solomon prevented that, however, his hand holding hers possessively. His arm rested firmly about her tiny waist.

"Dearly beloved . . ."

The minister began the ceremony and Jacinta lost touch with everything surrounding her. It was as though she were outside herself looking down on what was taking place.

"Do you Jacinta, take Solomon to be . . ."

She did manage to respond to the minister's questions, though she could neither feel nor hear herself speaking the words.

"I now pronounce you husband and wife."

The minister spoke the words that sealed her fate.

"Mister Dikembe, sir, you may kiss your bride."

Amidst shouts of best wishes, Jacinta felt her mouth captured in a sweet, deep kiss, and she fainted.

CHAPTER 14

When Jacinta opened her eyes, she felt pillows and crisp bed linens surrounding her body. Golden candle-light flickered all around—its shadow danced on the walls of the darkened bed chamber. She snuggled deeper into the bed and sighed.

A dream, she thought, a satisfied smile tugging at the natural curve of her lips. It was all a dream, she told herself. The terrible lunch had never occurred; Solomon Dikembe was not her husband. Still, as she reached the acknowledgement, she couldn't deny feeling a small twinge of disappointment twist in her stomach.

Jacinta closed her eyes and tried to drift back to sleep. Smiling contentedly, she thanked whoever removed the confining, elaborate white gown for the baby blue shift she now wore. White gown . . . her eyes widened then.

"No!" she snapped, shaking her head against a pillow before whipping back the covers and sitting up.

"Feeling better, love?"

The deep voice rumbling close behind forced a shriek past her lips and Jacinta turned. Crouching on her knees, she found herself looking into Solomon's handsome face. He lounged in the huge armchair situated next to the wardrobe. He looked rested, uncommonly gorgeous and impossibly sexy with his gray linen shirt unbuttoned to reveal the massive expanse of his chest.

"What the hell are you doing in my room?" she demanded, hoping anger would keep her mind, and her eyes, off his chest.

Solomon's one dimpled grin appeared and he rested his hands back against the chair. "Where else would a husband be on his wedding night?"

"Husband?" Jacinta breathed, her voice catching on a gasp as she spoke.

Solomon pretended to be concerned by her shock. "I'm truly hurt now. Surely you remember our wedding this afternoon, love?"

Jacinta moaned, her fingers weakening where she clutched the bed linens.

"Is there something the matter?" Solomon inquired, smiling at her reaction.

"Don't!" Jacinta ordered, extending her hand to ward him off when he rose from the chair. "Just . . . just don't. I want you out of my room. *Now*, Dikembe."

Solomon left the armchair anyway. "I can't do that, love."

"Damn you. You concocted this entire scheme," Jacinta hissed. She had never been so angry in her life.

Solomon was enjoying his moment of triumph. He took his place on the edge of the bed, resting against the headboard. One trouser-clad leg relaxed upon the bed while the other dangled along the side.

Jacinta leaned closer to him. "Get out," she demanded, her smoky brown eyes filled with disgust.

Solomon shrugged. "You were there this afternoon. Don't tell me you've forgotten becoming my wife?"

"Bastard. That was no real ceremony."

"Real enough."

"Go to hell."

"Not just yet," he countered, his gaze appearing more unsettling amidst the firelight.

"Damn you," she spat across her shoulder while scrambling from the bed. She stormed from the bed and twisted the knob, only to find it would not give. Refusing to accept what she knew as fact, she tugged it a few more times before resting her head against the door. "Where's the key?" she asked, receiving silence for her answer. At last, she turned to Solomon. Seeing the arrogant, smug grin gracing his face was her undoing. A roar of laughter passed Solomon's lips when his wife charged towards him. Her beautiful hair flew about them in glorious disarray as they tussled upon the bed. Solomon laughed the entire time, easily dodging the blows aimed for his face. Jacinta pounded his chest with all her might, deciding to use her nails when her husband appeared unscathed.

"No, you don't," Solomon growled, catching her wrists before she could graze his skin. In one easy move he pinned her beneath him. Her breathing caused her breasts to heave in an unconsciously seductive manner.

"Calm down," Solomon urged, his voice soft and coaxing as he settled between her parted legs. "Calm down," he repeated, lowering his head to the crook of her neck, where he lavished her satiny dark skin with brief kisses.

Jacinta's lashes fluttered and she turned her face away, which only succeeded in giving Solomon's mouth more room to roam.

Solomon's large hands tightened about her wrists as she flexed her fingers to the limit.

"I'm asking you not to—" Jacinta never finished her statement. Solomon's mouth slanted across hers and he silenced her with one smooth thrust of his tongue.

A helpless sound lodged in Jacinta's throat, and she could feel herself melting into the heavy linens covering the bed. Solomon kissed the fight out of her, weakening her strength and ability to resist with the intense mastery of every possessive lunge. He released her wrists to massage her hips and thighs beneath her flowing, baby blue gown. He parted them to accommodate his body more comfortably.

Jacinta gasped, feeling the power of his steel length pressing against the center of her body. She heard Solomon chuckle as he deepened the kiss, and berated herself for allowing him to disarm her so easily.

"I don't want this," she murmured when he released her bruised lips to outline their full shape with his tongue.

Solomon raised his head just slightly. The bottomless depths of his obsidian stare appeared as though they could completely absorb her. "You don't want this?" he questioned, his tone blatantly doubtful as one hand left its position around her thigh. He smoothed the uneven hem of her gown higher and gently insinuated his hand between their bodies. "You're certain?" he challenged, seeing her lashes flutter when his thumb stroked the extra-sensitive petals which guarded her womanhood. "Jacinta?" he called, when she tugged her bottom lip between her teeth and closed her eyes as though she were savoring the sensation.

With an expert's touch, Solomon gently probed her sex with the tip of his middle finger. He felt her instantly tense and pressed his lips to her ear. "Relax," he commanded softly, deepening the caress. Jacinta's soft gasps aroused him to the brink of madness, but he restrained himself. Soon, his finger was bathed in her moistness. The deeper he probed, the more volume her gasps gained.

At last, Solomon pulled away to favor other areas of her body with his touch. His kisses were hard and heated by the urgency of desire. Jacinta writhed each time his mouth touched her. It was as if he were worshipping her with his kiss. His hands curved around her hips to keep her on the bed. When the tip of his nose brushed the riot of black curls forming at the triangle of her thighs, Jacinta tensed in response.

"Solomon—"

"Shh . . ." he urged. This time his nose brushed the silky feminine loveliness he had caressed with his fingers just moments earlier. He continued to nudge her there until the need for more satisfactory pleasure reigned supreme.

Jacinta felt his tongue stroke her once in an intimate manner. Her eyes widened and she tried to free herself from his hold. Of course, Solomon wouldn't allow that and held her more firmly. Jacinta's legs trembled uncontrollably, but Solomon simply continued his maddening assault.

"Wait . . ." she moaned, feeling the tip of his tongue at the entrance of her love. "Solomon . . ." she sighed, losing what remained of her speaking ability when his tongue delved inside her repeatedly.

Small, tortured sounds filled Solomon's chest as he had his way with the voluptuous chocolate beauty he held. His hands left their place around her thighs and smoothed across her flat, silken stomach. He heard her groan when his hands closed over her breasts to squeeze and fondle the firming nipples.

Jacinta arched herself into the scandalous kiss. Her fingers curled into her hair in much the same manner as her toes did into the bed coverings.

"Solomon—Solomon wait . . . oh please, wait . . ." she gasped, all the while desperate to feel him ease the ache he'd stoked inside her. Her eyes widened in surprise and frustration when he promptly obeyed.

"I won't take you until you ask," he explained, once his large frame covered her smaller one on the bed.

Jacinta's chocolate gaze flashed with stunned disbelief. "I'll never give you the satisfaction of hearing that," she swore.

Solomon graced her with a smile that simultaneously exuded boyish charm and intense sensuality. His head bowed, his dark eyes following the trail of his fingers as they returned to their favorite destination. "Somehow I doubt that," he predicted, his middle finger pleasuring her shamelessly until he saw the toughness fade from her face to be replaced by arousal.

"Let me go," she managed to whisper despite the sensations overwhelming her.

Solomon leaned close. "Never," he vowed, dropping a quick kiss to the tip of her nose.

Jacinta's own fingers curled into the bed linens and she was sure she could have torn them to pieces. She was frustrated beyond mention, but not because of the unorthodox wedding ceremony. Solomon Dikembe was drawing dangerously close to endearing himself to her— if he hadn't already. That was the one thing she could not allow. She'd never survive knowing she'd added more power to his already intolerable amount of confidence.

"Listen," Solomon urged, one hand closing over her fists to still their frantic pounding against his chest. "Stop upsetting yourself. You should rest."

"Humph," Jacinta grunted, glaring up at him with knowing eyes. "Mmm, yes, I'm sure having me in an unconscious state would make things easier for you," she accused, her heart somersaulting when his rich laughter erupted.

Solomon removed his fingers from their intimate hideaway and pulled Jacinta's gown back into place. "I promise that I have no intention to take you in such a helpless state."

"And I should believe this?"

"You should," he confirmed, curving his fingers beneath her chin. "When I make love to you, I damn well want you to remember it." With that said, he sat up, taking her with him.

Jacinta smiled, realizing his intent was to settle her beneath the covers. Her gaze was soft as she watched him concentrate on making her comfortable. She allowed herself to look beyond the devastating features to the man beneath. What she saw there brought on a rush of contentment that she would never admit to. When Solomon left the bed and began to disrobe, that 'contentment' became a distant memory. "What are you doing?" she called, moving to a sitting position.

"Undressing."

"Here?"

"Where else?"

"Your room."

"This is my room."

"You're mistaken."

"You're my wife, are you not?"

Jacinta's lips thinned. "In name only, by force and trickery."

"Name only . . ." Solomon sighed, pulling the shirt from his powerful torso as he strolled back to the bed. "Not for long. I can promise you that."

Jacinta lost a bit of her confidence as her warm brown gaze focused on the powerful male before her. "You promised . . . you promised to wait," she saw fit to remind him.

Solomon shrugged. "I've not forgotten."

Jacinta swallowed and calmed a little, but her gaze was still apprehensive as she watched him. The lump lodged in her throat seemed to grow when he removed his trousers. Every inch of his body appeared taut, riddled with muscles. He looked even more magnificent than he had the day at the pond. Smothering the moan which clamored for release, she closed her eyes and scooted down in bed.

While Jacinta begged sleep to arrive swiftly, Solomon slipped beneath the covers. He quickly closed the distance between them, his arm snaking around his wife's waist to pull her back against him.

Jacinta stifled a cry and held her breath. Solomon shielded his face with her loosened hair, inhaling the fresh scent clinging to the black locks. A grunt of satisfaction passed his lips as he nuzzled his face deeper into the healthy tresses. Jacinta's breathing now resembled quick pants that caused her breasts to heave against his hands. Solomon reached up to untie the tassels securing the front of the flowing gown.

"Mmm—" Jacinta moaned, before turning her face into a pillow to smother any other outbursts. Solomon had reached inside the gown to cup and fondle her breasts. His fingers massaged the nipples until they stood as erect as small gems.

"Solomon . . ." Jacinta whispered, squeezing her eyes shut as though that would stop the pleasure from overwhelming her. Her every breath simply pressed the rigid, sensitized buds deeper into his palms.

Solomon had pushed the gown from her shoulder and was bathing her chocolate skin with moist, open-mouth kisses. One hand left her chest to ease down her torso to her thighs. That move, combined with his kisses against her shoulder and his suckling on her earlobe, weakened her legs. His fingers were granted the access they sought.

She gasped, turning onto her back then. What remained of her statement was smothered by his kiss. She melted, eagerly returning the sultry lunges of his tongue. Her hands reached up to stroke his collarbone, her head left the pillow as she kissed him with wild abandon.

Solomon moaned into her mouth as his fingers played in the moist, tight heat of her sex. He imagined his stiffened arousal there in place of his fingers and the vision set his hormones aflame. Suddenly, he pulled away and pressed his mouth to her ear.

"Tell me not to stop," he ordered, kissing and suckling her lobe as he spoke.

Jacinta squeezed her eyes shut. "I can't," she whispered, knowing he wanted her complete surrender.

Solomon bowed his head against her shoulder. He took several deep breaths in an attempt to quell his powerful desire for her. "You know where I am when you can," he told her, then left her alone on her side of the bed.

Sleep was a long time coming.

Jacinta woke feeling just as exhausted as she had before bedtime. It had been the same for the past two nights. She and Solomon shared the same passion-tensed bed. Each night, he carried her to the brink. But then, he withdrew and urged her to come with him. And how she wanted him, but could not make herself speak the words. They would be leaving for Charleston that afternoon— confined to the *Lariat* for at least two days.

The thought pushed Jacinta to leave the bed. She had yet to pack, and decided to get on with it.

Solomon had awakened several hours before his wife and had taken his breakfast on a secluded veranda. He was in a vicious mood and feared he would snap at the first person who approached him. He knew the plan to break down her wall of resistance was working. Unfortunately, it didn't seem to be working fast enough for his satisfaction. His need for her had risen to such a level he could hardly sleep. When he was granted a few hours to slumber, the time was as torturous as his waking hours. All he dreamed of was bedding her and hearing her confess her love for him as they shared the pleasure of their bodies. From his place on the veranda, he could see the *Lariat's* crew toiling away as they stocked the ship for the voyage back to Charleston. Feeling the need to work off his frustration, Solomon set out to offer his assistance.

"Oh, I'll miss you!" Esa cried as she pulled Jacinta into another hug. "Please don't wait so long before visiting again."

Jacinta backed away. Tears sprinkled her lashes. "I won't," she promised, pressing a hard kiss to Esa's cheek.

Esa's expression grew more solemn. "Thank you, Jaci, for forgiving me."

"For—forgiving you?" Jacinta stammered, clearly confused.

"The wedding. I know it wasn't what you wanted."

Jacinta pressed one index finger; encased within a pristine white glove, across Esa's lips. "Now, now, there's no need for apologies. We've known each other too long to lose touch over something like that. I know you felt it was for the best."

Esa smiled, glancing over at Solomon, who stood with Ibn near the dock. "I may not know much, but you should give that man a chance. He loves you."

Jacinta would have laughed had it not been for the serious expression Esa wore. "And this is what you know? That Solomon Dikembe loves me?" she inquired doubtfully.

Esa shrugged. "It is."

Her certainty rattled Jacinta's nerves, but there was no time to dwell upon the remark. Esa was kissing her friend's cheek and ushering her toward the dock. The evening was cold—bitterly so. The crew and its passengers remained within their quarters. Dinners were eaten inside cabins. Jacinta had secretly hoped Solomon would dine with her, but he never arrived in the cabin. Obviously he'd opted for separate quarters for the trip back. She wondered if that decision would extend to their living arrangements back in Charleston.

Jacinta ceased brushing her hair and leaned back upon the bed. She acknowledged that she had no idea what their situation would be back in Charleston. Did Solomon mean to live there? Did he mean to take her away? The later possibility was unsettling; Jacinta shook her head as though that would remove it from her mind. Thankfully, she had no time to let it rile her; the bath she'd requested had arrived.

Solomon had, in fact, decided to take separate quarters from his wife, but hadn't realized his bags were stored in her cabin until he was preparing to turn in for the night. He braced himself for her mood, not bothering to remove the stony glare from his face as he approached her door.

The knob gave when he twisted it and Solomon uttered a brief prayer, thankful she had not set the lock. His dark eyes narrowed when he noticed the firelight on the walls once he'd stepped inside. An inviting fire blazed in the brick hearth, while candles offered additional illumination from their scattered locations.

Solomon did a double take, his gaze returning to the fireplace. A helpless look crossed his handsome face when he found his wife nude and kneeling in a tub of bubbly water. The drip of the water as she squeezed a saturated sponge across her skin added to the allure of the moment. Solomon stood entranced by the way the golden light enhanced the rich, chocolate tone of her skin. A tortured sound rose in his throat as his feet carried him forward with a mind of their own. His feet, encased in a pair of black leather thigh boots, made no sound as he tread the red woven rug covering the floorboards.

Jacinta's head was bowed, one arm extended as she appeared to be reaching out. Solomon noticed a water pitcher on the simple wooden chair set next to the tub.

Her hair teemed with bubbles, so Solomon took that as his hint. Kneeling beside the tub, he reached the pitcher just as her fingers grazed the porcelain handle. The move startled Jacinta and she looked up. Seeing her husband filled her with surprise and unease. She calmed when she saw that his intent was to rinse her hair.

Solomon's expression was guarded as he poured the water over Jacinta's head. She moaned her appreciation as the liquid penetrated her scalp. The throaty sounds of delight were almost Solomon's undoing, but he remained a gentleman. His black eyes followed the path of the water as it cleansed her hair of the suds. Tentatively, his free hand wound into the midnight mass. He could have sat for hours enjoying the feel of the lukewarm water and Jacinta's healthy locks against his skin.

When the bubbles were thoroughly rinsed away, Solomon watched her gather her hair in both hands. She twisted the locks into a long rope and squeezed to remove the excess water. Solomon rolled his eyes and stood, unable to take another moment alone with her. He set the pitcher to the floor with a harsh clatter. This time, his boots fell heavily along the floorboards as he headed toward the door.

"Solomon? Wait."

His hand was but an inch from the knob when he heard her voice. He turned, meeting her wide stare. An instant later, he bounded across the room to lift her from the soapy water. His mouth came down on hers to punish her with a heart-stopping kiss. Jacinta thought her neck would snap beneath the force of it. Solomon's hands flexed around her upper arms, drawing her closer while his tongue thrust deeply, repeatedly, inside her mouth. He carried her to the bed in the corner, settling her to the center before covering her with his fully clothed frame. He broke the kiss to drop harsh, wet kisses to her cheeks, collarbone and shoulders. His hands cupped her breasts, squeezing, fondling and taking turns suckling each nipple.

"Solomon . . ." Jacinta whispered, arching into his touch. "Solomon?"

He closed his eyes to ward off the sound of his name. Wishing her silent, he buried his face into the side of her neck, knowing he was about to hear her turn him away again. He prayed for the strength to leave her.

"Solomon?"

"Yes?"

"I'm telling you not to stop."

The gentle yet firm admission brought Solomon's head up with a snap. He blinked once, his dark eyes searching every inch of her round, lovely face. Jacinta blinked steadily, waiting for his response. Solomon's stare lowered to appreciate the appearance of her unclothed and willing in his arms. His head lowered, this time the kisses were soft and taunting. His tongue darted out infrequently, bathing her dark skin with languid strokes. He outlined the full mounds of her breasts, and then applied the same treatment to the dark clouds surrounding each nipple. Jacinta tugged her bottom lip between her teeth and arched her back to force the bud deeper into his mouth.

Solomon breathed her name, savoring the feel of her body grazing his tongue. His huge hands eased beneath her hips to slide up her back and draw her closer.

Jacinta gasped, feeling a heavy ache settle deep within her. The petals of her femininity tensed and relaxed in response to Solomon's attentions. In spite of her inexperience, she was an eager participant in their seductive scene. Tentatively, her small hands spanned the width of his chest. Her fingers curved around the pectorals that flexed beneath his shirt. He was beautifully crafted, and she could feel herself responding to the mere sight of him.

Solomon moved to sit up above her. He quickly doffed his clothing and returned to her without haste. Jacinta's tiny cry of pleasure filled the room when she felt him shelter her bare form with his own. She began to bathe his flawless, vanilla-toned skin with kisses that were slow and uncertain at first. Then, as he began to moan in response, her kisses became more confident. Her head rose from the pillow as her lips closed around one nipple. Her body twisting and rubbing against him caused Solomon's maleness to stiffen to a painful state. Jacinta's actions slowed when she felt the powerful organ nudging her womanhood.

"What do I do?" she whispered, knowing their lovemaking was reaching the most crucial point.

Solomon smiled at her innocence. He kissed her ear, his hands encircling high about her thighs to spread them further.

Jacinta's expression was even more apprehensive when she gained the courage to meet his intense black stare. "I don't know what to do," she admitted.

Solomon tugged her earlobe with his perfect teeth. "I'll show you," he promised. His seductive mouth grazed the soft line of her jaw, and then covered her lips briefly before his tongue thrust inside. The fervent lunges of his tongue made Jacinta feel as though he were seeking to taste her very essence.

"Love?" he murmured, during their kiss.

Jacinta twined her fingers into his gorgeous hair. "Mmm?"

"This may be uncomfortable at first," he prepared her.

Jacinta was too absorbed by the sultry mastery of the kiss. "Mmm . . ." she responded.

Solomon squeezed his eyes shut tight. Never had he been so aroused by the act taking place as well as the woman he held. With his arousal positioned at the very entrance he craved, he pressed forward.

Jacinta's lashes fluttered at the slight intrusion. "Mmm . . ." she moaned at the delicious sensation it created. Her fingers weakened in Solomon's hair as she focused on what was happening elsewhere. She tried to liken the pleasure to that which occurred when he put his fingers inside her, but this went far beyond that.

Solomon pressed onward, sheathing more of him within her body. A well of moisture began to bathe his manhood and he lowered his head to moan into her neck. He pressed deeper.

A tiny furrow wrinkled Jacinta's brow and her lashes fluttered as she opened her eyes. The sweet pleasure now mingled with a dull pain. As terribly as she yearned for the pleasure, the pain could not be denied. Solomon raised his head when he felt her hands against his chest. This time, they were curved into fists and lightly pounding. He kissed her hairline to soothe her. "Shh . . . it's all right."

"Solomon . . ."

"It won't hurt for long," he said, easing more of his length inside her.

"Solomon . . . I—I can't," she moaned, feeling as though she were about to burst. "I can't . . ."

Solomon was past the stopping point. He could have remained positioned as he was and enjoyed the satisfaction it provided. But he had waited too long to have this woman—to share such an incredible experience with her. This night he would make her his. Preparing himself for her scream, he held her thighs in an iron grasp and buried his lengthy shaft deep within.

Her anticipated scream was buried beneath his kiss. Solomon withstood her fisted blows to his chest and back. He moved over her in wicked fashion, lunging mercilessly as he carved his place inside her.

Tears streamed from Jacinta's face and disappeared into her damp hair. Striking Solomon's chest was like pounding the trunk of a tree, so she ceased and prayed for an end to the torture. Then, she gasped and gasped again when another sensation surged deep within the bruised walls of her sex. Solomon's thrusts were now soothing away the pain and replacing it with indescribable pleasure. Jacinta's hands fell above her head, as her hips began to undulate in an age-old rhythm. Her breathless gasps, mingled with soft cries and moans. The silken steely ridge of his erection stretched her awakened womanhood.

Solomon freed her thighs, allowing her legs to lock around his back. He threaded his fingers through hers and pressed her hands to the bed. He increased the speed of his thrusts and shuddered her name as the feel of her creamy sheath squeezed, then released, his arousal. Unable to resist, he embraced the satisfaction that beckoned him.

Jacinta woke after a short nap and cried out at the delightful emotions coursing through her. Her thighs trembled beneath Solomon's erotic torture, but he held her fast. His tongue was thrusting at a frantic pace. Just briefly did he pause to rotate it playfully, before the thrusting resumed. Jacinta's cries gained volume and she turned her face into a pillow. Solomon was a most generous lover. He was determined to see that she experienced as much or even greater fulfillment than he. He carried her to the brink of complete satisfaction, then let her down easily only to bring her back again.

When he buried himself inside her for the second time, her total pleasure was his only agenda. He loved her until her entire body quivered in orgasmic waves. He allowed her but a moments rest, before pulling her back into erotic bliss.

Jacinta woke after their fifth round of lovemaking to find a tray laden with delectable treats set on the nightstand next to the bed. She pushed herself up in the middle of the tangled covers while brushing strands of hair away from her face. She smiled demurely at Solomon when he handed her a warm sweet roll. They ate in silence, Jacinta in the middle of the bed, Solomon reclining against the headboard. Both wanted to talk, but feared it would spoil the enchantment it had taken them so long to find. After long moments, however, Jacinta smiled and fixed her husband with a cunning look.

"We've been locked away in this cabin so very long," she noted, "Poppa may be worried."

Solomon shrugged and set his hot tea to the tray. "I doubt it," he replied.

"That's right . . . he was your accomplice in all this."

"Well . . . not *all* this."

Jacinta laughed. Solomon simply watched her, enjoying the sound.

"I suppose we should join him for dinner," she suggested, sobering a bit beneath his intense gaze.

Solomon's hand closed over her wrist and he pulled Jacinta across his lap. "Perhaps breakfast," he decided, grinning when his wife nodded her agreement.

CHAPTER 15

"Ah! We were afraid we'd have to leave you two on the boat. We'll be arriving shortly in Charleston, you know?" Jason teased the newlyweds when they arrived on deck for breakfast. The older man was full of smiles, for it was obvious his daughter and her husband had become much closer.

Through Jason's contentment, however, Jacinta could tell something wasn't quite right. "Poppa, I think you should get more rest once we're home. I'll handle any business that needs tending," she decided.

Jason squeezed her hand when she leaned down to kiss his forehead. "I thank you, love, but I can promise you I'm fine. A good night's sleep in my own bed will make all the difference."

"Poppa—"

"Besides, you have a husband to tend to. The two of you will be setting sail for home soon."

Jacinta's eyes narrowed and she fixed her father with a curious smile. "Now I know you haven't been getting enough rest. Have you forgotten we're sailing for home at this very moment?"

Jason reclined in the high back wooden chair he occupied, realizing he'd spoke hastily. He glanced toward Solomon, who sat in the chair opposite his. After a moment, Jacinta was also staring in Solomon's direction.

"We set sail for New York in one week," he informed her, his dark stare daring her to argue.

Jacinta was speechless, but only for a moment. "I won't be going," she decided simply, shaking her head to send a slew of curls flying into her dark, pretty face.

"This isn't open for discussion or debate."

"What?" Jacinta whispered, feeling a slight shiver of rage surge along her spine.

Solomon prepared a cup of tea. "You heard me."

"How dare you—"

"I think I'll take my daughter's advice and get a bit more rest," Jason interjected, eager to avoid the coming argument.

"If you think you can just *tell* me we're going and that's final—"

"That's exactly what I think," Solomon admitted tiredly, leaving the table to prepare a plate of scrambled eggs, fried steak, grits and gravy.

Jacinta rose from the table as well, easing her hands into the side pockets of her red velvet riding dress. "Perhaps you're unaware of this, Dikembe, but I don't give a damn about who you are in the North. You pull no weight down here."

"Perhaps not, but you're still my wife," he reminded her sweetly.

"So you believe because we've consummated our marriage—"

"That gives me every legal right to do or say as I please where you're concerned."

"Horse's ass," Jacinta hissed, her hands clenched into fists.

Solomon finished preparing his plate. "That's no way for a wife to address her husband, love."

"I'll address you any way I see fit, you conceited, scheming son of a jackal!" she fearlessly continued, marching right up to Solomon and poking her index finger into the dark woven fabric of his suit coat.

Solomon sighed, setting his plate to the buffet. He turned, advancing on his wife and forcing her to retreat until the table behind her prevented further movement.

"Know this, Miss McIver—excuse me, *Mrs.* Dikembe. You are mine. *Forever.* Nothing can change that now," his rough voice grated. "You can either accept this or spend your time bitter and angry. Your choice. Bitter and angry, however, are not attitudes I'm willing to tolerate indefinitely," he warned, then turned away, collected his plate and left the deck.

❦

That afternoon, the *Lariat* docked and the Dikembes and Jason McIver boarded a carriage for McIver Estate. Jacinta remained silent during most of the trip, barely speaking when she was spoken to. Once the threesome arrived home, she took her journal and opted for a walk instead of going into the house.

"She is tough, my boy," Jason noted while he and his son-in-law watched Jacinta stroll down a tree-lined pathway. "And you are still surprisingly calm in light of her attitude," he added.

"Humph," Solomon acknowledged with a grunt, his eyes hooded in aggravation. "I'm even surprised that I've held my temper this long," he admitted.

Jason shook his head. "It'll be better for you both once you're on your own," he predicted, patting his hand against the front of the black linen shirt Solomon wore.

The younger man wasn't so convinced. "I've counted on the company of others to prevent me from wringing my wife's pretty neck," he muttered, before storming toward the main house.

Jason let loose a howl of laughter, inwardly congratulating himself for making the right choice for his daughter. Jacinta would be far too busy attempting to triumph over her husband's strong will to focus on much else. He was sure of it.

Jacinta had located a private spot and managed to fill several pages of her journal before she was interrupted. It was however, an interruption she was most delighted by.

"The island meetings were so successful I just can't tell you," she raved, as she strolled the path with Hosiah Basa, a local carpenter and loyal Vesey supporter.

"Mister Vesey was sure they would be," Hosiah said, nodding his satisfaction.

"We collected a staggering amount of signatures. The coming weeks promise to be even more successful," Jacinta was saying as they rounded the path's curve and the main house came into view. Suddenly, Hosiah grabbed her hand and pulled her into the shelter of the trees.

"Hosiah, what—"

"Shh! That man, Jaci. That man can't be trusted."

"Who?" Jacinta queried, frowning as she squinted in the direction Hosiah glared. "Oh," she remarked, grimacing as her brown eyes scanned the porch. "Solomon Dikembe," she sighed in a knowing tone.

Hosiah was shaking his head. "No, Jaci, not Solomon."

Jacinta did a doubletake, her frown returning. "But the other man is Paul Vinson. You know him, Hosi."

"And I also know he was the man who betrayed Jore Sula and his family to Chuck Wallens."

"Are you certain?" Jacinta breathed, her eyes wide with disbelief.

Hosiah hooked his thumbs around his overall suspenders. "I rent my services to ol' Wallens and I seen Vinson there many times, includin' day before Chuck and his boys visited your house."

Jacinta's head whipped around, her expression now wild with fury. She studied the small mulatto with renewed interest. She'd never cared for the man and shouldn't have been surprised to hear of his betrayal. But she was thinking of more than that now. She was remembering the day she saw Solomon in conversation with the man, and there they were again.

"I wonder," she whispered.

Jacinta waited until Paul Vinson finished his conversation with her husband, then followed Solomon upstairs to the bedroom he'd occupied since arriving in Charleston. He strolled several feet ahead of her, and Jacinta was certain he had no idea of her presence.

"Is there something on your mind, wife?" he inquired just as Jacinta approached the doorway.

Jacinta gasped as Solomon turned to face her.

"Shut the door and talk to me," he persuaded softly.

"Oh, you are a calm devil, aren't you?" she sneered as she slammed the door.

Solomon was removing his cuff links. "Is there any reason I should be otherwise?"

"Twice, Dikembe. Twice I've seen you in conversation with Paul Vinson."

Solomon frowned as a measure of surprise clouded his face. "Paul Vinson?" he repeated, intrigued by the suspicion in her voice.

Jacinta mistook Solomon's surprise for guilt, and it fueled her suspicions. "I should've known," she sighed.

"Is there some problem with my socializing with your neighbors?"

"There is when that neighbor betrayed a guest in my home to a monster!"

"Explain yourself," Solomon's deep voice grated, his easy mood evaporating like mist.

"I know for a fact that it was Paul Vinson who informed Charles Wallens about Jore being here," Jacinta explained, crossing her arms over the button-down front of her riding dress. "Not only that, but I've seen you in cozy conversation with the snake on more than one occasion. Coincidence, husband?"

Solomon's long lashes fluttered over his eyes, his temper rising. "Fool," he breathed.

Jacinta cast off the scathing tone of his raspy voice. "This rebellion will bring so many changes," she raved, pacing the room with all the regality of a queen. "I believe you half-whites will have more problems with blacks being freed than your pure white idols."

"I told you you'd regret continuing to involve yourself in this rebellion."

"And I told *you* that I don't care one damn about your opinions toward the way I live my life!" Jacinta spat, bracing her fists against her hips. "You thought that farce of a wedding would make you lord and master over me, Dikembe? Think again!"

"I only expect you to master three things," he returned. "How to be a lover, wife and mother."

"Mother?" Jacinta repeated the word as though it put a bad taste in her mouth. Her smoky brows narrowed as her anger got the better of her. "Mother. No way will I ever give birth to one of your half-white bastards!" she raged, gasping the instant the sentence touched her ears. Even she was appalled by the ugliness of the spontaneous remark. She could see the hurt clearly in Solomon's dark eyes, and she knew her words had cut him deep.

Solomon's reaction lasted but a moment. "That's it," he muttered, pulling open the door and storming out into the hall. "Mary!" he called, beckoning one of the upstairs maids.

The young woman hurried over, eager to see to her employer's beloved houseguest. "Yes, Mister Solomon?"

Solomon's voice was soft in spite of the anger roiling inside his body. "I want you to get started packing all Miss Jacinta's things. Get help if you need it. I want this done quickly," he instructed.

Mary curtsied. "Yes, sir," she promised before rushing off.

"What are you doing?" Jacinta demanded.

Solomon didn't bother to look her way. "Preparing to take you home."

"I *am* home."

"My home. Your new home."

"Never."

"You'd prefer me to take you by force then?" He suggested, finally turning a stony glare in her direction. "Because as badly as I'd like to throttle you right now, I'd be most agreeable to it."

Thoroughly unnerved by the savage gleam in his pitch-black stare, Jacinta made a mad dash for the front door. Solomon caught her easily, one arm snaking around her waist while he kicked the door shut with the tip of his boot.

"Dammit! Solomon!" Jacinta hissed, struggling against him, her legs flailing wildly behind her. "Stop!" she insisted, sounding breathless as his arm beneath her breasts threatened to cut off her air supply.

Solomon turned her in his arms just as he approached the bed.

"Let go!" Jacinta commanded, preparing herself for the collision when he suddenly dropped her to the center of the bed.

"Never will you be mother to my children?" Solomon taunted, ripping the shirt from his back before going to work on his trouser fastening. "We shall see about that," his voice grated, and he hated that she had managed to rouse the vicious temper he always tried to hide.

Jacinta kicked out, but Solomon caught her ankles and pulled her down to the center of the bed. "Get off!" she bellowed, bucking her legs against him when he'd settled between her thighs. "Solomon . . . damn you." She continued to fight even as the tingle of pleasure surged through her.

Solomon was forceful, yet even more appealing. Jacinta cursed him and herself as she succumbed to the throbbing urges. When it was over, he did not pull her close. Instead, he moved to his side of the bed, his back toward her. Jacinta cried herself to sleep, torn between the growing love she felt for the man and fear of leaving the only life she'd ever known.

Early morning sunlight fought past the heavy dark green drapes. Jacinta squeezed her eyes shut tightly, hoping to ward off the glare beaming against her eyelids. She could have slumbered several hours longer, but it was not to be. She felt the bed shake and raised her head to find that Solomon had slammed a heavy case upon it.

Jacinta turned amidst the disarray of covers. She winced at the aches that pulsed to life in the intimate areas of her body. Her cheeks burned as memories of their rapacious lovemaking surfaced in her mind. In his embrace, she would always be wanton, in a constant state of desire for his touch and affection. In his embrace, she forgot about their differences, her responsibilities, his aversion to the way she led her life. All that mattered was the cloud of pleasure upon which they floated.

The beautiful vision brought a slow frown of concern to her face. Sadly, they could not spend an eternity in a passionate embrace. A marriage certainly couldn't survive on it, and Solomon seemed intent on their marriage being real in every way. Did she dare hope that his feelings could go deeper than the physical? Did she dare hope the same for her own?

"We leave in the morning," his voice resounded in the quiet room. "I suggest you use the day to spend time with your father. You'll not be seeing him for quite a while."

"You've got my father fooled by this caring gentleman act of yours, but I know you're simply a conniving jackass only satisfied when getting your way," she snapped, the reality of leaving making her feel sour on the inside.

Solomon shook his head. "You always pay so dearly for that sharp tongue," he sighed, dropping a shirt into the case. "What a shame you never think to curb it."

Jacinta flopped back down into the bed and slammed her fists against the covers. "Solomon, please reconsider this," she whispered, using her most needy tone of voice. "If you won't stay for me, think of Poppa. It'll be Christmastime soon, and with everything else going on it would be nice for a bit of warmth and cheer." She shrugged, her gaze drifting off into the distance. "As much cheer as one can have in the midst of such circumstances," she added.

Solomon stood still, his strong fingers curved over the edge of the case. His stare was riveted on her face, and he was utterly captivated by her sweetness.

Jacinta saw him staring and eased up, bracing her weight on one elbow. "Please, Dikembe, for Poppa?"

The enchantment on Solomon's face faded into a look of smug wickedness. "Your Poppa wants you out of Charleston more than anyone," he informed her happily.

Jacinta blinked. "You lie," she breathed.

Solomon closed the case then moved over to where his wife lay on the bed. There, he sat next to her, bracing his fists on either side of her body. "Your father, Esa and myself included, were aware of your presence at the Vesey meetings during our stay on Regal," he shared, smiling when he glimpsed her smoky gaze widen briefly. "It was one of the reasons for such an unplanned wedding ceremony." He leaned closer. "Your father wants you out of this town—out of the South as far as you can go."

Jacinta blinked, the trail of her gaze faltering on the bed linens. She felt stunned and angry. Most of all, she felt remorseful. She had put her father through so much. Now he was frightened—truly frightened for her safety. Jason McIver knew Solomon Dikembe was the only man who could take her away and keep her safe. Keep her safe and love her.

Jacinta looked up to search Solomon's intense stare with her own. "What were the other reasons?" she whispered.

Solomon blinked and shook his head. "Other reasons?" he queried, clearly confused.

Jacinta hesitated before speaking. For a moment, she was fixed on the lone dimple that flashed in Solomon's cheek each time he spoke. "You said my outings on Regal were but one of the reasons for the quick ceremony. What were the other reasons?" she whispered.

Solomon bowed his head, and Jacinta could see the vibrant muscle dancing its wicked jig in his jaw. Solomon was definitely contemplating. He knew that to tell her he loved her would only give her the power to hurt him more deeply.

"You should dress," he urged, leaning forward to drop a quick kiss to her mouth.

Jacinta seized the moment of tenderness. Her tongue darted past his lips and she heard his surprised moan. His fists braced against the bed as he leaned into the kiss. Jacinta was kissing him in wild abandon, her lips suckling his tongue, caressing it with her own.

"Jaci . . ." he breathed, kneeling upon the bed to take her into his arms. He broke the kiss to trail his mouth along her temple and the line of her jaw.

Jacinta smoothed her palms against the fine material of his blue gray shirt. Her nails grazed the cords of his neck before her lips followed the same sensuous path.

Solomon massaged her bare back. He continued to lavish her dark skin with wet, worshipping kisses that showered her collarbone and the tops of her breasts. Jacinta felt a rush of confidence at the sound of the helpless sighs rising from the chest of the powerful man who held her so tenderly. Once his lips closed over an aching nipple, she cupped his head to savor the caress. Solomon pleasured the bud with his teeth and tongue, nibbling and bathing the peak while she gasped her appreciation.

"Poppa, are you certain about this? Is this what you truly want of me?" Jacinta was asking Jason later that afternoon when they strolled the grounds of McIver Estate.

Jason smiled, gathering his daughter close as they walked. "It is most certainly what I want."

"To leave you?" she whispered, turning to face him with tearful eyes.

"Now, now . . ." Jason hushed, using both thumbs to brush the moisture away from her cheeks. "You'll never leave me, and I'll never leave you—not really. You know that," he said, peering deeply into her eyes.

Jacinta knew what he meant, but she was still emotional. "I'm sorry, Poppa."

Jason kissed her cheek, pulling her close again as they cuddled against a brisk November wind. "I understand you're uncertain and a bit frightened, but Solomon Dikembe is a good man. I believe you know this. I love you, and I would never have chosen to give you to him if I didn't truly believe he wouldn't love, protect and adore you."

Jacinta hid her hands within the folds of her wrap and bit her tongue. She didn't want to tell her father how on edge she was about leaving her home. It was important that she remain the dutiful and cooperative daughter— she owed her father that at least.

"Poppa, just promise me you'll be safe," she said instead, turning to squeeze his hands into hers. "You don't want to discuss this, but the rebellion is as much as set. You're a powerful man in this town, and your involvement will certainly be sought."

Jason patted her cheek. "I know this, my dear. I've been approached several times already," he revealed, chuckling at the surprise in her brown eyes. "I'll be fine here, but I don't want you to dwell on the goings-on in Charleston. Occupy your time with thoughts of your husband. You have a lot to learn about allowing a man, other than your father, to care for you."

Again, Jacinta bit her tongue to stifle telling her father that she could very well take care of herself. She kissed him instead, hugging him tightly and praying he could not feel her heart about to pound out of her chest.

CHAPTER 16

February 1822

When the *Sheba* docked in New York Harbor, the Dikembes were completely on edge. Solomon had crafted the stunning water vessel into the coziest, most sensual thing Jacinta believed she had ever seen.

The *Sheba,* with its grand cabins and massive dining hall, was one of the few luxurious ships of its kind. Of course, the fact that it was owned by a black man, commanded by another black man, and crewed by an entirely black crew, made it even more exquisite.

Solomon had wanted to acquire the ship ever since stories of Paul Cuffe reached his ears. Cuffe, a free black man, owned a 69-ton schooner that he sailed to purchase cargos of vegetables and other stock. White people were filled with alarm at the sight of a black man in complete command of such a possession, not to mention his charge of an all black crew. It had been an unprecedented occurrence in the mid 1700s. People wondered and worried over what impression this would have on their slaves. A black man with such a powerful tool could easily incite blacks in bondage to escape, or worse, rebel. Paul Cuffe, however, was angered by this assumption. Still, he refused to allow the views of whites, or anyone else, to interfere with his work. He considered himself a businessman pure and simple, conducted his affairs and left others to frustrate themselves over whatever underlying motives they might have had.

Solomon was inspired by this and strived to live his life, both personally and professionally, in much the same fashion. He was determined to carve out his place in the world and do his best to ignore the rumblings of those who feared the power he would acquire.

Jacinta did not fear her husband's power, in spite of the fact that it had played a huge role in her father choosing him as her partner. Moreover, she celebrated the fact that men such as Solomon existed, black men who weren't afraid to stand up against the brutality they faced. Men determined to reach out for the prosperity and well being in their grasps. If the *Sheba* were a testament to Solomon's determination, then she had married a very ambitious man. Sadly, however, being surrounded by the beauty and luxury of the vessel had its drawbacks. With its color scheme of burgundies, golds and brownish hues, the *Sheba* instilled a sense of sensuality and comfort. The lavishness only fueled the urges which rested between the Dikembes—urges they'd made silent decisions not to act upon.

Solomon knew his wife wasn't completely secure in the idea of leaving her home. Moreover, he knew her feelings had not a fraction of the depth of his feelings for her. Therefore, he kept his distance, hoping time would make all the difference.

Of course, this made the voyage seem much longer. Christmastime and the onset of a New Year came and went with little pomp and circumstance. Jacinta missed her home and her father more with each passing day. She dreaded thinking of what she would find to occupy her time in her strange new life.

When the ship docked early one February morning, Jacinta received a shock. New York's climate was terribly cold for one of her southern blood. She instinctively cuddled close to her husband when he assisted her from the *Sheba's* deck. Thankfully, the breathtaking ankle-length sable coat, with a matching hat and hand warmer, kept her very toasty. Still, the biting wind managed to chill her to the bone.

Solomon kept a protective arm about his wife's tiny frame as they made their way along the harbor. Jacinta's eyes were wide like a child's as she observed the sights. New York was a town on a grand scale which, in her opinion, far exceeded anything Charleston had to offer. The harbor teamed with bodies and smelled of fish, musk and men. Their loud rough voices carried in the chilly air and mingled with the sounds of gulls overhead. Ship's crews issued orders as their vessels arrived to port. Jacinta was intrigued by the new visions and by the fact that she was in the midst of it. Ensconced in Charleston all her life, she realized that she'd never given any real thought to the lives led by others.

"Steady . . ." Solomon urged, keeping his big hands secured around her upper arms as he guided her through the narrowing space along the harbor. The chilly wind kissed the water-slicked wood of the dock to produce a sheer coating of ice that could easily cause a fall. Solomon tried to keep his mind focused on getting them safely to the carriage awaiting them. He found his thoughts wandering, however, to the soft fragrance of coconuts that followed Jacinta and teased his nostrils. Though she was covered by the thick fur, its sensuous touch only reminded him of the way her bare skin felt beneath his fingertips. Over the last several weeks, he had been slowly going out of his mind. Despite their tender encounter just before leaving Charleston, their emotional distance had remained. Solomon didn't trust himself to not want to throttle her for whatever complaint she might make. So he stayed away from her—watching her become more desirable as the long weeks passed.

"Cold?" he asked, watching as she raised her hands to warm her cheeks against the sable hand warmer.

"I'm fr-freezing," Jacinta admitted, before pressing her lips together to prevent her teeth from chattering.

"Freezing?" Solomon parroted in an incredulous manner. " 'Tis quite refreshing in my opinion," he said, grinning when his wife fixed him with a sour glance. "New York's weather can be a bit rough, especially on those who've lived their lives in warmer spots."

"Is it always like this?" Jacinta asked, unconsciously snuggling deeper into Solomon's hard frame.

Solomon's broad shoulders rose beneath his heavy black wool cloak. "This is nothing—wait until tonight," he warned, chuckling when she groaned. "You'll feel better once we get inside the carriage. We'll get some hot tea inside you and you'll be fine."

The promise brought a happy smile to Jacinta's lips and gave her the strength to brave the cold. "Do you have a home he-here?" she asked while they walked.

"I've been thinking about it," Solomon said, tugging on the brim of his black top hat as he spoke. "I don't really do much business here, and so I usually stay with friends," he explained.

Jacinta felt a rush of glee as they approached the street lined with carriages. "Are we heading there now?" she asked, almost screaming in delight when Solomon responded with a nod.

"Thomas," Solomon greeted a finely garbed young dark man.

"Mister Solomon," Thomas replied, smiling broadly as he shook hands. "I pray your trip was satisfactory?"

"Very much," Solomon confirmed with a nod, before turning. "I'm afraid my wife is a bit unused to the temperature. By chance would you have anything warm inside the carriage?"

"Even better—I have brandy," Thomas proudly announced, appreciating the hearty clap Solomon placed upon his shoulder. "This way, Mrs. Dikembe," he instructed, his soft gray stare twinkling as he appraised the tiny dark beauty in his presence.

"Thank you, Thomas," Jacinta whispered, accepting his hand.

"Very beautiful, Mister Solomon," Thomas saw fit to add once Jacinta was inside the cab.

Solomon's grin was a combination of pride and appreciation. "Very," he agreed and followed his wife.

Thomas checked to ensure the curtains were secure before the cab's windows, then shut the door and went to take his place at the front. Meanwhile, the Dikembes settled onto the plush black velvet cushioned seat. Solomon settled a thick, gray blanket across their laps, taking extra care to tuck Jacinta in. Then, he poured two snifters of the rich brandy.

The fragrant liquid warmed Jacinta' insides like the fuzzy blanket surrounding her. A wonderful shiver of warmth brought a look of contentment to her face. Solomon had dropped his arm about her shoulders and she cuddled back against him, but not for warmth.

"Tell me about your friends," she urged him, hoping to keep at bay the sexual energy crackling and popping about them.

Solomon cleared his throat and smiled. "Taurus and Monique Mandela. They run their own business and live in a home Monique inherited from her father on Whitehall Street," he shared.

"Is that where all the blacks live?"

The innocent question forced Solomon to laugh. "Very few blacks live there, love."

Jacinta fixed Solomon with a curious stare. "I take it these friends of yours are rebels in their own right?"

"You could certainly say that. I think you'll find a lot in common," Solomon added, before continuing in his discussion of the Mandelas. In truth, the young couple was only one of a miniscule percentage of blacks who dwelled in New York's most fashionable district.

The west side of Manhattan was also the city's most exclusive quarter. Had Monique not acquired the property on Whitehall from her father, she and her husband would have most certainly dwelled in a less noted area.

With its four-story Federal-style mansions, elm tree-lined streets, beautiful walkways skirting the water's edge and the sheer elegance of the buildings which housed the city's most respected businesses, lower Broadway garnered raving comments from all who visited.

"I think you'll be quite impressed by them," Solomon went on, a smile adding a more sensuous element to the curve of his mouth.

Jacinta watched her husband as he spoke. She traced his profile with intent eyes. She memorized every facet of his appearance, from the sleek line of his extremely long brows to the dark shadow of a beard which added that roughish element to his good looks. Dammit, she mourned, why did they always have to be at odds with one another?

Solomon was still talking, when he felt Jacinta's head drop to his chest. He heard her low, steady breathing shortly after and knew sleep had finally claimed her. Love and desire radiated from his eyes and he leaned down to press a tender kiss to her forehead.

Stretching like a lazy feline while snuggling deeper into the cushiony bed, Jacinta woke feeling relaxed for the first time in weeks. The gorgeous four-poster bed was huge and dressed with heavy linens, warm blankets and at least six goose down pillows. She could only force her eyes half opened, but saw there was a fire raging across the room. The brick hearth was flanked by two deep burgundy armchairs which sat on a beautiful emerald rug trimmed in the same color as the chairs. Jacinta forced herself to turn over and found the white drapes pulled back partially and revealing frost-covered windows.

"Mmm . . ." she purred, stretching her toes beneath the covers and her fingers high above her head. The sound of low giggling in the room caused her eyes to widen. Jacinta saw a slender white woman with pitch black, heavily coiled hair standing across the room. She'd been stocking the cabinets beneath the washstand with soaps and bath oils, but ceased her chore when she heard Jacinta awaken.

"I do hope I didn't wake you. I apologize if I did," she said softly, clasping her hands as she approached the bed on tentative steps. "I'll take your moan to mean you had a good nap?"

Jacinta's smile returned and she slowly pushed herself up in the bed. "No, it's all right. Please don't apologize," she insisted, finding it oddly refreshing to find that this white woman was so friendly and hospitable. "I fell asleep in a carriage and never expected to awaken in such comfort," she went on.

"Oh, I'm so happy to hear you say that," the woman gushed, clearly pleased by the comment.

"Such a beautiful room," Jacinta whispered, her warm chocolate gaze floating around the cozy fire-lit chamber. Another yawn claimed her then and her eyes drifted longingly across the bed.

"You're welcome to sleep longer. Supper won't be for hours, and I could even have it sent up if you prefer to dine here."

Jacinta was already waving her hand and shaking her head no, even as she resisted the urge to accept the offer. "I couldn't possibly," she told the polite young woman. "These people are my husband's good friends and I wouldn't want to appear rude by remaining in my room all evening."

"Oh, you won't give that impression, I assure you."

Jacinta wasn't convinced. "I've never met them, and I'd never forgive myself for casting a bad impression."

The young woman moved to take a seat on the edge of the bed. "As I said, you won't give that impression. You've already passed muster with the hostess, and the host is a big ol' sweet bear."

Jacinta frowned in confusion even as a huge smile began to brighten her face.

The young woman leaned close while extending her hand. "Monique Mandela," she announced, grinning broadly when she saw the shock in the eyes of her guest.

Jacinta's eyes had widened to the size of small moons. "Mandela? But you . . ."

"Are a white woman?" Monique supplied in a playful, knowing tone. "No, just a bit on the light side," she explained.

Jacinta bowed her head and smothered a curse. "I am sorry," she groaned.

Monique waved her hand. "It's quite all right. I assure you that I'm used to it."

Jacinta could only shake her head until a quick laugh escaped her.

"What?" Monique inquired, laughter still coloring her own voice.

"I'm just remembering something my husband said about us having a lot in common."

"And now you've realized exactly what he meant?" Monique guessed.

"Mmm . . . have you all known each other long?" Jacinta asked, leaning back against the pillow-lined headboard.

"I've known Solomon all my life," Monique shared, propping both hands behind her on the bed.

"Is that how you met your husband?" Jacinta inquired.

Monique's smile promised there was a story to be told. "Actually Solomon and Taurus were involved in some business. Solomon always stayed with my parents whenever he visited New York. One evening in particular, Solomon invited Taurus to drinks at the house. They rounded the corner in time to see me involved in a nasty argument. Actually, I was only listening while the offensive *gentleman* voiced his nasty opinions of me and 'my kind'."

Jacinta's eyes closed briefly. "I'm sorry," she sighed.

"Oh, don't be," Monique drawled, with a coy look. "Taurus came to my rescue with Solomon at his heels. But Taurus was the real hero. When it was all over, that

275

gentleman was standing in a puddle, and it wasn't rain-water."

Jacinta was laughing so hard, her eyes streamed tears.

"Well, that was certainly a fine way for Taurus to endear himself to your parents."

Monique wiped a tear from the corner of her eye. "Indeed. They loved him right away. Especially my mother."

"Mmm . . . I can imagine. Her little girl wedding a handsome suitor," Jacinta spoke in a dreamy tone.

Monique's dark doe shaped eyes reflected sadness for the first time. "Yes . . . I suppose she was just as happy to see that happen for me. Although I know it made her think back over the way things happened in her own life."

"Well . . . wasn't she with your father?" Jacinta slowly inquired, praying Monique wouldn't take offense to the question.

Monique smiled in understanding. "The man who raised me was the only father I ever knew. He was a black man. My mother had me before she ever met him. She was raped by a white man. I was the result."

Jacinta's round face reflected horror. "Oh, Monique," she gasped, leaning across the covers to brush her fingers against the woman's crisp, maroon skirts. "I'm so sorry. I didn't mean to pry."

"It's all right, Jacinta. It was a long time ago," Monique soothed, squeezing Jacinta's hand in both of hers. "This is why I've known Solomon for so long. My mother was mulatto. She was well educated and Solomon's grandparents, the Hamptons, arranged for her to be Miss Sheba's companion." Monique blinked as tears spiked her very long lashes. "Mama was seeing a young white man who didn't know she had black blood. When he made the discovery . . . his reaction was very violent." Monique sniffled a bit, then fixed her new friend with a refreshing look. "Anyway, Solomon and I were practically raised together until Mama met Poppa and he brought us to New York."

The tale held Jacinta in awe. She was still shaking her head and watching Monique in disbelief when a soft knock fell upon the bedchamber door. The knob twisted slowly and, a moment later, Solomon looked inside.

"Are you all right?" he asked in a quiet tone, making his rough voice even raspier.

"Fine," Jacinta whispered back, a gentle smile gracing her lips.

"You slept well?" Solomon persisted, his long brows drawn close in concern.

Jacinta shivered against the protective tone she heard in his voice and witnessed in his enveloping stare. "Everything was wonderful, really," she reassured him.

Solomon seemed satisfied. He scrutinized her seated demurely near the front of the bed. Her hair was tousled most provocatively, and the unintentionally seductive white ruffled gown beckoned his gaze to her bosom, just visible where a few buttons were left unfastened. Clearing his throat, he forced himself to look away. "Moni, Taurus sent me to find you," he announced, scarcely able to keep his eyes on the woman who was like a sister to him.

Monique responded with a soft yet unladylike snort. "There's no escaping that bear," she mockingly complained while pushing herself from the bed.

"You two seemed rather involved in conversation," Solomon noted, approaching the bed once Monique had gone.

Jacinta shrugged and leaned back against the pillows. "She's a lovely person. I never expected to wake up and meet someone so sweet."

Solomon appeared impressed by the statement. "Even though she's a 'half white'?" he chided, stepping toward the dressing table near the windows.

Jacinta took no offence. "I suppose all of you aren't so terrible," she teased back, smiling when Solomon bowed his head.

"I'm glad to hear it," he responded absently. "Will you be coming down for dinner? It's to be served shortly," he announced, his head still bowed while he focused on toying with the fringe of the cream silk scarf Jacinta had worn that day.

Jacinta expelled a dramatic sigh and fell back onto the bed. "Mmm, I haven't decided yet," she purred, lying with one arm thrown above her head. "I'm quite tempted to remain in this heavenly bed all evening," she debated, stretching lazily amidst the disheveled covers.

Solomon turned and leaned against the dressing table. He tried to smile at the remark, but he couldn't get past the alluring picture she made. He left her scarf dangling against the bureau and settled to the bed. Jacinta opened her eyes, startled, but Solomon was already covering her body with his—her mouth with his. Jacinta forgot any thoughts of refusing-not that she'd had any-and decided to enjoy the moment.

CHAPTER 17

The Mandelas had prepared their more intimate dining room for dinner with their guests. The small area was adjacent to both the main dining room and the kitchen. It boasted coziness, elegance and relaxation. The brightly candlelit room smelled of roasted beef with herb-seasoned vegetables, fresh baked bread and wild rice. The aromas wafted in from the kitchen as Taurus and Monique prepared to indulge in a bit of wine.

"I believe there is tension between them, Tauri. It was as if they wanted to be in each other's embrace, but were waiting for the other to act upon the desire."

Taurus chuckled, his molasses-toned face appearing less fierce with humor. "And this you ascertained by being in their presence for the better part of three minutes?" he teased, reclining in the massive Chippendale chair he occupied at the head of the table.

Monique tossed a napkin toward the giant dark man seated to her left. "Even in that time, I could see how much they mean to each other."

Taurus reached for the goblet of fragrant red wine. "And since when are you such an authority on affairs of the heart?"

Monique leaned close to her husband and giggled when he brought his dark face close to hers. "I've become such an authority since I managed to win the heart of one very stubborn, very infuriating publisher."

"Mmm, don't forget huge and handsome."

Monique's dark eyes sparkled with love as she giggled again. "Oh, I could never forget that," she breathed, her gaze faltering to Taurus's mouth.

The couple's passionate, lingering kiss was called to a halt a short while later when the Dikembes arrived. Solomon interrupted his friends by noisily clearing his throat. Taurus and Monique broke apart, looking embarrassed and acting more like two children caught being naughty instead of a married couple of almost eight years. When they rose from the table, Monique left her husband's side and rushed over to Jacinta. Quickly, she introduced her husband to their newest houseguest.

Jacinta had always regarded Solomon as the most powerfully built man she had ever seen. Taurus Mandela, however, was a huge, dark giant, pure and simple. Still, he and Solomon were tied in the fierce looks category.

"It's quite an honor to meet the woman who can tolerate Solomon Dikembe!" Taurus bellowed, and everyone joined him in laughter.

Jacinta fixed her husband with a sly look. "Believe me when I say that I am often torn between tolerate and strangle," she replied, joining in when more laughter erupted.

"Are you two finding everything to suit you?" Monique inquired, a mixture of concern and happiness filling her dark eyes.

"Oh, Monique, everything's beautiful. I was telling Solomon on the way down how I admired the artwork lining the walls along the banisters," Jacinta complimented.

"The artist lives right around the corner on Greenwich Street, you know?" Taurus was saying as he waved his huge hands toward the table in silent instruction that his guests be seated.

"In truth?" Jacinta breathed, her brown eyes widening at the fact that she was in the midst of such creativity.

Taurus nodded. "The area isn't far from here. I can't tell you how pleased I was to discover that after Niqui and I moved here."

"Oh? Why was that?" Jacinta questioned.

Monique leaned across the table. "Greenwich Street and many of the streets adjacent to our area populate a small number of free blacks."

"Mmm as you can imagine some of our neighbors were a little perturbed by that fact," Taurus jibed, letting a dash of wicked laughter follow his words.

"I suspect they were equally perturbed to discover the two of you living even closer," Jacinta added.

"Quite!" Taurus confirmed. This time the rumbling roar of his laughter filled the air and beckoned everyone else to join in.

"We'll have to visit the area before the end of your stay, Jacinta," Monique suggested once the volume of laughter had decreased. "There are so many wonderful shops. I think you'd enjoy it."

"I'm sure I would," Jacinta agreed, "though I'm enjoying myself just being in your home. It's so cozy, I may be reluctant to leave."

Monique clasped her hands to her mouth. "I'm so happy to hear you say that. You're sure the bedroom will suit your needs?" she had to ask.

"I think we're both finding it very comfortable," Solomon decided to reply, his slightly suggestive tone earning him a warning glare from his wife.

Monique was pleased and pushed her chair from the table. "Well then, if you gentlemen relax here, dinner will be served shortly. Jacinta, would it be in poor taste to ask for your help?"

"Of course not!" Jacinta responded quickly, joining her hostess at the dining room's swinging door. In the short time she'd known Monique, she found her to be delightful company.

Alone in the warm, elegant dining room, Taurus helped himself to another swig of wine. "She's a true beauty," he complimented after a few silent moments. "Was it a love match?" he queried when he spied the slow, wicked smile cross his friend's mouth.

"Is there any other kind?" Solomon challenged.

Taurus's uncommon hazel gaze narrowed then. "I suppose you can still tolerate my speaking frankly?"

"Tauri, I'd think you ill if you didn't."

Taurus bowed his head. "All right . . . was it a love match, or did you simply find it to be the easier route to get her into your bed?"

Solomon nodded. "Lust wasn't the only motivator, but it was a definite factor."

"And love?"

"Love . . . I'd rather not say."

"You're in love with her, aren't you?" Taurus whispered, his voice full of certainty. "And you don't believe she feels the same?" he guessed.

Solomon's shoulder rose in a slow shrug beneath the fabric of his black suit coat. "I believe she could, if she would let go of certain . . . realities."

"Your color?"

Then Solomon's glare darted to his friend's face in a manner that was all too telling. Clearly he was stunned that his great friend had guessed his thoughts so quickly. He did not respond, only turned his face away and began to gnaw inside his jaw.

"Is that why you brought her here?" Taurus asked, trailing his thumb around the mouth of the wine goblet, "to spend time around Niqui and me?"

Solomon's smile reappeared and he waved his hand toward his friend. "I commend your intelligence, but that wasn't the reason. I really wanted her to spend time with Moni. Charleston is a beautiful place that pulses with a hatred I can't describe. Horrific tensions exist between white and black, yet they are nothing compared to those existing between black and mulatto. A situation like that could be their downfall if certain opinions aren't changed."

"I see," Taurus whispered, stroking the ridge of his square jaw. "I certainly held those very same opinions. Even though you and I were friends, I didn't realize how deeply those opinions ran until I met Monique."

Solomon leaned back in his chair and tapped his fingers against the embroidered lilac tablecloth. "I want my wife to see that all people of mixed race are not consumed by pleasing the white, but that they are just as consumed by the need to see their people free and prosperous."

"And if she feels this way about Monique, perhaps she will have these feelings about you?"

Solomon shrugged. "As I said, you are an intelligent man, my friend."

"Sol tells me you're a writer," Monique was saying as she transferred the seasoned wild rice from a pot to a more decorative porcelain serving dish.

Jacinta responded with a modest smile. "I keep a journal. Nothing's been published. Basically I record the experiences of slaves—their pasts, their hopes, the horrors they've survived," she explained, clearing her throat to mask the quiver in her voice.

Monique stood still next to the iron stove. Her expression stated that she was both intrigued and curious. "What it must be like to speak of such painful things," she breathed, turning to carve a few slices of the tender roasted beef. "Sometimes I can't even bear to *think* of the painful experiences in my past."

Jacinta tossed the herb seasoned vegetables with two wooden spoons. "They speak of things I can only imagine," she shared.

"Some events in my life have mirrored the ones in Solomon's, but . . . it's different for a woman—a girl."

"Humph, I know so very little about Solomon's experiences," Jacinta admitted, shaking her head in regret.

Again, Monique turned. This time, her expression reflected surprise. "He doesn't like to speak of it . . . have you ever tried to encourage him to talk about them?"

"Once . . ." Jacinta sighed, toying with the flaring lace sleeve of her silver blue satin gown. "He closed himself off to speaking on it," she said, omitting the fact that she'd made comments that had most likely deterred him.

"He's suffered so much pain, suppressed so much," Monique lamented, never noticing the sorrow in Jacinta's eyes. "I've always wanted him to speak with someone he could *really* talk to. In talking with me, so much is understood it doesn't need to be verbalized. I believe it would benefit him to speak with someone in the manner that I can speak with Taurus. Do you understand what I mean?" she asked, fixing Jacinta with an expectant stare.

Quickly, Jacinta nodded. Silently, she berated herself for adding to her husband's despair.

Monique finished with the meat. "I've always wanted that for him. I fear that his feelings, if left unshared, could one day explode, and the results would be terrible," she said.

"Niqui!"

"Oooh!" Monique cringed at the sound of her husband's bellow. "I'm coming, you bear!" she bellowed back, before winking at Jacinta. "Let's get this supper to the table."

"I assure you they are simply writings in a journal, much like a diary a girl would keep."

"Diary, ha!" Solomon expressed from his place at the table. "Don't let her fool you. The woman's work is a far cry from any schoolgirl's musings, I can tell you that."

Jacinta bowed her head, hoping to hide the happiness over her husband's admiration. Much of the dinner conversation focused on her writings. She'd learned that Taurus was publisher of his own paper. *The Obsidian Beacon* was formed after he'd made his money in farming.

"I think I'm more interested in hearing how Taurus decided to become a newspaper man after a lifetime as a farmer."

"The *Beacon* is a sounding board," Taurus began, "a tool for expressing not only newsworthy occurrences of the day, but also to express the feelings and concerns of the party concerned."

"The black population," Jacinta guessed, watching Taurus nod. "My . . . an entire newspaper dedicated to the issues of our people. Quite impressive."

Taurus shrugged. "Alas, I'm not a writer; I simply offer a means for them to showcase their work. I suppose that's one reason why I started the publication, to be in the midst of those who could do something I wanted to do, but couldn't."

Jacinta propped her chin upon her palm and fixed him with a skeptical look. "I think everyone's born with the ability to write. You simply have to find that which speaks to you and only you."

"Well, something must definitely be speaking to you, Mrs. Dikembe, if you can create the sort of work my friend raves about," Taurus remarked, cutting his hazel stare toward Solomon. "Tell me, have you ever considered seeing your work in print?"

Jacinta was never more stunned. She sat watching Taurus with wide eyes, torn between wanting to laugh and gasp. "I—I've . . . never considered it actually. I love to write but . . . I don't know if it's perfected enough for public reading."

"Let me decide that," Taurus said, adding more of the roast's flavorful juices to his bed of wild rice. "Would you consider reading for us after dinner?"

Jacinta cast her rich, brown gaze towards her lap and sat staring at her hands, which were clasped within the folds of her gown. "You would simply rave to prevent bruising my feelings," she accused softly.

Taurus's bold, deep laughter erupted as his wife giggled.

"She don't know me, do she, love?" he asked.

Monique reached over to pat Jacinta's hand. "My husband can be painfully honest, you just rest assured."

"My wife is an exceptional writer," Solomon suddenly spoke up. "She writes from her heart, and it is captivating."

Again, Jacinta was shocked by her husband's candor. She smiled in response to the compliment, not bothering to mask the adoration dwelling in her eyes when she looked his way.

"Not only an ambitious land baron, but also a literary connoisseur!" Taurus teased, joining in when everyone else laughed.

"Ambitious land baron, yes. Literary connoisseur, no. I only know what I like," Solomon clarified, his eyes focused on Jacinta and bringing a more sensual tone to his words.

Jacinta regarded the Mandelas beneath the heavy fringe of her lashes. Thankfully they didn't sense the suggestive turn in the conversation. "Solomon just purchased land in South Carolina. Did he tell you?" she asked Taurus and Monique, hoping to spark more general conversation.

"Mmm, Michigan, Ohio, New York and now South Carolina. You certainly are staking your claims," Monique teased, watching Solomon shrug.

"I've often inquired about his intentions for such possessions," Jacinta interjected.

Solomon added another slice of the succulent roast to his plate. "One can never have too much land."

"True," Taurus agreed, rubbing his fingers through the dark waves of his hair. "Of course, we know it means more than that for you."

"The land in Charleston has the potential to affect much change," Solomon explained, his gaze shimmering with determination and optimism. "It's enough to comfortably employ scores of the enslaved to cultivate the property's resources and perform other tasks. I'm committed to seeing my people work as free men and women."

The room was bathed in silence as everyone nodded their agreement and admired Solomon's vision. Dinner went on to be a wonderful success, due as much to the fantastic results of Monique's culinary talents as to the stirring conversation. Later, coffee and cake were served in the sitting room.

Jacinta closed her eyes to savor yet another sip of the creamy coffee. Never had she tasted a brew with such a particular flavor. Monique revealed that a spicy mint had been added to the pot, accounting for the intriguing taste. The foursome enjoyed a moist apple cake while seated in cushioned, deep armchairs situated before a massive brick stone fireplace. Politics were the main topic, drawing Jacinta's attention and opinions. Of course, her first inquiries focused on the Northern perception of slavery in the South. Taurus and Monique were quite candid as they spoke on the subject, its dehumanizing affects and those who perpetuated the way of life.

"Yet another reason I began the paper," Taurus was saying as he accepted a second slice of the apple cake. "I'd been a landowner all my life, as was my father and grandfather. When I came to New York and had my first taste of real prejudice, it sickened me. White men didn't believe a baboon, much less a black man, had an inkling of the brain power necessary to operate a business." His dark, handsome features twisted with sinister intent. "My first desire was to kill as many white masters as I could find."

"What did you do?" Jacinta questioned, her face radiating interest as she followed his story.

Taurus grinned, revealing double dimples and the whitest teeth. "Thankfully good sense, a better idea and the encouragement of friends prevailed," he told her, then smiled at Solomon.

"A black man in complete ownership of a business is a rarity where I come from," Jacinta shared, setting aside her porcelain cup and saucer. "If a master discovered his slave even possessed aspirations of such a goal it could mean his or her death. They make their living by their wits, using whatever *free time* they have to rent out their labor and craft products to sell."

"She's right," Solomon agreed, crossing his legs at the ankles while regarding his wife thoughtfully. "But actually, love, entrepreneurship among blacks had existed since the early 1770's. Perhaps earlier. I was always inspired by the black merchant Jean Baptist Du Sable. He established the first settlement in Chicago around that time."

"In truth, Jacinta, black people have prospered in almost every segment of enterprise—construction, transportation, manufacturing, real estate . . ." Monique said.

"*And* publishing," Taurus added, "which brings me back to you," he said, turning to face Jacinta more fully. "We've persuaded you to bring down your journal. Might we persuade you to share a passage?"

Jacinta's lashes fluttered and she visibly cringed at the request.

"Please, Jacinta," Monique urged, her slender fingers curving over the upholstered arms of the chair.

Jacinta looked to Solomon for rescue, but he simply waved his hand towards their hosts. With a grimace, she retrieved the journal from where it was tucked away between her and the chair she occupied. At first, she fidgeted in her seat, while turning to pages in a slow, uncertain manner. Of course, only one passage called to her. She'd known it would be the one to share since Taurus requested the reading earlier that evening. As she scanned the entry, she prayed for courage, which had suddenly deserted her. Then, clearing her throat, she began.

"This entry was recorded by Miss Lula, a slave of the Wallens Plantation. It was written three years ago when

Lula was sixteen. . . . The words are Lula's. A bit of it I've reworded so that it may be better understood by those who cannot comprehend her dialect."

" *'My mother and brother were sold away years back. So far back I can't remember their faces. How can a child forget the face of its mother? In the slave life, though, there are many thoughts to take the place of the vision of a mother's face. I stayed behind on the plantation, raised by another slave family. Even at four, I worked the land like I was a big woman—picking cotton, working in the rice fields . . . fields so sticky in the summer time, you scratching as much as you working. All I wanted to do was take a rest. Once I rested . . . overseer saw me—I don't remember his name—only that he was an old man. So old, I think he might fall off that big horse he ride. Old or not, he had strength of ten men when that lash come down on my legs. After that, I rest when I get back to the cot in my shack. From that day, I was always afraid, workin' hard so I won't get beat like that no more. I think nothin' so bad as that. As I get older, I learn they be worse things . . . going back to the shack after workin' from before daylight 'til after dark sometime . . . still hot and sweaty with rice and grass and mud stickin' to you, feeling ready to fall out right on the ground you so tired. Then, I hear 'em . . . laughin', talkin' foul and lookin' my way. I try to walk fast, but it no use. They grab me—same overseers who spittin' at us, callin' us names and whippin' us like we animals . . . now they kissin' on me, they hands rippin' 'way my dress that already torn. They keep me in the shed, some talkin' and drinkin' while the other ones on top of me, hurtin' me so bad I scream for 'em to stop and get kicked in the head . . . that happen just some days back, Miss Jacinta—could be longer. I ain't sure. All I can think while this bein' done to me, is why? I ask God why He let this happen and when it gone end?'"*

Jacinta closed the journal as gently as she'd opened it. She pressed her lips together, feeling the pressure behind her eyes and knowing a good cry was seconds away. She managed to suppress the urge, however, and fixed her audience with a refreshing look. "My father purchased Lula's freedom. She's now married to a free man, living in Charleston with their three children. She is happy," she added, noticing that the group was still on edge. Monique sat in her chair teary-eyed and upset, while Solomon and Taurus remained stone-faced and silent. After a few moments, Taurus stood.

"Jacinta, if you would do me the great honor of allowing me to read the entire journal, I will guard it with my life," he swore, one hand resting across his wide chest in a gesture of sincerity.

"Yes," she whispered, passing him the book, which he took in both hands and held it as though it were a precious gem.

Taurus nodded, then turned and assisted his wife from her chair. The Mandelas said their goodnights and left the Dikembes alone in the sitting room.

Solomon stood and moved to take a seat in the chair closest to Jacinta. He didn't care for the set look on her lovely face as she stared into the fire. "Will you talk to me?" he asked.

Jacinta smiled and sent her husband a quick, soft glance. "Just a little down spirited, that's all."

"From the passage?"

Jacinta shrugged. "In part. Reading it only makes me wonder what I'm doing here, enjoying lavish dinners and cozy lodgings when there are children being ripped from their families . . . and worse."

Solomon flexed his fingers and then clenched them into a fist. He shared his wife's feelings, but knew it would do her no good to dwell upon them. "I suppose I'll have to lift your spirits, then," he teased.

Jacinta appeared skeptical. "It would take quite a feat to accomplish that tonight, I'm afraid."

"Well, why don't you leave that concern to me, hmm?" he spoke in a raspy whisper, his seductive eyes caressing her face with unmasked appreciation.

Jacinta tugged her bottom lip between her teeth when Solomon stood to gather her in his embrace. They left the sitting room. Solomon crossed the lower level to the staircase. No words were spoken as they journeyed through the quiet, candlelit house. Jacinta wound her arms about her husband's neck and rested her head against his chest.

Inside their guest room, Solomon bypassed the bed and carried Jacinta to one of the massive red velvet armchairs before the fire. He ignored her look of confusion, which faded to one of desire when he began to disrobe. Jacinta gasped as more of his magnificent form was revealed to her view.

The orange glow of the firelight enhanced the chiseled beauty of his vanilla toned body. Jacinta felt her fingers curving into the chair's cushioned seat, her lips parted as she unconsciously beckoned his kiss. Solomon pulled her from the chair and took her place there. Jacinta found herself seated astride his lap, her frilly under things doing nothing to diminish the rigid, delicious feel of his arousal pressing against her.

Solomon's entrancing black stare slid past his wife's lovely dark face and lower. His big hands curved around her breasts, outlined so prominently against the bodice of her gown. Jacinta's excitement had caused her nipples to harden, forming the most adorable impressions against the material of her dress. Slowly, his thumbs began to manipulate the tiny jewels until Jacinta moaned and her head fell back amidst swirls of sensation. He teased her unrelentingly, taking great pleasure in seeing passionate delight softening her features.

Soon, Solomon craved something more satisfying. He began to tug at the fat ties securing the front of the gown. Deftly, his fingers released the black strings from their criss-crossed positions. At last, the material slackened and he peeled it away.

"What is it?" Jacinta queried in breathless fashion when she noticed him grimacing.

Solomon's eyes were narrowed. "All this damned clothing," he muttered, dexterously unbuttoning the chemise she wore beneath her dress. Finally, he grunted and made her stand before him. "Take this off," he commanded quietly.

Jacinta complied, completing the task of loosening the ties and letting the long rope fall to the rose-colored rug beneath her feet. In one movement, she freed herself from the dress, allowing it to meet the same fate as the rope tie. Solomon's intense stare unnerved her so, at first, she could barely look his way. As more of her clothing hit the floor, however, she grew increasingly confident. The helpless, wanting look in his sweet dark eyes aroused her more than any touch.

Solomon's lashes fluttered as his loins tightened to an almost painful state. Jacinta had absolutely no idea how her disrobing was affecting him. He could do nothing more than watch and feel his manhood lengthen and swell with every part of her body that was revealed.

Jacinta stood nude before her husband and slowly removed each pin from her hair until the mass fell to her waist in a hoard of thick, black curls. Stepping from the pool of material, she reclaimed her position astride his lap. Solomon's hands hung limply past the arms of the chair. He appeared exhausted as though he were already spent from the exertions of lovemaking. Therefore, Jacinta decided to take it upon herself and assume the lead. She knew it would be a task she would definitely enjoy.

She began to lavish him with kisses to his cheeks and the curve of his hard jaw. Her nipples grazed his sleek, hard chest and she gasped at the delicious friction the act provided. Solomon jerked in reaction to the touch and she smiled. Her hair provided a lover's curtain when she slanted her mouth across his and teased him with quick pecks. Her lips journeyed lower nipping and stroking his neck. Her slender fingers toyed with his male nipples, torturing him as he had done to her only moments before.

"Jacinta—"

"Shh . . ." she urged, knowing he was tortured by passion when she positioned her femininity against the tip of his maleness. She cupped his handsome face in her hands and kissed him long and deep. Her tongue stroked his wantonly, suckling and dueling as she sheltered more of his stiff length inside her body.

"Dammit . . ." he growled, his large hands tightening about her waist to hasten the process.

"No . . ." she pleaded, folding her smaller hands over his. Once his grip loosened, she took in more of his throbbing sex as a reward.

When, at last, she was securely impaled upon the iron organ, Solomon's hands tightened once more. He squeezed his eyes shut, wincing amidst the pleasure of being sheathed within the creamy walls of her love. Jacinta's gasps mingled with soft, throaty sounds. A roguish smile added a devilish element to Solomon's magnificent looks as he relished the sound of the purely feminine cries filling his ears.

Jacinta tossed her head back, threading her fingers through her hair. The movement thrust her breasts proudly before her husband. Solomon accepted the gift, outlining the dark mocha globes with his nose, then his mouth. His lips fastened onto a rigid peak and he alternated between gently pinching the nipple with his perfect teeth and comforting it with his tongue.

Jacinta fastened her teeth around her bottom lip in an attempt to stifle the cries which threatened to become screams. Her hands folded over the high back of the chair as she moved up and down Solomon's unyielding length. They spoke in whispers, words of desire and need. Their movements gained intensity and heat, before they simultaneously collapsed exhausted and content.

Later that night, Solomon enfolded his wife in a protective embrace as they shared the warmth of the huge bed across the room from the fire that still raged. They spoke in whispers and were more relaxed than in all the time they had known one another. It was then that Jacinta felt at ease enough to ask Solomon about his upbringing. He was candid in his remarks, yet surprised that he was not angered as he recalled his childhood.

"My mother and I were truly blessed," he acknowledged, toying with a lock of Jacinta's hair that lay across his chest as he spoke. "We were taken in by a family who truly wanted to care for and love us. I never knew my father, but I believe he did love my mother if the way his family treated us was any indication. I had the finest of everything," he shared, his gaze suddenly turning guarded. "Unfortunately, with all the blessings or, as I later came to call them, trappings, I found that my people, the people of my black heritage, hated me."

Jacinta winced as she reached up in an attempt to smooth the furrows of dismay from his brow.

". . . I remember as a child being given a mud bath. This was done in an attempt to make me black," he explained, with a rueful smile that provided him with a sinister look against the firelight. "Then, to 'turn me white' again, the children washed me in the river. I almost drowned," he said, sighing heavily as he looked toward the ceiling. "The adults weren't any better. I can't recount the things that were said about my mother with regards to her relationship with my father. So many cruelties . . . all at the hands of the people I loved and most wanted to identify with."

Jacinta listened. All the while, her heart ached at the pain so evident in Solomon's raspy voice.

"Couldn't they see that, Jacinta?" he asked, his soulful dark eyes glistening in the firelight while he looked at her. "Couldn't they see that my skin was only white on the outside? That inside my blood pulsed with the same yearnings for freedom and equality that theirs did?"

"Solomon, shh . . . shh . . ." Jacinta soothed, covering his face with showers of kisses as she hugged him tight. "But look at you now," she commanded, lying completely across him in order to look deep into his eyes, "you've accomplished so much for yourself. You've not only employed your people, you've given them freedom. *That* I've seen with my own eyes."

Solomon attempted to smile, but only succeeded in producing a weary glare. "And as incredible as all that felt, being down there only reminded me of earlier times."

Jacinta bowed her head, squeezing her eyes shut against the tears pressuring them. She realized then, what her cruel words and suspicions had put him through, and she hated herself for it. Leaning closer, she nuzzled her face into his neck. "I am so very sorry. I love you, and I should never have put you through that."

Solomon's hands tightened around her upper arms and he forced her back a bit. "What did you say?" he whispered, his ruggedly beautiful face a picture of curiosity.

Jacinta searched his eyes with her own. "I love you."

Solomon was speechless, only able to watch her in disbelief. "I've loved you for a very long time," she went on. "At first, I believed it was because you'd made me feel things I'd never felt before. Then, I realized it was simply because of *you* and the beautiful things—things I wouldn't allow myself to dwell upon—that filled my mind when you were near."

"Why didn't you—"

"Tell you then?" she asked, smiling and shaking her head. "I knew that would've given you a power over me that I didn't want you to have."

Solomon laughed then. "We are too much alike, you and I. I'm guilty of doing the very same thing."

Jacinta's sweet chocolate gaze widened. "Then you—"

"I love you. I believe I did from the moment I knocked that cap from your head when you were leaving that meeting near the Santee."

"Since then?" Jacinta breathed, gasping when he pulled her impossibly closer.

"Since then," he confirmed, "I love you," he spoke against her mouth.

They made love until the early hours of the morning.

CHAPTER 18

The Dikembes and the Mandelas got a late start the next day. The group set out for a tour of Taurus's news house, the *Obsidian Beacon*. Jacinta was like a giddy child as her vibrant brown gaze absorbed the sights of the breathtaking city.

"You own this entire building?" Jacinta breathed, when the carriage drew to a halt before a tall, brick establishment.

"Every corner, I'm proud to say," Taurus boasted as he jumped to the ground and reached up to escort his wife.

"I know so many who could thrive in their own businesses back home. If only they realized the true value of their services," Jacinta was saying as Solomon assisted her from the carriage.

Taurus kept a protective arm about Monique's waist as they crossed the sidewalk to the double cherry wood doors. "I think they are aware of it. I doubt they'd even have the desire to rent out their services if they didn't have some inkling about how valuable they were. It's just as you said last evening about slaves living by their wits. It's the same, dealing with the whites here, especially in relation to business. To be *very* successful one must be shrewd and a bit ruthless when it comes to maneuvering around the restrictions set to keep black entrepreneurs in their place."

Jacinta fixed Taurus with a sly grin. "And would you care to share your maneuverings?" she asked, drawing laughter from the group.

Taurus tugged on the lapels of his mushroom-colored suit coat. "Well, because my business is news and information, I want to be as visible as possible. Of course, there are those stories many don't want me to print. They discuss the delicate sensitivities of those in the North," he explained, as they stepped onto the main level of the paper. "You're right, Jacinta, to question the northern views of slavery. There are those who believe such hardships couldn't possibly exist. After all, many of them keep slaves whom they treat almost like members of the family. Hell, in many cases they *are* members of the family!"

"What sort of writings do you publish?" Jacinta asked when the laughter over Taurus's previous statement had quieted.

"Pertinent matters of the day," he shared as they headed towards a winding iron stairwell situated in the middle of the floor. "Elections, taxes, crime; however, our main focus is the institution of slavery and its abolishment. But we also speak of the accomplishments our people are making in education, medicine and entrepreneurship."

"I had no idea such accomplishments would be numerous enough to fill the pages of an entire publication," Jacinta admitted, her eyes riveted to the imposing printing presses, stacks of paper and other machinery that filled almost every area of the establishment.

The group talked and toured until they arrived at Taurus's office. There, Jacinta was introduced to members of the staff. Jacinta was stunned to see a white man in Taurus's employ. They spent another hour touring the paper, until Taurus announced that lunch had been provided on the first floor. The group became better acquainted over a spread of sautéed shrimp and scallions on a bed of rice, hot moist cornmeal bread and white wine. Jacinta was having a fine time until Taurus made mention of her work and, to her further dismay, produced her journal. He began to read from a passage from Jore Sula that had been recorded during his stay at McIver Estate. Jacinta placed her napkin upon the table and covertly observed her lunch partners as they listened to the reading.

" '. . .*the meeting went on longer that we all expected. I knew I be in a mess of pain if Mistuh Wallens find out where I been. I don't care 'cause this important work we be doin'. This rebellion can change things for us. For all us. I think they knew I was gone 'cause they be waitin' for me when I come through the back gate. It hardly used, mostly hid by grass and bushes most us who work the land think ol' Wallens forget it be there. He ain't forget . . . ol' man probably left it like that hopin' somebody be fool enough to try it. They grab me and take me to one of the barns. Soon as my hands tied, they starts whippin'. I ain't neva been beat before, and the pain like none I ever feel. I just wanted to sleep and forget the pain. My eyes keep closin' and they keeps on whippin'. Later I feel them untie me and put me in a wagon. I hear Mistuh Wallens say the Work House, and I know I be a dead man. But sometime later, I wake up alive*

*as I ever been. I'm at the Work House and they beatin' me
again. That lash come down on skin already sliced and
bleedin'. But you know what, Jaci? Through all that I'm content. I hardly cry out—maybe that why Massa Chuck send
me to the Work House. I don't cry out, 'cause all I think of
be Mister Vesey and this great day he promisin'. The day
when we have our justice—have our freedom.'"*

Taurus closed the journal and gave it a reverent shake.
"Who can tell me this work doesn't deseve to be read by
the masses?" he challenged.

"Extraordinary," Cullen McCortle, the only white
person at the table said.

Taurus grinned at his editor. "My sentiments exactly."

"You can't be serious?" Jacinta breathed, nervously
fidgeting with the lace cuffs of her green woolen dress.

"Mrs. Dikembe, Cullen's right," Sherman Moser, the
Beacon's managing editor interjected. "This is extraordinary work. To publish it would bring great awareness and
a truer sense of the horrors of this abomination."

"Jacinta," Taurus called, leaning across the table, "you
cannot tell me you've never thought of having others see
your writings?"

Jacinta rolled her eyes toward Monique. "Has he
always been so persistent?" she asked.

Monique shook her head. "Always . . ."

At last, Jacinta looked toward Solomon. She prayed
her husband would give her just a hint of his feelings.
When he nodded, Jacinta smiled, shivering with the
warmth that suddenly surged up her spine. Finally, she

turned back to the dark, imposing man to her left. "I accept," she announced, raising her hand when Taurus and his staff expressed their satisfaction. "You must promise that there will be no mention of Mister Vesey or the rebellion. I completely support him, and I'd not want to betray him because my work happened to be read by the *wrong* eyes."

Taurus nodded. "Any changes made to any of the passages will be by your hand only. The paper is published bi-weekly, and all we ask is that you write introductions for each piece, telling our readers a little about the person you're recording and so forth."

"Agreed," Jacinta said, laughing when Taurus extended his hand for her to shake. She felt as though her head was spinning out of control and it was a wonderful feeling.

The next few weeks were very busy. Jacinta found that her words flowed so freely until she had a commitment to fill. She could see the words so clearly in her mind, but when the pen was poised for writing, nothing would come.

Of course, that wasn't completely true, she admitted only to herself. The melancholy she'd been experiencing had finally begun to affect her work.

Solomon entered the bedchamber to find his wife staring out at the late evening skies. The stately, cobblestone streets, lined with expertly manicured trees, handsome carriages and majestic buildings, provided a breathtaking scene beneath the orange, purple and bluish hues of the city. Still, Solomon knew the view had nothing to do with his wife's set expression.

Jacinta smiled when she felt her husband's arms encircle her waist like steel bands. She savored the closeness, resting back against his hard chest and allowing herself to be lulled by the strong beat of his heart.

"Tell me what's wrong?" Solomon asked, cuddling her close as he pressed his face into her neck.

Jacinta closed her eyes for a moment. "So many stories . . ." she sighed, letting her gaze rest upon the desk in the corner. "I've recorded so many and felt truly fulfilled in doing so."

"But?"

"But . . . I—I guess I'm now realizing that I've yet to record my own."

"Well, love, you have to admit your life has been quite different from those that you've written about."

"But the things I've seen," she stressed, curling one hand into a fist. "And I've seen both sides of it. As a child growing up, things have often become confusing. Listening to you speak the other night about your childhood . . . I realized that I've not only seen and experienced hatred from whites toward blacks but hatred from blacks towards other blacks. Those are feelings that should be exposed." She felt cold penetrate the luxurious folds of the heavy deep purple dressing gown she wore. "If we can't love ourselves, then what is the point of it all, Solomon?"

Solomon's long brows drew close as he held Jacinta more tightly. "Are we speaking of the rebellion?" he asked, reluctant to breach the subject but knowing he had to.

Jacinta nodded against his chest. "I can't believe it's not a cause every person of color would seek to be part of. But I've heard the talk, and I know there are those who root for Mister Vesey's failure. It wouldn't surprise me in the least if those very people betrayed him to those who hold so many of us enslaved."

Solomon understood and agreed with her point. But, at the moment, he was concerned by other things. He didn't care for the weary look around her eyes or the grim set of her mouth.

"Listen to me," he said, turning her around to face him. "Why not put work aside for the night and come to bed?" he proposed.

Jacinta didn't need much coaxing and did as her husband suggested. She was nude beneath the robe. It was a custom she had taken to weeks earlier. Feeling the crisp linens directly against her skin was a most intoxicating sensation.

Solomon couldn't have been more pleased. He remained clothed, helping Jacinta into bed, where he directed her to lie on her stomach. He brought his hands down on her body and began to press and rotate his fingers into her skin.

"Mmm . . . Solomon . . . what is this? What are you doing?"

"Shh . . . clear your mind. This is a massage."

"Mmm," Jacinta moaned, her eyes closed against the exquisite sensations. She could feel every single one of his fingers stroking away the tension in her neck, shoulders and back. When his thumbs focused on soothing the small of her back, her entire body weakened. "Massage," she purred. "I'd like very much for you to do this to me again," she requested lazily.

A slow smile intensified Solomon's devastating features. "I think that can be arranged."

"Mmm . . ." Jacinta moaned again. The promise added to the erotic delight of the massage. She was so completely relaxed that she melted into a deep sleep.

March 1822

Incredibly, over a month had passed since the Dikembes arrived in New York. Jacinta's creative juices had been restored and she completed the introductory writings to her book of recordings. It pleased her to know that her talent for writing lay not only in copying the words of others, but for creating her own original thoughts. This pleased her so, unknown to anyone else, she began to record her own writings into a work she had tentatively entitled *Insights From A Free Black Woman of the South.*

Of course, working on such a task made her miss home all the more. She commanded herself not to speak a word of such longings to Solomon. Since their first night in New York things had continued to progress so beautifully for them. Words of love rolled from their tongues so sweet and free. Jacinta never dreamed she would come to feel so deeply for any man.

Taurus and Monique organized a party to call attention to the paper's newest feature. Friends of many races flocked to the Mandela's home one brisk March evening for a night of eating, drinking, dancing and enlightenment. The place was vibrant with conversation flowing from some of the city's most noted scholars to those who earned their living in more humble, yet equally respected, positions as chefs and landscapers. Also in attendance was the noted boxer Tom Molineaux. Molineaux, a former Virginia slave, had earned his freedom by triumphing over other slave boxers, which resulted in his former owner's great profit. Most recently the famed pugilist had fought English champion Tom Cribb. Though Molineaux lost the England fight in round thirty-three of a controversial decision, he was still considered a 'champ' amongst his people and much of the general population.

"How do you feel?" Solomon asked, as he twirled his wife around the crowded dance floor.

Jacinta shrugged and smiled her contentment. "At this moment, quite pleased," she sighed.

Solomon chuckled. "I have no trouble believing that. You're in some very fine company tonight, Mrs. Dikembe. Educators, doctors, lawyers—"

"A famed boxer," Jacinta added. In truth, she'd been more impressed meeting Tom Molineaux than any of the other distinguished guests.

Solomon's laughter continued. "This is true, but you're still the toast of the evening," he pointed out.

Jacinta's expression harbored a twinge of uncertainty. "I still can't believe there's been so much fuss all due to the writings of a sheltered girl."

"A sheltered, yet insightful, woman," Solomon corrected, his face carrying a look mixed with firmness and love. "A woman with a sense of obligation to her people," he added.

Jacinta smiled, her fingers curving around the crisp, high collar of the stark white shirt worn beneath a worsted black three-quarter length coat. "Do you ever run out of such delightful things to say?" She stood on her toes and spoke against his mouth.

Solomon dropped a kiss to her nose. "Not when I have you as my inspiration," he whispered.

Somewhere in the distance, a glass clinked over the talkative crowd. A call was made for everyone's attention. Even the soothing, delicate melodies from the string quartet, had silenced.

Taurus Mandela stood at the front of the ballroom with his wife by his side. "Several weeks ago, Monique and I had the pleasure of meeting a young woman. She is the wife of our dearest friend, but in time she became more than that. We realized she was not only a compassionate and courageous person, but also a gifted writer. Her work, both important and beautiful, focuses on a topic we are all aware of—slavery. A topic we all hope to live to see the end of. For this reason, I decided to include an insertion of her writings into each edition of the *Obsidian Beacon*. Now I would like to introduce to you the extraordinary young woman who has made this possible. Friends, Mrs Jacinta McIver Dikembe!"

Her stomach suddenly swimming in a sea of nerves, Jacinta clutched Solomon's hand. Her smile appeared when he started to escort her through the crowd. Once on the makeshift stage alongside Taurus and Monique, Jacinta stood smiling out at the crowd, who applauded her rigorously.

"Jacinta, if you would honor us with a reading," Taurus urged, already handing her the familiar brown leather journal.

Jacinta cleared her throat and chose the passage from Nambia Sula. The recording from the slave and grandmother continued for at least five pages. Jacinta read with such passion that the already potent words seemed to intensify with every syllable that was uttered. The crowd was entranced. Once the reading had concluded, the guests resumed their rigorous applause and cheered for more.

"I'm afraid you all will have to wait for the next edition of the *Obsidian!*" Taurus called playfully. Someone booed his decision, and laughter ignited.

Jacinta beamed from pride and happiness as she maintained her place on stage. Again, she reached for Solomon's hand and snuggled against him when he pulled her close.

Later that evening, Jacinta felt a little less on edge having been so well received by the crowd of learned scholars, businessmen and abolitionists. She mingled, joining several conversations, and was even asked to sign autographs.

"Charleston is such an extraordinary city," said Louise Portman, wife of Gerald Portman the *Beacon's* printer. "One would never believe such a beautiful place could mask such evils."

"I'm afraid it does," Jacinta confirmed, unable to hide the sorrow in her tone. "Unfortunately those evils increase by the day."

"I've heard the black population outnumbers the white by well over fifty percent," Abner Moss, a local attorney mentioned. "You would think the people would have rebelled several times by now."

"And won," Gordon Finch, Abner's partner, added.

"The people are becoming more aware of the power they wield each day," Jacinta shared, taking great care in the manner she phrased her words.

"Could we expect recordings from you should such a revolt ever take place?" Louise Portman teased.

"You most certainly could," Jacinta vowed in her own teasing tone, though her decision was quite serious.

Solomon approached the small group as Jacinta was speaking. At first, he barely paid attention. He was focused on the enjoyable sight of his wife as she spoke and moved in the mocha colored satin dress with its high collar and low-cut bodice. The gown had teased his senses from the moment he'd watched her don it earlier that evening.

Slowly, however, his relaxed expression turned fierce when he overheard his wife speak of returning home to record the events of the revolt (should there ever be one). Without a care for the surprised looks he received, he caught Jacinta's upper arm in his steely grasp and led her out of the party.

"What are you doing?" Jacinta snarled, through clenched teeth. "Solomon!" she called, trying to produce a tight smile on her lips. "Dammit!" she hissed, making a move to wrench her arm from his grip without alerting the onlookers that there was any sort of problem.

Solomon was unresponsive as he led the way to a deserted sitting room at the back of the house.

"You are such a fool!" he scolded, his magnificent features twisted with sinister intensity. "Speaking of this rebellion—"

"Oh, that?" Jacinta interrupted with an airy wave. "Sweetheart, I didn't tell them anything that could have been used against Mister Vesey. As far as they are concerned, the rebellion is an event they've concocted in their own minds."

Solomon massaged his neck, hoping to dispel the tension gathered there lest he completely lose his temper. It didn't work. "As I said, 'a fool'. Listen to me *clearly*, wife. You are to forget this nonsense about returning to 'take part' in that rebellion. Is that understood?"

"No, it is not," she retorted, easing out from the small space Solomon had backed her into. "Should this rebellion take place, you couldn't possibly expect me to stay away and—"

"That is exactly what I expect."

"You have no right to—"

"I have every right!"

Stomping her foot, Jacinta fixed him with her harshest glare. "I suppose I was right all along. You can't possibly understand how important this is."

Solomon pulled her back to face him. "I understand all too well, but it's not important enough for me to risk losing you."

"But I have no intention to fight."

Solomon rolled his eyes at the naïve argument and turned away. "I'm done debating this with you."

Jacinta boldly stepped before him. "You can't just decide the end of the conversation. I'm your wife, Dikembe, not your slave."

"Your involvement down there is out of the question," he whispered, bringing his face very close to hers. "If you continue to press the issue, I'll see that you never return home."

"Bastard," she gasped, the word barely audible because she was so breathless with anger.

Solomon sent her a lazy smirk and rose to his full height. "You've called me worse."

"Dammit, why are you doing this?" she cried, hating the helplessness coloring her words.

Solomon's glare bore deeply into her lush brown eyes and he ordered himself not to be swayed by their allure. "You are my wife," his raspy voice grated in a deep pensive tone. "Your place is with me in my home, occupying yourself with the duties of a wife, and you will damn well tend to every one of your responsibilities. Is that clear?"

Jacinta's anger would not allow her to submit. "My responsibilities are—"

"With me, and since you're having such difficulty understanding that, it's time we get the hell out of here."

Jacinta cursed the tears streaming down her face as she slapped them away. "You can't treat me like this, dammit!"

Solomon took both her upper arms in a none-too-gentle hold. "I'll do what is necessary to keep you safe," he breathed, keeping her stationary before him.

"And you believe that keeping me away from the South is best because you believe this is a southern issue," Jacinta spoke in a surprisingly calm manner, her expressive gaze searching her husband's face. "I don't know what will become of Mister Vesey's rebellion, Solomon. I do know that the day will come when everyone in this nation will have to choose a side and fight. If not for freedom, then for their way of life. The horror of slavery will not last. The God I believe in wouldn't permit such an evil to prevail forever," she vowed, glancing down at his hands covering her arms. "Now, if you've finished with me, I should like to return to the party your friends have been so kind to give in my honor." With that said, she waited. Once Solomon released her, she left him with a curt nod, turned and strolled out of the moonlit room. The graceful folds of her skirt sashayed behind her.

Solomon's anger diminished and he couldn't help but smile and shake his head. The courageous beauty leaving the room possessed ability unlike any other woman he had ever known: the ability to captivate him with both her body and her mind.

CHAPTER 19

March 1822

Solomon and Jacinta left New York and began their journey home to the Michigan Territory. From New York, they journeyed by covered wagon and boarded a ship just outside the town of Cheektowaga, New York. With such a lengthy trip ahead, Jacinta spent a great deal of time working on her book of thoughts and studying the beautiful land she traveled. The ship docked every other evening, and Jacinta was amazed to discover how many people knew her husband. She was even more amazed by the amount of land he had acquired at such a young age.

One evening they made port and traveled to what appeared to be a huge farm positioned just outside the town of Toledo, Ohio.

"Monro and Agnes Duley, my wife, Jacinta Dikembe."

"A pleasure to meet you! She a right pretty thing, Mister Sol," Monro commented slyly.

Jacinta laughed, while shaking hands with the short, stocky couple.

"Welcome to our home, Missus Dikembe," Agnes Duley greeted, clasping one of Jacinta's slender hands in both her chubby ones.

"Please call me Jacinta," she urged, her almond brown stare riveted on the stunning view of the setting sun. "This is a truly beautiful home you have," she breathed, mesmerized by the view.

Monro grinned, his pride very evident. "We have Mister Solomon to thank for that. He give us a home deeded to us and a future when all we could think 'bout was livin' to see 'nother day under the overseer whip."

Jacinta's attention was drawn to her husband then. "Yes, he is quite a man," she agreed softly, smiling when he cast his gaze to the ground as though her words embarrassed him. In truth, Jacinta believed she would only continue to be astonished by the gestures of the man she'd married. Not only had he provided numerous slaves with the chance to earn a safe, honest living, but he presented them with opportunities to purchase the property they settled and become landowners. The group spoke for only a short while longer. Then, while dinner was being completed and the ship was being cared for, Jacinta took advantage of the quiet and strolled the gorgeous landscape.

Solomon offered to assist Monro and his men with the horses and enjoyed a bit more time chatting with his old friend. Afterwards, he went to find Jacinta. His easy expression harbored concern when he found her on a remote stretch of the property that offered the most spectacular view of the river and setting sun. On silent steps, he headed over.

"I love you," he murmured against her ear, his arms slipping about her waist.

Jacinta smiled and settled back as though she'd been expecting his company. "It's so amazing, so beautiful," she raved, her eyes riveted on the sun setting against an orange, purple and blue-streaked sky. "Do you own very many places like it?" she asked.

Solomon shrugged, more intrigued by the pulse beating below her earlobe than the incredible vision of the setting sun. "Perhaps. I scarcely pay attention to the view when deciding on a land purchase."

"Yet here it is," Jacinta sighed, her gaze hooded as complete contentment showered her. "So many admirable things you've done for the people, but especially in allowing them to own a part of something so incredible, something they probably never dreamed of."

"I've been acquiring land since seventeen. That's when I first realized its worth." He cast his eyes toward the horizon. "When I understood the power it wielded and what that power would allow me to do for those in bondage . . . there was no swaying my dedication to see it happen, and there's still much left to do."

"You're a man of many surprises, Solomon Dikembe," Jacinta praised. The magenta folds of her skirts rustled when she turned in his arms. "I find that very appealing." Her eyes lowered to his mouth, then back up to his probing black stare.

Solomon captured her parted lips in the sweetest kiss. His big hands delved into the loosened, fragrant locks of her hair. Jacinta gasped when he cupped her breasts in a fleeting manner, before moving on to massage her back with achingly delicious strokes. Their tongues taunted and teased amidst hushed words of desire. The sensual interlude lasted only a few moments past sunset. Then, hand in hand, they practically floated back to the main house.

After a few days, the caravan set off. Their next stop was the town of Sibley in the lower region of the Michigan territory. Jacinta's smoky stare narrowed out of sheer awe at the glorious stretch of land before her eyes. If possible, the area was even more breathtaking than the previous property they'd visited.

"Solomon? Is that?"

"Hmm?"

"Can't be . . ." Jacinta whispered, knowing she had to be mistaken by what she saw.

Solomon pretended to be engrossed with the news journal he read. "What is it, love?" he inquired absently.

Slowly, Jacinta's confusion cleared, taking on a more curious gleam. How could anyone there be even remotely familiar? she asked herself, tilting her head as one of the figures in the yard ventured closer to the carriage.

"Zambi?" Jacinta whispered, happiness illuminating her face when she raced out of the carriage to embrace her dearest friend.

"Is this real?" Jacinta cried, hugging Jore Sula and his sister at once. "What are you doing here? How—"

"Jaci, you knew Mister Solomon was takin' us away," Jore said.

"But I had no idea . . . we are in Michigan, correct?" she asked, looking back at Solomon, who nodded. "And you all are so close!" Tears of delight streamed down her dark face. "This is wonderful!" She hugged the elder Sulas when they joined the reunion. Questions abounded, and more hugs were in order as the rest of the family came to greet the new arrivers.

"Why didn't you tell me you were having the Sulas taken to Michigan?" Jacinta asked Solomon later, when some of the excitement had died down.

Solomon folded his arms across the white linen shirt he wore and continued to rock the chair he occupied on the Sulas' front porch. "I wanted to surprise you," he finally revealed.

Jacinta's mouth curved upwards into a knowing smirk. "I would have come along more willingly had I known they were here."

"I know."

"Then why didn't you tell me?" she persisted, propping her hands on her hips.

"One reason was because I wanted to know that you were happy to be here because of me—not for the promise of being reunited with lost friends," he admitted, his dark eyes raking her curvaceous figure, which was encased in a black button-down riding dress. "My other reason was because you are my wife and I want to spend my life making you happy. I knew seeing the Sulas would do that."

"Solomon . . ." Jacinta murmured affectionately. She took his hand when he extended it.

"And this is truly their home? They own it?" she questioned, once securely seated on his lap.

"They own every acre."

"But how? They had nothing."

"They had a determination for a better life. Besides, Mister Sula and his brothers are determined to cultivate this land for produce and livestock. I'll have all the beef and corn I can tolerate for the rest of my life!" he raved, drawing Jacinta's laughter.

The dinner bell sounded before their closeness could result in a kiss.

Dinner was a spectacular gathering. Zambia admitted the family had been anticipating Solomon and Jacinta's arrival. The incredible meal consisted of sweet golden cornbread, seasoned chicken and roasted beef prepared in the kitchen's stone hearth, fresh greens, stewed potatoes and onions topped off with a delicious peach pie. Jacinta felt the pressure of tears behind her eyes many times as the evening progressed. Such a spread would have been unthinkable during the Sulas life on Wallens Plantation. Now, the family had a beautiful warm spacious home and enough food for the entire Sula clan. They had been blessed beyond their wildest hopes and thanked God each day for changing their status in life.

Of course the loveliness of the evening brought on hearty conversation. Talk of the rebellion soon rose, and the Sula men were especially eager to hear all news regarding Denmark Vesey's progress. The conversation lasted quite a while. Jacinta gave her thoughts on the subject, though her husband did much of the talking.

Surprised, Solomon noticed his wife wasn't full of her usual conversation.

"You our first guest, Jaci, and we gone treat you as such. Now git. We call you for dessert directly."

Jacinta laughed at the order voiced by Mirinda Sula, wife to one of Mingo Sula's brothers. Jacinta did as she was told and left the rest of the Sula women to clear the dishes from the long, pine wood table. She contented herself in the sitting room just off from the dining room. There, she stood warming her hands before the fierce fire that raged in the brick hearth. Solomon found his wife and studied her stance with concern. Then he clapped his hands and walked on into the room.

"Smells good in there!"

Jacinta smiled at the sound of her husband's voice. "Miss Nambia makes the best peach pie. I can't wait for them to call us back for dessert."

"Thinking about dessert," Solomon sighed, easing his arms about her waist, "is that why you're in such a quiet mood?"

Jacinta frowned. "Am I? I hadn't noticed."

"You barely said a thing while your favorite topic was being discussed," he said with a shrug. "Talk of the rebellion always draws your fire."

Jacinta shook her head against Solomon's chest. "It's been a long day. I suppose I'm just not in the mood for conversation."

"Mmm . . ."

"Solomon Dikembe," Jacinta drawled, turning in her husband's arms as she laughed and fixed him with a playful glare. "This I can't believe. You're on edge whether I participate in conversation about the rebellion or not."

Solomon nodded, accepting her soft ridicule. "So are you up for more socializing?" he finally asked, his bottomless stare unwavering as he watched her.

Jacinta was happy that he'd read her thoughts. "Do you suppose there will be any of Miss Nambia's pie left in the morn?"

Solomon chuckled. "We can request she save a few slices for us," he teased, pulling her into a tight embrace.

Their goodnights said, the Dikembes headed upstairs arm in arm as they ascended the wide majestic staircase.

Inside their warm, isolated bedchamber, Jacinta began to disrobe, having no regard for the heated stare that followed her every move. When she was in her shift and reaching for her gown, she was scooped into an ironclad embrace.

"Dikembe, what are you up to?" she drawled, her mouth curved into a sensual smile.

"Time to work off some of the tension from the trip," he explained, his long strides covering the distance to the bed.

Jacinta snuggled deeper into the embrace. "But our trip isn't over," she reminded him in a sly tone.

"All the more reason to work off some tension."

"Ah I see . . . and am I work to you?"

"Work of the most satisfying sort," he clarified, his mouth trailing her temple as he laid her down.

After several weeks of travel, the caravan finally arrived in the town of Oakwood. They traveled from the Sula's home near Sibley to Oakwood by way of covered wagon. Nearly everyone, including the horses, felt the weight of the strenuous journey.

Jacinta, however, felt a strange calm and succeeded in completing several pages in her journal of thoughts. Visiting new places and meeting people who had already overcome tremendous obstacles in obtaining and maintaining their freedom filled her with a sense of exhilaration and stimulated her creativity. Unfortunately, so much writing also weighed on her energy. When Jacinta wasn't writing, she slept. The arrival in Oakwood was met with great celebration, as it was also Solomon's first visit in almost a year. Jacinta was introduced to everyone and praised as the woman who had finally claimed the much sought-after title of Solomon Dikembe's wife. Sheba Dikembe was no less excited as she welcomed her son's wife. Jacinta battled between wanting to remain sociable and wanting to fall right into a deep sleep.

"Nonsense, you will most certainly rest before you even consider coming down to visit with anyone."

Jacinta sent a grateful smile toward the beautiful, dark woman who spoke with the authoritative yet kind tone. Sheba Dikembe was as kind as she was regal. Everyone in the Dikembe household, not to mention neighbors and friends to the family, revered her. Her strength and courage proved valuable to all who knew her.

"I should be bursting with energy. I managed to sleep quite a bit on the wagon."

"Wagon, ha!" Sheba retorted with a quick shake of her head. "A young woman traveling such a distance needs her rest. *Proper* rest," she said, fixing her daughter-in-law with a look that oozed motherly wisdom.

Jacinta smiled brightly as thankful for the woman's hospitality as she was for the fact that Sheba was truly a kind wonderful person. "This house is amazing," she noted when they approached a grand staircase carpeted in a rich, deep blue. The oak case spanned two floors before branching off to opposite wings of the house.

"Thank you, love. I think so, too," Sheba reminisced, smiling up in contentment as her dark eyes traced the spectacular chandelier in the high ceiling. "When I was a child I thought the Hamptons house only appeared so huge because I was so small. Now I know that it was as huge as I've always believed it to be. Still, it was surprisingly small compared to all this."

Jacinta joined Sheba in laughter. "I can just imagine Solomon racing through the house as a boy," she confided, her warm gaze observing the colorful tapestries that decorated the walls.

"You love my son very deeply. I can tell," Sheba spoke in a hushed tone, nudging Jacinta's shoulder with her own as they strolled the stairway.

"I never thought I would feel this way about him," Jacinta admitted with a wavering smile. "I did everything to convince Solomon, and myself, that I was very unimpressed by him."

Sheba's laughter was like that of a young girl and mirrored the sparkle in her youthful face. "All women do this. But I think the harder we try to convince ourselves the more we realize this man is the one."

Jacinta studied Sheba closely as though she could see the memories mingled with the words. "Solomon should be happy that his parents were so much in love."

Sheba pulled Jacinta closer as they turned down one of the second story corridors. "We were *very* much in love . . . I'd never felt so alone when Kenneth died."

"But you were fortunate and very blessed to have his family embrace you as they did."

"Yes, and then Solomon came and my life took on new meaning," Sheba spoke in a refreshing tone, before favoring Jacinta with a playful look. "I tried to give him all the things I never had. Unfortunately, a love like what his father and I shared, that I couldn't give. I'm so thankful to you, Jacinta."

"Me?" she spoke in a tiny voice.

When Sheba nodded, the beads wound through the heavy braid that snaked around her head sparkled merrily. "I see a new happiness shining on his face, genuine happiness that can't be obtained from the purchase of a new property or money. He loves you so much, and I am so happy because I believe he is truly loved in return."

"Oh, he is, Miss Sheba. He is. I love him so," Jacinta vowed, her eyes brimming with tears.

"Now, enough of this. Let's get to your room," Sheba decided, squeezing her daughter-in-law's hands before she turned to open the double oak doors.

The room was beautiful and dimly lit by the afternoon sunlight flowing past the wide-paned windows that spanned almost the entire wall of the room. The huge, African print rug in the center of the floor matched the drapes and heavy quilt covering the inviting bed in the corner. A fire had already been started in the stone hearth to ward off the chill the evening promised.

"I'll fetch someone to wake you shortly before dinner," Sheba was saying, then she pressed a kiss to Jacinta's forehead and left the room.

For a few moments, Jacinta enjoyed the sight of the green hills and leafless trees in the distance. Then she yawned, removed her dress and fell, face first, onto the bed.

ঔ৸৹

Solomon found his wife asleep a few hours later. He'd wanted to show her the estate and was hoping she was up from her nap. Of course, the fact that she was still sleeping when he entered the room only left him with the delightful task of waking her.

Jacinta rested on her stomach, and removing her shift took a bit of maneuvering. Solomon handled the duty effortlessly. He removed the garment, along with the frilly underthings she wore beneath.

"Mmm," Jacinta grunted when Solomon pulled the pins from her hair and spread the healthy onyx mass over the pillows.

For a while, he simply enjoyed the sight of her, so unconsciously alluring amidst the tangle of crisp sheets and the quilt. Slowly, his lips trailed her shoulder blades, before his tongue traced the line of her spine. He paid special attention to the small of her back, tonguing the inviting dip in the most possessive manner. His lips caressed the generous swell of her bottom and he smiled when she shifted beneath the quick kisses he dropped across the dark, satiny cheeks.

Jacinta gasped in her sleep when Solomon added his hands to the interlude. They curved around her upper thighs to urge her legs further apart.

"Solomon . . ." Jacinta murmured, still dozing while her husband took advantage of her prone state.

The quick pecks Solomon placed to his wife's bottom became lengthier and more intimate. His nose nuzzled against her femininity and his own sex stiffened to an almost painful state as her scent threatened to drive him mad with desire. His tongue darted out to stroke her womanhood from behind, and then he lunged deeply rotating his tongue inside the moist recesses of her love.

Jacinta's lashes fluttered open and the full force of delicious sensations engulfed her body. "Solomon, what—" she gasped, silencing her questions when his fingers played in the crisp curls at the junction of her thighs before they eased lower to manipulate the silky folds of her anatomy. The delight of the double caress wreaked havoc on Jacinta's ability to breathe.

"What-what are you doing?" she cried into a pillow, having believed Solomon had already introduced her to every form of pleasure imaginable.

"Waking you," he replied, bringing a halt to the scandalous kiss and turning Jacinta onto her back.

"We-we can't," she said, her lashes still fluttering in response to the sensations heating her body. "It's the middle of the afternoon. The house is filled with people."

"And?" Solomon challenged, removing his shirt to toss it to the floor where his coat and boots had already been discarded.

"Solomon—"

"We're married. *Newly* married, at that," Solomon argued, covering her with his body while he unfastened his trousers and kicked them from his long legs. "I stifled my urges enough when I first met you. I'll be damned if I'll be plagued by such torture again," his rough voice grated in her ear, the feel of his breath sending the most wondrous shivers through her body.

Completely nude, Solomon settled his powerfully chiseled form across Jacinta's body. His long lashes closed over his deep-set eyes and he relished the feel of her small, silken form beneath him. His large hands molded and skirted across her as though he were worshipping her. His lips paid homage to the line of her collarbone and neck before his tongue favored the dip of her throat. Jacinta tilted back her head to enjoy more of the touch, but Solomon had moved on. Tiny groans of sensual torture escaped his throat as he was consumed by the feel and scent of her.

Slowly, his tongue glided across the rise of her breasts, then drove into the valley between. Meanwhile, his hands cupped the dark cocoa mounds, his thumbs brushing the nipples until they stood out like tiny gemstones.

Jacinta ached to have him quell the heavy ache forming deep within her, an ache that grew heavier each moment. Solomon, however, was more involved with the sight of his wife as she trembled beneath his touch. His beautiful stare caressed her, reveling in the flawless appearance of her dark skin and incredible hair.

"I love you," he whispered as he settled more snuggly against her.

"I love—" Jacinta's reply caught on a gasp when she felt him inside her body. Her toes curled into the bed coverings and she had never felt so complete.

Solomon was in a state of bliss as well. He could feel every nuance of Jacinta's femininity as she gripped and released his rigid length. He thrust slowly, hoping to extend the indescribable pleasure for as long as possible.

"Mmm," Jacinta purred much later. The promise of sleep after such an enjoyable love session brought a smile to her lips. She wanted nothing more than to curl into her husband's arms and doze the rest of the day away.

"No time for sleep, love," Solomon was saying just then, his lips murmuring the phrase against her temple.

"What do you mean?" she asked, barely raising her head from his chest.

Solomon chuckled. "The welcome dinner Mama planned . . ." he reminded her, and turned to gnaw upon her shoulder.

"Oh . . ." Jacinta groaned, closing her eyes as though it pained her to think about it. "Do we have to?"

"No, but the house is going to be filled with people wanting to meet you. I know Mama won't mind if you

329

want to remain here for the night. It was a rather long trip."

"No, no, I can't do that," she sighed, slowly pushing herself up in bed. "She's gone to so much trouble. It would appear ungrateful to turn down such hospitality. "Besides," she whispered, pressing a kiss to the tip of his nose, "I'm eager to meet the people you know."

Solomon watched her closely. "You're certain? I was only teasing, you know. It's fine if you'd rather rest here."

"I'll be all right," she insisted, but glanced back towards the array of pillows tousled against the headboard. "I'll be even better if you tell me we have time for a quick nap before dinner."

"We have time for something better," Solomon spoke in a mysteriously challenging tone.

Jacinta felt her heart race.

"I want to show you the estate, and I won't take no for an answer."

Hoping his idea involved them remaining inside their bedchamber—in bed, preferably—Jacinta sighed. She seriously doubted her legs could withstand a tour of the extensive property. Rather than rouse her husband's concern, though, she nodded in agreement to the tour.

Solomon's home was indeed an exquisite place. Jacinta had first assumed it was where he grew up, but learned it was his own—bought when he'd made a profit from his first land deal. Of course, the fact that he'd been able to afford it at all was due to his affluent background.

"I always felt cursed by the fact that their blood ran through my veins. They loved me unconditionally," he said as they took a walk through the flower garden.

"You loved them, too," Jacinta guessed, her hands clasped behind her back as they strolled.

Solomon shrugged. "They were my family. My only connection to my father. I loved them, but always felt I should hate them," he explained, then shook his head as though the summation was far too complex for anyone to understand. "Finally, I told myself it was their white blood that I hated, not them. Convoluted, perhaps, but it helped me accept things as they were. I suppose those feelings were my first inspiration to use my money to help those less fortunate."

"And now?" Jacinta inquired, tugging on the sleeve of his gray woolen suit coat.

He responded with a half smile. "Now I don't feel cursed, but blessed and with blessings to share."

Jacinta stopped walking and tugged again on Solomon's sleeve to urge him closer. "You're generous and good and intelligent. It's all so very appealing," she murmured, standing on her toes to speak the words against his hard jaw.

"How appealing?" Solomon inquired wickedly, his molten black stare brimmed with desire.

Jacinta answered the question by spreading her hands across his broad chest and pulling him into a kiss. The sultry act weakened her legs while their tongues fought an erotic battle. Her legs were so weakened, she almost dropped to her knees when Solomon released her.

"Whoa," they whispered simultaneously.

"Are you all right?" Solomon asked, searching her face with his eyes.

Jacinta nodded rapidly then began to laugh. Solomon joined her.

"It may be best to save the rest of the tour," he decided, slipping one arm about his wife's minute waist as they headed back toward the house.

The celebration was in progress when the newlyweds arrived in the backyard. There appeared to be scores of people-all eating, dancing and having a grand time. Jacinta had never seen so many black landowners, teachers and other professionals in one place—not even at Taurus and Monique Mandela's posh New York home. It was all quite refreshing and Jacinta believed that evening alone would give her scores of new thoughts to add to her journal. She met a family from Charleston and they spoke of how unchanged things were in the south. Needless to say, the conversation distressed the family greatly. Jacinta couldn't help but inform them of the pending rebellion—after she made sure her husband was nowhere in sight, of course.

"Enjoying yourself?" Solomon asked when they shared a dance sometime later.

Jacinta's brown eyes sparkled as she studied the array of guests waltzing, mingling and laughing. "I am thoroughly enjoying myself. Thank you for not letting me sleep through it."

"But you are all right?" he persisted, a hint of concern dwelling in the depths of his gaze.

"Solomon, for the last time, I'm fine." Jacinta assured him firmly and rolled her eyes. Just then, the exhaustion she wouldn't admit to reasserted itself and she collapsed in her husband's arms.

"Jacinta?" Solomon's voice seemed to echo when the crowd was stunned silent. He appeared as uncertain as a small boy and knelt to lay his unconscious wife to the ground. "Jacinta?" he whispered again, his heart beating in his ears so loudly he couldn't hear his own voice.

Someone had found a doctor and, in moments, Melvin Gill was pushing his way through the crowd. Dr. Gill had received his training under the doctor he'd been sold to as a teenager. He and Solomon became fast friends, as Melvin also knew what it was like to be in the care of whites who wanted to contribute to his success and not to his destruction. Moreover, Melvin knew what it was like to have his own people hate him for it.

"What's happened?" Melvin asked, having knelt alongside Solomon.

Solomon was shaking his head, opening his mouth as though he had some explanation. "I . . ." was all he could manage.

Melvin rubbed his friend's shoulder. "Has this happened before?" he asked, smoothing one hand across Jacinta's wrist to search for a pulse.

Again, Solomon shook his head. "She stumbled . . . earli-earlier. She . . . hasn't had much sleep since the trip began," he slowly confided, watching helplessly as Melvin checked the rate of her pulse.

"Right now I suggest you get her into bed. Her pulse is weak. She's completely exhausted and needs rest with no disturbances," Melvin diagnosed, helping Jacinta into her husband's arms. "I'll arrange to give her a complete examination tomorrow."

Solomon nodded, though his expression was soft and questioning. He felt dazed. He had never seen Jacinta appear so helpless. Silently, he cursed himself for not allowing her more rest.

Solomon wandered in from walking about aimlessly once the party began to thin. In no mood for further socializing, he set out immediately after putting Jacinta to bed.

Sheba was on her way down the opposite end of the corridor, where she'd been seeing off the last of the guests. She saw Solomon and quickly hurried to pull him into a reassuring embrace.

"Come sit," she urged softly, tugging on the gray sleeve of his woolen coat.

Solomon followed his mother to the sitting room like an obedient child. His handsome face reflected a weariness and helplessness simultaneously. Sheba couldn't recall having ever seen her son appear so lost.

"You love her very much," she said to him, smoothing the back of her hand across his square jaw.

Solomon responded with a self-loathing smirk. "I love her so much, I didn't listen when she told me how tired she was. All I could think of was myself and what I wanted."

"Shh . . ." Sheba insisted, pulling him close. "How can you blame yourself for loving her too much to stay away from her?"

"I could have waited. My taking advantage that way had nothing to do with love—only lust."

Sheba pulled back to study her son with amusement lurking in her luminous dark eyes. "To see you so in love with one woman . . . it makes me so very happy. I thought you were doomed to flit carelessly from one adoring set of arms to the next."

Solomon bowed his head to rake all ten fingers through the silky dark waves of his hair. "Aren't I doomed anyway? It can't be healthy to be so far gone over any woman," he looked up at his mother with questioning eyes, "one woman who holds so much of my heart. All of my heart," he admitted.

"It is only unhealthy if you believe she doesn't love you in return. From what I've seen that young woman is just as in love with you as you are with her."

"It's taken us so long to get here," he groaned, "I don't think I could stand knowing her feelings were not as deep."

"Have you any reason to believe that?"

Solomon bowed his head. "No."

Sheba reached out to cup his chin. "Then why torture yourself?"

"I suppose some part of me is still . . ."

"Afraid of being disappointed by someone you feel so strongly for?"

Solomon couldn't prevent a grin from spreading. "Sometimes I wish you did not know me so thoroughly."

Sheba tapped his knee. "But I do, and I also know something else—these are concerns best shared with your wife. Perhaps then you can truly focus on the happiness your future promises."

Solomon nodded and would have said more had it not been for the high-pitched screams which riveted through the house at that moment. He bolted from the settee and raced upstairs with the rest of the house either ahead of him or at his heels.

Solomon found a group gathered outside Jacinta's room door, where the screams had originated. He burst inside, his gaze growing wider and more incredulous at the sight which met his eyes.

Jacinta lay motionless on the floor where she'd collapsed seconds before her husband burst into the room. The bed was tangled, the top sheets stained with streaks of crimson and the bottom sheet was soaked with it. Solomon felt his heart threatening to beat right out of his chest. He could barely move, and it was Sheba who eventually brushed past him to investigate the scene. She hurried over to Jacinta and pressed both hands to her cheeks. Then she looked down and gasped. The lower half of the girl's gown was soaked in blood that still flowed and pooled on the rug beneath.

"Martha, Josie, get a fresh gown and wash towels! Annie, draw me some hot water and lye soap! Get the fire stoked in the next chamber and turn down the bed! Solomon . . . Solomon! Solomon!" she finally bellowed to retrieve her son's attention. "Fetch Doc Gill! Now!"

CHAPTER 20

Jacinta woke the next evening and found it to be a chore to open her eyes. When she did manage to do so, she found Solomon at her bedside. He appeared relaxed in the tanned velvet arm chair he occupied. His coal black gaze, however, was alert and focused on her.

"What is it?" she whispered, frowning at the hollow sound of her voice. "What's the matter?"

"What do you remember?"

Jacinta frowned, thinking her husband's voice sounded even drearier than her own. Her brown eyes narrowed as she struggled to recall the events of the previous evening. Suddenly, a picture of stained sheets flashed to mind. The memory of rippling pain searing through the base of her belly forced a gasp from her lips.

"No!" she breathed.

Solomon moved from the chair. He clutched Jacinta's trembling hand and folding it between his chest and hers as they embraced.

"What . . . happened?" she inquired tentatively, sounding as though she already knew.

Solomon buried his face in her hair. "You miscarried."

Jacinta's trembling stopped, but then began all over again in a more frantic manner. No, she mouthed, her eyes tearing when no sound came. Again, she tried, but her voice had deserted her. She began to shake her head in an awkward fashion against Solomon's chest.

"Shh . . ." he soothed, rocking her gently.

Solomon, she mouthed again. She kept forming his name on her lips until her voice had returned. "Solomon, I didn't know," she finally blurted, "I didn't know, I didn't . . ." she moaned, her words beginning to mingle with sobs. "Nooo . . ."

"Love, please, please . . ." Solomon urged, attempting to console her by increasing the speed of his rocking embrace. "This was not your fault. It could have been prevented if only I had . . . had let you rest more, I was selfish. I should have suspected something, realized you were more than just a little weary from the trip, but I couldn't see that. I should have left you alone instead of making love—"

"Shh, Solomon no . . ." Jacinta whispered, pressing her fingertips against his mouth.

Solomon pulled away her hand and kissed her palm. "Don't focus on me now. Mel says you're to get much rest," he told her as he stood and tucked her back beneath the covers. He placed another quick peck to her forehead and left the room.

Alone, Jacinta let her tears flow in an uncontrolled wave.

The following weeks were quiet ones. Jacinta rested to regain her strength while Solomon avoided his wife at all costs. It was a feeling like no other to discover you are about to be a father, then to discover it is not to be in the same moment, he thought. Solomon Dikembe was like a dazed man as he performed his responsibilities as overseer of his business interests.

Sheba knew her son was hurting and let him be. She hoped he would share his feelings with his wife, if no one else. Slowly, Jacinta returned to herself, but no one would allow her to overexert herself. She kept to her room, the sitting room or the garden working on her book of thoughts. A great birthday celebration at the home of a neighbor was to empty much of the house that weekend. Solomon and Jacinta would remain behind.

"No, no, don't stand. I only wanted to come and say goodbye."

Jacinta set aside her journal anyway and stood to greet Sheba. "What a beautiful shawl," she complimented, eyeing the colorful wrap covering the vibrant coral dress the woman wore.

Sheba gave a dramatic twist to show off her attire. Then she laughed and pulled Jacinta close. "I hope this gathering will be worth all my fixing up," she sighed.

"Well, it's wonderful that they've invited all the house staff to come along."

Sheba waved her hand. "Fred and Beulah Rhodes love many people at their affairs, child. But I still put in a special request to take everyone along—give the two of you some time alone."

Jacinta's lovely cocoa gaze sparkled briefly in realization. "I don't know what change a few days would make."

"Why, none, if you remain here in this garden writing and he remains inside trying to find things to occupy his time."

"Sheba—"

"Nonsense," the woman scoffed, patting Jacinta's arm as they strolled toward the waiting carriage, "take comfort in being close," she urged, "you've both been terribly hurt, and this is the time to be together, not apart."

Jacinta only smiled and nodded. The carriage pulled away shortly and she waved the high-spirited group on their way. What motivation she may have had to talk with her husband rode away with Sheba. Jacinta had no idea what to say to the man. How could she tell him how very sorry she was for losing a life they created together?

Solomon had been avoiding everyone and only happened into the garden when he heard the partygoers venturing off in the carriage. He approached the clearing near the bushes that would bloom with fragrant roses in a short while. A lone, iron chair and coordinating round table sat there. He smiled, recognizing his wife's work space. Her book of thoughts lay on the chair, and he reached for it. The faint scent of her dusting powder brought a deeper smile to his lips when he thumbed through the sheepskin pages. He decided to read a bit, hoping Jacinta's creativity and gift for story telling would soothe his frazzled nerves. His smoldering gaze narrowed as he focused on the latest entry. Sadly, it did anything but soothe him.

. . . to go on with myself each day and not realize the life I carried in my womb—a life created with Solomon . . . I

try to recall those days, try to recall if there was a moment that I should have felt it—should have realized, but there was nothing. I suppose it was a good thing not to know, not to have the slightest awareness of it. Surely it was a good thing. Even a blessing, perhaps. Yes, perhaps it was a good thing this child never entered the world . . .

Solomon could read no more, and dropped the book as though it burned him to touch it. His mind swam as dizziness overcame him, his lashes fluttered uncontrollably. He recognized the burning sensation he felt behind his eyes as tears that would not come. He backed away from the book, eyeing it in the manner one would a snake. His hands clenched into massive fists. The muscle in his jaw performed its wicked dance. His heart raced and filled his ears with an unbearable throbbing sound and his soul was filled with rage.

Jacinta returned to the garden, deciding to continue her writing where she'd left off before Sheba arrived. She paused for a moment, finding it odd that the journal lay on the ground instead of the chair. Dismissing it, she shook off the book and reclaimed her seat to finish the passage.

. . . I realize that I am only trying to convince myself with these words. If I write often enough perhaps I will truly come to believe them—come to believe that this happened for the best. How could it not be for the best? This world so beautiful, yet so disappointing. How I long to bring my child into a world where his people are free, not living in

*fear of being beaten or sold away from their families. Still
. . . my heart is saddened—my soul aches. I wanted my husband's child—my child in spite of the ills of the world.
Nothing would have been more elating than to bring a new
life into this world—a child with the ideals of his father. A
new generation to usher in a new era for the Negro people.
An era of hope.*

*Yes, I would have wanted to know my child existed
within me even if he weren't meant to be a part of this world.
To experience the joy of knowing that Solomon and I were to
bring about a life together—a life created in love that would
have made this tremendous pain I feel so much easier to
bear—easier if only for a moment. I love my husband so, and
I fear I've killed a part of him because of this loss.*

The pen slipped from Jacinta's fingers as though
somehow signaling that this passage was complete—that
there was nothing more to be written. She was about to
proof the entry, when a loud noise rose from somewhere
inside the house. Jacinta gave a start, dropping her
journal when the deafening boom was followed by a loud
crash and subsequent crashes. She bolted from the
garden, the chair she'd occupied teetering in her wake.

"Solomon? Solomon?" she cried, racing in and out of
rooms like a madwoman. She was about to head upstairs,
when she decided to check the study at the far end of the
corridor. "Solomon!" she called once more, but received
no response. Bravely, she followed the sound of the
ruckus, hoping her husband had already found the
destructive intruder. She couldn't have appeared more

stunned than when she walked into the grand study to find that it was her husband demolishing the room.

For a while she watched, horrified at the sight of him tearing wooden panels from the walls as though they were paper. His desk was covered with crumpled papers and spilled ink. The elegant drapes, which shielded the study from the sometimes blinding noonday sun, looked as though they had been shredded.

"Solomon?" she spoke in an uncertain manner, swallowing past the swell in her throat when he did not answer. "Solomon, please!"

He stopped then, his massive hands flattened against the wall. He did not turn to face her. But it as easy to tell from the room's appearance and his heaving back and shoulders that he was enraged.

"Solomon? What—what is it?"

"Get out."

Instead, Jacinta stepped further into the room, her hands twisting inside the flaring sleeves of her olive green and gold laced housedress. She pressed her lips together, her maple brown gaze impossibly wide as she studied the magnificent expanse of his back. The black material of his linen shirt threatened to burst at the seams under the effects of his heavy breaths.

"Solomon—"

"Get the hell out of my sight!" he ordered then, his charcoal glare as savage as the sound of his deep, rough voice.

Jacinta closed her eyes, hoping to keep her own temper cooled. "What is this? Why would you destroy your study this way? What's happened?"

"I don't want to talk about this," he muttered, going to the windows to peer past the tattered drapes.

Jacinta wouldn't back down. "Well, I *do* want to talk about this," she persisted. Still, her heart lurched when he fixed his black stare on her.

"No wife, you most certainly *don't* want to talk about this."

Jacinta blinked, realization beginning to glare on her round lovely face. "It's me? You're upset with me, aren't you?"

"Jacinta—"

"Why? What have I done?" she pleaded for an answer, her hands curved toward her chest in a helpless gesture.

Solomon wasn't convinced. "There's nothing you need to say. Believe me, you've 'said' enough."

"What does that mean?" Jacinta cried, despising the powerless tone to her words. Solomon spoke in a riddle—a riddle she had no idea how to solve. She watched him open the liquor cabinet and extract a bottle. He guzzled down a good deal of bourbon, unmindful of the brownish liquid streaming out the sides of his mouth and down his neck. Once he'd nearly emptied the heavy glass container, he hurtled it across the room.

Jacinta screamed when it shattered on a far wall.

"Now get out," Solomon ordered once more, his black stare focused and deadly.

Jacinta formed no arguments. Gathering the flowing skirts of her dress, she left the study.

CHAPTER 21

From the day of Solomon's fitful rage, Jacinta tread carefully, determined not to excite his suddenly quick temper. She cast cautious glances across her shoulder and around every corner in hopes of not running into him. Solomon's mood had steadily worsened over the weekend and well into the following week. Sheba had sent word by messenger that she and the rest of the staff would be away a bit longer than they had originally planned. Jacinta knew her mother-in-law was only trying to help, but she dreaded the change in plans. She felt so uneasy being alone with her husband that it was even difficult for her to focus on her writings. A few times, she managed to gather her courage and approach him, hoping to extract some bit of information that would explain his mood. Solomon remained silent, scarcely acknowledging her presence. When Jacinta entered a room, he would leave. The couple dined and slept separately.

"Afternoon, Missus Dikembe!"

"Afternoon, Cecil!" Jacinta called, waving to the messenger as he trotted his Chestnut Hackney up the bush lined path to the front porch.

"Letter addressed to you, ma'am," Cecil announced, as he swung off the back of the stunning horse.

"For me?" Jacinta breathed, her eyes widening at the unexpected treat. She spoke a short while with Cecil, and that conversation—her first in days—combined with the letter, put something of a sparkle back in her eyes.

When Cecil rode away, Jacinta turned over the envelope and studied the front. A small gasp of happiness passed her lips, and she was even more elated to see that the correspondence was from Charleston.

Ripping into the crisp paper, Jacinta read all the news with hungry eyes. Of course most of it was quick and cursory. Shannel Benjamin and her husband Muro had twins, Vesta Simmons's son Grady had been caught stealing pears off McIver Estate—again. The rebellion was still the biggest talk . . . Jacinta enjoyed the reading, though she found it strange that the letter had been written by head housekeeper Dot Simons and not her father. After a bit more reading, she understood why.

. . . he been ill for some time, child. He didn't want you to know lest you be frettin and fussin over him and that'd make him even more sick. Doc say he need rest now, but you know your Poppa, gal. 'Cause of his stubbornness, he getting sicker every day. Come home, child. I believe you the only one who can make him listen . . .

The letter slipped from Jacinta's weakened hand. The thought of her father being ill sent her into a fit of nervous shakes. She took a seat right on the ground, her legs too weak to continue supporting her. She couldn't lose him . . . he was all she had.

"Get up," she ordered herself in the coldest tone. Blinking away the tears that blurred her eyes, she headed into the house. She knew what she had to do, though it was the last thing she wanted to do. Unfortunately, she had to go through her husband if she was to ever get back home. Of course, she could set out by foot, which was just as dangerous as it was foolish.

Bracing herself, Jacinta entered the quiet house, which now seemed eerie in its grandiose stature. Quietly, she walked the corridors, peeking into each room in hopes of locating her husband. On the second floor, she literally ran into him at their bedroom doorway.

Solomon's hands closed quickly around Jacinta's upper arms to steady her. Their eyes met, and the simple touch brought a rush of suppressed longing to the surface. Clearly, they were starved for one another. Solomon's features were drawn into a helpless, desire-filled expression. Jacinta's entire body tingled with arousal at the feel of his touch. Then, Solomon's hands fell away as if he had no strength left to hold her.

"I received a letter today, from home," she announced, twisting the edge of the envelope between her fingers. "It's my father. He's . . . ill," she said, her heart lurching at the concern sparkling to life in Solomon's black eyes. The look gave her the strength to voice her request. "I'd like to return home. Under the circumstances—"

"Impossible. I can't allow that."

Jacinta was stunned, but not by his quick refusal. She felt a measure of happiness dawning. Could he want to keep her near? Could his feelings be softening?

"Why do you really want to go, wife?"

The question started to douse the happiness that was beginning to take root. "Why?" she inquired slowly.

Solomon simply folded his arms across his chest and waited for her response.

"My father is ill—gravely ill. Haven't you been listening?" Jacinta snapped, anger beginning to replace her happiness and patience.

"Is it really that? Or simply an excuse to become involved with the rebellion again?"

"How could you even suggest such a thing? Do you think me *that* heartless?"

"Don't make me answer that."

"You're a cold man, Solomon Dikembe," Jacinta breathed, shaking her head as though she didn't recognize him. "What's happened to you?"

Solomon's black eyes only raked his wife's small form with unmasked hatred.

Jacinta continued to shake her head. "I know you've been upset about . . . the baby, so have I."

"Humph."

"You doubt that?" Jacinta probed, stepping closer. "Solomon what is this about? I demand to know?"

"You demand?"

"Yes. And I damn well intend to have answers. I believe I'm due at least that much!"

"If you only realized what you are due," Solomon breathed, bringing his face to within inches of Jacinta's, "believe me, wife, you would certainly not be asking for it."

Cold washed over her at the soft threat, but she would not be swayed. "Why are you doing this?" she asked.

"I know how you felt about the baby."

Jacinta took a step back. "What?" she countered, completely taken off guard by his words.

Solomon rose to his full height. "I know how you felt about having my child." His words were soft and full of hurt.

"What are you talking about?"

"In your own hand," he began to clarify, his expression hardening as memories of the day resurfaced. "I'd hoped your words would comfort me. What I read did anything but comfort me. I know you viewed the loss of our child as a blessing."

Suddenly, a picture of her journal lying on the ground flashed before Jacinta's eyes. That's what he'd seen! "Solomon you're mistaken, I—"

"What? Someone else wrote those words? It was someone else writing that our child didn't deserve to be brought into this world?"

"Solomon, please! Please, you have to let me explain," Jacinta begged, rushing after him with her hands clenched to the bodice of her peach silk housedress.

"You told me so many times, and I wouldn't listen. You said you would never give birth to any of my 'half-whites', remember that?" he challenged, his ebony gaze a mixture of hurt and anger.

Jacinta bowed her head. "Solomon, please . . ."

"What?" he snapped, pinning her with his bottomless dark eyes. "You deny speaking those words as well?"

349

"No. I-I don't deny saying those things—"

Solomon muttered a nasty curse and smoothed a shaking hand across his dark, wavy hair.

"I can't deny that I said those things or the fact that I wrote about my not wanting to bring the child into this world," she bravely went on, watching him pace the study like an enraged lion. "I said and I felt those things, but there's more."

"No," he raised his hand, "I don't need to hear more. You can't show me the logic or reason behind such feelings other than the fact that you didn't want my child."

The pressure of sobs began to build in Jacinta's throat. Tears cascaded down her cheeks and she felt powerless to remove the loathing from his eyes.

"I think it would be best for you to leave," he decided in an eerily refreshing tone as though he had decided to rid himself of her. "I'll arrange passage. You should be able to leave by steamboat in two days."

Though terribly concerned for her father, Jacinta had no desire to leave her marriage in such a perilous state. She watched Solomon go to the liquor chest and extract a bottle. Knowing she would never get through to him once the alcohol clouded his mind; she turned and practically dragged herself from the room.

Solomon uncorked the whiskey bottle. Then, realizing his wife had gone, he set it aside and buried the heels of his hands against his eyes.

Jacinta chose not to dwell on the situation that was slowly driving her mad. Instead, she packed for her trip. She packed thoroughly, not knowing when, or if, she would return. She was just finishing the task the following morning when Sheba and the rest of the house staff returned.

Sheba had been searching for her son, but was just as pleased to locate her daughter-in-law first. "You're looking well!" she called from the open bedroom doorway. Her tone was cheery, but curiosity sparkled in her dark eyes at the sight of the young woman packing.

Jacinta dropped a lace camisole into the case and ran around the bed to embrace her mother-in-law. "I've missed you so," she whispered, burying her face in Sheba's shoulder.

Concern now mingled with Sheba's curiosity. "You appear as though your strength has returned," she noted slowly.

Jacinta nodded. "I'm feeling much better."

Sheba smiled. "That's quite obvious, if all these packed cases are a result of your efforts."

Jacinta's shoulders seemed to slump a little. "My father's taken very ill. I'm packing to go home," she explained.

"Oh, Lord," she gasped, closing her eyes to utter a brief prayer. "Will he recover?"

"They don't know," Jacinta spoke as she returned to her bed to continue packing. "He won't rest as he should. They hope I can convince him."

"My prayers are with you and your father, child," Sheba spoke while glancing around the room. "Is my son all packed?"

Jacinta cleared her throat. "He won't be going," she announced in a matter-of-fact tone.

"Not going?" Sheba whispered, stepping closer to the bed. "Surely he's not about to let you take such a trip on your own?"

Jacinta was silent.

"What would possess him to allow that? It's far too dangerous for a young woman to—" Sheba silenced when Jacinta burst into tears.

"There, there . . . that's it . . . get it all out. That's it," Sheba soothed later when the girl's emotions showed signs of calming. Jacinta had just told her everything that had happened.

"I'm sorry," Jacinta spoke through her sniffles, "I haven't talked with anyone about this. Solomon won't discuss it, he's barely said a thing."

"I've always urged him to control his temper—it's something I've come to regret," Sheba confided while holding Jacinta in a rocking embrace. "I suppose I urged him more in adulthood because he's such a large man and that, combined with his mixed heritage, has earned him much unwanted attention. Has he ever spoken to you of an incident regarding a mud bath?" Sheba inquired, offering a sad smile when she felt Jacinta nod against her chest. "I fear I've taught him to suppress his emotions to the point that when he explodes, it's a devastating scene."

"He had every right to be enraged," Jacinta championed.

"Perhaps. But he has no right to send you off to Charleston alone with no protection," Sheba countered.

Jacinta's tears were returning. "It's best for me to go. I think maybe Solomon and I were fooling ourselves . . . perhaps we weren't meant for each other."

"Now stop this!" Sheba ordered, her hands tightening around Jacinta's arms to force her to sit up. "I'm going to find that boy."

Solomon had gone for the day. When he returned, the house had settled for the night. He journeyed to the sitting room for a drink. He'd lost count of how many times he had imbibed that day. He found his mother there in the dark, waiting for his return.

"How was the party?" Solomon asked, clearly disinterested.

Sheba held her hands clasped atop her multi-colored skirts. "Very nice. How are things here?"

"I'm sure you know, so let's not discuss it," he decided, slamming a heavy whiskey bottle to the window-sill behind the bar.

"I understand Jacinta's taking a trip?" Sheba coolly mentioned, watching her son decide against using a glass to partake of his whiskey. "I also understand you've decided to let her travel alone?"

"That's right," Solomon threw back, taking another swig from the bottle.

Sheba closed her eyes, frustrated by her son's mood, yet knowing it was important to appeal to his sense of manhood and duty to his wife. "How can you allow that?" she questioned, when he brushed past her.

"She'll go whether or not I allow it," Solomon retorted, whipping the blue linen coat from his shoulders. "You know how she is," he added.

"That's not what I mean and you know it!" Sheba raged, finally losing her patience with her only child. "You know how dangerous it is for a woman to travel alone. It is especially perilous for a black woman—a young, beautiful black woman. Now you think on that," she ordered before storming out of the fire-lit room.

Alone, the reality of his mother's concerns doused Solomon like a dash of cold water. He knew, despite whatever difficulties existed between him and Jacinta, it was his place to keep her safe. Besides, he knew he would die if anything ever happened to her.

Jacinta took a light breakfast in her room and then headed downstairs to meet the carriage that would carry her to the dock where she would board the steamboat.

As her gloved hands trailed the polished stairways with their majestic carvings and plush carpeting, her eyes were set on the warmth and décor of the house. She did not want to leave! Her life was there, her heart was there, her husband was there, she thought. Solomon was there and she loved him desperately. Now that she loved him so completely, it was too late.

"Morning, Jacinta!"

"How are you?" Jacinta greeted upon seeing Joseph Ells on her porch. The man was one of her husband's business associates, and they'd become friends the moment they met.

"Leaving us so soon?" Joseph asked, glancing back at the driver who was loading the carriage with Jacinta's belongings.

She shrugged, hoping to keep the sadness from her eyes. "It's my father. I have to be with him."

"Of course, and my prayers go with you," Joseph said, and pressed a gallant kiss to the back of her hand. "Solomon," he said, his tone more firm when he turned toward the man, "we'll see you upon your return."

Solomon grinned, taking Joseph's hand in a firm shake. "Take care," he said.

Jacinta's spirits were soaring. He was coming with her! She was as surprised as she was hopeful.

"You changed your mind?" she whispered, when they stood alone on the porch.

Unfortunately, Solomon's coldness had returned. "It means nothing," he grumbled, taking her elbow in a stiff, unaffectionate embrace. "Let's go," he ordered.

Solomon retained every bit of gallantry he possessed as he helped his wife into the carriage. As they walked, however, the coldness he fought to hold on to melted away as irresistible desire took root.

Jacinta thought she would swoon at the feel of his powerful hand encircling her upper arm. At times, she could have sworn she felt him massaging her gently through the pink satin sleeves of her dress.

The ride was set to be a lengthy one. Essentially, they would retrace the route of their journey into Michigan. Sadly, this trip would be bereft of the numerous stops and social events that colored their previous travels. Jacinta was grateful her strength had returned, for the trip would be even more taxing than before. Since much of the ride would be by covered wagon, Jacinta had the opportunity to don her tattered male clothing, as it would make for far more comfortable travel attire. She had planned to write between naps in the wagon, but she dared not pull out the book in the presence of her husband.

"Solomon, why did you change your mind?" Jacinta dared to ask one afternoon, when they had been riding in silence for the better part of fifteen minutes.

"It's dangerous—a woman traveling alone," was all he said. *A beautiful woman*, he added silently, his dark eyes tracing the face visible beneath the wide brim of the tattered brown hat she wore.

Jacinta was still pleased. At least he had cared enough to accompany her, she thought. That was enough for her. The notion relaxed her, and she settled back against the cushioned blue velvet long seat. The view from the small square windows held her gaze, until sleep visited.

When they arrived in New York and boarded the steamboat that would take them into Charleston, South

Carolina, Jacinta found herself thinking of the Mandelas. She wished there was time to visit with Taurus and Monique and couldn't help but recall how close she and Solomon had become during that time.

Forcing those thoughts from her mind, she focused on keeping up with Solomon as they made their way along the busy dock. Jacinta felt completely secure, enjoying the feel of Solomon's arms about her shoulders as he guided her. It was amazing, she thought. She had never been a woman to expect, or be in need of, such niceties. Oftentimes, she found it weak that a woman couldn't make her own way without male assistance. Now, she realized that it wasn't out of weakness that a woman craved those things. It was the simple appreciation and wondrous feeling of support from another—a lover that made all the ills and hardships of the world seem bearable.

The beautiful steamboat *Greenshaw* housed a lovely café on deck. The Dikembes enjoyed a light supper there while their bags were being carried to the room. They were oblivious to the interested glances, or glares, thrown their way from other white passengers. Of course, many of those looks harbored more curiosity than animosity. Solomon and Jacinta were indeed a beautiful pair, they practically shrieked confidence and noble stature without having to utter a word.

Jacinta felt neither confident nor noble as she tried to consume the delectable slices of beef roasted to tender perfection, along with baked sweet potatoes and fresh crusted bread. Her eyes settled several times upon her husband's powerful hands. Her mind raced with memories of his sweet gentle touch. Her memories grew so bold, her fingers weakened around the cutlery and a soft moan rose from her throat.

"Are you ill?" Solomon asked, there was no trace of harshness in his deep voice, as he was unable to mask the concern in his tone or his dark gaze.

Jacinta cleared her throat. "No." She spoke in a hushed tone and barely looked up at him.

The rest of the meal passed with no further discussion.

Following supper, Solomon escorted Jacinta to their cabin, but he did not remain there with her. When three quarters of an hour passed without his return, Jacinta felt at ease enough to bring out her writings. She lost track of the time and fought her disappointment at the reality of her husband choosing separate sleeping quarters. She prepared for bed, simply choosing to sleep in the soft shift she'd worn beneath her clothing that day. She was just closing her eyes when the lock turned; Solomon had come back. She listened, afraid to move or breathe, lest he set out again. She could hear him, even though his steps were barely audible as he moved about preparing for bed. The mattress gave beneath his weight and she pressed her lips together and prayed that he would call out to her, pull her close and snuggle her into his safe embrace. Sadly, she realized her prayers would not be answered that night. The low steadiness of his breathing told her that he was sleeping. In time, she, too, gave into the exhaustion that weighed her eyelids.

Solomon, however, was not sleeping, but very much awake. How could he rest peacefully with her there next to him in a bed that was far too small to keep an adequate distance between them? Her hair brushed his arms and shoulders and her alluring scent teased his nostrils. God, he wanted her! He missed her in spite of the way she had hurt him. What he'd feared had happened. He had let down his defenses and allowed himself to love her and to be enchanted by her and he had been wounded—wounded heart and soul.

The wind howled incessantly the following morning. Rain beat the deck in blinding sheets. Solomon woke from his slumber; he barely recalled closing his eyes. He had gone through the night restless, frustrated and aroused. That arousal rose to greater heights when he realized that during the night, Jacinta had wound herself about him like a silken sheet. Her thin shift covered little as she snuggled against his nude form. Solomon could think only of taking her again and again. Unable to deny the urges rampaging his senses, he allowed himself just a brief touch of her satiny, chocolate form.

A heavy tendril of her dark mane fell across her eyes and he smoothed the lock between his thumb and forefinger before inhaling the fresh scent which clung to it. Her breasts were prominently outlined against the shift that was twisted between their bodies. The ample, dark mounds spilled from the tops of the garment, making the mocha clouds surrounding her nipples just visible. Solomon turned, dropping moist quick kisses along her neck and collarbone as he traveled closer to her chest. There, he scooped one breast from its confinement and encircled its shape with the tip of his nose. He could feel his manhood further extend and moaned as his lips entrapped one of the rigid buds.

Jacinta woke with a silent gasp. She saw Solomon's head moving against her chest as he pleasured her aching nipples with his incredible kisses. She tugged her lower lip between her teeth to quiet the screams she wanted to reveal. She was so afraid he might stop, that she ordered herself to remain unresponsive.

That order was impossible to obey when Solomon added his fingers to the torture. They glided along her thigh and insinuated themselves within the sweet joining between. Instinctively, her legs parted, weakening beneath the probing caress. Solomon squeezed his eyes shut tight as his fingers were bathed deep inside a well of moisture. Moisture that increased when he added another finger to the intimate massage.

"Solomon . . ." Jacinta gasped on a whimper, arching her slender form towards him. Her small feet tangled into crisp bed linens and she opened herself to more of the overwhelming treat. She could feel his powerful length nudging her thigh, and she forced herself not to demand that he delight her with that area of his anatomy. She wanted nothing to spoil the sensuous moment. The closeness was desired and very much missed and needed. When Solomon's restraint was spent, he rose, pulling

Jacinta with him. He held her back against his chiseled frame as they knelt in the center of the bed. With his handsome face buried in the mass of coal black tresses, Solomon brought his hands around to cup her breasts once more. His thumbs and forefingers alternated between stroking the buds into hard peaks and manipulating them as she writhed in pleasure.

Jacinta nudged her bottom against his pronounced erection, silently begging that he provide her with ultimate fulfillment. Solomon's hands left her chest to venture past her flat stomach. Briefly, he played in the crisp, dark curls sheltering her womanhood. Then, he gripped her hips and situated her to his satisfaction. Within seconds, Jacinta felt the smooth, hard intrusion of his sex as it invaded her yearning femininity. She could have fainted from the pleasure, but Solomon held her fast. One hand cupped a full breast, while the other remained firmly planted at her hip. His thrusts were slow. He deliberately taunted, making her want to beg for more. Jacinta's hands covered his at her breast as she met the force of each thrust. Her hair enveloped them in a cloud of smoky black. Their bodies rocked in time to the sway and dip of the ship, it seemed. Jacinta's heart raced with delight as she reveled in the confident manner Solomon handled her body. He took her several times as they made love late into the morning. His passion thoroughly spent, Solomon laid across Jacinta, his heavy frame completely shielding her petite body. Jacinta didn't mind at all. She felt the warmth of happiness embrace her as she lay curled in her husband's arms.

Sadly, however, the sexual interlude had not removed the tension between them. Once Solomon's arousal had lost its stiffness and his breathing slowed, he left her. Jacinta realized nothing had changed, and tears pooled her eyes.

⸎

The day was indeed a dreary one. Rainstorms plagued the passengers and crew off and on. For Jacinta, the weather was a perfect match to her mood. The comfort she'd experienced in realizing Solomon needed her physically was fleeting. She needed more. She wanted to talk to him—to explain that he was wrong to think that she didn't want his child.

She remained close to the quarters, not caring for the way men's eyes raked her face and form. The blatant lust in their eyes certainly enraged their female travel companions. The women regarded Jacinta disdainfully, as though she were to blame for the men's incessant stares. Thankfully, the cabin had a small balcony complete with a little wooden tea table and two matching swayback chairs. Grateful for the solitude, she draped her black shawl across the arm of the chair and took refuge in the serene view of the Atlantic.

Some time later, Solomon returned to the cabin. He masked the concern on his face before entering. He had been searching for his wife, and had seen nothing of her since he left that morning. Morning, he thought, stifling a grunt as pleasurable thoughts sent a familiar tightening below his waist. He had missed her so, and the closeness they'd shared had been heaven-sent. Still, knowing she harbored such feelings about his heritage hit him like a dash of cold water once the heat of passion was spent.

A look of contentment softened his striking features when he found his wife napping on the balcony. Not caring for the way she slept slumped down in the chair—and wanting a reason to hold her-he carried her to the bed. Jacinta didn't stir, and Solomon went back to the balcony to collect her shawl.

He found her book of thoughts in the opposite chair. Against all his adversity to the material, he couldn't stop himself from picking it up and scanning its contents. More had been written since he last read, but Solomon only wanted to see the dreaded passage again. He turned right to the entry as though it had called out to him from inside the crisp pages.

His lips tightened as he read the lines which were burned into his memory. A frown began to tug at his sleek brows as he read on. He glanced toward his wife, half expecting to see her smiling–smug over the fact that she was succeeding in fooling him again.

No, she was oblivious to it all. He told himself it was a trick, a ruse to put her back in his favor. But the way the words flowed in feeling . . . he knew he had misjudged her. He had read an unfinished thought. He had intruded upon her privacy, her creative flow, and he was ruining their marriage because of it.

Solomon brushed his fingers across the words and shook his head to ward off the tears pressuring his ebony eyes. Jacinta wanted his child and she was blaming herself for the loss. She was hurt and confused by his mood and believed he blamed her as well. She believed he did not love her anymore.

Solomon replaced the book where he'd found it. Tightening his grip on the shawl, he approached the bed and draped it across her legs and stocking feet.

"Jacinta . . ." he whispered, and then brushed his cheek against hers before he left the cabin.

CHAPTER 22

June 1822

No matter the depth of blood and tears that teamed below the oyster white sand of Charleston's city streets, Jacinta felt exuberant. Being home again after so many months was a feeling like no other. The feeling was short-lived, however, when she saw the men in chains and those with welted backs, hefting trunks and other baggage from the steamships that had recently arrived into port. She was so absorbed by the scene it startled her when Solomon's hands closed over her shoulders.

"Stay close to me while I see to the bags," he whispered against her cheek.

Jacinta nodded, managing an easy smile even as her brown eyes misted with confusion. She didn't trust herself to accept that Solomon had been behaving quite differently during the last weeks of the trip back to South Carolina. He treated her as though they were strangers—friendly acquaintances. It was as though he were uncertain about how to approach her. She felt none of the coldness he had shown towards her. Could he be having a change of heart? Was he finally ready to listen to her explanations?

Jacinta heard her name across the wharf and frowned. Setting her hand against her brow, she frowned against the mid-morning sun and her mouth formed a perfect O when she spied a familiar face from McIver Estate.

"Beta!" she cried, rushing forth to reach for the housemaid's outstretched hands. "Oh, Beta," she sighed, hugging the girl tightly.

Beta's lovely, caramel-toned face appeared even more radiant when she laughed. "Oh, Jaci, it's so good to have you home!" she said, pulling back to look into her friend's face.

Jacinta hoped her smile appeared genuine.

"Everyone so excited 'bout seeing you. They all so envious when Mister Jason choose me to come with Mitchell to town to fetch you," Beta went on, referring to the driver who waited in the carriage a ways off. Her animated expression dimmed just a bit then. "I wish your visit could come at a better time," she lamented.

Jacinta was nodding. "Yes, I pray Poppa's health will take a turn for the better during my stay."

"Oh, Jaci, it has!" Beta cried, brushing her gloved hand across Jacinta's arm. "He's getting' back more of his old strength, and he even taking a few meals outside his bedchamber. The doctor say he still need more rest, but even he know that's hard with all that's happening."

In spite of such wonderful news, Jacinta's lovely round face was a picture of confusion. "Beta, I don't understand. You say Poppa's much better, what more could be happening?"

Beta glanced toward the passing whites quickly before lowering her eyes to the slick wooden slabs on the deck. "The great man has been betrayed."

Jacinta's heart lurched and she glanced suspiciously at passersby. She made certain that Solomon wasn't near to overhear anything pertaining to the subject. "How?" she asked.

Beta was shaking her head. "It happened in May . . . a Peter Desverneys and George Wilson. We believe they was the ones."

"Why?" Jacinta breathed, quickly recalling that one of the men Beta spoke of was mulatto. She shook her head to dismiss the thought.

Beta was wringing her hands. "They live good lives, so they think. It was probably too much for them to think on. I b'lieve some slaves just as afraid to be free as white people is to let 'em free."

"Oh, no," Jacinta sighed, feeling a rush of tears pressure her eyes. She knew it would be unwise to display such emotions in broad daylight and suppressed the urge to submit to a good cry. Still, her mind swam with the reality of what had happened.

In fact the betrayers were both slaves, well cared for in their opinions and by the standards in which most slaves were treated. Actually, one might understand their concern over an uprising that may bring harm to their owners. The slave Desverneys belonged to a Colonel Prioleau of Charleston. He was a "house servant", and it was well known that the class of slaves fared far batter than their less fortunate brethren who toiled in the fields of rice and cotton with only the lash of the overseer as a 'reward' for work.

Once the two slaves were off and running to their masters with news of the coming revolt, the city was turned inside out.

At first, little credence was given to the story. There were no news articles or rampant arrests. Though the city council did question several 'suspicious slaves', they managed to keep the community ignorant of the plot. Of course, the newspapers were soon full of the story after a number of arrests had been made. The plot was foiled, a public investigation commenced and Denmark Vesey's name was on everyone's lips.

"We'll discuss this later," Jacinta told Beta when she noticed Solomon heading towards them.

"Beta!" he greeted her, leaning down to drop a jovial kiss to the young woman's cheek.

"Mister Solomon!" Beta gushed, her caramel-toned face darkening when she blushed.

"The carriage is packed and ready to take us back," he announced, offering Beta his arm while dropping an arm across his wife's shoulders and pulling her into a closer embrace.

The air was breezy and warm, yet Jacinta felt a shiver race her spine in response to her husband's contact. "Thank you," she whispered, having summoned the courage to speak. "Thank you for coming with me," she clarified.

Solomon stared straight ahead as they walked along the crowded wharf. "Your beauty would do anything but keep you safe."

The compliment forced her to smile, but she didn't remark upon it. "It's just that with all your concerns . . . your business is so vast."

Solomon held her back and allowed Beta to precede them. "You are my business," he told her.

The look in his eyes left no doubt in Jacinta's mind that his cold demeanor was melting.

Not wanting to ruin whatever was happening between them; Jacinta remained silent during the walk to the carriage. Solomon spoke with Beta, who blushed profusely when he laughed over her comment about the way everyone was bustling about in preparation for the return of 'Mister Jason's handsome houseguest.

The mood inside the carriage was warm and gay, but Jacinta found that she could not thoroughly enjoy it. Not when she looked out the window towards the Work House. The overseers were like foreboding beasts towering above from their positions on horseback. Behind the massive animals, black men trudged along with their hands and feet bound in rusting iron shackles.

Solomon could see the dismay on his wife's face and cursed himself for having to bring her back there. Unfortunately, he had to acknowledge that Charleston was her home, and it was only natural and right that she would be concerned over its condition. He took her gloved hand, which was balled into a shaking fist. Tenderly, he unclenched her fingers, entwining his own between them to give her hand a reassuring squeeze. Jacinta closed her eyes against the horror past the window and drew strength from the sweet gesture. She'd never treasured anything as much.

The travelers arrived at McIver Estate, and Jacinta rediscovered her exuberance. The place was unchanged and even more enchanting. Jacinta raced out of the carriage, unmindful of her fancy rose blush dress with its lace trimmed hem, sleeves and bodice, The matching hat had fallen from her head and only hung on thanks to the gauzy cream bow that was still tied about her neck. She was too busy hugging, kissing, talking and laughing with the house staff of McIver Estate, the people who comprised her family. She glanced around to see Solomon helping to unload the bags before setting off to locate her father. Of course, she found Jason McIver in the last place he needed to be—his office. Papers cluttered every square inch of the sturdy pine desk surrounding Jason and his assistant, whose head was bowed as he scribbled furiously to keep up with the rapid dictation from his employer.

"Well, isn't this a familiar and completely impermissible sight!"

Both Jason and Herman Sims looked up at Jacinta's bellow. In moments, Jason was on his feet and rushing forward to greet his only child.

"My love," he sighed, enfolding her in the tightest embrace. He laughed when he heard her sobs of happiness. "There, there love."

"Poppa, I missed you so," Jacinta's voice was like a shudder as she inhaled the scent of brandy and pipe smoke clinging to her father's black linen shirt.

"Shh . . ."

"I didn't know what to think," Jacinta said, pulling back enough to look into her father's kind cinnamon brown face. "I was so worried that something would happen before I could get back-the trip was so very long and—"

"Shh, Jaci, shh . . ." Jason urged, patting her cheek that time. "Curse Dot and that 'I know what's best' mind of hers!"

"Poppa," Jacinta scolded.

"Bah!" Jason spat with a quick wave. " 'Twas only something minor. There was no need for 'em to pull you away from your new home."

"I would've been very upset had they done otherwise," Jacinta assured the man while untying the gauzy bow in order to remove the elaborate hat. "It is my place to be here," she added.

"Your *place* is with your husband," Jason corrected, noticing a strange glint flicker in his daughter's eyes. "That's all for now, Herme," he called to his assistant.

Herman figured as much and had already gathered his belongings. "Good to see you home, Miss Jaci," he whispered, reaching out to squeeze one of her hands within his frail looking one.

"Thank you, Herme," she said, covering the man's slender hand with her other.

"I shouldn't be surprised to find you working, but I'd hoped this would convince you to stop pushing yourself so," Jacinta told her father once they were alone in the office. "What ails you?" she asked.

Again, Jason waved his hand. "Doctor says fatigue, stress and poor diet contributed."

"Poppa, how many times have we begged you to pay attention to all those things and—"

"Jaci, Jaci, please. My word, anyone who lives here knows how impossible it is to rest these days."

Jacinta bowed her head, pressing her lips together. "I understand."

Jason heard the underlying meaning in her words. "How much do you know?"

"Beta says Mister Vesey was betrayed by slaves, no less—the very people he wanted to help."

"The irony is so very bitter," Jason admitted with a slow, defeated shake of his head.

Jacinta began to remove her gloves. "How bad is it?"

"You mean, 'have there been any hangings'?"

"Oh Poppa, surely—"

"I can promise you it will most certainly come to that."

"Beta said one of Colonel Prioleau's slaves, Peter Desverneys, was a betrayer. I believe I've seen him on occasion," Jacinta said, tossing her gloves to where the hat lay on a long chair. "He's mulatto, isn't he?"

Jason pulled all ten fingers through the unruly head of gray hair that already appeared to be standing on end. "I think that hurt most of all. This will put an even deeper rift within the race."

Jacinta gave a noticeable swallow past the ball of emotion lodged in her throat. Her father noticed.

"How is Solomon?" he asked.

"He's well."

The simple response, combined with her reaction to his earlier mention of her marriage, told Jason much. Clearly Jacinta was in no mood to discuss it, so Jason decided there would be plenty of time later to approach the subject.

Later that afternoon, Jason enjoyed drinks outdoors with his son-in-law. They spoke of business, and that conversation soon glided into talk of the revolt. It was the first Solomon had heard of the betrayal, and he wondered if Jacinta knew.

"She does," Jason confirmed while reaching into the breast pocket of his coat for his pipe. "You should know that at least one of the men is mulatto."

Other than the brief flex of the muscle in his jaw, Solomon kept his emotions masked. He realized why his wife had chosen not to speak on it. "The betrayers . . . was it the same who gave over Jore Sula and his family?"

Jason was shaking his head. "No, Desverneys is a cook for a Colonel Prioleau, who lives in town. He even prefers to be called by the white man's last name. Wilson was quite trusted among the black population in spite of his mixed blood." Jason took a long drag from his pipe and leaned back against the rain-washed rocker. "Many believe rumors had already reached the white man's ears long before they had anything as concrete as word from the mouth of a slave."

Solomon tapped his fist to the worsted hunter green fabric of his trousers. "How bad do you believe it will become?"

"I believe it will become very bad, very bloody," Jason replied without hesitation. He noticed the unease on the younger man's face and cursed his thoughtlessness. "Son, I apologize for the house staff acting in haste," he explained, smiling when Solomon looked at him. "In their concern for me, they thought of nothing but getting Jacinta back here. I'm afraid they did not stop to think of the danger."

"I'm grateful for their foresight, sir," Solomon assured his father-in-law. The look in his dark eyes was sincere. "I pray you won't be insulted, but I believe it's high time we all leave Charleston behind."

Jason appeared as though he had reached the conclusion long ago. "Pray tell, what will you do to convince my daughter?"

One corner of Solomon's mouth tilted upwards in a lazy grin. "Rest assured, you may leave her to me."

"And I have no doubt you'll succeed," Jason responded with a chuckle that lasted only a moment. "Still, something tells me that all is not right between you two."

Solomon's easy expression faded into a scowl, and he stood. "You're right," he said, already heading down the front porch steps, "it's a situation I intend to rectify this very day."

"At least you can be there, Mea—this will surely be worthy of noting."

"Let's just pray my brothers won't notice my tracking them through the woods to Bulkley Farm."

Jacinta chuckled. "They haven't yet, and it's been what? Two years?"

Mea Riley was a young woman with the same drive and dedication as Jacinta. She and her family worked a plantation on the other side of the Wallens place. It was rumored that Mea was one of the children of Frank Riley, the master of the plantation. It was denied, of course. However, Mea was the only child that was allowed inside the big house frequently. Townspeople gossiped she had even been educated right alongside Riley's legitimate offspring. Mea and Jacinta had made each other's acquaintance during a meeting they'd both 'invited' themselves to. Mea was just as infatuated by the rebellion to be led by Denmark Vesey, and had once gone so far as to cut her brown, waist-length curls in hopes of maintaining a more boyish disguise.

"Are the authorities aware of the meetings that have taken place there?" Jacinta asked, referring to Bulkley Farm where scores of secret gatherings had been held. Many of Vesey's most spiritually passionate speeches had been spoken on the farm.

Mea appeared uncharacteristically afraid. "They know much. We can only hope the Bulkley location hasn't been compromised."

"And if it hasn't yet, it soon will be," Jacinta groaned, then fixed Mea with an apologetic smile. "I shouldn't be saying this. I'm sure you're unsettled enough."

Mea shrugged. "The rebellion's been ruined. We all must accept that. The punishments will be swift and brutal. I'm sure of that. Men are being questioned, more each day. If Mister Vesey hasn't been detained yet, he soon will be."

"I wish I could go with you," Jacinta whined, her lush brown gaze filled with disappointment. "Instead I'm standing here like some helpless fool waiting for tidbits of information to come my way."

"Jacinta, you've done more than enough, and you know it," Mea said, rubbing her small hand across Jacinta's forearm. "Besides, the men are very firm about us women remaining in the background," she added, rolling her eyes toward the pale blue. "I'm sure your husband feels the same. He doesn't look like the sort of man to make light of his wife's safety," she added.

Jacinta's brows rose several notches. "You're right about that," she sighed.

"And you're a blessed woman to have such a man in your life," Mea said, setting both hands to her friend's shoulders. "You should take pride in that."

A single tear escaped the corner of Jacinta's eye as she nodded. "I do, Mea. I do every day," she swore.

"Then, I'm off," Mea decided, dropping a worn brown hat that was several sizes too big across her thickly coiled brown hair that was slowly, but surely, returning to its original length. She left Jacinta with a quick hug and then she disappeared into the woods that began a few yards shy of the gate.

Jacinta's gaze was longing as she watched Mea— recalling when she herself raced out on a whim. It had seemed so long ago and she felt as though she were a different person then.

Leaves crunched close by as they were crushed beneath a heavy boot. Jacinta turned to find Solomon approaching. Her heart lurched in her chest as she watched him. Even beneath the expensive tailoring of the linen chestnut slacks, matching three-quarter length suit coat and a high-collared cream shirt, the quiet power of his physique was clearly evident. The set look on his handsome face caused her nerves to grate. She prayed he was not cross with her.

"Walk with me?" he softly requested, his head bowed and hands clasped behind his back.

Jacinta silently complied and for a while they enjoyed the serenity of the estate. She could feel a ball of emotion cause her throat to swell against the choke collar of the lovely peach frock she wore with a matching linen long coat. The day held an eerie chilliness that hinted at the possibility of a storm and made her attire all the more comfortable. Her lashes moistened with tears as she studied the landscape as far as she could view it. Though she had lived there all her life, it was still impossible to fathom such evil and sorrow could exist in so perfect a place.

"Why didn't you tell me about Vesey's betrayal?"

The sound of Solomon's rough voice against the silent air stunned her almost as much as his question. "I didn't think you'd appreciate hearing me speak on such things."

"Why not?"

"Solomon, I know you don't approve of my involvement or even my interest in the revolt."

"And is that the only reason?" he asked, his dark eyes cast toward the ground.

Jacinta turned her gaze there as well and offered no response.

Solomon didn't press. "This situation is perilous—too perilous," he told her instead. "Your father agrees that it's time to close the house and leave."

"Close the house?" she questioned, her steps slowing a bit.

"It's time, love," he spoke softly, knowing the true meaning of what he was telling her would be difficult to accept. "You and I, your father, the entire household. We have to leave. At any moment your door could be knocked upon."

"And you're frightened by this?" Jacinta challenged, pinning him with a stony look.

Solomon regarded her closely. "Never."

"Neither am I," she swore. "I've never been frightened by those cowards, and I have no qualms about facing them," she declared.

"And what of your father?" Solomon challenged, standing back on his long legs and folding his arms across his chest. "Do you think he would survive their . . . questioning?"

Jacinta stopped walking and slumped against the trunk of a nearby elm tree. Her dark, pretty face held a defeated expression.

Solomon leaned next to her. "I'm sorry for upsetting you. I know this is a lot to handle, and the last thing I want is to put you through anything more unpleasant."

Jacinta raised her hand then. "You have nothing to apologize for. You're absolutely right."

Stunned by her admission, Solomon could only watch her in silence.

"You were right about everything from the very beginning. What you said about my writing being some form of entertainment. At first it was. I wanted to do something I thought would be completely exciting and completely inappropriate. I believed it was the one way to get my father's attention," she admitted, her rich cocoa stare becoming sorrow filled. "He was so depressed after my mother died, and he just seemed to forget I was there." She shook her head and leaned back against the tree as she gazed up through its heavy limbs. "Then while I was 'entertaining' myself with these horrific stories, my ears and my heart opened to them and something inside would not let me rest until these voices were heard. I couldn't rest until I knew their pain was on the hearts and minds of those with the power to change things. Humph," she gestured, brushing an escaped tear from her cheek, "I was foolish enough to think I could march right up to the most powerful white man in Charleston and demand he read my work. Surely things would change then—or so I foolishly told myself."

Solomon leaned closer to reach for a loose tendril of hair that whipped against her cheek. "Have you forgotten your writings and how well they were received in New York? Your work has been embraced by the most powerful state in the Union. You know it hasn't been in vain."

"I haven't forgotten." She pulled his hand into hers. "But there's so much more to be done. Still, I must remember that my first allegiance is always to my family. I should have always known that, and I'm so very sorry that it's taken me so long to come to the realization." She searched Solomon's face for forgiveness.

He only shook his head and pulled her into a tight hug. Jacinta held on as though he were her lifeline.

CHAPTER 23

Jacinta visited her father's bedchamber that night, hoping to find him still awake. She was pleased to see him up, reading in bed.

"Perhaps one day you'll be reading a book with my name on the cover," she teased, knocking lightly upon the door while she stepped inside the room.

"That's something I can hardly wait to see," he said, waving his hand to beckon her towards the bed.

Jacinta took her place, and for a moment she and her father enjoyed the silence marred only by the intermittent pop and fizz from the candles on the nightstand next to Jason's bed.

"Solomon told me what you'd decided about the house," she finally admitted.

"And how do you feel about that?"

Jacinta shook her head. "It's hard to imagine just . . . abandoning my home. But I know it's for the best."

"It makes me so happy to hear you say that, little girl," Jason whispered, leaning close to squeeze her hand beneath his larger one.

Jacinta relished the gesture and bowed her head to press a hard kiss to the back of her father's hand. Then, growing overwhelmed with emotion, she turned to kneel at his bedside. Her wide eyes were filled with tears as she clutched his hand to her chest. "Poppa, please forgive me, please . . ."

Jason began to frown and moved to sit up straighter against the headboard. "Jacinta, what—"

"Poppa, I've been so difficult and I am so sorry. I never obeyed your orders to stay close to home. I foolishly cast off the danger you always warned me about—"

"Shh, shh, love, it's alright," Jason consoled, extracting his hand from her clutch in order to cup her chin. "In spite of my warnings and heavy handedness, I always understood you. You're a young woman who has experienced much sorrow at a very young age. You've lost your mother, seen your closest friends in shackles and beaten, and the one person you should have been able to come to at *any* time was always involved with business or off someplace mourning the loss of his wife."

Jacinta saw the sorrow in her father's hazel eyes and inched closer to the bed. "Oh, Poppa, don't. Please don't blame yourself, not when *I'm* to blame for putting you through so much aggravation. Perhaps you wouldn't have taken ill if I hadn't been so—"

"Jacinta, stop."

"Poppa, is this why you wanted me to become involved in your business?" she questioned, her breath coming in shuddery gasps.

"No, Jacinta," was Jason's firm response.

She shook her head, lowering it to the crisp linens that smelled of fragrant lye soap and her father's favorite tobacco. "Poppa . . ." she sighed, "I am so sorry. So very sorry. Will you forgive me?" she pleaded, looking up at him with weary eyes.

Jason laughed shortly, "What for, child?"

"Poppa, please! I know what a terror I've been. I should have been more obedient."

"Shh . . . love you were the only way you could have been," he assured her, his voice dropping an octave and growing more assuring in its softness. "I've raised a strong woman—of that I am most proud. Whatever happens, I feel content leaving you now."

Jacinta was horrified, "Poppa, no!"

"Shh . . . you'll have the whole house upon us," Jason ordered, amused by his child's hysterics. "I plan to be around a good long time, Lord willin'. But Jaci, you have come full circle. Your courage continues to strengthen, but now you have the wisdom and level headedness to fortify that courage. Your bravery will allow you to do many things, including fighting for the survival of your marriage."

Jacinta's lashes flickered, but she maintained eye contact with her father.

"Be good to Solomon, love," Jason urged, tossing a lock of Jacinta's unbound hair back across her shoulder. "The poor boy is almost mad, he loves you so much. And as firm as he tries to be, such love could hurt him deeply if taken for granted. Be wary of that," he warned. "For you most certainly have great influence over that young man. He is deep in love with you, and I see you are just as far gone over him. Build your lives around that. Respect your love and each other and the two of you will have many happy years, regardless of anything that may have happened in the past."

Jacinta smiled at the kiss her father planted against her temple. As they hugged, her gaze drifted off someplace distant and thoughts of the lost baby came to mind.

"Get your rest now," she urged in a whisper, forcing the sadness from her voice and expression. Bidding Jason a good night, Jacinta left him to his reading.

Jacinta stepped into her bedchamber and found her husband awake as well. He was working on something at the desk in the corner and turned when the thick wooden door creaked open.

"Sorry," she whispered, smiling when he shook his head.

"No need. I'm finishing up this letter for Cuffe to be sent by messenger in the morning," he explained, already creasing the letter which he placed in a bound leather cover.

Jacinta removed her emerald green robe and placed it at the edge of the bed. Smoothing her hands across the capped sleeves, she slipped beneath the covers. She leaned back against the head board, drawing her knees to her chin as she debated.

"Do you feel up to a talk?" she asked, after watching Solomon for almost two full minutes.

"All right." He pushed himself away from the small cherry wood desk. He left the candle burning and began to undress for bed.

Jacinta cleared her throat as his garments were discarded. Realizing how important the conversation was, she focused her eyes on something other than her husband's body.

Solomon was just as captivated by his wife as she sat up in bed. The emerald satin was beautiful against the rich chocolate tone of her complexion. She struck him as a pretty confection atop a cake, and he wanted nothing more than to gather her close and love her throughout the night. With a soft grunt, he commanded himself to remain focused on this 'talk' she wanted to have.

"You want to discuss leaving Charleston, I suppose?" he asked, once situated beneath the covers.

"Mmm, no," Jacinta replied, deciding it was safe to turn and face him again, "I understand that. It's safer for us to go. Safer for everyone. I won't argue."

Solomon gave a slow nod, and then allowed his ebony gaze to falter. "Were you trying to protect my feelings by not telling me about the betrayal or the betrayers?" he heard himself asking.

Jacinta didn't want to risk another falling out, but she knew it was time for honesty. Complete honesty. "Yes," she spoke firmly with a decisive nod, "I was trying to protect you—and myself. I didn't want you to think I held you responsible. I didn't want to draw more of your anger," she admitted in a tiny voice.

"Jac—"

"Solomon, wait," she urged, raising her hand as she turned fully toward him in the bed, "I have to explain about the book. I know you found it and read it . . . but you completely misunderstood what was written—you must have. I never completed the passage. Your mother was leaving for the weekend party and I left my writing to see her off. When I returned, I saw the book on the ground and it never occurred to me that you'd read it. I sat back down and finished the passage." She leaned her head back to focus on the ceiling in hopes of keeping her tears at bay. "I want you to read the completed version, but I know you'll probably feel that I'm trying to win your favor by adding something to justify what you read." She pulled all ten fingers through her hair as though it were getting in the way of the explanation she was desperate to share. "When I wrote that I didn't want to bring a child into the world, I meant it, and not because it would carry white blood, but Solomon, this world is so cruel, so evil. I've listened to you speak of your childhood—" She paused to slap away her tears. "I couldn't bear to see our child go through those things and I couldn't bear to see you relive that awful time."

"Shh," Solomon urged then, his hand covering hers. "Please stop talking now," he insisted quietly.

"Solomon—"

"I know that you wanted our child."

"But—"

"One night on the ship, I found you asleep on the balcony in our cabin." He stroked the back of her hand and studied the invisible pattern his fingers traced there. "I felt compelled to pick up the book again. At first, I did believe your words were untrue." He cleared his throat when a wave of emotion constricted his chest. "I know differently now."

"Solomon, I'm so sorry that I put you through that," Jacinta apologized, moving to her knees to look him directly in the eye.

Solomon smothered both her hands in his own. "I apologize as well for losing my temper and allowing it to almost ruin our life together."

"And do we still have a life together?" She was almost afraid to hear his response.

Solomon cupped her cheek, bringing her close. "We have a life together for as long as you'll have me."

Jacinta pressed her forehead against his. "Then we shall have an eternity."

"I love you," he swore in the fiercest tone.

She kissed the tip of his nose. "I love you. Always."

That night, they relished sleeping in each other's arms.

Hours later, frantic knocking woke the Dikembes. Instantly alert, Solomon pulled on a long, heavy black robe and bounded toward the door. He found head housekeeper, Dot Simons, in the blackened corridor.

"Forgive me, Mistuh Solomon," she whispered and curtsied.

"What is it, Dot?" Solomon inquired quickly, drawing the older woman into the warmth of the bed-chamber.

Dot's usually unruffled demeanor was quite the opposite as she squeezed her hands in a nervous manner.

"It's late in the night, Mistuh Solomon, but please come down to the back sittin' room."

Wasting no more time with words, Solomon did as she asked. Of course, Jacinta was right at her husband's heels. When the couple arrived in the remote sitting room, they were stunned to find hoards of men, women and children there. Many ran to Jacinta when they saw her. Eyes wide, she stared at Solomon, who looked to one of Jason McIver's men for answers. In moments, stories filled their air of husbands, brothers and fathers—freed and enslaved—being forced away into the night. Women were crying, children appeared frightened, and while it was the thing Jacinta's had most anticipated, most feared, she had no idea what to do about it. She had no need to worry.

"Dot?" Solomon beckoned the head housekeeper to his side. "Fetch the letter from the desk in our bed-chamber. It's written in my hand and addressed to a Moses Cuffe."

"Yes, sir." Dot obliged with a bow.

"Lucas," he called, waving toward one of Jason McIver's lookouts, "when Dot returns with that letter, I want you to take it to Cuffe—my ship's captain. He's still docked here at Blake's Lands. Place this letter in no one's hand other than Cuffe's, understood?"

Lucas tipped the brim of the worn black cap atop his head. "I understand."

"Just take your time and be careful," Solomon instructed, setting his hands across the young man's shoulders as he sought to quell his excitement.

"Remember, the boat is docked at Blake's Lands. Can you get there undetected?"

Again, Lucas nodded briskly. "You can trust me, Mister Solomon."

Jacinta's face was a picture of bewilderment. She watched Solomon issue requests to the house staff and felt as though she were inside a dream.

"We need to get the group someplace safe," he was saying to her then. "Surely they're already being hunted down."

"What is your plan?" Jacinta asked.

Solomon's onyx glare was hard as he scanned the soft speaking crowd. "Get the group moved and we'll speak later," he decided.

Before Jacinta could move, Solomon cupped her face in his wide palms. He kissed away the tears streaking her cheeks, and then brushed his nose across hers. "I love you," he whispered before sending her on her way.

"Good morning! I hope everyone had a bit of sleep. I know this past night has been hard for you all. I'm sad to say it may get harder before it becomes easier, but have faith and we will see this through."

Jacinta and Solomon stood alongside Jason as he addressed the families and the house staff. Though everyone had slumbered in the most comforting quarters and dined on a wonderful breakfast, the unease on their faces was impossible to mask. In spite of Jason's hearty words of encouragement, the group remained silent. That silence was punctuated by a light pelting of rain against the tall windows of the grand ballroom where the group had rested the previous evening.

Jacinta had often dreamed of the day when the room would be filled with her people. She never imagined it would be under such circumstances.

"I've sent word to my ship's captain," Solomon began, his words followed by the soft echo of thunder grumbling in the distance. "He's preparing the ship to sail. We're all leaving Charleston this night."

A hush fell over the room. Even the thunder and rain seemed to have gone silent in the wake of the announcement.

"The ship will take us to Regal—a sea island under the protection of McIver Estate," Solomon went on to explain, his hands hidden within the pockets of his salt and pepper woven trousers. "We'll be there no longer than fourteen days before heading north. You need only pack the necessities—not enough to raise suspicions," he advised the lookout men and the house staff, as the families were already packed and ready.

The meeting adjourned and Jacinta moved closer to her husband, circling her arms about his lean waist. Solomon turned to envelop her in his own embrace as he bowed his head to capture her mouth in a sweet kiss. Jacinta gasped, allowing him the entrance he craved. The kiss was filled with love and lust that swirled in one fiery wave of desire. For a moment, the two completely forgot that they weren't alone.

"Thank you, Solomon. Thank you so much," Jacinta breathed, once they'd reluctantly ended the kiss.

Solomon helped himself to another taste of her mouth. "No need for thanks. Kissing you is something I very much enjoy doing."

Jacinta slapped her hand against his forearm when she spied the teasing smile cross his lips. "I wasn't referring to that," she retorted playfully.

"I know what you were referring to."

"For the first time, I can see real hope shining on their faces. It's wonderful," she whispered.

"Well, I'm not done," Solomon was saying, his handsome face a picture of fierce determination as he looked out across the room filled with people, "once the group is taken to safety, the *Sheba* will return for another group and another . . ."

Jacinta's eyes registered concern. "That's so dangerous," she warned.

Solomon shook his head. "I can accept the danger if it means sparing the life of just one man."

June 22, 1822

The storm that had simmered all day blew in at full steam that night. Thankfully, the group worked diligently to pack everything and was ready to leave by nightfall. Dinner was served, but the delicious roast duck, wild rice, oven-roasted herb-seasoned vegetables and cornmeal bread barely went tasted and felt more for show in hopes of keeping up the pretense at normalcy. When a thunderous knock sounded on the door, everyone went still.

Solomon remained cool as he went to answer the door. Outside, he found a robust short man who may have been a bit taller had his back not been humped in a show of humbleness.

"Good evening," Solomon greeted.

"Beg pardon, suh, but I'm a friend of Mister Jason's. Might he be at home?"

Jason, who had followed Solomon to the foyer, stepped forward. "Girard?" he inquired, almost not recognizing Girard Stalings, a free man who lived in town. "What's happened?" he went on to ask.

"Jason, thank the Lord," Girard praised, his brown eyes appearing even more weary and sunken, though his relief had begun to show signs of life.

"Girard, tell me what's happened," Jason persisted.

Girard closed his eyes as though he were uttering a silent prayer. When he spoke, his usual robust tone sounded strained and hopeless. "I'm here with my family, old friend. We be needin' shelter for the night if you can spare—"

"Surely we can. Come, come," Jason ordered, waving in the man's wife, Aeris Stalins, and their four children. "Jacinta," he called, watching as his daughter got the mother and her children settled.

"The city gone mad, Jason," Girard revealed as he headed towards the grand ballroom where everyone had gathered. "They arrestin' innocent people and takin' 'em to the Work House. They even sent Cap'n Dove and Fred Wesner to arrest Mister Vesey. They tracked him to his wife's house."

"Good Lord," Jason breathed, knowing the old man's fate was thoroughly sealed.

In fact, the entire group realized the same. It was well known that Fred Wesner, a local builder, hoped to seal an appointment as chief warden at the Work House. Playing a part in the capture of Denmark Vesey would almost certainly grant him the post. The notorious Captain Dove had no hesitation when it came to shooting blacks, be they innocent or not, freed or enslaved. The City Guard commanding officer had led the search that Saturday evening through Charleston's narrow streets amidst the terrible storm until they found their man.

"We just be needin' shelter for the night, Jason. Then we set out 'fore day in the morn."

Jason observed Girard as though the man had lost his mind. "You may as well head in the direction of the Work House, then, for that is surely where you'll end up," he scoffed, drawing Girard into a small huddle. "We are preparing to close the house and set out tonight."

Girard's expression cleared as he realized the scope of what Jason was saying. His full lips tightened into a thin line as his hand covered Jason's where it rested upon his shoulder.

Though the rest of the night grew rainier and windier, the group set out, dispersing into the woods and praying for the Lord to see them safely through. They regrouped at Blake's Lands, somewhat relieved as the area's gruesome history kept it lightly policed and able to be crossed. Quickly and silently, they boarded the *Sheba* and set sail for Regal.

Once the ship was at sea and everyone was safely tucked away inside their quarters, Jacinta allowed herself to breathe a bit easier. She stared unseeingly into the night looming past the cabin's porthole window. Though her expression belied it, her thoughts were racing. A measure of contentment settled, however, when Solomon pulled her back against the warm, solid wall of his chest.

"You feel like heaven against me," he spoke next to her ear, his deep voice rumbling in the most sensual manner.

Jacinta smiled, curving her hands over his forearms. "I love you," she sighed.

Solomon's dark, deep set eyes narrowed and he nuzzled his handsome face into her neck. "What is it?"

Jacinta gave a nervous laugh that he could read her thoughts so easily. "It's nothing," she said with another laugh.

"Tell me," he insisted.

Closing her eyes, Jacinta inhaled deeply. She didn't want to confide, feeling she should have been overjoyed at the accomplishments they had made that evening. "The rebellion," she sighed, shaking her head against her husband's chest, "it promised to be a bloody battle and the innocent may have been slaughtered with the evil, but it makes me sad to know it's not to be. Solomon, do you think freedom is just fanciful thinking? Will it ever be real? I guess I'll always wonder if I could have played a greater role in the rebellion? Perhaps, I could have done something more—"

"Listen to me," Solomon interrupted, his hands tightening around her body when he turned her to face him, "how many times will you forget your writing? Because of you and many like you, this story and others like it will live on. Others will be inspired, and one day the freedom we all seek will be a reality."

Jacinta's lovely dark face still harbored the depression claiming her heart. "Freedom will never be a reality if something isn't done about the hate—the sheer hate of it all," she hissed out of frustration, her vibrant brown stare sparkled as a result. "Hate I witnessed each day in the place where I played as a child who was filled with innocence and wonder. Hate you faced as a child. Hate I've held in my own heart. What good will freedom bring if we can't look past the hate in ourselves?" Her eyes searched Solomon's as if the answer lie somewhere in their bottomless depths.

Solomon had no answers, none that would bring the light back to his wife's beautiful face. "Shh . . ." he could only urge, while pulling her into a rocking embrace.

October 1822—Michigan Territory

Jacinta had experienced bittersweet days in the time since they'd left Charleston. Solomon decided to store a new ship on the property he had purchased in South Carolina. All were welcomed to come aboard the *Jaci*. The vessel was thought to be a slave ship, as the crew was all white and boasted of their business. They were, however, loyal friends to Taurus Mandela as well as Solomon, not to mention staunch supporters for the abolition of slavery.

The *Jaci* had already returned from its first run with passengers bound for freedom. Sadly, many opted to remain in their lives of bondage. Fear, uncertainty, or simply a desire to remain in the only home they knew, kept the masses from venturing away. This reality took its toll on Jacinta's writing, but she was thankful for her husband, who lavished her with attention and love each day.

Jason McIver had decided upon residence in New York, and he flourished in the bustle of the city. Jacinta knew she and her family had much to be grateful for. Still, her book of thoughts called to her, but Jacinta felt she had nothing to give.

"Jacinta?"

"Out here, Dot!"

Dot Simons who had decided to settle herself in Michigan, rushed out to the sitting room balcony to find the young woman enjoying a rather nippy October evening.

"You need more about those slender shoulders than such a thin shawl," Dot scolded. "For you," she announced, handing Jacinta an envelope.

"Why don't you and Sheba join me?" Jacinta urged, knowing the two women had been virtually inseparable since Dot's arrival in Michigan.

"Bah!" Dot scoffed with a wave of her hand. "We're baking, and I have more chores to tend to afterwards."

"Oh, Dot . . ." Jacinta drawled, laughter tingeing her words. She and Solomon had insisted the woman allow herself to be taken care of for a change. Dot Simons, however, wouldn't hear of it. She watched the woman hurry off mumbling something about how busy she was. Jacinta shook her head and focused on the envelope that had arrived. She went still at the sight of Mea Riley's name scrawled across the front. After a moment, Jacinta's trembling fingers tore through the package.

Jacinta, my friend, I pray this letter finds you and your family well. As you are aware, the rebellion was betrayed. Charleston has restored itself in the time since your departure. Sadly, Mister Vesey was killed on July 2, 1822. He was, of course, found guilty after his farce of a trial. They were determined to strip him of any greatness by hanging him at Blakes Lands like some criminal instead of a good man willing to fight for the survival of his people. His accusers— those cowards—were questioned outside his presence. Mister Vesey was never granted the right to face the men who betrayed him. He never had the chance to question them. As I said, Charleston has restored itself, and while its appearance remains unchanged the same does not hold true for its people. While many of us harbor unease at the thought of escaping to freedom, we now have tangible proof that it can be a reality. Seeing so many of our sisters and brothers leave us on ships and secret passages bound for a new life . . . this gives the people hope. The whites are more wary, more intrigued by us now. Gone are their perceptions that we are as children needing to be cared for. They know that, in spite of this setback, we will continue to organize and fight for our freedom. Believe me, my friend, one day we shall be victorious.

> *Truly,*
> *Mea Riley*

Jacinta traced her fingertips across the words on the page and closed her eyes. She felt as though some power from the expressions voiced so strongly in the black ink was being absorbed into her skin, into her very being. She folded the letter, reinserting it inside the envelope, and then headed indoors. For the first time in months, she made an entry to her book of thoughts.

"What's this?" Solomon called, when he entered the bedroom he shared with his wife. Surprise and delight illuminated his features when he saw her scribbling away at her desk.

"I haven't been able to stop writing since earlier this afternoon," Jacinta almost cried, sounding as though she were just as surprised as her husband.

Solomon closed the distance between them and enfolded her small form within his steely embrace. His heart soared to find her so happy for the first time in so long.

"Feeling optimistic?" he inquired, nuzzling his face into her loosened hair.

Jacinta set her pen aside and turned to face him in the chair. "Optimistic and loved," she told him, cupping his face in her palms as she pressed the sweetest kiss upon his lips.

EPILOGUE

Christmas 1822

Taurus and Monique Mandela's annual Christmas gala was in progress amidst a powerful snowstorm that had raged for almost one week. Inside their cozy home swirled the sights and sounds of the festive season. Sheba Dikembe was in attendance, as was Jason McIver, Ibn and Esa Obu and, of course, Solomon and Jacinta.

During the merriment, time was taken for readings of poetry, letters and thoughts. Jacinta was introduced and brought to the stage last, where she read from a provocative piece entitled "Passion's Furies".

". . . my hope now rests on the future," she continued, approaching the final paragraphs of the work. "I am filled with passion to see a new world—a world changed for the better. With this passion, this zeal to see the abolishment of slavery, we must never forget or underestimate its potential to cast negative affects on what we all hope to accomplish. I was disappointed by the inside betrayal and subsequent failure of the rebellion to be led by Denmark Vesey. The hopes and dreams of a great many people were dashed when the great plan was foiled.

"However, there is much we may take from this unfortunate turn in events. We *must* realize the importance in coming together as a people—a people of many backgrounds—a people of many shades. From the darkest Negro to the lightest skinned mulatto, we must look past it all to see our brother, our sister, our family. If we ever hope to triumph over this evil that has destroyed our lives, our dignity, our humanity . . . slavery will not be a lasting evil. It will one day be a thing of the past, but we must live beyond that day and we must know when our zeal is pushing us towards negative territory.

"The passion for love and the passion for hate appear equal—as is our passion for freedom. Only as we forge ahead is it revealed whether the arrival of that freedom is a testament to love or hate."

Solomon went to find his wife when she had been gone from the party a bit too long for his liking. She had retreated to a quiet room at the end of the main corridor and stood before a wide row of windows against the back wall where she enjoyed the sight of snow falling in waves of gleaming silence.

"You have a house full of admirers waiting to shake your hand," Solomon spoke against her shoulder once he had pulled her back against him.

"I won't keep them waiting any longer," Jacinta promised, reluctant to leave the serene security she found within her husband's embrace.

Solomon's long lashes shielded his dark gaze from view as he inhaled the peach fragrance rising from Jacinta's hair and the material of her alluring crimson gown. "Tell me what you're thinking," he requested softly.

Jacinta turned to fix him with a dazzling grin that sparkled as brightly as the mischievous glint in her chocolate stare. "I was thinking that it's time we return to Michigan," she purred against the line of his jaw as her lips caressed him there. "There are some changes I'd like to make to the house," she murmured, smoothing her hands across the dark fabric of his tailored three quarter length suit coat.

Solomon's dimples flashed when he heard the naughtiness in her voice. "Can you be more specific about these changes?"

"Mmm," Jacinta gestured, with a lazy shrug and lowering of her eyes. "Well, I'd definitely like to get some things done in the bedroom," she shared, giggling madly when Solomon began to gnaw at her neck. She tilted back her head as his mouth raced her cheek before coming to suckle at her earlobe. "And then there's the nursery," she drawled.

Solomon's head raised quickly, his black eyes widening in disbelief. His legs felt weak and he took refuge in a nearby armchair. "What are you telling me?" he whispered, once he pulled her onto his lap.

Jacinta giggled again enjoying the way his uncertainty made him all the more handsome. "What do you think I'm telling you?" she leaned close to whisper against his ear. "I'm pregnant. I'm going to have your child and I can hardly wait. I love you."

Solomon nuzzled his face against hers. His heart raced at a frantic speed. "I love you. Forever, I love you," he swore.

They cuddled on the arm chair, forgetting about the party and, for a time, forgetting about the troubles of the world. They watched the snow fall and they were optimistic. They were optimistic of the future that lay ahead.

SOURCES

1. International Library of Negro Life and History Series: Introduction to Black Literature in America. 1746–Present (1968).
2. Denmark Vesey: The Buried History of America's Largest Slave Rebellion and the man who led it. Author: David Robertson.
3. Black Charlestonians: A Social History 1822-1885. Author: Bernard E. Powers Jr.
4. Charleston Houses and Gardens. Author: Evangeline Davis.
5. Hilton Head Island: A Perspective.
6. History of American Costume 1607–1870. Author: Elizabeth McClellan.
7. Shepherd's Historical Atlas 9th Edition. Author: William R. Shepherd.
8. New York facts: A comprehensive look at New York today, county by county. Author: John Clements.
9. The Food Timeline.
10. The History of Steamboats: Authors: John Fitch and Robert Fulton.
11. The Holy Bible.

ABOUT THE AUTHOR

AlTonya Washington is a native of South Carolina and a 1994 graduate of Winston-Salem State University in North Carolina. She has received numerous awards and nominations for her work including the Romantic Times Best 1st Multicultural nomination in 2003 and the Romantic Times Reviewer's Choice Award for Best Multi-cultural Romance in 2004. AlTonya resides in North Carolina where she works as a Senior Library Assistant. *Passion's Furies* is her second novel for Genesis Press.

2008 Reprint Mass Market Titles

January

Cautious Heart
Cheris F. Hodges
ISBN-13: 978-1-58571-301-1
ISBN-10: 1-58571-301-5
$6.99

Suddenly You
Crystal Hubbard
ISBN-13: 978-1-58571-302-8
ISBN-10: 1-58571-302-3
$6.99

February

Passion
T. T. Henderson
ISBN-13: 978-1-58571-303-5
ISBN-10: 1-58571-303-1
$6.99

Whispers in the Sand
LaFlorya Gauthier
ISBN-13: 978-1-58571-304-2
ISBN-10: 1-58571-304-x
$6.99

March

Life Is Never As It Seems
J. J. Michael
ISBN-13: 978-1-58571-305-9
ISBN-10: 1-58571-305-8
$6.99

Beyond the Rapture
Beverly Clark
ISBN-13: 978-1-58571-306-6
ISBN-10: 1-58571-306-6
$6.99

April

A Heart's Awakening
Veronica Parker
ISBN-13: 978-1-58571-307-3
ISBN-10: 1-58571-307-4
$6.99

Breeze
Robin Lynette Hampton
ISBN-13: 978-1-58571-308-0
ISBN-10: 1-58571-308-2
$6.99

May

I'll Be Your Shelter
Giselle Carmichael
ISBN-13: 978-1-58571-309-7
ISBN-10: 1-58571-309-0
$6.99

Careless Whispers
Rochelle Alers
ISBN-13: 978-1-58571-310-3
ISBN-10: 1-58571-310-4
$6.99

June

Sin
Crystal Rhodes
ISBN-13: 978-1-58571-311-0
ISBN-10: 1-58571-311-2
$6.99

Dark Storm Rising
Chinelu Moore
ISBN-13: 978-1-58571-312-7
ISBN-10: 1-58571-312-0
$6.99

2008 Reprint Mass Market Titles (continued)

July

Object of His Desire
A.C. Arthur
ISBN-13: 978-1-58571-313-4
ISBN-10: 1-58571-313-9
$6.99

Angel's Paradise
Janice Angelique
ISBN-13: 978-1-58571-314-1
ISBN-10: 1-58571-314-7
$6.99

August

Unbreak My Heart
Dar Tomlinson
ISBN-13: 978-1-58571-315-8
ISBN-10: 1-58571-315-5
$6.99

All I Ask
Barbara Keaton
ISBN-13: 978-1-58571-316-5
ISBN-10: 1-58571-316-3
$6.99

September

Icie
Pamela Leigh Starr
ISBN-13: 978-1-58571-275-5
ISBN-10: 1-58571-275-2
$6.99

At Last
Lisa Riley
ISBN-13: 978-1-58571-276-2
ISBN-10: 1-58571-276-0
$6.99

October

Everlastin' Love
Gay G. Gunn
ISBN-13: 978-1-58571-277-9
ISBN-10: 1-58571-277-9
$6.99

Three Wishes
Seressia Glass
ISBN-13: 978-1-58571-278-6
ISBN-10: 1-58571-278-7
$6.99

November

Yesterday Is Gone
Beverly Clark
ISBN-13: 978-1-58571-279-3
ISBN-10: 1-58571-279-5
$6.99

Again My Love
Kayla Perrin
ISBN-13: 978-1-58571-280-9
ISBN-10: 1-58571-280-9
$6.99

December

Office Policy
A.C. Arthur
ISBN-13: 978-1-58571-281-6
ISBN-10: 1-58571-281-7
$6.99

Rendezvous With Fate
Jeanne Sumerix
ISBN-13: 978-1-58571-283-3
ISBN-10: 1-58571-283-3
$6.99

2008 New Mass Market Titles

January

Where I Want To Be
Maryam Diaab
ISBN-13: 978-1-58571-268-7
ISBN-10: 1-58571-268-X
$6.99

Never Say Never
Michele Cameron
ISBN-13: 978-1-58571-269-4
ISBN-10: 1-58571-269-8
$6.99

February

Stolen Memories
Michele Sudler
ISBN-13: 978-1-58571-270-0
ISBN-10: 1-58571-270-1
$6.99

Dawn's Harbor
Kymberly Hunt
ISBN-13: 978-1-58571-271-7
ISBN-10: 1-58571-271-X
$6.99

March

Undying Love
Renee Alexis
ISBN-13: 978-1-58571-272-4
ISBN-10: 1-58571-272-8
$6.99

Blame It On Paradise
Crystal Hubbard
ISBN-13: 978-1-58571-273-1
ISBN-10: 1-58571-273-6
$6.99

April

When A Man Loves A Woman
La Connie Taylor-Jones
ISBN-13: 978-1-58571-274-8
ISBN-10: 1-58571-274-4
$6.99

Choices
Tammy Williams
ISBN-13: 978-1-58571-300-4
ISBN-10: 1-58571-300-7
$6.99

May

Dream Runner
Gail McFarland
ISBN-13: 978-1-58571-317-2
ISBN-10: 1-58571-317-1
$6.99

Southern Fried Standards
S.R. Maddox
ISBN-13: 978-1-58571-318-9
ISBN-10: 1-58571-318-X
$6.99

June

Looking for Lily
Africa Fine
ISBN-13: 978-1-58571-319-6
ISBN-10: 1-58571-319-8
$6.99

Bliss, Inc.
Chamein Canton
ISBN-13: 978-1-58571-325-7
ISBN-10: 1-58571-325-2
$6.99

2008 New Mass Market Titles (continued)

July

Love's Secrets
Yolanda McVey
ISBN-13: 978-1-58571-321-9
ISBN-10: 1-58571-321-X
$6.99

Things Forbidden
Maryam Diaab
ISBN-13: 978-1-58571-327-1
ISBN-10: 1-58571-327-9
$6.99

August

Storm
Pamela Leigh Starr
ISBN-13: 978-1-58571-323-3
ISBN-10: 1-58571-323-6
$6.99

Passion's Furies
AlTonya Washington
ISBN-13: 978-1-58571-324-0
ISBN-10: 1-58571-324-4
$6.99

September

Three Doors Down
Michele Sudler
ISBN-13: 978-1-58571-332-5
ISBN-10: 1-58571-332-5
$6.99

Mr Fix-It
Crystal Hubbard
ISBN-13: 978-1-58571-326-4
ISBN-10: 1-58571-326-0
$6.99

October

Moments of Clarity
Michele Cameron
ISBN-13: 978-1-58571-330-1
ISBN-10: 1-58571-330-9
$6.99

Lady Preacher
K.T. Richey
ISBN-13: 978-1-58571-333-2
ISBN-10: 1-58571-333-3
$6.99

November

This Life Isn't Perfect Holla
Sandra Foy
ISBN: 978-1-58571-331-8
ISBN-10: 1-58571-331-7
$6.99

Promises Made
Bernice Layton
ISBN-13: 978-1-58571-334-9
ISBN-10: 1-58571-334-1
$6.99

December

A Voice Behind Thunder
Carrie Elizabeth Greene
ISBN-13: 978-1-58571-329-5
ISBN-10: 1-58571-329-5
$6.99

The More Things Change
Chamein Canton
ISBN-13: 978-1-58571-328-8
ISBN-10: 1-58571-328-7
$6.99

Other Genesis Press, Inc. Titles

Other Genesis Press, Inc. Titles (continued)

Blaze	Barbara Keaton	$9.95
Blood Lust	J. M. Jeffries	$9.95
Blood Seduction	J.M. Jeffries	$9.95
Bodyguard	Andrea Jackson	$9.95
Boss of Me	Diana Nyad	$8.95
Bound by Love	Beverly Clark	$8.95
Breeze	Robin Hampton Allen	$10.95
Broken	Dar Tomlinson	$24.95
By Design	Barbara Keaton	$8.95
Cajun Heat	Charlene Berry	$8.95
Careless Whispers	Rochelle Alers	$8.95
Cats & Other Tales	Marilyn Wagner	$8.95
Caught in a Trap	Andre Michelle	$8.95
Caught Up In the Rapture	Lisa G. Riley	$9.95
Cautious Heart	Cheris F Hodges	$8.95
Chances	Pamela Leigh Starr	$8.95
Cherish the Flame	Beverly Clark	$8.95
Class Reunion	Irma Jenkins/	
	John Brown	$12.95
Code Name: Diva	J.M. Jeffries	$9.95
Conquering Dr. Wexler's Heart	Kimberley White	$9.95
Corporate Seduction	A.C. Arthur	$9.95
Crossing Paths, Tempting Memories	Dorothy Elizabeth Love	$9.95
Crush	Crystal Hubbard	$9.95
Cypress Whisperings	Phyllis Hamilton	$8.95
Dark Embrace	Crystal Wilson Harris	$8.95
Dark Storm Rising	Chinelu Moore	$10.95

Other Genesis Press, Inc. Titles (continued)

Other Genesis Press, Inc. Titles (continued)

Other Genesis Press, Inc. Titles (continued)

Last Train to Memphis	Elsa Cook	$12.95
Lasting Valor	Ken Olsen	$24.95
Let Us Prey	Hunter Lundy	$25.95
Lies Too Long	Pamela Ridley	$13.95
Life Is Never As It Seems	J.J. Michael	$12.95
Lighter Shade of Brown	Vicki Andrews	$8.95
Love Always	Mildred E. Riley	$10.95
Love Doesn't Come Easy	Charlyne Dickerson	$8.95
Love Unveiled	Gloria Greene	$10.95
Love's Deception	Charlene Berry	$10.95
Love's Destiny	M. Loui Quezada	$8.95
Mae's Promise	Melody Walcott	$8.95
Magnolia Sunset	Giselle Carmichael	$8.95
Many Shades of Gray	Dyanne Davis	$6.99
Matters of Life and Death	Lesego Malepe, Ph.D.	$15.95
Meant to Be	Jeanne Sumerix	$8.95
Midnight Clear	Leslie Esdaile	$10.95
(Anthology)	Gwynne Forster	
	Carmen Green	
	Monica Jackson	
Midnight Magic	Gwynne Forster	$8.95
Midnight Peril	Vicki Andrews	$10.95
Misconceptions	Pamela Leigh Starr	$9.95
Montgomery's Children	Richard Perry	$14.95
My Buffalo Soldier	Barbara B. K. Reeves	$8.95
Naked Soul	Gwynne Forster	$8.95
Next to Last Chance	Louisa Dixon	$24.95
No Apologies	Seressia Glass	$8.95
No Commitment Required	Seressia Glass	$8.95

Other Genesis Press, Inc. Titles (continued)

No Regrets	Mildred E. Riley	$8.95
Not His Type	Chamein Canton	$6.99
Nowhere to Run	Gay G. Gunn	$10.95
O Bed! O Breakfast!	Rob Kuehnle	$14.95
Object of His Desire	A. C. Arthur	$8.95
Office Policy	A. C. Arthur	$9.95
Once in a Blue Moon	Dorianne Cole	$9.95
One Day at a Time	Bella McFarland	$8.95
One in A Million	Barbara Keaton	$6.99
One of These Days	Michele Sudler	$9.95
Outside Chance	Louisa Dixon	$24.95
Passion	T.T. Henderson	$10.95
Passion's Blood	Cherif Fortin	$22.95
Passion's Journey	Wanda Y. Thomas	$8.95
Past Promises	Jahmel West	$8.95
Path of Fire	T.T. Henderson	$8.95
Path of Thorns	Annetta P. Lee	$9.95
Peace Be Still	Colette Haywood	$12.95
Picture Perfect	Reon Carter	$8.95
Playing for Keeps	Stephanie Salinas	$8.95
Pride & Joi	Gay G. Gunn	$15.95
Pride & Joi	Gay G. Gunn	$8.95
Promises to Keep	Alicia Wiggins	$8.95
Quiet Storm	Donna Hill	$10.95
Reckless Surrender	Rochelle Alers	$6.95
Red Polka Dot in a World of Plaid	Varian Johnson	$12.95
Reluctant Captive	Joyce Jackson	$8.95
Rendezvous with Fate	Jeanne Sumerix	$8.95

Other Genesis Press, Inc. Titles (continued)

Revelations	Cheris F. Hodges	$8.95
Rivers of the Soul	Leslie Esdaile	$8.95
Rocky Mountain Romance	Kathleen Suzanne	$8.95
Rooms of the Heart	Donna Hill	$8.95
Rough on Rats and Tough on Cats	Chris Parker	$12.95
Secret Library Vol. 1	Nina Sheridan	$18.95
Secret Library Vol. 2	Cassandra Colt	$8.95
Secret Thunder	Annetta P. Lee	$9.95
Shades of Brown	Denise Becker	$8.95
Shades of Desire	Monica White	$8.95
Shadows in the Moonlight	Jeanne Sumerix	$8.95
Sin	Crystal Rhodes	$8.95
Small Whispers	Annetta P. Lee	$6.99
So Amazing	Sinclair LeBeau	$8.95
Somebody's Someone	Sinclair LeBeau	$8.95
Someone to Love	Alicia Wiggins	$8.95
Song in the Park	Martin Brant	$15.95
Soul Eyes	Wayne L. Wilson	$12.95
Soul to Soul	Donna Hill	$8.95
Southern Comfort	J.M. Jeffries	$8.95
Still the Storm	Sharon Robinson	$8.95
Still Waters Run Deep	Leslie Esdaile	$8.95
Stolen Kisses	Dominiqua Douglas	$9.95
Stories to Excite You	Anna Forrest/Divine	$14.95
Subtle Secrets	Wanda Y. Thomas	$8.95
Suddenly You	Crystal Hubbard	$9.95
Sweet Repercussions	Kimberley White	$9.95
Sweet Sensations	Gwendolyn Bolton	$9.95

Other Genesis Press, Inc. Titles (continued)

Other Genesis Press, Inc. Titles (continued)

Order Form

Mail to: Genesis Press, Inc.
P.O. Box 101
Columbus, MS 39703

Name _____
Address _____
City/State _____ Zip _____
Telephone _____

Ship to (if different from above)
Name _____
Address _____
City/State _____ Zip _____
Telephone _____

Credit Card Information
Credit Card # _____ ☐ Visa ☐ Mastercard
Expiration Date (mm/yy) _____ ☐ AmEx ☐ Discover

Qty.	Author	Title	Price	Total

Use this order

form, or call

1-888-INDIGO-1

Total for books	
Shipping and handling:	
$5 first two books,	
$1 each additional book	
Total S & H	
Total amount enclosed	

Mississippi residents add 7% sales tax

199